Collins | English for Exams

絕對攻略
TOEFL
iBT 新托福閱讀＋寫作

Skills for the TOEFL iBT Test
Reading and Writing

STEP ①

STEP ②

掃描書中 QRCode

快速註冊或登入 EZCourse

STEP ③

STEP ④

STEP ⑤

請回答以下問題完成訂閱

一、請問本書第65頁，紅色框線中的英文＿＿＿＿是什麼？

答案 請注意大小寫

二、請問本書第33頁，紅色框線中的英文＿＿＿＿是什麼？

答案 請注意大小寫

送出

回答問題後送出

完成訂閱

點擊個人檔案

依系統指示（題完或題目與大小寫）

點書右側需顯示「已訂閱」，
表示已成功訂閱，
即可點選播放本書音檔。

查看「我的訂購記錄」
並顯示已訂購本書，
點選封面即刻本書線上收聽。

目次 Contents

本書使用說明
How to Use This Book

《絕對攻略 TOEFL iBT 新托福閱讀＋寫作》提供了應考托福測驗的全面指南。使用本系列書籍準備托福考試，能夠幫助你在測驗中獲得高分並提高被排名前段的大學錄取的機會。

無論你的英文程度如何，《絕對攻略 TOEFL iBT 新托福閱讀＋寫作》提供順利通過測驗所需的內容。以下是本書的章節內容介紹：

- 挑戰及解決方法：提供測驗的策略和技巧，幫助你學習如何克服測驗中最常碰到的困難。
- 快速指南：每個章節開始會提供題型的簡短介紹，並以易於閱讀的表格形式呈現，讓你迅速了解回答該題型所需知道的策略。
- 題型範例：呈現你在考試中可能會看到的問題類型、段落文章和回答。預先知道會出現什麼樣的題型是準備考試的重要環節。
- 掌握要領：概述在各個題目上正確作答的重要技巧和練習。
- 題型練習：閱讀和聆聽特定的資訊內容，勾選筆記和練習題目，並注意選項為何正確或錯誤。
- 綜合演練：練習更多題型和研究題目選項的解析，這能幫助你獲得測驗技巧和信心。
- 實戰演練：提供仿真測驗題，讓你練習目前所學。
- 答案解析：教你如何排除錯誤的題目選項，並選出最佳答案。
- 模擬試題：利用模擬試題來檢驗你的能力。這有助於找出你的弱點，才能知道考試前應該將重點放在哪裡。
- Test Tips：為如何應對特定的題型提供最佳建議。
- 字彙：提供柯林斯高級英語詞典（Collins Cobuild Advanced Dictionary）的釋義來幫助你理解單字，並提升你在托福測驗和美國大學的教科書和課堂中常見的學術詞彙的知識。
- 學術字彙表：由科斯海德（Coxhead, 2000 年）編輯的學術字彙表包含 570 個經常出現在各個學術文本的詞彙。許多大學教授都會推薦此學術字彙表給他們的學生。認識並練習這些單字有助於擴充你的詞庫，幫助你理解和使用更多的學術英文字彙。

- 講稿和解答：在準備托福測驗時練習和檢查答案。
- 音檔：本書音檔提供了寫作試題的內容。

通過托福測驗的訣竅 Tips for Success

制定計畫，並執行以下方法：

- 提早報名：確認欲申請大學的申請截止日期，一定要在截止日期前提早報名托福測驗，以確保你的成績能及時送達。
- 了解欲申請大學的分數要求：學位課程通常會在其網站上公布最低分數要求。
- 提早開始學習：練習得愈多，技巧就提高得愈多。給自己至少一個月的時間來複習本書題目並完成所有練習。每天至少花一個小時學習，不要放棄。
- 計時：在完成本書的練習和模擬測驗時計時。
- 反覆聆聽聽力講稿和口說回答範本，直到你理解本書所教導的概念。
- 在書上完成練習。同時不要害怕在書本上做筆記。記下你不知道的單字的定義，這有助於記憶。
- 在聽力部分，完成題目後不要回頭去看，這能幫助你習慣實際的測驗過程。
- 在口說部分，回到前面的提示，並嘗試想出新的回答。練習能夠在有限的時間內輕鬆作答。

什麼是托福網路測驗 What is the TOEFL iBT ® Test?

這項測驗能夠準確評量你在大學課堂中閱讀、聽力、口說和寫作英文的能力。這有助於你自信的脫穎而出，並讓你具備明顯的外語優勢，亦即各大專院校知道你已經準備好以流利的英文交流。

托福網路測驗提供三種測驗方式，你可以選擇最適合你的需求和喜好：

- TOEFL iBT test 托福網路測驗：在授權的考試中心使用電腦進行測驗。
- TOEFL iBT Home Edition 在家考托福：在家中使用電腦進行測驗。
- TOEFL iBT Paper Edition 托福網路測驗紙筆版：2024 年 1 月後停辦。

托福網路測驗（在考試中心）The TOEFL iBT® Test (at a Test Center)

你會在 2 個小時以內完成托福網路測驗。測驗分為四個部分：

- 閱讀評估你閱讀課堂上的教材及文章之理解能力：35 分鐘；20 題
- 聽力評估你在大學校園中對口語英文的理解能力：36 分鐘；28 題
- 口說評估你在學術環境下使用英文表達的能力：16 分鐘；4 題
- 寫作評估你能否適當的使用英文寫作的能力：29 分鐘；2 題

托福測驗強調整合技巧，幫助你確認已經準備好在課堂上就所讀到和聽到的內容，用英文表達自己的想法。整合題型要求你綜合多項技巧，題目將要求：

- 讀，聽，接著以口說回答問題
- 聽，接著以口說回答問題
- 讀，聽，接著以寫作回答問題

測驗的每個部分都有時間限制，如果你提前完成了某項，你可以繼續往下，但不能返回已經完成或時間已經結束的部分。不過在閱讀部分，你在時間內可以返回到先前的段落。

在閱讀和聽力部分的題目，你應該迅速且仔細的作答。有些題目比較困難，但請盡量回答每一道問題。如果對答案不確定，請盡量猜測最佳答案。

口說和寫作部分的每道題目都單獨計時。請嘗試在規定時間內盡可能完整的回答。請根據指定的主題回答，如果文不對題，你的答案將不計分。

在家考托福 TOEFL iBT Home Edition

「在家考托福」與你在考試中心參加的托福網路測驗相同，只是你可以在自己家裡或其他私密的環境中進行，並由線上監考人員監控。只要能考托福網路測驗的地方都能選擇在家考試。在報名「在家考托福」之前，請確定你已檢查過居家考試所需要的設備和環境，並且符合要求。你需要為你的電腦進行系統檢查，檢查是否有不當使用的軟體。更多訊息請參考網站 https://www.ets.org/toefl/test-takers/ibt/about/testing-options.html

「在家考托福」在內容、格式和螢幕體驗上與在考試中心進行的測驗完全相同，每週四天，全天候提供報名。

托福網路測驗概述
Overview of the TOEFL iBT® Test

以下是有關托福網路測驗內容的更多資訊。托福網路測驗分為四個計時的部分：閱讀、聽力、口說和寫作。每個部分都測驗你在英語圈的大學就讀所需的關鍵技巧。

閱讀部分 Reading Section

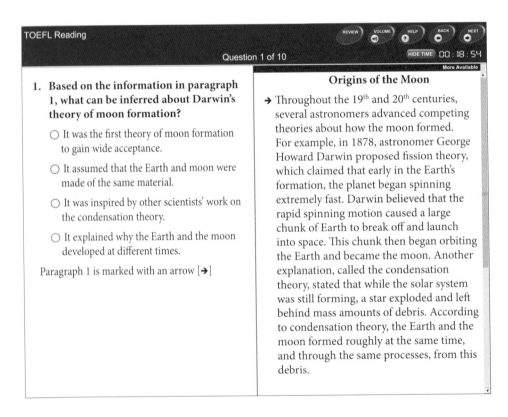

閱讀是托福測驗的第一部分，透過呈現一系列學術文章來測試你的閱讀理解能力，你要根據每篇文章回答一組問題。此部分測試以下能力：

- 判斷主旨
- 理解主要細節
- 推論

- 理解文章的組織結構
- 利用上下文的線索來判斷關鍵詞的定義

每個閱讀部分有 2 到 4 篇學術文章，文章數量取決於你報名的托福測驗方式為何。每篇文章的篇幅介於 600 到 750 個單字之間。在閱讀完文章之後，要回答一組問題，每篇文章有 10 個問題。這個部分允許返回先前回答過的問題，去檢查或修正答案。

聽力部分 Listening Section

聽力是托福測驗的第二部分。為了測驗你的聽力理解能力，首先你會透過耳機聆聽一段講座或對話，接著你要根據每個聽力段落回答一組問題。此部分測試以下能力：
- 判斷聽力段落的主旨或目的
- 理解主要細節
- 推論
- 判斷說話者的目的

聽力部分會有 5 個聽力段落。每個聽力段落的長度介於 3 到 5 分鐘之間。在聽完聽力段落之後，你要回答一組問題，每個段落有 5 到 6 個問題。聽力部分不允許查看先前回答的問題。

口說部分 Speaking Section

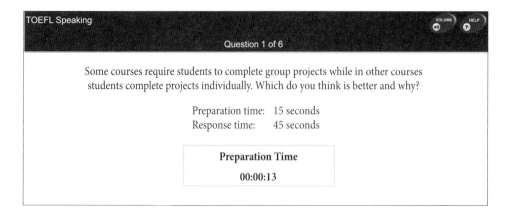

Some courses require students to complete group projects while in other courses students complete projects individually. Which do you think is better and why?

Preparation time: 15 seconds
Response time: 45 seconds

Preparation Time
00:00:13

口說是托福測驗的第三部分。在這一部分，你要對著麥克風針對各種題型作答。這些題型要測試各方面的口說能力，包括：

- 表達意見
- 理解並回答課堂上的問題
- 參與學科的討論
- 結合來自兩個來源的資訊
- 報告別人的看法
- 與大學校內職員互動

這一部分包含 4 個口說題：1 個獨立題和 3 個整合題。

每個口說題需要不同的技能，包括閱讀＋聽力＋口說；聽力＋口說；以及僅有口說。

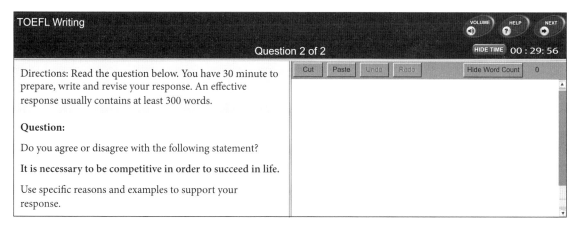

寫作是托福測驗的第四部分。在這一部分，你要在電腦上輸入或是用筆寫出每個項目的回答。這些題型測驗以下能力：

- 規劃和組織一篇文章
- 根據示例或具體細節用書面文字回答
- 使用各種語法結構和詞彙
- 使用正確的拼寫和標點符號

寫作部分包含兩大題：第一大題是整合寫作題，第二題是學術討論題。學術討論題要你根據題目提供的資訊和自己的想法，來回答教授的提問。

快速指南 QUICK GUIDE

TOEFL iBT Test		
測驗	內容	考試時間
閱讀部分	文章篇數：2 篇文章 問題數量：20 個問題	總計：35 分鐘
聽力部分	5 個聽力段落：3 段講座，2 段對話 問題數量：28 個問題	總計：36 分鐘
口說部分	問題數量：4 題 1 個獨立題，3 個整合題	總計：16 分鐘
寫作部分	問題數量：2 1 個整合題 1 個學術討論題	整合題：19 分鐘 學術討論題：10 分鐘 總計：29 分鐘

電腦鍵盤：托福網路測驗考試中心使用標準的英語鍵盤（QWERTY）。QWERTY 的名稱來自鍵盤第三行的前六個字母，如果你以前未使用過這種類型的鍵盤，請在參加考試之前用這種鍵盤練習。某些考試中心所在區域的常用鍵盤設置為 QWERTY，他們會為每位考生提供一個模板，以幫助查找位於不同位置的幾個按鍵。

替代格式資料（Alternate Format Materials）：如果你需要其他格式的考試準備資料，請直接聯繫美國教育測驗服務社（ETS）身心障礙服務部門。

身心障礙或有健康問題考量的考生：

- 為符合 ETS 要求的身心障礙或有健康問題考量的考生提供協助。如果要申請協助，必須在報名考試之前取得許可。
- 如果要尋求協助，請盡早提出申請。ETS 收到申請和填妥的文件之後，大約需要四到六週的審查時間。

報名 Registration

托福網路測驗的報名方式有好幾種，最簡單的方式是透過你的 ETS 帳號。還可以透過電話或郵件，使用托福網路測驗報名表 PDF 報名。

如果在報名之前還沒有 ETS 帳號，可以在 www.ets.org/mytoefl 或使用托福官方應用程式（TOEFL® Official App）申請。

確定你在報名時所使用的姓名拼寫，與你帶到考試中心的身分證明文件上的姓名完全一致。閱讀你所在地區的具體要求（如果有的話），在報名考試時要準備好你的身分證明文件。

透過網路或托福官方應用程式報名：

- 如果還沒有 ETS 帳號，可以透過線上、托福官方應用程式或電話申請。
- 無論透過何種方式申請帳戶，請務必完成所有必填欄位，你提供的資訊將被完全保密。
- 確認你的個人資料。你會看到一個確認頁面，顯示你提交的所有資訊。

- 姓名和出生日期一旦輸入後就無法更改，請確定你輸入的資訊與你攜帶到考試中心的身分證明文件完全一致。

電話報名：
- 可以透過電話報名，並使用信用卡／簽帳金融卡或以美元支付的電子支票。
- 常規的電話報名在考試日期前七天截止。逾期的電話報名則在考試日期前一天、考試中心當地時間下午 5 點截止。如果在「考試前七天」截止期限之後報名，將收取逾期報名附加費。
- 可以到 www.ets.org/s/toefl/pdf/iBT_reg_form.pdf 查看報名表，以查看致電時所需要的其他資訊。

郵寄報名：
- 可以透過郵件寄送考試報名表，表格請至 www.ets.org/s/toefl/pdf/iBT_reg_form.pdf
- 在表格上填寫所有資訊，包括信用卡／簽帳金融卡資訊，或以美元支付的支票或匯票。將填寫完整的表格郵寄到表格上所顯示的地址，必須在最早的考試選擇日期前至少四週寄達。
- 屆時將根據你在表格上提供的資訊來分配你的考試日期、時間和地點（僅限考試中心）。

重要報名需知 Important Things to Know When You Register
- 公告的考場和考試日期可能會更改。有關考場、日期和其他報名資訊的最新消息，可透過你的 ETS 帳號得知。
- 並非所有的考場都在所有的考試日期開放。
- 選擇日期範圍和地點時，你會看到該區域的考場列表。如果要尋找未列出的特定考場，請嘗試不同的日期範圍。
- 在報名期間，可以選擇最多四個免費的成績單寄送地點。
- 盡早報名，考試日期可能很快就被選完。
- 盡早參加考試，讓學校能夠及時收到你的成績單，並在考慮你的學校申請時使用。
- 報名不可轉讓，不能讓其他人使用你報名的場次。
- 不提供現場報名服務。
- 請在考試前一天利用網路或透過應用程式進到你的 ETS 帳號查看考試詳情，或許會有一些更動，例如不同的建築物或考試開始時間。

考試日期 Test Dates

托福網路測驗在全球合格的考試中心或在家中提供每週最多六天的考試機會。在報名時，要選擇適合你需求和偏好的托福網路測驗選項：在考試中心、在家裡或使用紙本試卷。你可從你的 ETS 帳號查看考試日期。並非所有地點都開放給所有考試日期。

考試地點 Test Locations

可在你的 ETS 帳號查看考試地點的最新資訊。增加考場是常有的事，座位的相關資訊可能會隨時更改，無需事先通知。

只要是能考托福網路測驗的地方通常都會提供「在家考托福」選項。

報名截止期限 Registration Deadlines

考試日期可能很快被選完，因此建議提前報名才能選到最理想的考試地點和日期。大約在考試日期前 6 個月開放報名。

常規的電話報名在考試日期前 7 天截止。逾期的電話報名則在考試日期的前一天、考試中心當地時間下午 5 點截止。逾期網路報名在考試日期的前兩天截止。例如你想要的考試日期是星期六，那麼你能夠報名的最後一天是星期四。如果在「考試前 7 天」截止期限之後報名，將收取逾期報名附加費。

評分 Scoring

你可以在考試的前一天，於考試中心當地時間晚上 10 點之前免費選擇最多四個成績單寄送地點（接收你成績的機構）。在超過時間之後，寄送成績將收取費用。

過了晚上 10 點的截止時間之後，不能增加、更改或刪除寄送地點。

你不能在考試中心選擇成績單寄送地點。

了解托福網路測驗分數 Understanding Your TOEFL iBT Scores

在完成托福測驗之後，會收到 4 個分科分數和 1 個總分。每個分科分數的範圍是 0-30，這些分數相加得到 0-120 的總分。每個測驗項目有 4 到 5 級熟練程度，你能從分數上得知你在該項目上的熟練程度。

項目	程度
閱讀	Advanced (24–30) High-Intermediate (18–23) Low-Intermediate (4–17) Below Low-Intermediate (0–3)
聽力	Advanced (22–30) High-Intermediate (17–21) Low-Intermediate (9–16) Below Low-Intermediate (0–8)
口說	Advanced (25–30) High-Intermediate (20–24) Low-Intermediate (16–19) Basic (10–15) Below Basic (0–9)
寫作	Advanced (24–30) High-Intermediate (17–23) Low-Intermediate (13–16) Basic (7–12) Below Basic (0–6)

托福拼分 MyBest® Scores

自 2019 年以來，托福出版商還推出了一項新功能，稱為托福拼分（MyBest scores 或超級分數）。透過結合你在過去兩年內所有考試中最高的分科分數來呈現你的最佳總體表現。這表示你或許能以較少的考試來滿足所申請機構的分數要求，更早實現你的目標。所有的托福網路測驗成績報告，都會顯示出你所選擇的那場考試的傳統分數和你的超級分數。愈來愈多大學和其他機構接受托福拼分，建議直接與要申請的機構聯繫，以確認其托福分數要求。

如何評分？ How is the Test Scored?

托福測驗只透過一個集中評分的網絡進行評分，而不是在考試中心評分。閱讀和聽力部分由電腦評分，口說和寫作部分則由人工智慧評分系統和多名受過培訓的人工評分員共同評分。更多資訊請參閱托福官網。

可以從你的 ETS 帳號查閱你的托福成績。何時可查閱成績結果，取決於你參加考試的方式：

在考試中心：考試後 4-8 天

在家考托福：考試後 4-8 天

成績的有效期限為兩年，你可以下載並列印 PDF 格式的成績報告，在你從 ETS 帳號收到成績兩天後便可下載。

你指定的成績單寄送地點何時收到成績，取決於你參加考試的方式以及他們所使用的成績寄送方法。

考試之前 Before Your Test Session

以下資訊適用於參加 TOEFL iBT 的考生。在考試之前，有幾件重要的事項應該做：

- 確認你的考試地點和報到時間。考試地點和報到時間有時候可能會變動，請在考試前 24 小時檢查你的 ETS 帳號。
- 檢查你的身分證明文件。如果沒有適當的文件，就不能進入考試中心。請確定你在報名時所使用的名字與身分證明文件上的名字完全一致。
- 查看測驗簡章和考場指南。
- 穿著舒適，為當天室溫做好應變措施。如果你在考試期間需要脫掉一件衣物，例如毛衣，考場人員會指示你將其放在考場提供的置物區。如果沒有可用的置物區，可以將物品掛在椅子的後面。如果你離開考場前往置物區，這會被視為非休息時間離開，考官會要求你在離開考場時簽名離開，並在返回考場時出示你的身分證明文件和簽名入場。在非休息時間不會停止考試計時。

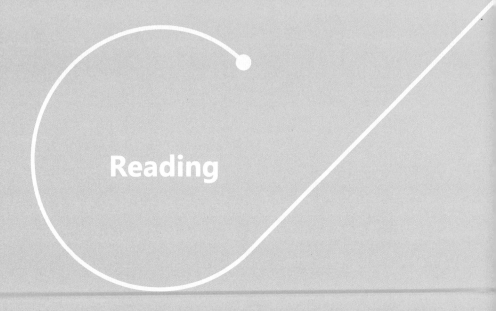

Reading

Part 1 閱讀

Unit 1

閱讀測驗指南
Guide to Reading

1-1　閱讀測驗概述

閱讀部分是托福網路測驗（TOEFL iBT）的第一部分。這部分會有幾篇文章，並根據每篇文章提出一系列的問題，來測試你對書面英文的理解能力。

閱讀測驗概述

內容	閱讀部分測試你理解書面學術英文（written academic English）的能力，其中包括各種不同類型和學術主題的文章。
須具備的能力	為了在閱讀測驗拿下高分，你必須能夠： • 理解文章裡的基本學術字彙。 • 快速掃視一段文章，理解其主旨和支持細節。 • 理解資訊的組織架構。 • 理解推論、關係、釋義和文章的目的。 • 在規定的時間內回答問題。
聽力段落	閱讀部分包括兩篇文章，每篇文章的篇幅通常是 650 至 700 字。每篇文章都會出現在你的螢幕上，並且在你作答時依然持續顯示。 閱讀測驗有三種不同類型的文章：說明文、論說文和歷史類文章。此外，每篇文章都會按照特定的結構呈現，包括比較與對照、因果關係、問題與解決方法、理論與支持，以及分類。
問題	每篇文章有 10 道選擇題，通常可以分為以下幾種類型： • Detail 細節　　　　　　• Referent 指涉 • Negative Fact 挑錯　　• Function 功能 • Inference 推論　　　　• Vocabulary 字彙 • Sentence Summary / Simplification 句子摘要／簡化 • Passage / Prose Summary 段落／文章摘要 • Insert A Sentence / Text 文句插入
計時	你有 35 分鐘的時間閱讀並回答兩篇文章的問題。

在閱讀部分，你看到的文章會類似於北美的大學生可能讀到的文字內容。文章的主題涵蓋了廣泛的學術科目，包括：

- anthropology 人類學
- archaeology 考古學
- art history 藝術史
- astronomy 天文學
- botany 植物學
- biology 生物學
- education 教育學
- engineering 工程學
- environmental science 環境科學
- geography 地理學
- geology 地質學
- history 歷史學
- literature 文學
- marketing 行銷學
- music 音樂
- paleontology 古生物學
- photography 攝影學
- psychology 心理學
- sociology 社會學
- urban studies 城市研究

閱讀部分有三種類型的文章：說明文、論說文和歷史類文章，通常每種類型的文章至少包含一篇。

Expository 說明文	定義	為一個主題提供概括性的說明
	主題範例	- Types of Camouflage 保護色的類型 - Adaptations of Deep Sea Fish 深海魚的適應 - Important Traditions of the Bambara Culture 班巴拉文化的重要傳統
Argumentative 論說文	定義	提供一個觀點，並提出幾個理由來支持該觀點
	主題範例	- Evidence of Contact Between Pacific Cultures and Indigenous Americans 美洲土著與太平洋文化接觸的證據 - Recuperation Theory vs. Circadian Theory of Sleep 復元理論vs.睡眠晝夜節律理論 - How Non-Native Species Hurt Local Habitats 非本土物種對本土棲息地的傷害
Historical 歷史類文章	定義	聚焦於過去的事件
	主題範例	- History of the Telescope 望遠鏡的歷史 - The Effects of the Norman Conquest 諾曼第征服英格蘭的影響 - Journalism and Social Change in the Twentieth Century 二十世紀的新聞業與社會變革

結構方式：每篇文章通常都會採用特定的結構，以此呈現出文章的觀點是如何舖陳。

結構	描述
Classification 分類	描述某個事物的兩、三種不同類別
Compare / Contrast 比較／對照	討論兩個或多個事物之間的相似性和差異性
Cause / Effect 因果關係	討論兩個或多個事物之間的因果關係
Theory / Support 理論／支持	提出一個理論，並且提供對它的支持性觀點
Problem / Solution 問題／解決方法	提出一個問題，並且討論解決方法

1-3　挑戰及解決方法

挑戰 1

文章或題目中有許多我不認識的單字。

解決方法 1　擴充詞彙。有好幾種工具可以幫助你擴充詞庫，提供學術環境中常見用語的字彙表是其中之一。艾維里科斯海德（Averil Coxhead）編製的學術字彙表（Academic Word List / AWL）囊括了大學入門教材中常見的 570 個單字。熟悉這些單字有助於在考試中表現得更好，並為進入英文授課課程做好準備。

解決方法 2　學習時使用學習者的詞典。像柯林斯高級英語詞典（Collins Cobuild Advanced Dictionary）提供了清楚的定義、例句、文法、插圖和照片來幫助你擴充知識，以及學會日常和學術字彙的用法。在本書中，你會看到具有挑戰性或不熟悉單字的定義，這些單字可能會在托福網路測驗的文章中出現。單字的定義就是來自柯林斯高級英語詞典。

解決方法 3　利用前後文線索（Context clues）。前後文線索就是圍繞著關鍵詞的單字和詞組，可以利用這些線索幫助你確定不熟悉單字的含義。作者可能會使用多種方式為關鍵詞提供前後文線索，包括舉例說明關鍵詞，將關鍵詞的含義和與其相反的概念作對照，或是提供關鍵詞的間接定義。關於這些方式的更多資訊，請參考 83 頁的表格。另外也可以試著閱讀報紙或大學教科書中大約 300 字的文字段落，來練習找到並使用前後文線索。閱讀時請注意作者用來幫助你理解困難單字的方式。

利用前後文線索的方法		
注意出現在醒目標示單字附近的舉例。如果你熟悉這些舉例，就可以利用它們來確定醒目標示單字的含義。	關鍵詞	▪ such as 比如 ▪ including 包括 ▪ consists of 由…組成 ▪ this includes 這包括 ▪ like 像
	例句	The photographs show banal activities, like going to the grocery store or doing household chores. 這些照片呈現了平凡的活動，比如去雜貨店或是做家務。
找出與前一個觀念呈現差異的關鍵字。如果你知道前後句中字詞的意思，你就會知道醒目標示單字的反義。	關鍵詞	▪ Unlike X... 不像 X ▪ On the other hand, X... 另一方面，X… ▪ While... 儘管… ▪ But... 但是… ▪ However... 然而…
	例句	Unlike most mammals, few of which are venomous, the platypus produces a noxious substance that can cause extreme pain in humans. 和大多的哺乳動物不同，只有很少數有毒，鴨嘴獸會分泌出一種能夠在人類身上引起極度疼痛的有害物質。
在醒目標示單字前後的句子中尋找術語的間接定義。定義可能是更簡單同義詞，或者是幫助闡釋其含義的資訊。	關鍵詞	▪ and 並且 ▪ meaning that 表示
	例句	In the southwestern United States, the sunflower is ubiquitous, and it is difficult to find a garden that doesn't include the plant. 在美國西南部，向日葵到處都是，很難找到一處不栽培這種植物的花園。

學習觀察單字的組成，例如字首和字尾，來確認單字的含義。許多英文單字是利用字首和字尾來組成的，字首置於單字的開頭，字尾置於單字的尾部。透過學習常見的英文字首和字尾的含義，你就能夠推測單字的定義。更多資訊請參見第 84 頁的表格。

✎ 挑戰 2

常常在我完成所有問題之前，時間就用完了。

解決方法 1　使用略讀（skimming）和掃視（scanning）技巧尋找問題的答案。略讀是指快速閱讀一篇文章，只關注最重要的概念。藉著略讀，你通常可以在短時間內判斷出許多問題所詢問的重要觀念。如此一來，就可以避免考試時間不夠用的問題。

為了有效略讀，你一定要知道在哪裡找到文章的重要觀念。無論文章的結構如何，重要觀念通常會出現在相同的地方。請參考下表。

文章組成	略讀技巧
Introduction 引言	▪ 閱讀引言的最後二至三行，這裡通常會描述文章的主旨。
Body Paragraphs 主體段落	▪ 閱讀主體段落的前二至三行，這些句子會描述段落的主旨。 ▪ 閱讀主體段落的最後二至三行，這幾行通常會說明各段落與段落主旨之間的關係，它們還會幫助你理解各個主體段落之間的關係。

「掃視」是指為了找到特定的關鍵詞或概念而快速閱讀文章。在閱讀題目及選項之後，你應該注意所有關鍵詞或概念，例如名稱、術語或數字，這些資訊有助於你回答問題。接著掃視文章，專注尋找這些關鍵詞。

請記住，在略讀或掃視文章時，不需要完全理解每個單字。最重要的是找到需要的資訊，以便快速和正確的回答問題。

要練習略讀和掃視，可以從大學教科書上找一篇 600-700 字的文章。先略讀文章，在紙上記下最重要的觀念，接著試著掃視文章，找出關鍵詞和日期。練習略讀和掃視的次數愈多，速度和準確性就會愈高，所以要盡量每天練習。

解決方法 2　注意螢幕上的計時器。計時器顯示你在該部分剩餘的時間。當你答題時，一定要偶爾看一下計時器。在閱讀測驗，你可以稍後回答之前未答的問題，所以一定要利用這個功能。如果你在一個題目上花了兩分鐘以上的時間就先跳過，稍後再回來。這能幫你避免卡在同一個題目上浪費時間。

🔍 **挑戰 3**

文章通常很複雜和讓人混亂，有時候我讀著讀著就茫然了。

解決方法 1：　了解托福閱讀文章常見的基本結構。如果你在閱讀時無法專注或感到困惑，只需要思考文章的結構就能重新找到方向。請利用下表來了解文章的常見結構，以及文章中資訊的常見顯示方式。

	Introduction 引言	Body Paragraphs 主體段落
Classification 分類	介紹將在文章中分類的事物	為被分類的事物提供 2-3 種不同的類型或特徵
Compare / Contrast 比較／對照	介紹兩個概念、事物或事件	第一段描述第一個事物的幾個特徵。在接下來的段落裡，作者提出第二個事物的相應特徵，指出這些特徵與第一個事物的相似或相異之處。
Cause / Effect 因／果	介紹一個事件或過程	第一段描述一個事件或過程的 1-2 個原因。接著作者描述這些原因的效應或結果。
Problem / Solution 問題／解決方案	介紹一個問題	提供 2-3 個解決問題的方法
Theory / Support 理論／支持	介紹一個理論	提供 2-3 個證據來支持理論

請閱讀本書中的每一篇文章來練習，看看你是否能分辨每篇文章的結構。請注意文章的主體段落是怎麼組織的。

解決方法 2：　在閱讀時尋找轉折詞（transition language）。轉折詞是用於連接不同句子想法的單字和詞組。例如有些轉折詞是導入新主題（Another example of X is… 另一個 X 的例子是…），而有些則指出過程或事件的順序（First… 首先…）。轉折詞通常出現在新段落的開頭，不過也可能出現在段落的中間。注意轉折詞及其使用方式，有助於你更加了解文章的內容，避免被文章中的資訊混淆。關於轉折詞的詳細介紹以及練習，請參考 65 頁。

要記住的資訊太多了！

解決方法 1. 不要擔心記不住文章中的每個細節。當你答題時，文章會一直顯示在螢幕右側。題目所根據的段落會以箭頭 [ ] 標記，你可以在回答問題時滑動文章，以找到你可能需要的任何資訊。

解決方法 2. 在紙條上迅速概述一下文章大綱。雖然在答題時可以檢視文章，但在某些情況下寫筆記仍然很有幫助。例如在略讀文章時，可以把閱讀中的基本重點做成大綱。利用縮寫來寫大綱就不會花太多時間。你可以在答題時使用大綱作為快速參考。大綱不需要包含文章的所有細節，但應該包含主旨，而且大綱在幾乎所有的問題類型上都很有幫助。請參考以下的範例大綱，它所根據的是第 51-52 頁的文章。

Fossey 佛西
- studied and protected the mountain gorilla 研究並保護山地大猩猩
- started a new approach to conservation 開創了一種新的保育方法
- worked in Rwanda 在盧安達工作
- established research center 成立研究中心

Threats 威脅
- hunters 獵人
- loss of habitat 棲息地喪失
- tourism 觀光業

Fossey's work 佛西的工作
- saved the gorillas from extinction 拯救了大猩猩免於滅絕
- began 'active conservationism' 開始了「積極保育主義」
- supported local population 支持當地人口
- showed humans and natural world can work together
  證明了人類和自然界可以共同合作

這個大綱雖然非常精簡，但仍包含了文章中最重要的概念。此外，這個大綱反映了文章的基本結構，對於段落／文章摘要題尤其有幫助。無論你正在做什麼類型的題目，寫下這些資訊可能會讓你更容易理解文章的基本概念，和更清楚的記住它們。

在閱讀題目和選項時,寫下關鍵字和論點。有些人在閱讀時會發現把關鍵字做醒目標示很有幫助。不過在考試當天,你無法在電腦螢幕上標記任何文字。因此,可以改成把任何能幫助你記住題目或選項中重要概念的關鍵字寫到便條紙上。接著你可以參考你的關鍵字列表,快速掃視文章,把關鍵字找出來。

挑戰 5

我很難分辨主要支持細節和次要事件之間的區別。

試著理解細節在文章中的作用。去理解你感到困惑的細節與文章中的論點有什麼關聯,你才能夠區分主要細節(major details)與次要想法(minor ideas)。利用下表中的步驟來理解文章中細節的作用。

區分主要支持細節(Major Supporting Details)和 次要事實(Minor Facts)的步驟	
步驟 1	略讀第一段,找到主題句(topic sentence)。主題句是表達一篇或一段文章主題的句子。無論文章類型或結構如何,每篇文章都會有一個它想呈現的主要論點。 引言(introduction)通常會提供主題的簡要背景,並提出一個總結文章主要論點的主題句。
步驟 2	略讀主體段落(body paragraphs),找到每一段的主題句。主題句通常位於主體段落的前二到三行內。 找到主題句,你便可以理解文章的主要論點,以及作者如何將每個想法組織起來。
步驟 3	一旦找到主題句,而且你也將文章的主要論點弄清楚了,就馬上回頭去看你不確定的細節。同樣的,當你檢視細節時,為了節省時間,要用掃視的方式在文章中尋找與這些細節相關的關鍵字。
步驟 4	當你讀到的句子包含你不確定的細節時,問自己以下問題:如果你省略了該特定細節,文章的主旨是否會變得薄弱?如果答案是肯定的,那麼該細節可能是一個主要細節。另一方面,如果省略該細節不會明顯改變或削弱文章的主旨,那麼該細節就是一個次要事實。

沒有一個答案選項「感覺」是正確的。

解決方法①　要熟悉不同的題型和回答每種題型所需的技巧。閱讀測驗有十種可能的題目類型。熟悉每種測驗題型的答題技巧，你才更容易了解如何找出正確答案，這有助於提高你對正確答案的直覺。仔細閱讀本書各節的「快速指南」。

解決方法②　了解正確的答案選項為何成立。雖然閱讀部分的正確答案在許多方面各不相同，但請記住，正確選項的一個共同特徵是「對關鍵資訊的改述」。正確選項一定會包含你在文章中讀到的關鍵資訊。不過這些資訊通常是混雜的，以避免正確答案選項使用與文章相同的措辭。換句話說，正確選項會包含文章的改述資訊。選項中的資訊可能透過以下方式改述：

- 更換關鍵詞（即使用同義詞）
- 包含文章中所詳述概念的一般資訊
- 將語氣從主動改為被動（或反過來）。被動語態通常是 be 動詞 + 過去分詞形成的。

為了練習判斷改述資訊，請完成本書閱讀測驗的一道練習題，並試著辨別一些選項中所使用的改述類型。這也許有助於提高你辨識正確答案和錯誤答案的能力。

解決方法③　使用排除法。排除法需要仔細閱讀每個選項，並且排除錯誤的選項。通常你可以排除包含以下內容的選項：

- 與文章中提出的事實和細節相互矛盾的資訊
- 答非所問的資訊
- 與文章中一模一樣的措辭。請記住，正確答案通常是從文章中改述的資訊，因此包含相同措辭的選項可能是錯誤的。

解決方法④　跳過你不確定的題目。請記住，閱讀部分你可以返回到前一個題目。但是你用來回答所有題目的時間相當有限。對於某些人來說，如果有多一點時間去思考，會更容易回答困難的問題。因此如果你發現你在一個問題上花費太多時間，而且你不確定答案，就跳到下一題或下一篇文章。你或許會發現，等你稍後回頭去看時，原本困難的題目變容易了。

題目類型	內容
Detail 細節題	要求你根據文章中呈現的事件資訊提供答案。
Referent 指涉題	要求你判斷一個單字或詞組指的是什麼——通常是代名詞。
Negative Fact 挑錯題	要求你根據文章辨識出錯誤的選項。
Function 功能題	問你作者所使用的修辭策略。作者是試圖舉例、解釋或闡明某事、挑戰某個觀點等等。
Inference 推論題	根據文章中呈現的資訊，要求你做出結論。
Vocabulary 詞彙題	要求你選出最貼切描述文章中醒目標示單字或詞組的定義。
Sentence Summary / Simplification 句子摘要／簡化題	要求你選出最能概括文章中的醒目標示句的答案。
Passage / Prose Summary 段落／文章摘要題	呈現一段文章的介紹敘述，並要求你選出三個最能概括文章主旨的選項。
Insert A Sentence / Text 文句插入題	給你一個句子，要求你把它放在段落中最適合的位置。

Unit 2 細節題 & 指涉題
Detail Questions and Referent Questions

2-1 細節題

細節題問的是文章中所呈現的事件資訊，這是閱讀部分中最常見的題型。

細節題可能用以下方式表達：

- According to paragraph 1, what is true about X? 根據第一段，有關 X 的說法何者為真？
- According to paragraph 2, why was the discovery of X significant?
  根據第二段，為什麼發現 X 是重要的？
- What do X and Y have in common? X 和 Y 有什麼共同之處？
- According to paragraph 3, which of the following was responsible for X?
  根據第三段，下列哪一個因素導致了 X？
- In paragraph 4, what does the author say about X? 在第四段裡，作者對於 X 有什麼看法？

細節題快速指南

內容	細節題會問文章中支持主要觀點（main points）的重要事實（important facts）。細節題通常是根據支持性事實（supporting facts）、關鍵詞的定義，以及文章中描述的事件順序出題。
須具備的能力	為了正確回答細節題，你必須能夠： ▪ 分辨文章的主要觀點（main points）以及用來支持它們的細節。並準備好回答有關次要細節（secondary details）的問題。 ▪ 理解兩個事件或概念之間的關係（X是否是由Y引起的？X是否在Y之後發生？X是否比Y更重要？）。 ▪ 仔細閱讀題目，理解它所要求的資訊。 ▪ 掃視文章，以尋找可以用來確定正確答案的具體細節。
正確答案	細節題的正確答案包含了在文章中呈現的事件資訊。正確答案通常可以在文章中的一兩個句子中找到，並且通常包含了改述的資訊。
錯誤答案	注意可能包含以下內容的選項： ▪ 與文章所提供的資訊相互矛盾 ▪ 使用與文章一模一樣的措辭，但並未回答問題。正確答案通常會改述資訊。 ▪ 包含文章中並未提到或支持的資訊

2-1-1　掌握要領：細節題回答技巧

Ⓐ 快速閱讀以下的細節題範例，在題目和選項中，用底線標示出能幫助你確定正確答案的任何關鍵字。

1. According to paragraph 2, what is true about the repetition strategy used in ancient India?
   ○ It allowed users to add new details to narratives.
   ○ It is more complex than other repetition methods.
   ○ It required people to read the sentences out loud.
   ○ It required users to remember entire paragraphs at a time.

Ⓑ 現在閱讀一篇有關於文學的文章。在閱讀時，用底線標出你認為有助於回答 A 部分題目的單字或詞組。當你完成後，在以上選項裡標記出正確答案。

Oral Narratives

1　Oral narratives are stories that are communicated through speech and not through the written word. Most cultures have important oral narratives that allow them to pass on traditional stories to younger generations. Amazingly, these can survive for many years without experiencing significant changes. Oral narratives remain unchanged for many years due to specific memorization techniques that help storytellers preserve the original form of the narrative.

2　One such technique is repetition, which involves saying the words of a story many times. For instance, a storyteller might repeat the same sentence many times until he or she remembers it. Once one sentence is memorized, the storyteller repeats the next sentence until it, too, is committed to memory. Thus, sentence by sentence, one can learn a complete narrative. Of course, some forms of repetition are more complicated than the method just described. For example, in ancient India, people memorized texts by repeating the words in a different order. If a sentence read, "She went to the river to wash her clothes," a person might memorize the sentence by repeating the words like this: "She went she, went to went, to the to," and so on.

3　Another important way to memorize oral narratives is through the use of musical memory, which refers to a person's ability to remember pitch. Like notes in a song, some words in a story have higher or lower pitch than the surrounding words. Someone listening to an oral narrative might remember these changes in pitch, and this can help the person remember the changes in the story. If one part of the story is exciting, the storyteller's voice may become higher in pitch. The listener will record this in his or her musical memory, and when the listener retells the story, his or her voice will become higher at the same moment.

中譯
口述敘事

1　口述敘事是透過言語傳達，而不是書寫下來的故事。大多數文化都有重要的口述敘事，讓他們能夠將傳統故事傳遞給年輕的一代。令人驚訝的是，這些口述敘事可以保存多年而不歷經顯著的變化。口述敘事能多年來保持不變是由於特定的記憶技巧，這些技巧能幫助說故事的人保留敘事的原始形式。

2　其中一種技巧是複述，它牽涉到將故事的詞句重複多次。例如，一個說故事的人可能會重複同一句話很多次，直到他／她記住為止。一旦一個句子被記住之後，說故事的人就會重複下一個句子，直到下一句也被記住。如此逐句重複，人們便可以學習完整的敘事。當然，有些複述形式比前面描述的方法更複雜。例如在古印度，人們會以不同的順序來重複詞句，藉此記憶文字內容。假如句子是「She went to the river to wash her clothes」，那麼一個人可能這樣重複詞句來記住這個句子「She went she, went to went, to the to」，依此類推。

3　另一種記憶口述敘事的重要方法是透過音樂來記憶，這是指一個人記住音調的能力。就像歌曲中的音符一樣，故事中有些字詞的音調比前後字詞的音調更高或更低。聽口述敘事的人可能會記住這些音調的變化，這有助於他們記住故事中的變化。如果故事的某個部分很刺激，說故事者的音調可能會變得較高。聽的人將把這部分記錄在他們的音樂記憶中，當他們重述故事時，他們的音調也會在同一個地方變得比較高。

字彙 POWERED BY COBUILD
oral 口的：uttered by the mouth or in words 由口中發出或以言語表達
pitch 音調：how high or low a sound is 一個音有多高或多低

2-1-2　掌握要領：細節題回答技巧

技巧 1
仔細閱讀題目。細節題的措辭千變萬化，所以一定要仔細閱讀題目，並確實了解它要問的是什麼。是在問主要細節還是次要細節？問的是事件發生的時間，還是在問兩個事件之間的因果關係？

練習① 在第 33 頁的問題中，用底線標示出有助於你理解回答問題所需資訊的單字或詞組。

技巧 2
掃視題目依據的段落。細節題的答案通常可以在文章中的一兩個句子裡找到。當你掃視題目依據的段落時，要尋找有助於你回答問題的關鍵字。

練習 2 在第 33 頁的第二段，用方框標示出有助於你選擇正確答案的單字或措辭。

技巧 3

當心與文章措辭相同的選項。細節題的正確答案通常含有閱讀內容的改述資訊。請注意含有和文章中相同措辭的選項，它們可能不包含題目所要求的資訊。

練習 3 在33 頁的題目，畫線刪掉一個與閱讀內容措辭相似的選項。

技巧 4

根據文章中的資訊刪除錯誤的選項。細節題依據的必定是文章中的事實。因此，根據文章中的資訊，任何內容錯誤的選項都不正確。

練習 4 在第 33 頁，根據文章中的資訊，從剩餘的選項中刪除兩個內容錯誤的選項。

技巧 5

明智的猜測！細節題通常會問你能夠支持主旨的細節。如果你在選擇正確答案時遇到困難，請根據題目所依據段落的主旨（main idea），選擇與其一致的答案。

練習 5 在第 33 頁的第二段圈出一個句子，概述整個段落的主旨。你的正確答案是否支持這個主題句？

TEST TIP!

不要在一個題目上花太多時間。記住，在閱讀部分，只要你有時間，就可以回頭去看前面的題目。因此如果你遇到一個比較難的題目，不要害怕跳到下一題。只要寫下題目編號，你就會記得稍後要回頭去看

指涉題要求你判斷一個單字所指向的另一個單字或片語。最常見的指涉題通常會包括代名詞，代名詞是句子中取代名詞或名詞片語的詞。在托福網路測驗中，人稱代名詞（personal pronouns）是最常考的。不過指涉題可能偶爾也會考關係代名詞（relative pronouns）、指示代名詞（demonstrative pronouns）或反身代名詞（reflexive pronouns），以及其他字詞。請參考下表的例子。

代名詞或其他字詞	舉例
人稱代名詞：I, you, he / she / it, we, they, me, him / her, us, them	**Susie** went to the lab. She didn't come back until later. **蘇西**去了實驗室，她直到稍後才回來。
關係代名詞：which / that, who / whom / whose, whatever, what	Rick replaced the **window** that was broken during the storm. 瑞克換掉了風暴期間被打破的那扇**窗戶**。
指示代名詞：this, that, these, those	The **apples** were in the bowl. Alan used these to bake a pie. **蘋果**在碗裡，艾倫用這些（蘋果）來烤派。
反身代名詞：myself, yourself, herself, himself, itself, ourselves, themselves	The **baseball players** entertained themselves by singing. **棒球選手們**透過唱歌來娛樂（他們）自己。
其他字詞：any, so, one	Mia and Kate went to buy **supplies** at the store. They couldn't find any. 米亞和凱特去商店買**用品**，他們找不到任何東西。

備註：在這些例子中，代名詞加底線，指涉對象加粗體。

基本上，每篇文章不會超過一個指涉題。

指涉題可能用以下方式表達：

- The word X in paragraph 2 refers to...
第二段中的 X 指的是…

內容	指涉題會在文章中指定一個代名詞,並以醒目標示來強調。答案會是文章裡的單字或詞組,你必須選出與醒目標示的代名詞相關的選項。
須具備的能力	為了正確回答指涉題,你必須能夠: ▪ 理解名詞和代名詞的文法一致性。 ▪ 確定文章中醒目標示的代名詞所指涉的對象。
正確答案	指涉題的正確答案會定義醒目標示的代名詞的指涉對象。指涉對象在數量、性別或屬格上與醒目標示的代名詞一致。在大多數情況下,文章中的指涉對象會出現在代名詞之前。
錯誤答案	注意包含以下資訊的選項: ▪ 在數量、性別或屬格上與醒目標示的代名詞不一致 ▪ 緊接出現在醒目標示詞前面。雖然正確答案通常出現在代名詞之前,但指涉對象通常不是直接出現在代名詞之前的名詞。 ▪ 改變句子的意思,使其與文章中呈現的事實相互矛盾。

2-2-1　指涉題範例

Ⓐ 快速閱讀以下的指涉題範例,在題目和選項中,用底線標示出能幫助你確定正確答案的任何關鍵字。

TOEFL Reading

Question

1. The word it in paragraph 1 refers to
   ○ the fifteenth century.
   ○ Venice, Italy.
   ○ Europe.
   ○ a top producer.

2. The word they in paragraph 2 refers to
   ○ the city's legacy.
   ○ printers.
   ○ books.
   ○ historians.

Ⓑ 現在閱讀文章範例。在閱讀時,用底線標出包含上述選項字詞的句子。完成後,標記出正確答案。

Printing in Venice

1   In 1455, a German goldsmith named Johannes Gutenberg invented the printing press, changing the way that people received new information thereafter. Not long after that, hundreds of print shops had opened throughout Europe. However, one city in particular emerged as the leader in printing by the end of the fifteenth century: Venice, Italy. Printing nearly a quarter of all books in Europe during the 1490s, **it** was a top producer of books. This success, which continued well into the 1500s, was due to several factors.

2   Long before the first print shop opened in Venice in 1469, the city was known as a major trade capital in Europe. For centuries, Venice had been an important stop on many trade routes, allowing Venetian merchants to establish partnerships with businesses based in many international locations across Europe and Asia. The city's legacy as a trade hub proved useful for printers in the fifteenth century because it was relatively easy to sell and distribute the books that **they** produced. According to historians, many printers in Venice created books specifically for export to other countries.

3   Another factor that allowed Venetian printers to flourish was the abundance of skilled and educated workers who resided in the city. Indeed, throughout the 1400s, Venice was home to a large and diverse population of scholars. These scholars not only provided manuscripts for printing, but were able to edit works created by other people as well. As a result, editing and printing a manuscript in Venice was relatively inexpensive. In some cases, printing costs in Venice were a third of what they were in other printing centers in Europe.

中譯

威尼斯的印刷業

1   在 1455 年，一位名叫約翰尼斯・古騰堡的德國金匠發明了印刷機，改變了人們接收新資訊的方式。不久之後，歐洲各地開了數百家印刷店。然而在十五世紀末，特別有一座城市以印刷業領頭羊的姿態出現：義大利的威尼斯。威尼斯在 1490 年代幾乎印刷了歐洲四分之一的書籍，它是書籍的頂尖生產者。這項成就一直持續到十六世紀，有幾個原因。

2   在 1469 年威尼斯第一家印刷店開業之前，這座城市就已經以歐洲的主要貿易中心聞名。幾個世紀以來，威尼斯一直是許多貿易路線的重要中途站，使威尼斯商人與位於歐洲和亞洲許多國際地點的企業建立合作夥伴關係。該城市貿易中心的地位是留給後世的資產，對十五世紀的印刷業非常有幫助，因為他們所生產的書籍相對容易出售和分銷。據歷史學家說，許多威尼斯印刷業者所生產的書籍，是專門為了出口到其他國家的。

3   威尼斯的印刷業蓬勃發展的另一個因素是，這座城市裡住著大量技術純熟和受過教育的工人。事實上，在整個十五世紀，威尼斯擁有大量各式各樣的學者。這些學者不僅提供印刷品的手稿，還

能夠編輯由其他人創作的作品。因此在威尼斯，編輯和將手稿拿去印刷都相當便宜。在某些情況下，威尼斯的印刷成本是歐洲其他印刷中心的三分之一。

2-2-2 掌握要領：指涉題回答技巧

技巧 1

重新閱讀醒目標示的單字所在的段落。當這樣做時，一定要注意選項裡的名詞。同時，找出能幫助你排除錯誤選項的前後文線索。

練習① 掃視 38 頁文章的第一和第二段。在第一段裡用底線標記出 4 個用在第 1 題選項裡的單字或措辭。在第二段裡用底線標記出 4 個用在第 2 題選項裡的單字或措辭。

技巧 2

試著用每個選項來替換醒目標示的單字。當這麼做時，可以排除以下選項：

- 與文章事實相互矛盾。你也許會發現好幾個選項都可用，不過其中一個選項可能會改變句子的意思，使它不符合文意。

- 與代名詞在數量、性別或屬格方面不一致。請參考下表，以了解在一致性（agreement）的簡要說明。

Number 數量	說明	名詞和對應的代名詞是單數還是複數
	舉例	The **students** sat in the classroom. They didn't know when the class would start. 正確：**學生們**坐在教室裡。他們不知道什麼時候開始上課。 The **students** sat in the office. He didn't know when the class would start. 錯誤：**學生們**坐在辦公室裡。他不知道什麼時候開始上課。
Gender 性別	說明	名詞和對應的代名詞是男性還是女性
	舉例	The **man** left his keys on the table, where he could find them easily. 正確：那位**男士**把鑰匙留在桌上，那是他可以輕鬆找到的地方。 The **man** left his keys on the table, where she could find them easily. 錯誤：那位**男士**把鑰匙留在桌上，那是她可以輕鬆找到的地方。

Case 屬格	說明	名詞和對應的代名詞是受格還是主格
	舉例	**Peter** arrived late, so he couldn't find a seat. 正確：**彼得**遲到了，所以他找不到座位。 **Peter** arrived late, so him couldn't find a seat. 錯誤：**彼得**遲到了，所以他被找不到座位。

練習 2　在 37 頁的第 1 題裡，畫線刪掉在替換代名詞的時候，意思變得與文章事實相互矛盾的選項。在 37 頁的第 2 題裡，畫線刪掉與代名詞的數量不符的選項。

TEST TIP!

在閱讀部分，指涉題是唯一與文法有關的題型。如果你不確定如何使用英文代名詞，請務必在考試前熟悉這個主題的文法講解。

掃視關於劇院的短文，用底線標出每個段落的主旨。

English Renaissance Theater

1   As European societies changed dramatically in the sixteenth and seventeenth centuries, artistic expression changed as well. England offers a clear example—in the early sixteenth century, a new type of theater, called English Renaissance theater, flourished there. English Renaissance theater was popular until the mid-seventeenth century and featured the work of famous playwrights like Christopher Marlowe and William Shakespeare. This new theatrical style, sometimes also referred to as Elizabethan theater, developed because of a number of changes in England.

2   One major reason for the popularity of English Renaissance theater was that it reflected the cultural changes that were occurring in England at the time. One such change was the ongoing attempts to distinguish the practices and beliefs of the English from **those** of cultures in mainland Europe. In the theater, this was accomplished by breaking from the types of plays that were trendy at the time throughout Europe. Most of these were morality plays which were intended to teach the audience moral lessons. These were common in English theater until the early sixteenth century. However, as social change occurred in the 1500s, morality plays became less prevalent in England. Instead, theater companies borrowed heavily from classical Greek tragedies and comedies to create new Renaissance-style pieces. The plays of William Shakespeare are well-known examples—he wrote about tragic love stories, comedic love stories, and the histories of royal families. These themes, which prioritized entertainment over moral lessons, became widespread throughout England.

3   During the same period, English theater companies and performance spaces also underwent a number of changes that helped bolster English Renaissance theater. Before the sixteenth century, theater groups in England consisted of traveling companies that went from town to town performing the same morality plays. But starting in the mid-sixteenth century, English nobility began funding the construction of theaters throughout the country. These public spaces housed companies of actors, who enjoyed the support and sponsorship of different noble families. Many theaters became recognized as public spaces devoted to entertainment, and gradually, the traveling companies of morality actors disappeared completely. Moreover, because many acting companies received

financial support from noble families, **they** had the resources to create more and more Renaissance pieces and perform them in these spaces.

英國文藝復興劇院

1　在十六和十七世紀，歐洲社會發生了巨大變化，藝術表現也隨之改變。英國供了一個明確的例子——在十六世紀初，一種被稱作英國文藝復興劇院的新型態劇院，開始蓬勃發展。英國文藝復興劇院在十七世紀中期之前很受歡迎，並呈現了著名劇作家如克里斯多福・馬洛和威廉・莎士比亞的作品。這種有時也被稱為伊莉莎白時代劇院的新戲院風格，是由於英國一連串的變化而發展出來的。

2　英國文藝復興劇院受歡迎的一個主要原因是，它反映了英國當時正在發生的文化變遷。其中一個變化，是不斷嘗試將英國的習慣和信仰與歐陸文化區分開來。實踐在劇院上，就是脫離了當時整個歐洲所流行的戲劇類型，其中大多數是旨在給予觀眾道德訓誡的道德劇，而這些在英國十六世紀初的劇院中很常見。然而，隨著十六世紀社會變革的發生，道德劇在英國變得不那麼普遍。取而代之的是，劇團大量借用了古典希臘悲劇和喜劇，創作出新的文藝復興風格作品。威廉・莎士比亞的劇本就是眾所皆知的例子——他寫過悲劇愛情故事、喜劇愛情故事以及皇室家族的歷史。這些主題優先考量的是娛樂而不是道德教訓，它們在整個英國逐漸流行起來。

3　在同一時期，英國的劇團和表演空間也經歷了一連串的變化，有助於強化英國文藝復興劇院。在十六世紀之前，英國的劇團由巡迴劇團組成，他們在一個接一個的城鎮裡表演相同的道德劇。但是從十六世紀中葉開始，英國貴族開始資助全國各地的劇院建設，這些公共空間容納了各種貴族家庭贊助的演員劇團。許多劇院被視為專門用於娛樂的公共空間，漸漸的，道德劇演員的巡迴劇團完全消失了。此外，由於許多演員劇團得到了貴族家庭的資助，他們有資源在這些空間裡創作愈來愈多的文藝復興作品，並且表演出來。

trendy 時髦的：something that is fashionable and modern 時尚且現代的事物
bolster 加強：to increase or strengthen something 增加或強化某個東西

Ⓑ 仔細閱讀題目。它們屬於哪種題型？在題目和選項中用底線標記你在回顧文章時要尋找的關鍵詞，接著開始作答。留意正確答案，並且閱讀答案解析的原因解釋。

1. According to paragraph 2, which of the following best describes popular theater in mainland Europe before the 1500s?

   ○ It was based on Greek plays.

   ○ Its primary goal was to teach lessons.

   ○ It featured the work of William Shakespeare.

   ○ It was enjoyed by royal families.

1. 根據第二段，下列哪一項最能描述十六世紀前的歐洲大陸所流行的劇院？

    ○ 它依據的是希臘戲劇。

    ✅ 它主要的目標是教導訓誡。

    ○ 它呈現威廉·莎士比亞的作品。

    ○ 它受到皇室家族的喜愛。

答案解析

▶ 題型：細節題

    ○ 作者指出，是英國文藝復興劇院借用了希臘戲劇，而不是歐洲劇院。

    ✅ 文章提到，道德劇在歐洲很受歡迎，它們教導了一些道德教訓。

    ○ 文章提到，十六世紀後的英國文藝復興劇院呈現了莎士比亞的作品。

    ○ 作者提到，莎士比亞寫了有關皇室家族的劇本，但這與題目無關。

2. The word those in paragraph 2 refers to

    ○ cultural changes.

    ○ ongoing attempts.

    ○ practices and beliefs.

    ○ the English.

中譯

2. 第二段裡的「those」指的是

    ○ 文化變遷。

    ○ 不斷嘗試。

    ✅ 習慣和信仰。

    ○ 英國人。

答案解析

▶ 題型：指涉題

    ○ 如果用「文化變遷」取代該代名詞，則該句子沒有意義。

    ○ 如果用「不斷嘗試」取代該代名詞，則該句子沒有意義。

    ✅ 該代名詞指的是習慣和信仰。

    ○ 記住，指涉題的答案很少是最靠近代名詞的名詞。

3. According to paragraph 3, what role did noble families play in the growth of English Renaissance theater?

○ They discouraged the production of morality plays.

○ They formed traveling companies that could perform new plays.

○ They provided inspiration for new types of plays.

○ They paid to have public theater spaces built.

中譯

3. 根據第三段，貴族家庭在英國文藝復興劇院的發展中扮演了什麼角色？

○ 他們不鼓勵道德劇的創作。

○ 他們組織了能夠演出新劇的巡迴劇團。

○ 他們為新型態的戲劇提供靈感。

✅ 他們支付了公共劇院空間的建設費用。

答案解析

▶ 題型：細節題

○ 作者說貴族家庭支持英國文藝復興劇院，而不是試圖阻止道德劇。

○ 作者說巡迴劇團消失是因為貴族家庭支持當地的演出團體。

○ 在第二段，作者提到英國文藝復興劇院的故事是關於皇室家庭，但這與貴族家庭不同。還有，題目指出答案出現在第三段裡。

✅ 作者說貴族家庭資助了公共劇場的建設。

4. The word they in paragraph 3 refers to

○ public spaces.

○ morality actors.

○ acting companies.

○ noble families.

中譯

4. 第三段中的「they」指的是

○ 公共空間。

○ 道德劇演員。

✅ 表演團體。

○ 貴族家庭。

答案解析

▶ **題型：指涉題**

○ 公共空間在句子的末尾才提到（these spaces），因此這不可能是答案。

○ 作者說道德劇演員消失了。如果用這個選項取代代名詞，這個句子沒有意義。

✅ 這個代名詞指的是表演團體。

○ 雖然「noble families」在數量上與代名詞一致，但這個選項沒有意義。

A 掃視關於音樂的短文，並寫下每段的主旨。

1. _____

2. _____

3. _____

4. _____

Ástor Piazzolla and Nuevo Tango

1   Tango is a type of music that originated among immigrant communities in Argentina and Uruguay during the mid-1800s. Today, tango remains iconic in its countries of origin and can still be heard in the homes of many Argentines and Uruguayans, though some musicians have made efforts to modernize the genre. One such artist was Ástor Piazzolla, who based his nuevo tango, or new tango, on traditional Argentine tango. Piazzolla's nuevo tango retains elements of traditional tango, but **it** is also distinct in several ways.

2   Piazzolla was born to Italian parents in Argentina. However, he spent most of his childhood in New York City. Throughout his early years, Piazzolla missed Argentina and felt a connection to his native country's tango music, the lyrics of which often describe nostalgia for one's home country. Piazzolla began to explore traditional Argentine music by learning how to play the bandoneón, an accordion-like instrument that is often employed in tango music. At sixteen, Piazzolla returned to Argentina, where he was widely considered a highly skilled bandoneón player. In fact, he was often invited to play with Argentine orchestras and bands before his own music gained popularity. The bandoneón also featured prominently in his nuevo tango music.

3   While there were clear influences of traditional Argentine tango in his work, Piazzolla's nuevo tango also reflected the other types of music he was exposed to as a young man. For example, growing up in New York, he developed an interest in jazz. Not surprisingly, he often incorporated rhythms from **this music** into many of his pieces. Furthermore, he learned about classical music by composers like Johann Sebastian Bach through his parents and later through his musical studies. Piazzolla used classical ideas in his work, such as counterpoint, which is when two or more voices sing using different rhythms but work together to create the harmony of a piece. Between jazz and classical influences, Piazzolla's tango was very different from the traditional tango of Argentina.

4　Another unique element of Piazzolla's nuevo tango music is its experimental tendency. Piazzolla was always looking for new and interesting pieces to incorporate into his own music. In 1956, Piazzolla released an album that combined his music with the poetry of writer Jorge Luis Borges. Throughout the album, Borges's romantic and emotional poetry was narrated over Piazzolla's nuevo tango music. This unique collaboration sparked outcries from traditional tango musicians, who considered Piazzolla's style to be too experimental.

中譯

阿斯托爾・皮亞佐拉與新探戈

1　探戈是一種在 19 世紀中葉起源於阿根廷和烏拉圭移民社區的音樂類型。今日，探戈在其發源地仍然具有代表性地位，許多阿根廷人和烏拉圭人的家中仍然可以聽到探戈音樂，儘管一些音樂家已經致力使該流派現代化。阿斯托爾・皮亞佐拉就是其中一位，他以傳統阿根廷探戈為基礎，創作了自己的新探戈。皮亞佐拉的新探戈保留了傳統探戈的元素，但在幾個方面仍有自己的特色。

2　皮亞佐拉出生於阿根廷的義大利裔家庭，但他大部分的童年都在紐約度過。皮亞佐拉在早年一直懷念阿根廷，對他的家鄉探戈音樂有著特殊情感，這種音樂的歌詞常常描述一個人對家鄉的思念。皮亞佐拉開始藉著學習彈奏班多鈕來探索傳統阿根廷音樂，班多鈕是一種類似手風琴的樂器，常用於探戈音樂。皮亞佐拉在十六歲的時候返回阿根廷，他被普遍認為是一位技藝精湛的班多鈕演奏家。事實上，他在自己的音樂開始受到歡迎之前，經常受邀和阿根廷管弦樂團及樂隊一起演奏。在他的新探戈音樂中，班多鈕就扮演了重要角色。

3　雖然他的作品中明顯受到了傳統阿根廷探戈的影響，但皮亞佐拉的新探戈也反映了他年輕時所接觸到的其他音樂類型。舉例來說，他在紐約長大，對爵士樂產生了興趣。不意外的，他經常將這種音樂的節奏融入到他的許多作品中。此外，他透過父母以及後來他對音樂的研究，學習到約翰・塞巴斯蒂安・巴赫等古典音樂作曲家的作品。皮亞佐拉在他的作品中應用了古典音樂的概念，例如對位法，這是指兩個或更多聲部使用不同的節奏演唱，但共同創造出曲子的和諧性。在爵士樂和古典樂的影響下，皮亞佐拉的探戈與阿根廷傳統探戈截然不同。

4　皮亞佐拉新探戈音樂的另一個獨特元素是它的實驗性傾向，皮亞佐拉一直在尋找新奇有趣的音樂來融入到自己的音樂當中。1956 年，皮亞佐拉發行了一張專輯，其中結合了他的音樂與作家霍爾・路易斯・博赫斯的詩歌。在整張專輯中，皮亞佐拉的新探戈音樂伴隨著博赫斯浪漫且情感豐富的詩歌旁白。這種奇特的結合引起了傳統探戈音樂家的抗議，他們認為皮亞佐拉的風格太過實驗性。

字彙 POWERED BY COBUILD

iconic 代表性的：to be a symbol of something 成為某件事物的象徵

genre 流派：a particular type of literature, music, film, or other art that has special characteristics 有其特徵的特定類型的文學、音樂、電影或其他藝術

B 仔細閱讀題目，注意它們是指涉題或細節題並作答。於各個解析旁邊填入分別對應的題目選項。請注意，答案解析順序不依照題目選項順序排列！讀者需要判斷各選項為何正確或錯誤，並且找出該選項所對應的正確解析為何，再於解析旁邊填入編號。

1. The word it in paragraph 1 refers to

○ origin. [A]

○ the genre. [B]

○ nuevo tango. [C]

○ traditional tango. [D]

中譯

1. 第一段的「it」指的是什麼？

○ 起源 [A]

○ 流派 [B]

✅ 新探戈 [C]

○ 傳統探戈 [D]

答案解析

▶ 題型：指涉題

_____ ○ 作者指的是新探戈，而不是傳統探戈。

_____ ○ 如果用「origin」取代代名詞，這個句子沒有意義。

_____ ○ 這個代名詞指的是新探戈。

_____ ○ 將代名詞替換為「the genre」會改變句子的意思。

2. According to paragraph 2, what aspect of Piazzolla's nuevo tango is directly inspired by traditional Argentine tango?

○ His use of the bandoneón [A]

○ The lyrics of his music [B]

○ His tendency to write music for large orchestras [C]

○ The focus on childhood experiences [D]

中譯

2.根據第二段，皮亞佐拉的新探戈直接受到傳統阿根廷探戈哪一方面的啟發？

✅ 他使用班多鈕琴 [A]

○ 他音樂的歌詞 [B]

○ 他喜歡為大型管弦樂團譜曲 [C]

○ 對童年經歷的關注 [D]

▶ 題型：細節題

_____ ○ 文章提到了皮亞佐拉的童年，但沒有說這是皮亞佐拉音樂的一部分。

_____ ○ 作者提到班多鈕琴通常用於探戈音樂中，而且皮亞佐拉使用了這種樂器。

_____ ○ 作者提到這是阿根廷探戈的一個特點，但沒有說明皮亞佐拉是否在自己的音樂中使用這種歌詞。

_____ ○ 文章提到皮亞佐拉與阿根廷管弦樂團合作，但沒有說他是否為他們作曲。

3. The phrase this music in paragraph 3 refers to

○ Argentine tango. [A]

○ nuevo tango. [B]

○ jazz. [C]

○ classical music. [D]

中譯

3. 第三段裡的「this music」指的是什麼？

○ 阿根廷探戈 [A]

○ 新探戈 [B]

✅ 爵士樂 [C]

○ 古典音樂 [D]

答案解析

▶ 題型：指涉題

_____ ○ 是皮亞佐拉的作品創造了新探戈流派，所以這個選項不可能正確。

_____ ○ 該代名詞指的是爵士樂。

_____ ○ 「classical music」可以取代這個代名詞，但會改變句子的意思。

_____ ○ 儘管「Argentine tango」可以取代代名詞，但句子的意思會改變。

4. According to paragraph 4, the experimental quality of Piazzolla's work resulted in

○ the inspiration of a work of poetry. [A]

○ disapproval from traditional Argentine musicians. [B]

○ collaborations with musicians in various genres. [C]

○ his lasting popularity in his home country. [D]

4. 根據第四段，皮亞佐拉作品的實驗性導致了

○ 詩作的靈感。[A]

✅ 傳統阿根廷音樂家的反對。[B]

○ 與各種流派的音樂家合作。[C]

○ 他在祖國持續受到歡迎。[D]

答案解析

▶ 題型：細節題

＿＿＿ ○ 作者說皮亞佐拉與一位作家合作，而不是與其他音樂家合作。

＿＿＿ ○ 作者沒有說詩歌是由皮亞佐拉的實驗音樂所啟發的。

＿＿＿ ○ 最後一句說皮亞佐拉的實驗風格引起了傳統音樂家的抗議，意思就是他們反對。

＿＿＿ ○ 雖然皮亞佐拉在他的祖國很受歡迎，但他音樂的實驗性質卻讓一些人不喜歡。

Read the passage about a topic in conservation.

TOEFL Reading

Question

Dian Fossey's work with gorillas

1   Gorillas are amongst the world's most recognizable animals but in the 1980s, in Rwanda, there were just 250 mountbain gorillas left. Primatologist Dian Fossey feared they would be extinct by the end of the century and she was determined to save them. Arguably, Dian's work with the mountain gorillas prevented the loss of these timid and sociable animals by revealing their closeness and connection to humanity. Dian also changed attitudes to protecting wildlife and started a new approach to animal conservation.

2   Dian's journey to Rwanda wasn't straightforward. She spent the first part of her working life as an occupational therapist in Louisville, Kentucky. But from early childhood she was fascinated with animals and in 1963 she travelled to Kenya, Tanzania, and what was then called Zaire (which is now called the Democratic Republic of the Congo). In Tanzania she met archaeologist Louis Leakey, where they discussed the importance of long-term research into the great apes, and at that point she decided to devote her life's work to the study and conservation of gorillas. For the next 20 years, Dian lived and worked with gorillas in the Rwandan rainforest, living as the only human high on the mountains, coping with loneliness and fighting poachers who hunted the gorillas. In 1967 she established a camp called the Karisoke Research Center for her research. Because the subjects of her studies are naturally shy and only knew humans as hunters, getting close enough to study **them** was difficult, but by imitating their actions and sounds Dian eventually gained their trust and even befriended some individuals.

3   During her research Dian observed that gorillas are complex, social animals and called them *"dignified, highly social, gentle giants, with individual personalities, and strong family relationships"*. She discovered that gorillas have social hierarchies and live in groups of between two and 40 individuals. These groups are called troops and are led by the dominant male called a silverback and include other younger males, females and infants. Male gorillas lead their groups to the best places for feeding and resting and

during these periods the gorillas play and interact, making social activities extremely important. This means that communication within the group is well developed—gorillas vocalize sounds to show distress or alarm, or to coordinate the group. They may sing or hum when they find food and several often join together in the singing. When a gorilla wants to play, they make a 'play face' and make expressions similar to smiling or yawning—the first shows appeasement after a fight, the second displays anxiety or distress.

4 On her arrival in Rwanda, the mountain gorilla population numbered just 450. Dian identified humans as the direct cause of the decline in numbers. Gorillas were being killed by poachers, either directly by their hunting of infant gorillas or indirectly because of setting traps for other animals in which gorillas also became ensnared. In addition, the local population was destroying the natural habitat of the gorillas in order to clear **it** for farming to provide food for themselves. This brought them into conflict with the apes because they were entering their territory. Finally, gorillas were also dying because of contact with visiting tourists who transmitted diseases like influenza. Dian was also opposed to tourists having contact with the gorillas because it altered their natural behavior.

5 Dian's work had many far-reaching, longer-term effects and today there are estimated to be just over 1,000 mountain gorillas. Her book (and then film) *Gorillas in the Mist* publicized the plight of the mountain gorillas. She established the Karisoke Research Center to help conserve the gorillas and their environment and it now attracts researchers and students from around the world. Most significantly of all Dian started a new approach to protecting animals called *active conservatism*. This included finding and destroying poachers' traps and engaging the local community in preserving the gorilla population. Today the Karisoke Research Center provides programs in education and economic development for the local population, such as rebuilding local schools and providing a health clinic to improve the quality of life for people in the region. Dian's life and work showed our vital ties to the natural world and pointed to a new way of living together with nature.

字彙 POWERED BY COBUILD

primatologist 靈長類動物學家：someone who studies the life and behavior of apes and other primates 研究猿類和其他靈長類動物的生活和行為的人

plight 困境：a very bad situation that someone or something is in 某個人或某種事物所處的非常糟糕的情況

1. According to paragraph 1, what did the work of Fossey achieve?

○ The extinction of the mountain gorillas
○ Changing people's attitudes to preserving animals
○ Making gorillas shy and sociable
○ Closer ties between humans and gorillas

2. According to paragraph 2, why did Fossey decide to work with mountain gorillas?

○ Because she was interested in archaeology
○ Because she was interested in animals
○ Because she liked Africa
○ Because she had a life-changing conversation about the significance of studying gorillas

3. The word them in paragraph 2 refers to?

○ hunters
○ mountains mountain
○ gorillas
○ illnesses

4. According to paragraph 3, why did Fossey say that gorillas are complex social animals?

○ Because they live in structured family groups
○ Because the leader of the group is a dominant male
○ Because they make facial expressions
○ Because they have strong personalities

5. The word it in paragraph 4 refers to

○ the local population
○ food
○ traps
○ the natural habitat

6. According to paragraph 5, what does active conservationism involve?

○ attracting researchers to study the apes
○ getting the local people interested in helping the gorillas
○ publicizing the dangers to gorillas
○ building schools for the local communities

Unit 3

挑錯題 & 功能題
Negative Fact Questions and Function Questions

3-1 挑錯題

挑錯題要求你根據文章裡的資訊去分辨錯誤的選項。相較於其他題型,回答挑錯題可能會花上你更多的時間,因為你需要確認三個細節的正確性,而不只是一個。

挑錯題可能用以下方式表達:

- The passage describes all of the following EXCEPT:
  文章描述了以下所有內容,除了:
- According to paragraph 2, which of the following is NOT true about X?
  根據第二段,關於X的描述,下列哪個是錯誤的?
- In paragraph 3, which of the following is LEAST likely?
  在第三段裡,下列哪個是最不可能的?

挑錯題快速指南

內容	挑錯題要求你根據文章提供的資訊,從四個選項中選出一個錯誤的。這類題目通常是根據閱讀的其中一段,雖然在某些情況下,挑錯題可能根據文章中的多個段落。挑錯題所依據的通常是清單資訊的一部份。
須具備的能力	為了正確回答挑錯題,你必須能夠: • 理解文章的主旨(main ideas)和主要支持細節(main supporting details)。 • 快速掃視文章,以找到事實來支持題目的其中三個選項。 • 根據文章內容,找出一個包含錯誤資訊的選項。
正確答案	挑錯題的正確答案是與文章中的資訊相互矛盾的選項。選項通常會使用文章裡的關鍵字或詞組,但改變當中一個關鍵細節,使它對於文章來說是錯誤的。在有些情況中題目所根據的是一份清單,正確答案是未包含在該清單中的項目。
錯誤答案	注意包含以下資訊的選項: • 文章中的資訊經過改述。選項或許會重新表達文章中的事實,以使其看起來錯誤,但實際上卻是正確的。請記住,對於這種題型,你要尋找的是錯誤的答案。 • 主動語態轉換為被動語態(或反過來)。舉例來說,文章可能會說「The man ate the apple.」。在選項中,它轉換為被動語態,變成「The apple was eaten by the man.」。請注意,這兩句的意義是相同的。

3-1-1　挑錯題範例

🅐 快速閱讀以下的挑錯題範例，在題目和選項中，用底線標示出能幫助你確定正確答案的任何關鍵字。

TOEFL Reading

Question

1. According to paragraph 1, all of the following accurately describe dynamic pricing EXCEPT:

○ Its popularity started to decline at the end of the twentieth century.

○ It gives the buyer some control over the price of an item.

○ It is used by sellers in online auctions.

○ It means that sellers charge different prices according to the situation.

🅑 現在閱讀範例文章。在閱讀時，勾（✓）出 A 部分題目選項裡提到的事實。請記住，與文章裡的事實不符的選項才是正確的答案。當你完成後，在以上選項裡標記出正確答案。

The Return of Dynamic Pricing

1　Throughout the twentieth century, many businesses used fixed-price strategies, meaning that prices for goods or services are predetermined by the seller. If a store has fixed prices, customers are expected to pay the set price. More importantly, buyers do not have any direct input in regard to the price of the items that they wish to purchase. Over the past few decades, however, it has become increasingly common for many sellers to use dynamic pricing, a strategy that involves changing the price of an item based on an individual buyer's needs and the circumstances of the purchase. Unlike fixed pricing, dynamic pricing is more flexible and allows buyers and sellers to work together to come up with prices that both parties can agree on. For example, online auctions, which allow buyers to place bids on items, use dynamic pricing.

2　The rising popularity of dynamic pricing was, without a doubt, linked to developments in new technology and the increasingly widespread use of the internet in the late twentieth century. This made it easier for sellers to use dynamic pricing by giving them access to information that affects pricing decisions. For example, sellers could now access up-to-date market information at any time of the day online. They could now receive information showing that the demand for an item was rising or that the cost to make a specific product had dropped. Both these factors influence the price of the item, so knowing this information now allows sellers to update prices as often as they want in order to reflect market fluctuations.

3   E-commerce software also now allows companies to monitor the purchase history of inventory: a supply or stock of something individual buyers. Sellers can then use this information to make recommendations that are tailored to meet a particular customer's preferences. Furthermore, the seller can change prices according to the customer's desires. For instance, sellers might offer unwanted inventory at lower prices to customers who show interest in it. As a result, the buyer receives a better deal.

中譯

動態定價的回歸

1 在整個二十世紀，許多企業都使用固定價格的策略，這表示商品或服務的價格由賣方預先決定。如果一家商店有固定價格，他們就會期望顧客支付已經設定好的價格。更重要的是，買家對於他們想買的商品，沒有任何直接的價格影響力。然而，在過去的幾十年裡，許多賣家愈來愈普遍的使用動態定價，這是一種根據個別買家的需求和購買環境來改變物品價格的策略。與固定價格不同，動態定價更靈活，允許買家和賣家協力達成雙方都可以接受的價格。例如，允許買家對商品提出競標的網路拍賣就使用動態定價。

2 毫無疑問，動態定價的盛行與二十世紀末新技術的發展和網際網路的使用日益普及有關。這使得賣家更容易使用動態定價，因為他們可以獲得影響定價決策的資訊。舉例來說，現在賣家可以在網路上隨時獲取最新的市場資訊。他們現在可以收到顯示對某項商品的需求正在上升，或製造特定產品的成本已經下降的資訊。這兩個因素都會影響商品的價格，因此掌握這些資訊的賣家，可以隨時根據需要來更新價格，以反映市場波動。

3 電子商務軟體現在也允許公司監控個別買家的購買記錄，賣家可以利用這些資訊提出符合特定客戶喜好的建議。此外，賣家可以根據客戶的需求更動價格。例如賣家可能會以較低的價格，把不需要的存貨提供給感興趣的客戶。因此，買家可以得到更好的交易。

字彙 POWERED BY COBUILD

bid 競標：an offer to pay a particular amount of money for something 支付特定金額以購買某項物品的提議

inventory 存貨：a supply or stock of something 某種物品的供應或庫存

3-1-2　掌握要領：挑錯題回答技巧

技巧 1

在掃視文章之前先閱讀題目和選項。對於這類題目，你需要查看題目中指定的段落以檢查每個選項的正確性。在查看段落之前，要先閱讀題目和選項。你應該試著理解每個選項的完整意思，這樣你才可以根據文章中的事實來確定選項是否正確。還要注意選項中的任何關鍵字或詞組。接著掃視文章中適當的段落，找出這些關鍵字或詞組。這能幫助你快速找到答題所需的資訊。

練習 1　查看你在題目和選項中畫底線的關鍵字，掃視 55-56 頁的文章，並且在文章中圈出與每個選項相關的四個關鍵字或措辭。

技巧 2

檢查是否有根據文章內容的改述。這類題目的選項通常包含重新表達文章的資訊，使正確的選項看起來錯誤。如果你發現一個選項改述了文章中的資訊，請把它拿來與文章比較，表達的意思是否相同？如果選項得到了文章的支持，就可以排除它。

練習 2　在 55 頁，哪兩個選項改述了文章中的資訊？

技巧 3

尋找使用被動語態的選項。被動式由 be 動詞加上動詞的過去分詞構成。例如，句子「The company opened three new factories」是主動語態，「Three new factories were opened by the company」是被動語態。請注意，無論語態如何，句子的意思都不會改變。因此你應該注意那些改變句子語態的選項。舉例來說，如果文章裡有個句子是主動語態，而選項是被動語態，那它們可能表示的是相同的意思。

練習 3　第 55 頁的哪個選項使用被動語態來描述原本以主動語態描述的事件？

TEST TIP!

挑錯題通常比其他題型需要更多時間來回答，因為你必須確認每個選項的正確性。每個挑錯題預計需要 2-3 分鐘的時間。

功能題（也叫修辭題 rhetorical purpose question）會問你作者所使用的修辭手法。修辭手法有多種功能，包括舉例、解釋或闡明一個觀點、質疑或支持一個觀點等。這類題目的答案通常以不定式開頭，例如「to explain」和「to make a point」是常見的不定式詞組。

功能題可能用以下方式表達：

- Why does the author mention X in paragraph 1? 作者為什麼在第一段提到 X？
- Why does the author give an example of X? 作者為什麼舉例說明 X？
- How does the information in paragraph 2 relate to paragraph 1?
  第二段的資訊與第一段有什麼關係？

功能題快速指南

內容	功能題要求你確定文章中單字、詞組，甚至整個段落的目的。功能題有兩種類型，其中一種會要求你確定作者在文章中提及特定資訊的原因。例如，題目提出一個單字或詞組，你需要確定該單字或詞組在周圍句子裡的功能。另一種問你為什麼作者以某種方式組織文章中的部分資訊。例如，你可能需要解釋一個段落與另一個段落之間的關係。
須具備的能力	為了正確回答功能題，你必須能夠： • 分辨常見的修辭手法及其相關措辭。 • 確定作者提及某個資訊的原因。 • 確定每個段落的主旨，才能理解段落之間的關係。 • 理解被問到的單字、詞組或段落，與周圍句子或段落之間的關係。
正確答案	功能題的正確答案能正確定義作者提到某個資訊、或說明作者以某種方式組織段落資訊的動機。請注意，作者不會在文章中直接表示該功能。因此，你必須根據文章裡的線索和對文章的整體理解來確定。
錯誤答案	注意包含以下資訊的選項： • 文章中提及但未解釋說話者功能的資訊 • 文章中根本未提到的概念 • 與文章提供的資訊相互矛盾

3-2-1　功能題範例

Ⓐ 快速閱讀以下的功能題範例，在題目和選項中，用底線標示出能幫助你確定正確答案的任何關鍵字。

TOEFL Reading

Question

1. In paragraph 3, why does the author discuss the pyramid in Teotihuacan that featured the feathered serpent?
   - ○ To argue that the Mayans inspired the use of the feathered serpent in Teotihuacan
   - ○ To contrast the symbolic images used by the Teotihuacanos and the Maya
   - ○ To give an example of an archaeological technique used by the Teotihuacanos
   - ○ To point out that the symbol was popular in Teotihuacan before the Maya used it

2. How does paragraph 1 relate to paragraph 2?
   - ○ Paragraph 1 gives examples of an idea that is explained in further detail in paragraph 2.
   - ○ Paragraph 2 describes the background of one of the cultures mentioned in paragraph 1.
   - ○ Paragraph 1 defines a key term that is central to the theory refuted in paragraph 2.
   - ○ Paragraph 2 provides evidence to support a theory that is introduced in paragraph 1.

Ⓑ 現在閱讀範例文章。在閱讀時，用底線標出你認為有助於回答 A 部分題目的資訊。當你完成後，在以上選項裡標記出正確答案。

The Influence of Teotihuacan

1　　The city of Teotihuacan, located in the central region of modern-day Mexico, was one of the first urban civilizations in Central America. Due to its military strength and far-reaching trade partnerships, Teotihuacan became very influential, reaching the height of its power around the year AD 450. During this time, the people of Teotihuacan had frequent and direct contact with the Maya, a civilization whose territory extended from southwestern Mexico to the regions of El Salvador. Evidence suggests that the Maya were greatly influenced by the Teotihuacanos, especially in the areas of architecture and ideology.

2　　The Maya used a variety of architectural styles. However, one that was likely inspired by Teotihuacan was a technique called the slope-and-panel style. This technique involved stacking rectangular stone panels on top of stone slabs that had inwardly sloped sides. The largest stone panels were located at the base, and the size of the panels decreased at each level, giving the resulting structures their characteristic pyramid shape. According to archaeological evidence, the slope-and-panel style was used in Teotihuacan as early as AD 200. Experts observed the same style in several Mayan cities. Interestingly, the Mayan structures that used the slope-and-panel style were built much later than those at Teotihuacan. This suggests that the style developed first in Teotihuacan and that the Maya adopted the style as a result of direct contact with the Teotihuacanos.

3　There is also evidence that the Teotihuacanos influenced the ideology of the Maya. This is particularly apparent in the use of certain symbols. For example, one of the most important symbols in Teotihuacan was the feathered serpent. Between the years 150 and 200, the Teotihuacanos even built a pyramid that featured the symbol extensively. The same symbol has been found in Mayan texts. However, the Maya didn't use it before AD 1000.

中譯

特奧蒂瓦坎的影響

1　特奧蒂瓦坎城位於今日墨西哥中部地區，是中美洲最早的城市文明之一。由於其強大的軍事力量和廣泛的貿易夥伴關係，特奧蒂瓦坎變得非常有影響力，它的權力在公元 450 年左右達到了巔峰。在此期間，特奧蒂瓦坎人與馬雅人有頻繁且直接的接觸，馬雅文明的範圍從墨西哥西南部延伸到薩爾瓦多地區。證據顯示，馬雅人受到了特奧蒂瓦坎人的極大影響，尤其在建築和意識形態方面。

2　馬雅人使用各種建築風格，然而，其中一種被稱為「斜平板風格」的技術可能受到特奧蒂瓦坎的啟發。這種技術是將長方形石板堆疊在內側有斜面的石板上，最大的石板置於底層，而每層的石板尺寸逐漸縮小，使得最終的結構物呈現出特有的金字塔形狀。根據考古證據，斜平板風格早在公元 200 年就在特奧蒂瓦坎使用過了。專家們在幾個馬雅城市裡觀察到了相同的風格。有趣的是，採用斜平板風格的馬雅結構物比特奧蒂瓦坎的要晚得多。這表示，該風格是先從特奧蒂瓦坎發展出來的，馬雅人是因為與特奧蒂瓦坎人直接接觸而採用了這種風格。

3　還有證據顯示，特奧蒂瓦坎人影響了馬雅人的意識形態，這在某些符號的使用中特別明顯。例如，特奧蒂瓦坎最重要的符號之一是羽蛇神。在公元 150 至 200 年之間，特奧蒂瓦坎人甚至建造了一座大量採用該符號的金字塔。同樣的符號也出現在馬雅文字中。然而，馬雅人直到公元 1000 年之後才開始使用它。

字彙 POWERED BY COBUILD

urban 城市的：belonging to a town or city 屬於城鎮或城市的
serpent 蛇：a snake 蛇

3-2-2　掌握要領：功能題回答技巧

技巧 1

在你掃視文章之前先閱讀選項。在閱讀選項時一定要注意關鍵字，這有助於你在掃視文章時更快的找到重要資訊。

練習 1　查看你在第 1 題及選項中畫底線的關鍵字。掃視第 59-60 頁的文章，並在第三段裡圈出與第 1 題每個選項有關的四個關鍵字或措辭。

技巧 2

學習托福網路測驗常用的修辭手法。在閱讀部分，作者會使用許多常見的修辭手法來達成某些目的。下表列出了一些常見的修辭手法，以及文章中的可能措辭。

Give an Example 舉例	在文章中看到	For example... 舉例 That is to say... 也就是說 This shows how... 這表示
	答案可能的措辭	To provide / give an example of... 舉例來說 To describe X in more detail 為了更詳細的描述 X To show / illustrate / demonstrate . . . 為了顯示／呈現／證明 To provide evidence of... 為了提供⋯的證據 To describe... 為了描述
Compare or Contrast 比較或對照	在文章中看到	In contrast... 對照之下 For the same reason... 基於同樣的理由 Another similarity / difference... 另一個相似／相異處
	答案可能的措辭	To contrast X and Y 為了對照 X 和 Y To show the similarity / difference between X and Y 為了顯示 X 與 Y 的相似／相異處 To argue that X is the same as Y 為了主張 X 和 Y 一樣
Emphasize a Piece of Information 強調一項資訊	在文章中看到	In this sense, X could be seen as... 按照這個情況，X 可以被視為 Specifically... 尤其是 This is particularly apparent in... 這在⋯方面特別明顯
	答案可能的措辭	To note that... 注意到 To highlight that... 為了突顯 To make the point that... 為了強調

練習 2　在第 59-60 頁的文章中，圈出與上述常見修辭手法相關的一個詞組。在第 1 題的選項中，哪一個與此詞組有關？

排除與作者的目的沒有直接關聯的選項。在某些情況下，選項可能提到文章中的資訊，但未正確解釋作者的目的。

練習③　在第 59 頁第 1 題的選項中，劃掉一個在文章中提到的資訊，但未顯示作者目的的選項。

技巧 4

假如題目問的是兩個段落之間的關係，就需找出這兩個段落的主旨。通常每一段都會有一個描述該段落主旨的主題句。比較兩個段落的主題句能提供你段落之間相關性的線索。這一段是否反駁或支持了另一段所介紹的理論？那一段是否討論了這一段所介紹的想法？

練習④　在第 59-60 頁的文章裡，用底線標示出第一段和第二段的主旨。根據這些主題句，這兩個段落之間可能有什麼樣的關係？

掃視關於建築學的短文，用底線標出每個段落的主旨。

Active Design

1   Daily physical activity is an important part of a healthy lifestyle. For this reason, over recent decades many architects and designers have been working to create buildings that encourage people to make exercise a part of their ordinary routine. The movement to promote healthy activity through architecture is called active design. It began in 1998 as part of a university public health program, and it has since gained popularity in cities around the world. Active design uses a number of techniques to encourage the occupants of a building to be more active.

2   One of the most important strategies of active design is inspiring people to make walking part of their routine. A particularly successful tool for promoting walking is the skip-stop elevator. These elevators stop only on every second or third floor, leaving riders to take the stairs in order to reach their destination. Another strategy of active design is to make stairs more pleasant and inviting. Instead of creating dim stairwells that are located in isolated parts of buildings, active design uses well lit and centrally placed stairs to encourage more foot traffic. Skip-stop elevators and appealing stair design are both effective tools of active design because they offer incentive and opportunity for exercise. In fact, researchers studying a building that employs both skip-stop elevators and more attractive stair design said that 70 percent of building occupants reported using the stairs every day.

3   Active design encourages physical activity using not only the interior features of a building, but the relationship between a building and its surroundings as well. A building that employs active design may integrate outdoor space in order to make the environment more engaging and promote physical activity. Some elements that architects use to incorporate the exterior with the interior are glass walls, interior gardens or park spaces, and courtyards with open ceilings, all of which de-emphasize the boundaries between inside and outside. These elements make the building more physically and mentally invigorating. Similarly, by increasing the number of entrances and exits to a building, architects can help keep a building's users interested in their surroundings by providing a variety of routes for them to use. If people continue to be stimulated by new sights or experiences, they are less likely to choose the quickest and easiest path to their destination and may instead choose a more physically challenging route.

中譯

活力設計

1　每天的身體活動，是健康生活方式中重要的一部分。因此近幾十年來，許多建築師和設計師一直致力於創造能鼓勵人們將運動納入日常生活的建築物。利用建築來促進健康活動的運動被稱為活力設計。活力設計始於 1998 年，是某個大學公共衛生計畫的一部分，並且從那之後在世界各地的都市裡變得愈來愈受歡迎。活力設計使用各種技術來鼓勵建築物的居住者更加積極的參與活動。

2　活力設計中最重要的策略之一，是鼓勵人們將步行納入他們的日常生活。促進步行特別成功的一個工具是跳層電梯，這些電梯每兩層或三層樓才停留一次，並讓乘客走樓梯到達目的地。活力設計的另一個策略是使樓梯更舒適和吸引人。活力設計不在建築物的孤立部分建造昏暗樓梯間，而是使用照明良好且位於中心位置的樓梯來鼓勵更多的步行。跳層電梯和吸引人的樓梯設計都是活力設計的有效工具，因為它們提供了運動的動機和機會。事實上，研究人員研究一座同時採用跳層電梯和更吸引人的樓梯設計的建築，發現有 70% 的建築物居民每天使用樓梯。

3　活力設計不僅利用建築物的內部特點來鼓勵身體活動，也利用了建築物與周圍環境之間的關係。採用活力設計的建築物可能會整合室外空間，使環境更具吸引力並促進身體活動。建築師會使用玻璃牆、室內花園或公園空間，以及帶有開放天花板的庭院等元素，將室外與室內融合在一起。這些元素都降低了內外的分野，使建築物更具身心活力。同樣的，建築師可以透過增加建築物的出入口數量和提供各種路線選擇，來幫助建築物的使用者保持對周圍環境的興趣。如果人們持續受到新的景觀或體驗的刺激，他們就不太可能選擇最快最簡單的路線，而是可能選擇一條更具挑戰性的路線到達目的地。

字彙 POWERED BY COBUILD

incentive 激勵：encouragement to do something 鼓勵去做某件事
incorporate 融入：to include; to make a part of 納入；使成為其中一部分

B 仔細閱讀題目。它們屬於哪種題型？接著開始作答。留意正確答案，並且閱讀答案解析的原因解釋。

1. According to paragraph 1, all of the following are true about active design EXCEPT:

○ It began at the end of the twentieth century.

○ Promoting physical activity is its goal.

○ Architects and medical professionals created it.

○ It is becoming increasingly common in cities.

中譯

1. 根據第一段，以下關於活力設計的描述都是正確的，除了

　○ 它開始於二十世紀末。

　○ 促進身體活動是它的目標。

　✔ 它是由建築師和醫學專家創造的。

　○ 它在都市裡愈來愈普遍。

答案解析

▶ 題型：挑錯題

○ 根據文章，活力設計運動始於 1998 年，這是二十世紀末。

○ 文章中提到「通過建築促進健康活動的運動被稱為活力設計」。

✅ 儘管文章提到了建築師和健康專業人員，但並沒有表明建築師和醫療專業人員共同合作創建了活力設計運動。

○ 文章提到「它已經在世界各地的城市中變得愈來愈流行」。

2. Why does the author discuss dim stairwells in paragraph 2?

○ To demonstrate the differences between elevator and stairwell design

○ To make a point about why people don't use the stairs often

○ To describe one advantage of using skip-stop elevators in buildings

○ To argue that skip-stop elevators may lead to design failures.

中譯

2. 為什麼作者在第二段討論昏暗的樓梯間？

○ 為了指出電梯和樓梯設計之間的區別。

✅ 為了指出人們為何不常使用樓梯。

○ 描述建築物中使用跳層電梯的一個優點。

○ 主張跳層電梯可能導致設計失敗。

答案解析

▶ 題型：功能題

○ 作者並未提到電梯和樓梯間設計的差異。

✅ 作者提到設計良好的樓梯間可以鼓勵步行。提到昏暗的樓梯間是為了舉例說明人們為什麼不想使用樓梯。

○ 雖然作者談到使用跳層電梯的優點，但昏暗的樓梯間並不是其中一項好處。

○ 作者暗示昏暗的樓梯間是一種失敗的設計，而不是跳層電梯導致這種失敗。

3. According to paragraph 3, which of the following is NOT a way that architects eliminate the boundary between indoor and outdoor spaces?

○ Creating spaces with open ceilings

○ Using see-through materials

○ Creating more routes for entering and exiting

○ Building gardens inside the building

中譯

3. 根據第三段，以下哪一項並不是建築師消除室內與室外空間界限的方式？

○ 創造具有開放天花板的空間

○ 使用透明材料

✅ 創造更多的進出路線

○ 在建築內部建造花園

答案解析

▶ 題型：挑錯題

○ 作者在描述如何將室外空間融入室內時提到了「帶有開放天花板的庭院」。

○ 作者提到了「玻璃牆」，而玻璃是透明材料。

✅ 文章提到多創造幾個出入口，其目的在於使建築使用者持續受到刺激，而不是消除室內和室外空間的界限。

○ 文章提到了「室內花園或公園空間」。

4. How does paragraph 2 relate to paragraph 3 in the passage?

○ Paragraph 2 describes an early model of a design discussed in paragraph 3.

○ Paragraph 3 argues about the effectiveness of the technique from paragraph 2.

○ Paragraph 2 explains a technique, and paragraph 3 gives examples of how it is used.

○ Paragraph 3 introduces a different strategy that the one discussed in paragraph 2.

中譯

4. 第二段和第三段在文章中的關係是什麼？

○ 第二段描述了第三段中討論的一種設計的早期模型。

○ 第三段論述了第二段中該技術的效益。

○ 第二段解釋了一種技術，而第三段為它的應用舉例說明。

✅ 第三段介紹了一種與第二段不同的策略。

答案解析

▶ 題型：功能題

○ 作者並未討論任何設計的早期模型。

○ 第三段並未提到第二段所描述的該策略的效益。

○ 每個段落個別描述一個技術並且舉例說明，同一項技術不會分散在兩個段落中。

✅ 兩個段落都討論到在活力設計中所使用的個別策略。

A　掃視關於考古學的短文，並寫下每段的主旨。

1. _____

2. _____

3. _____

4. _____

Archaeological Dating

1　In the past, archaeologists had few precise ways of determining the age of artifacts. Some methods they used included researching written records, comparing objects to similar items, or analyzing the depth at which an object was buried. The limitations of such methods were numerous. For instance, though it may seem logical to assume that relics buried deep underground are older than those found closer to the surface, earthquakes, floods, and even rodents can change the position of artifacts. Thus, these methods could not provide the exact information that archaeologists needed. However, advances in technology have provided modern archaeologists with several methods that give them the absolute age of an object.

2　The most common absolute dating technique is radiocarbon dating. This process involves analyzing objects for a substance called radiocarbon. All organic material, or matter that was once part of a living organism, contains trace amounts of radiocarbon. For example, human remains, ash residue on cooking pots, or animal products used for clothing or tools all contain radiocarbon. Over time, the amount of radiocarbon in an object steadily decreases at a predictable and measurable rate. Thus, by determining the amount of radiocarbon present in a skull fragment, for example, archaeologists can calculate the age of that object.

3　However, many of the artifacts that archaeologists study are not organic. They also study the inorganic remains of human culture, like architecture, tools, jewelry, and pottery. For some inorganic remains, like pottery, archaeologists use a technique called thermoluminescence dating. This process measures radioactive decay, which is the breakdown and loss of atomic material that many inorganic remains experience. In rigidly structured matter, like the minerals often found in pottery, radioactive decay also results in the storage of small amounts of energy. When the minerals are heated to high temperatures, they release this stored energy as light, or thermoluminescence.

4   Thermoluminescence dating is particularly useful for dating pottery because of the process by which pottery is made. In order for clay to be converted into pottery, it must be fired. The clay is put into a special oven, called a kiln, and heated to very high temperatures. When pottery is fired, the minerals in the clay release the energy they have stored during radioactive decay. This resets the clock, and the minerals continue to undergo radioactive decay from the time of firing. When archaeologists heat a pottery sample, the amount of light it releases tells them how long ago it was fired. Because pottery is a common artifact of ancient cultures, thermoluminescence dating is a valuable tool for archaeologists.

中譯

考古學的年代測定法

1   在過去，考古學家很少有能夠確定文物年代的精確方法。他們使用的一些方法包括研究書面記錄、將文物與類似文物進行比較，或分析文物埋藏的深度。這些方法的限制很多，舉例來說，「埋藏在地下深處的文物比靠近地表的文物更古老」，這個假設儘管看似合乎邏輯，但地震、洪水甚至老鼠都可能改變文物的位置。因此這些方法無法提供考古學家所需的確切資訊。然而，技術的進步為現代考古學家提供了幾種可以測定物品絕對年代的方法。

2   最常見的絕對年代測定技術是放射性碳定年法。這個過程牽涉到分析物品中一種叫做放射性碳的物質。所有有機物質，或曾經是生物的一部分的物質，都含有微量的放射性碳。舉例來說，人類遺骸、烹飪鍋上的灰渣，或用於衣服或工具的動物產品都含有放射性碳。隨著時間的流逝，物品中放射性碳的含量會以可預測且可測量的速率穩定減少。因此，利用測定某物品——例如骷髏頭碎片——放射性碳的量，考古學家可以計算出該物品的年代。

3   然而，許多考古學家研究的文物並非有機物。他們也研究人類文化的無機遺留物，像是建築、工具、珠寶和陶器。對於一些無機遺留物，像是陶器，考古學家會使用一種叫做熱釋光測年法的技術。這個方法測量的是放射性衰變，即許多無機遺留物所經歷的原子物質的分解和流失。在結構嚴密的物質中，例如陶器中常見的礦物，放射性衰變也會導致少量能量被儲存起來。當礦物被加熱到高溫時，它們會釋放這些已存儲的能量作為光，或熱釋光。

4   由於陶器的製作過程，熱釋光測年法對於陶器的年代測定特別有用。為了將黏土轉換為陶器，必須燒製黏土。黏土被放入一個被叫做窯的特殊烤爐，並加熱到非常高的溫度。當陶器在燒製時，黏土中的礦物會釋放出在放射性衰變過程中所儲存的能量。這讓時間重設了，礦物從陶器被燒製的時候開始繼續進行放射性衰變。當考古學家加熱一個陶器樣本時，它所釋放的光的量，讓學者們知道它是多久以前被燒製的。由於陶器是古代文化的常見文物，因此熱釋光測年法對於考古學家來說是一種寶貴的工具。

字彙 POWERED BY COBUILD

relic 遺跡、遺物：something that was made or used a long time ago 指很久以前製造或使用的物品

trace 微量：very small amount 極小的量

B 仔細閱讀題目，注意它們是挑錯題或功能題並作答。於各個解析旁邊填入分別對應的題目選項。請注意，答案解析順序不依照題目選項順序排列！讀者需要判斷各選項為何正確或錯誤，並且找出該選項所對應的正確解析為何，再於解析旁邊填入編號。

1. The author discusses rodents in paragraph 1 in order to

○ explain the problem with one dating technique. [A]

○ argue that modern dating techniques are not accurate. [B]

○ describe how scientists use living organisms to date objects. [C]

○ give an example of a modern dating technique. [D]

中譯

1. 作者在第一段討論老鼠，是為了

✅ 解釋一種年代測定技術的問題。[A]

○ 主張現代的年代測定技術不精確。[B]

○ 描述科學家如何使用生物來對物品進行年代測定。[C]

○ 為現代的年代測定技術提供一個例子。[D]

答案解析

▶ 題型：功能題

_____ ○ 作者在第一段裡沒有提到用生物來對物品進行年代測定。

_____ ○ 當作者提到老鼠時，重點在於舉例說明早期的年代測定技術，而非現代的技術。

_____ ○ 作者說老鼠可能改變文物的位置，如果考古學家將埋藏的深度作為指標，會導致測定的年代不準確。

_____ ○ 作者主張早期的年代測定技術是不準確的，而非現代的技術。

2. Why does the author mention ash residue in paragraph 2?

○ To illustrate the accuracy of radiocarbon dating [A]

○ To show how radiocarbon can be destroyed [B]

○ To provide an example of an organic material [C]

○ To differentiate between organic and inorganic objects [D]

中譯

2. 為什麼作者在第二段提到灰渣？

○ 為了說明放射性碳定年法的準確性。[A]

○ 為了顯示放射性碳如何被破壞。[B]

✅ 為了提供有機物質的一個例子。[C]

○ 為了區分有機和無機物體。[D]

▶ 題型：功能題

_____ ○ 文章沒有提到灰渣與放射性碳定年法的準確性有關。

_____ ○ 作者在前一句中定義了有機物質，該句以「For example 舉例來說」開頭。

_____ ○ 作者並未指明放射性碳是否會被破壞，以及如何被破壞。

_____ ○ 該句僅提到有機物質，沒有提及無機物質。

3. According to paragraph 3, which of the following is NOT true about thermoluminescence dating?

○ It will likely replace radiocarbon dating methods. [A]

○ It measures how much radioactive energy has been stored. [B]

○ It works well for materials that have a rigid structure. [C]

○ It uses light as a measure of stored radioactive energy. [D]

中譯

3. 根據第三段，以下哪一項關於熱釋光測年法是錯誤的？

○ 它很可能取代放射性碳定年法。[A]

◉ 它測量儲存了多少放射能量。[B]

○ 它適用於結構堅硬的物質。[C]

○ 它利用光來測定已儲存的放射能量。[D]

答案解析

▶ 題型：挑錯題

_____ ○ 作者說，陶器的年代是根據它在加熱至極高溫度時釋放多少光。

_____ ○ 作者說放射性碳定年法對於無機物質不起作用，而不是熱釋光測年法會比放射性碳定年法更普及。

_____ ○ 作者說放射性衰變導致少量能量被儲存起來。

_____ ○ 作者說熱釋光測年法用於「結構堅硬的物質」，例如一些陶器中的礦物。

4. According to paragraphs 3 and 4, which of the following is NOT a way that pottery is well suited to thermoluminescence dating?

○ It is relatively easy to find compared to other artifacts. [A]

○ Pottery is made of inorganic materials. [B]

○ Pottery contains minerals that undergo radioactive decay. [C]

○ It has no stored radioactive energy from the time it is fired. [D]

4. 根據第三和第四段，以下哪一個不是陶器適合進行熱釋光測年法的點？

　✅ 與其他文物相比，相對容易取得。[A]

　○ 陶器由無機物質製成。[B]

　○ 陶器含有會進行放射性衰變的礦物。[C]

　○ 它在被燒製時沒有存儲放射性能量。[D]

答案解析

▶ 題型：挑錯題

＿＿＿＿ ○ 在第四段裡，作者解釋當陶器第一次被燒製時，它「讓時間重設了」，表示它沒有存儲放射性能量。

＿＿＿＿ ○ 在第三段裡，作者說熱釋光測年法對於測定一些像是陶器的無機物質來說，是很好的方法。

＿＿＿＿ ○ 雖然陶器是一種常見的文物，但這與它是否適合進行熱釋光測年法無關。

＿＿＿＿ ○ 作者說陶器中的礦物在陶器燒製時「繼續進行放射性衰變」。

Read the passage about a topic in psychology.

TOEFL Reading
Question

Nonverbal Communication

[1] The ability to share complex, detailed information through spoken language is frequently cited as the primary factor that distinguishes humans from animals. However, in addition to using a highly developed language system, people also share information nonverbally, without using words at all. Though speech is often considered the chief form of human communication, people also depend heavily on many types of nonverbal communication.

[2] One of the most common forms of nonverbal communication is body language. Body language can include facial expressions, gestures, and even eye contact. The human body is capable of a nearly limitless variety of expressions, postures, and gestures, all of which can carry meaning that can be used for the purposes of communication. Facial expressions are perhaps the most commonly recognized form of body language. Some studies even suggest that facial expressions showing feelings like anger, fear, surprise, happiness, and sadness could be universal, meaning that they are understood by people all over the world. For example, in some cases, even though two people may speak entirely different languages and come from widely divergent cultures, they can still share basic emotions by using facial expressions.

[3] It is important to recognize, however, that not all body language is universal and that the attitudes and norms of a culture play a large role in how some kinds of body language are interpreted. For instance, putting one's hands in one's pockets might indicate feelings of relaxation to members of one culture, but it could signal disrespect to members of another. Thus, the meaning of body language is often dependent on culture or personality. Despite the difficulty of interpreting what particular types of body language mean, studies of human behavior indicate that it forms a significant part of human life. Some researchers suggest that 50–70 percent of human communication consists of body language.

4 In addition to communicating through movements, expressions, or other visible body language, human beings also communicate nonverbally through touch, which is often referred to as the haptic sense. Research indicates that haptic communication is especially important in the development of infants. Before children develop language, parents or other caregivers can use touch to convey a number of ideas, such as attention, care, and safety. Touch remains an important means of communication for adult humans as well. It is a central part of establishing friendships and other cooperative relationships. That's because touch often indicates and encourages trust. However, in some cases, the haptic sense can also communicate less positive messages. For instance, physical violence is a form of haptic communication in which a person expresses their state of mind by threatening or harming another.

5 Though a majority of the messages sent and received through body language and interpersonal contact are subconscious, human beings use nonverbal communication consciously as well. People often choose certain aspects of their appearance, like their clothes, their hairstyles, or other forms of personal decoration, very carefully, and these choices are another form of nonverbal communication. One of the primary purposes of nonverbal communication through appearance is to indicate wealth or status. For example, a person can communicate wealth by wearing expensive clothes. Similarly, a person can show his or her status by wearing specialized types of clothing, like badges or uniforms. Appearance can communicate information about whether a person wishes to be considered serious or playful, conventional or odd, professional or casual. For instance, though the types of clothing that are considered formal differ widely from culture to culture, most societies recognize some difference between formal and informal dress. Most commonly, formal dress is apparel that shows respect for an important occasion. While most people exert some degree of control over what they wear or how they present themselves, there are some types of nonverbal communication that are unintentional. Studies have found that, in some cultures, taller people are regarded as being more impressive and often receive promotions over their shorter colleagues. In this case, nonverbal communication is not intentional and may even convey false information.

字彙 POWERED BY COBUILD

divergent 相異的：things that are different from each other 彼此不同的事物
convey 傳達：to cause information or feelings to be known or understood by someone 使資訊或感受被某人知道或理解

1. According to paragraph 2, which of the following is NOT true about body language?

   ○ It includes behaviors like gestures and facial expressions.
   ○ Some cultures use body language more than others.
   ○ It accounts for at least half of all human communication.
   ○ Some body language is thought to have the same meaning everywhere.

2. In paragraph 3, the author mentions putting one's hands in one's pockets in order to

   ○ explain a common way of using body language.
   ○ make a point about how body language can affect mood.
   ○ give an example of body language that can have multiple interpretations.
   ○ support the idea that the majority of communication is nonverbal.

3. How does paragraph 2 relate to paragraph 3?

   ○ Paragraph 2 presents a theory about some body language, and paragraph 3 demonstrates that the theory is not always true.
   ○ Paragraph 3 compares the two types of body language described in paragraph 2.
   ○ Paragraph 2 gives examples of body language, and paragraph 3 explains how body language is interpreted.
   ○ Paragraph 3 provides evidence for a theory about body language that was introduced in paragraph 2.

4. In paragraph 4, the author mentions all of the following functions of haptic communication EXCEPT:

   ○ Giving attention to infants
   ○ Promoting language development
   ○ Building trust among friends
   ○ Physically harming others

5. In paragraph 5, the author says that conscious nonverbal communication can be used for all of the following EXCEPT:

○ To indicate one's personality
○ To demonstrate how much money one has
○ To recognize members of the same group
○ To show respect in certain situations

6. Why does the author mention a study about height in the workplace in paragraph 5?

○ To illustrate how nonverbal communication can have unintended consequences
○ To suggest that people's impressions based on height are the same around the world
○ To provide evidence that most types of nonverbal communication are conscious
○ To show that using nonverbal communication can have a number of advantages

Unit 4 推論題 & 詞彙題
Inference Questions and Vocabulary Questions

4-1 推論題

推論題要求你根據文章中提供的資訊導出結論。推論題的正確答案絕不會在文章中出現直接的敘述。反之,你必須自己串連文章中的資訊才能進行推論。

推論題可能用以下方式表達:

- In paragraph 1, the author implies... 在第一段裡,作者暗示…
- According to paragraph 2, which of the following can be inferred about X?
  根據第二段,關於 X 可以推論出下列哪一項?
- Which of the following is implied about X in paragraph 3?
  在第三段裡,下列哪一項是關於 X 的暗示?
- Based on the information in paragraph 4, what can be inferred about X?
  根據第四段的資訊,關於 X 可以推論出什麼?

推論題快速指南

內容	推論題要測試你對文章中所隱含的概念或暗示的理解能力。雖然答案不會明確的在文章中敘述,但你要能夠藉著既有的資訊做出強而有力的推論。
須具備的能力	為了正確回答推論題,你必須能夠: • 理解隱含在文章中,並未直接敘述的論點。 • 根據前後文的線索來解讀文章中的概念。 • 快速掃視文章,找出支持你結論的資訊。
正確答案	推論題的正確答案要能夠正確的導出結論。正確答案的推論會得到文章內容的支持,但不會直接敘述出來。
錯誤答案	注意包含以下資訊的選項: • 是真實的結論,但不被文章內容支持。在考試中,推論題的正確答案必定是文章中所支持的資訊,你不需要依賴過去所知或外部知識來回答問題。 • 與文章的主旨或細節相互矛盾的資訊 • 與文章中一模一樣的措辭。正確答案通常會改述資訊。

4-1-1　推論題範例

Ⓐ 快速閱讀以下的推論題範例，在題目和選項中，用底線標示出能幫助你確定正確答案的任何關鍵字。

TOEFL Reading

Question

1. According to paragraph 2, what can be inferred about the abacuses used in Babylon?
   ○ They were the earliest calculators.
   ○ They did not have any educational value.
   ○ They were not easy to move around.
   ○ They inspired the invention of the wire abacus.

Ⓑ 現在閱讀範例文章。在閱讀時，用底線標出你認為有助於回答 A 部分題目的資訊。當你完成後，在以上選項裡標記出正確答案。

Early Calculators

1　Modern electronic calculators perform many complex mathematical functions. However, any device that helps compute mathematical values is a type of calculator. The earliest form of calculator was the human hand. In fact, a medieval English monk developed a system for using one's fingers to count all the way up to one million. But advanced tools are necessary for math that requires more difficult calculations than simple counting. Ancient cultures all over the world developed a variety of early calculators.

2　The most common type of early calculator was the abacus. An abacus is a device that uses stones or beads as markers to assist a person in basic calculations, like addition, subtraction, multiplication, and division. The earliest abacuses, which used grooves for holding stone markers, are also called counting trays. Merchants used them to determine prices, while government officials used them to keep official accounts and teachers used them to teach mathematics. Records suggest that the Babylonians created the first counting tray around AD 300. This type of abacus was used by Greeks, Romans, Egyptians, and other cultures for centuries. In the thirteenth century, Chinese thinkers invented the wire abacus, which uses beads mounted on wires and held within a frame. The wire abacus is more portable than the counting tray and can be used for more rapid calculations. In fact, despite advancements in technology, people all over the world still use the wire abacus.

3　Trade between people in China, India, Europe, and Africa explains the spread of early calculators in many parts of the world. However, the early inhabitants of the Americas actually created a calculator without these influences. Some scholars propose that the Inca, a South American empire that was powerful from about 1430–1533, used a device called a yupana for calculations. The yupana is a block of stone carved into many sections and levels that resembles a miniature model of a city. This device was most likely used to calculate amounts of stored resources, like grain or livestock, and some historians speculate that it may have been used for astronomical calculations. Unlike the wire abacus, the yupana is no longer in use.

中譯

早期計算機

1　現代電子計算機可以執行許多複雜的數學功能。然而，任何有助於計算數值的裝置都算是一種計算機。計算機最早期的形式就是人類的手，事實上，在中世紀有一位英國修道士發明了一種系統，可以利用手指計數到一百萬。但是比簡單計數更困難的數學計算就需要先進的工具。世界各地的古代文化發展出了各種早期的計算機。

2　最常見的早期計算機是算盤。算盤是一種以石頭或珠子作為標記的裝置，幫助人們做基本運算，如加法、減法、乘法和除法。最早的算盤使用溝槽來固定石頭標記，也被稱為計數盤。商人用它來確定價格，政府官員用它來記錄官方帳目，教師用它來教授數學。記錄指出，巴比倫人在公元前 300 年左右創造了第一個計數盤。這種類型的算盤被希臘、羅馬、埃及和其他文化使用了幾個世紀。在十三世紀，中國思想家發明了線算盤，它把珠子放在線上，並且置於一個框架內。線算盤比計數盤更方便攜帶，可以用於更快速的計算。事實上，儘管科技進步，世界各地的人們仍然使用線算盤。

3　中國、印度、歐洲和非洲人們之間的貿易，說明了早期計算機在世界上許多地方都很普遍。然而，其實美洲早期居民在沒有這些影響的情況下創造了一種計算機。一些學者提出，印加帝國——約 1430 年至 1533 年在南美洲的一個強大帝國——使用了一種叫做優巴納的裝置來計算。優巴納是上面被刻成許多部分和層次的石頭，類似於一個城市的微型模型。這個裝置很可能用於計算儲存的資源量，像是穀物或家畜，但有些歷史學家推測它可能用於天文計算。與線算盤不同的是，優巴納已不再被使用。

字彙 POWERED BY COBUILD

portable 可攜帶的：something that is easily carried or moved 可以輕鬆攜帶或移動的東西
miniature 微型的：something that is very small; a smaller version of something that is normally bigger 非常小的東西；某種普遍較大物件的縮小版本

4-1-2　掌握要領：推論題回答技巧

技巧 1

仔細閱讀題目和選項。當你閱讀題目時，注意你要推理的內容。並且要仔細閱讀選項，確定你理解每個選項的大意。

練習① 在第 77 頁的題目和選項中，用底線標示出五個關鍵詞組。當你掃視文章時，一定要牢記這些詞組，這樣才有助於你回答問題。

技巧 2

注意包含文章中關鍵字的選項！推論題的正確答案不會直接出現在文章中。而且，正確答案通常會改述所有的關鍵論點，因此要當心措辭與文章的用詞一樣的選項。

練習② 在第 77 頁裡，畫一條線刪去與文章中關鍵字一樣的錯誤選項。

技巧 3

刪去在文章中未得到支持的選項。你可能會看到一個看似正確的選項。但除非它得到文章資訊的支持，否則它不會是正確答案。此外，你只要根據文章的資訊來回答問題，不需要任何背景知識來回答閱讀部分的問題。

練習③ 在第 77 頁裡，畫一條線刪除未得到文章支持、但可能是正確推論的錯誤選項。

TEST TIP!

推論題所根據的往往是日期和數字。當你閱讀一篇文章時，要注意與日期相關的資訊。你或許需要對在特定日期之前或之後發生的事件做出結論。

詞彙題要求你選出最能夠說明文章中醒目標示的單字或詞組的定義。在大多數情況下，題目會要求你選出一個單字的定義，但偶爾也可能問你一個詞組的定義。

詞彙題可能用以下方式表達：

- The word X in the passage is closest in meaning to... 與文章中的字彙 X 最接近的意思是…
- The phrase X in the passage is closest in meaning to... 與文章中的詞組 X 最接近的意思是…

詞彙題快速指南

內容	詞彙題要求你從一段文章中判斷一個單字或詞組的定義，該單字或詞組會在文章中被醒目標示。用來測驗的字彙可能有好幾種意思，你必須選出最能夠說明該單字或詞組在該篇文章中的定義。因此，你不能只靠著單字表來準備考試。
須具備的能力	為了正確回答詞彙題，你必須能夠： • 理解單字或詞組在文章中的使用方式。 • 利用前後文線索來確定單字或詞組的意思。 • 熟悉常見的英文字尾和字首及其含義。 • 具有廣博的英文字彙知識。
正確答案	詞彙題的正確答案可以替換文章中醒目標示的單字或詞組，而不改變句子的含義或與文章的主旨相互矛盾。正確選項通常是醒目標示詞的同義詞。
錯誤答案	注意包含以下資訊的選項： • 與醒目標示詞結構類似的字詞，如單字 slather 和 gather。兩個單字看起來相似，並不表示它們有相同的意義。 • 與另一個選項的含義相反。如果有兩個選項的意思彼此相反，那麼它們兩個的答案可能都錯誤。 • 單字的定義正確，但用法不同。你必須選出能最適當描述該單字在文章中的意思的答案。

4-2-1 詞彙題範例

A 快速閱讀以下的詞彙題範例，並回答下列問題。依你認識的單字，寫下其簡短定義。

TOEFL Reading

Question

1. The word gradual in paragraph 1 is closest in meaning to
   - ○ hurried.
   - ○ continuous.
   - ○ slow.
   - ○ graceful.

2. The word imperceptible in paragraph 2 is closest in meaning to
   - ○ dangerous.
   - ○ insignificant.
   - ○ unnoticeable.
   - ○ impassible.

B 現在閱讀範例文章。在閱讀時，用底線標出你認為有助於回答 A 部分題目的資訊。當你完成後，在以上選項裡標記出正確答案。

Fast-Moving Glaciers

1　Glaciers are enormous rivers of ice that form in locations where snow accumulates more quickly than it can melt. These ice rivers are known for their **gradual** pace— on average, glaciers move a mere 30 centimeters a day. However, in some cases, glaciers move at a much faster rate. For example, one glacier travels at a speed of 111 feet a day. Fast-moving glaciers can have both local and more widespread consequences.

2　One result of increased glacial speeds is glacial earthquakes. When a glacier experiences a dramatic increase in speed, it can cause seismic waves, or waves of energy that travel through the earth. Because glaciers are usually located in uninhabited areas, glacial earthquakes are not particularly destructive. Furthermore, the seismic waves produced by glacial earthquakes are usually **imperceptible**, even to someone standing on the glacier as the earthquake occurs. However, some scientists hypothesize that a significant glacial earthquake could cause oceanic disturbances and perhaps even tsunamis.

3   While glacial earthquakes may currently have limited effects, fast-moving glaciers can also impact the environment in a more noticeable way. When a glacier moves at a fast pace, it loses massive amounts of ice. This causes the sea level to rise because the ice melts into the ocean. In fact, records show that melted ice from a single, particularly rapid glacier has caused the global sea level to rise by four percent. Higher sea levels can have disastrous effects not only for human beings, who frequently settle in coastal areas that could be flooded by rising oceans, but also for the complex ecosystems that are located in or near oceans and freshwater bodies. For example, many organisms live in tidal areas, or places that are underwater at high tide and above water at low tide. Rising sea levels could wash these habitats away altogether. Thus, by raising the sea level, increased glacier speed in extreme northern regions of the earth could be devastating for organisms in locations thousands of miles away.

中譯
快速移動的冰河

1   冰河是積雪速度超過融化速度時所形成的巨大冰塊河流。這些冰河以其緩慢的速度而聞名——平均而言，冰河每天僅移動 30 公分。然而在某些情況下，冰河的移動速度會快得多。舉例來說，有條冰河移動的速度每天可達 111 英尺。快速移動的冰河可能對當地和更遠的區域產生影響。

2   冰河速度增加的一個結果是冰河地震。當冰河的速度急劇增加時，它會引發地震波，即穿越地球的能量波。由於冰河通常位於無人居住的地區，因此冰河地震並不特別具破壞性。此外，由冰河地震所產生的地震波通常是無法察覺的，即使站在冰河上也難以感覺到地震。然而有些科學家也提出假設，認為重大的冰河地震可能會引起海洋擾動，甚至可能引發海嘯。

3   雖然目前冰河地震的影響有限，但快速移動的冰河也可能以更明顯的方式影響環境。當冰河快速移動時，它會失去大量的冰，並導致海平面上升，因為融化的冰進入海洋。事實上記錄顯示，光是來自一個移動特別快速的冰河的融化冰，已經導致全球海平面上升了百分之四。更高的海平面不僅對人類有災難性的影響，因為人類經常定居在可能被上升的海洋淹沒的沿海地帶，而且對位於或接近海洋和淡水資源的複雜生態系統也有嚴重影響。舉例來說，許多生物生活在潮汐區，也就是高潮時在水面下，低潮時在水面上。上升的海平面可能會完全沖走這些棲息地。因此，在地球極北地區快速移動的冰河會因為海平面上升，而可能會對數千英里外的生物具有極大的破壞性。

字彙 POWERED BY COBUILD
mere 僅僅、少的：a small amount or number of something 少量的、不多的
hypothesize 假定：to say what you think will happen because of various facts 根據各種事實說出你認為將會發生的事情

4-2-2 掌握要領：詞彙題回答技巧

技巧 1

檢視醒目標示字或詞組所在的段落。因為你必須選擇與段落中該單字或詞組的意思最接近的答案，你需要確切了解單字或詞組的使用方式。當你檢視單字或詞組及前後的句子時，要注意能夠幫助你理解意思的前後文線索。請參考下表，了解使用前後文線索來確定單字或詞組意思的方法。

<table>
<tr><th colspan="3">利用前後文線索的方法</th></tr>
<tr>
<td rowspan="2">注意出現在醒目標示單字附近的舉例。如果你熟悉這些舉例，就可以利用它們來確定醒目標示單字的含義。</td>
<td>關鍵詞</td>
<td>
• such as 比如
• including 包括
• consists of 由…組成
• this includes 這包括
• like 像
</td>
</tr>
<tr>
<td>例句</td>
<td>The photographs show banal activities, like going to the grocery store or doing household chores.
這些照片呈現了平凡的活動，比如去雜貨店或是做家務。</td>
</tr>
<tr>
<td rowspan="2">出與前一個觀念呈現差異的關鍵字。如果你知道前後句中字詞的意思，你就會知道醒目標示單字的反義。</td>
<td>關鍵詞</td>
<td>
• Unlike X... 不像 X
• On the other hand, X... 另一方面，X…
• While... 儘管…
• But... 但是…
• However... 然而…
</td>
</tr>
<tr>
<td>例句</td>
<td>Unlike most mammals, few of which are venomous, the platypus produces a noxious substance that can cause extreme pain in humans.
和大多的哺乳動物不同，只有很少數有毒，鴨嘴獸會分泌出一種能夠在人類身上引起極度疼痛的有害物質。</td>
</tr>
<tr>
<td rowspan="2">在醒目標示單字前後的句子中尋找術語的間接定義。定義可能是更簡單同義詞，或者是幫助闡釋其含義的資訊。</td>
<td>關鍵詞</td>
<td>
• and 並且
• meaning that 表示
</td>
</tr>
<tr>
<td>例句</td>
<td>In the southwestern United States, the sunflower is ubiquitous, and it is difficult to find a garden that doesn't include the plant.
在美國西南部，向日葵到處都是，很難找到一處不栽培這種植物的花園。</td>
</tr>
</table>

練習 1 在第 81 頁的段落中，在 gradual 附近用方框圈出一個間接定義（indirect definition）和表示對照的轉折詞（contrasting word）。根據這些前後文線索，哪一個選項可能是正確的？

✏️ 技巧 2

學習常見的英文字首和字尾。透過學習常見英文字首和字尾的定義,你便能夠分析一個不熟悉的單字並猜測它的意思。

字首	舉例	字尾	舉例
a- 沒有…的	amoral 沒有道德的	-able 能夠做	readable 可閱讀的
de- 去除	defog 去除霧氣	-acy 狀態	privacy 隱私
im- 不	improper 不適當的	-ate 使	activate 使活躍
mis- 錯的	misplace 放錯地方	-er / -or 工作職稱	actor 演員
pre- 在前	predate 早於…發生	-ful 充滿	merciful 仁慈的
re- 再做	redo 再做一次	-ish 有點	whitish 帶點白色的
sub- 在下面	subzero 零下的	-ment 狀態	fulfillment 實現、執行
un- 不	unhealthy 不健康的	-ness 狀態	happiness 幸福

練習 2 在第 81-82 頁的段落中,用方框圈出單字 imperceptible 的字首。這個字首在英文中的意思是什麼?

✏️ 技巧 3

嘗試用每個選項替換醒目標示字,接著閱讀句子。在插入正確的選項時,句子應該是合乎邏輯的,而且能支持段落的主旨。不合乎邏輯的選項應該被排除。

練習 3 在 81 頁第 1 題和第 2 題的選項中,刪除不合乎邏輯或與段落主旨相互矛盾的選項。

✏️ 技巧 4

在考試前增加你的字彙知識。使用字典和書末的學術字彙表來學習新單字的定義。學術詞彙表由科斯海德(Coxhead,2000 年)編製,包含了 570 個字彙群,這些字彙群在各種學術教科書中頻繁出現。了解和練習這些單字將有助於擴充你的字彙庫。

練習 4 用字典查 81 頁第 1 題和第 2 題的醒目標示字。

TEST TIP!

在考試當天,你可能會注意到文章裡有一些被畫上底線的單字。這些單字通常是專業術語,已經幫你寫好定義。若要查看定義,只需按一下畫底線的單字即可。

掃視關於氣候的短文，用底線標出每個段落的主旨。

The Climate of the Atlantic Archipelago

1   The Atlantic Archipelago is a group of islands located northwest of continental Europe. The largest island in the archipelago, Great Britain, covers nearly 90,000 square miles and is one of the most heavily populated islands in the world, with around 68 million inhabitants. Ireland, located west of Great Britain, is the second largest island in the group, with a land area of about 32,000 square miles and a population of just over 7 million. In addition to the two large islands, the Atlantic Archipelago consists of more than 6,000 smaller islands. The entire archipelago covers more than 120 square miles, and its location plays a large role in the climate of the region.

2   The latitude of the Atlantic Archipelago undoubtedly influences its climate. Latitude refers to how far north or south a place is in relation to the equator, the imaginary line that divides the north half of the world from the south half. Typically, the farther away from the equator a location is, the weaker the intensity of sunlight in that area. The Atlantic Archipelago is about 54 degrees north of the equator, similar to Russia and Canada. Yet, despite their northern location, the islands have a **temperate** marine climate that ranges from 32 degrees Fahrenheit in the winter to 90 degrees Fahrenheit in the summer.

3   The islands enjoy mild temperatures largely because of their **proximity** to the ocean. Ocean water heats up and cools down more slowly than land, so areas by the coast usually experience less extreme temperature swings in summers and winters. Furthermore, the Atlantic Archipelago benefits from being near the Gulf Stream. The Gulf Stream is an ocean current that begins in the Gulf of Mexico, flows up the east coast of North America, then crosses the Atlantic Ocean and reaches the Atlantic Archipelago. The water transported by the Gulf Stream ranges in temperature from 45–72 degrees, which is about twice as warm as the water surrounding the Gulf Stream. The islands in the Atlantic Archipelago constantly receive this warm ocean water from the Gulf Stream, which makes the climate about 10 degrees warmer than it would be otherwise.

大西洋群島的氣候

1　大西洋群島是位於歐洲大陸西北部的一群島嶼。該群島中最大的島嶼是大不列顛島，面積將近90,000 平方英里，是世界上人口最稠密的島嶼之一，擁有約 6,800 萬居民。位於大不列顛島西部的愛爾蘭是該群島中第二大的島嶼，面積大約 32,000 平方英里，人口約逾 700 萬。除了這兩個大島之外，大西洋群島還包括 6,000 多個較小的島嶼。整個群島總面積超過 120 平方英里，其地理位置對該地區的氣候有著重要的作用。

2　大西洋群島的緯度無疑影響了其氣候。緯度指的是一個地方與赤道的南北距離，赤道是把北半球和南半球分開的假想線。通常一個地方距離赤道愈遠，該地區的陽光強度就愈弱。大西洋群島大約位於赤道以北 54 度，類似於俄羅斯和加拿大。儘管位於北方，這些島嶼卻擁有溫帶海洋型氣候，冬季氣溫大約華氏 32 度，夏季氣溫大約華氏 90 度。

3　這些島嶼的氣溫溫和，主要是由於接近海洋。海水的升溫和降溫速度比陸地慢，因此沿海地區通常在夏季和冬季的溫度變化較小。此外，大西洋群島也因靠近墨西哥灣流而受益。墨西哥灣流是一股洋流，起始於墨西哥灣，沿著北美東海岸流動，接著橫穿大西洋，抵達大西洋群島。墨西哥灣流中的海水溫度是攝氏 45 至 72 度，大約是其周圍海域水溫的兩倍。大西洋群島的島嶼不斷接收來自墨西哥灣流的溫暖海水，使氣候比原本預期的還要暖 10 度左右。

字彙 POWERED BY COBUILD

climate 氣候：general weather conditions 普遍的天氣狀況
marine 海洋：relating to the sea 與海有關

Ｂ　仔細閱讀題目。它們屬於哪種題型？接著開始作答。留意正確答案，並且閱讀答案解析的原因解釋。

1. Based on the information in paragraph 2, which of the following can be inferred about sunlight?

　○ Its intensity is not affected by latitude.
　○ Areas north of the equator receive less sunlight.
　○ It is most intense near the equator.
　○ Places near the ocean receive more sunlight.

1. 根據第二段的資訊，關於陽光，可以推論出下列哪一項？
　○ 陽光的強度不受緯度影響。
　○ 赤道以北地區接收的陽光較少。
　✅ 陽光在赤道附近最強烈。
　○ 靠近海洋的地方接收的陽光較多。

▶ 題型：推論題

○ 作者說，地點離赤道愈遠，該地區的陽光強度就愈弱。這表示緯度確實影響了陽光的強度。

○ 作者說，地點離赤道愈遠，該地區的陽光強度就愈弱。這並不表示這些地區接收到的陽光較少。

✅ 作者解釋，距離赤道遠的區域陽光強度較弱。根據這個資訊，你可以推斷在赤道附近陽光最強。

○ 儘管大西洋群島被海洋環繞，作者並未說明這個因素影響了島嶼接收到的陽光量。

2. The word temperate in the passage is closest in meaning to

○ moderate.

○ extreme.

○ varying.

○ humid.

中譯

2. 在文章中，「temperate」的意思最接近於

✅ moderate（適度的）

○ extreme（極端的）

○ varying（多變的）

○ humid（潮濕的）

▶ 題型：詞彙題

✅ 同一句中的轉折詞 yet 和 despite 暗示了 temperate 與人們對於北方地區（即寒冷地區）的預期相反。在下一句中，作者提到這些島嶼氣溫溫和。mild 是 moderate 的另一種說法，或表示「缺乏嚴重極端的」。

○ temperate 指的是缺乏極端的溫度變化。

○ varying 這個詞在該句子也是可以接受的，但會改變意思。重點應該放在缺乏極端，而不是溫度變化的範圍上。

○ 這些島嶼可能有潮濕的氣候，但 humid 與 temperate 的意義並不相同。

3. The word proximity in the passage is closest in meaning to

○ dependence.

○ introduction.

○ significance.

○ closeness.

中譯

3. 在文章中，「proximity」的意思最接近於

○ dependence（依賴）

○ introduction（介紹）

○ significance（重要性）

✅ closeness（接近）

答案解析

▶ 題型：詞彙題

○ 這個選項是不合邏輯的。儘管可以說這些島嶼在某種程度上依賴海洋，但這種依賴不會對溫度產生影響。

○ 將 proximity 替換為 introduction 會造成句子意思混淆，這個答案是錯誤的。

○ 雖然 significance 可以放在該句中，但它改變了句子的意思，使結果不支持段落主旨。

✅ 作者提到大西洋群島被水包圍。此外，靠近海洋會影響溫度是合理的。

4. **Which of the following can be inferred about the Gulf Stream?**

○ It leads to warm water temperatures in the Gulf of Mexico.

○ It keeps its warmth as it crosses the Atlantic Ocean.

○ It carries cooler waters during the summer.

○ It ends when it reaches the Atlantic Archipelago.

中譯

4. 關於墨西哥灣流，可以推論出下列哪一項？

○ 它導致墨西哥灣的水溫升高。

✅ 當它橫越大西洋時依然保持溫暖。

○ 它在夏季所攜的海水比較涼。

○ 它在到達大西洋群島時結束。

答案解析

▶ **題型：推論題**

○ 作者提到墨西哥灣流源於墨西哥灣，但沒有資訊顯示這股洋流如何影響那裡的水溫。

☑ 作者說這股洋流橫越大西洋，而且大西洋群島從這股洋流中接收到溫暖的水。根據這項資訊，可以推斷這股洋流在橫越大洋時保持著熱能。

○ 作者提到大西洋群島不斷從這股洋流中接收溫暖的水，這表示水的溫度在夏季不會改變。

○ 作者描述了洋流到達大西洋群島前的移動，但這並不表示墨西哥灣流在那裡結束。

Ⓐ 掃視關於生物學的短文，並寫下每段的主旨。

1. _____

2. _____

3. _____

4. _____

Poison Sequestration

1   There are hundreds of thousands of poisonous organisms in the world, and many of these plants and animals are able to produce their own toxins. However, there is also a class of poisonous animals that cannot produce toxins independently. Instead, they use a process called poison sequestration in order to obtain toxins. By using this method, animals are able to save and use toxins that are produced by another organism, generally in order to defend themselves from predators. Given the advantages that toxins offer, many animals have developed multiple strategies for obtaining poison through poison sequestration.

2   One method of poison sequestration involves obtaining toxins from plant sources. This strategy is especially common among insect species, such as butterflies, beetles, and ants, but it's also employed by several larger species. One such animal is the African crested rat, a species native to West Africa that can grow up to fourteen inches long. The rat's spine is protected by long, absorbent fur that sticks up when the rat is threatened. This strip of fur is covered with poison that the rat obtains by chewing on the bark and roots of the arrow poison tree and coating the hairs on its spine with the chewed material. Thus, if a predator attacks the rat, it **inadvertently** ingests the poison, which causes heart attacks in many organisms.

3   Another poison sequestration strategy involves obtaining poison from other animals. Typically, this strategy is used by larger animals, like the European hedgehog, that are capable of hunting other organisms. In a manner similar to African crested rats, European hedgehogs chew the skins of poisonous toads and **slather** the remains onto themselves. However, some small species have developed methods of obtaining toxins from animals larger than them. For example, the blue sea slug, a creature that usually grows no larger than one inch, becomes poisonous by eating the tentacles of an aquatic animal called the Portuguese man-of-war. These tentacles are up to 100 feet long and contain a deadly poison. When blue sea slugs eat Portuguese man-of-

wars, they store the poisonous parts of the animal in special pouches so they can use it for defense at a later time.

4   It is also common for poison sequestration to progress up the food chain, meaning that many predators sequester poison from prey that have also sequestered poison. For instance, the tiger keelback, a species of snake, sequesters poison by eating poisonous frogs. In many cases, poisonous frogs become toxic by eating poisonous insects.

中譯

毒物截存

1   在世界上有成千上萬種有毒生物，其中許多植物和動物能夠自行產生毒素。然而，還有一類無法獨立產生毒素的有毒動物，牠們使用一種叫做毒物截存的過程來獲得毒素。透過這種方法，動物能夠保存和使用由另一個生物產生的毒素，其目的通常是為了抵禦掠食者。鑒於毒素帶來的好處，許多動物已經發展出多種藉由毒物截存來獲得毒物的策略。

2   毒物截存的其中一種方法是從植物來源獲取毒素。這種策略在昆蟲中特別常見，例如蝴蝶、甲蟲和螞蟻，但也被幾種較大的物種所採用。其中一種動物是非洲冠鼠，這是一種生長在西非的物種，可長達十四英寸。冠鼠的脊椎受到長而具吸收性的軟毛保護，當冠鼠受到威脅時軟毛會豎起來。這片軟毛上布滿了毒物，冠鼠藉由咀嚼箭毒樹的樹皮和根部，並把咀嚼的物質塗抹在其脊椎的軟毛上來獲取毒物。因此如果掠食者攻擊冠鼠，便會在無意間攝取到毒素，這種毒素會導致許多生物心臟病發作。

3   毒物截存的另一種策略是從其他動物獲取毒素。通常這種策略是被體型較大的動物採用，例如歐洲刺蝟，牠們能夠捕獵其他生物。與非洲冠鼠類似，歐洲刺蝟會咀嚼有毒蟾蜍的皮膚，並將殘餘物大量塗抹在身上。然而，一些小物種已經發展出從體型比牠們更大的動物身上獲取毒素的方法。舉例來說，身長通常不超過一英寸的藍色海蛞蝓，會吃下一種叫做葡萄牙戰艦（僧帽水母）的水生動物的觸手而變得有毒。這些觸手長達 100 英尺並含有致命毒素。當藍色海蛞蝓吃下葡萄牙戰艦時，牠們會將動物的有毒部分存儲在特殊的囊袋裡，以便日後用於防禦。

4   毒物截存通常也會沿著食物鏈進行，這表示許多掠食者也會從截存毒物的獵物那裡獲取毒素。例如，一種叫做虎斑頸槽蛇的蛇類，就是藉著吃有毒的蛙類來截存毒素。在許多情況下，有毒的青蛙是透過吃有毒昆蟲而變得有毒。

字彙 POWERED BY COBUILD

ingest 攝取：to eat or adsorb something 吃下或吸收某物
toxin 毒素：a poisonous substance 有毒的物質

B 仔細閱讀題目，注意它們是推論題或詞彙題並作答。於各個解析旁邊填入分別對應的題目選項。請注意，答案解析順序不依照題目選項順序排列！讀者需要判斷各選項為何正確或錯誤，並且找出該選項所對應的正確解析為何，再於解析旁邊填入編號。

1. The word inadvertently in paragraph 2 is closest in meaning to

○ suddenly. [A]

○ partially. [B]

○ accidentally. [C]

○ harmlessly. [D]

中譯

1. 在第二段裡，「inadvertently」的意思最接近於：

○ suddenly（突然）[A]。

○ partially（部分的）[B]。

✅ accidentally（意外的）[C]。

○ harmlessly（無害的）[D]。

答案解析

▶ 題型：詞彙題

_____ ○ 雖然 suddenly 可以用在這個句子裡，但它不符合文章的整體意思。

_____ ○ 這種毒素會導致一些動物心臟病發作，所以吃下這種毒物並非無害。

_____ ○ 這個選項不合邏輯，因為沒有理由說掠食者只會吃下部分的毒物。

_____ ○ 攻擊冠鼠的動物並不知道牠有毒，因此牠是意外吃下這種毒物的。

2. What can be inferred about poison sequestration?

○ A small animal is more likely to sequester poison from plants than animals. [A]

○ Poison sequestration is a common defense strategy among large animals. [B]

○ Poison that is sequestered by animals is usually stored in special pouches. [C]

○ Small animals are typically able to produce their own poisons. [D]

中譯

2. 關於毒物截存，可以推論出下列哪一項？

✅ 小型動物比較有可能從植物中截存毒物。[A]

○ 毒物截存是大型動物常見的防禦策略。[B]

○ 被動物截存的毒物通常會儲存在特殊的囊袋中。[C]

○ 小型動物通常能夠產生自己的毒物。[D]

▶ 題型：推論題

_____ ○ 文章中沒有任何暗示說毒物截存在較大型動物中更為常見。

_____ ○ 作者描述了幾種小型動物截存毒物的情況，因為牠們無法自行產生毒物。

_____ ○ 作者僅提到一種動物將毒物儲存在特殊的囊袋中。

_____ ○ 作者提到大型動物較容易透過捕獵其他生物來獲取毒物，因此推測小型動物更有可能從植物中獲得毒物。

3. The word slather in paragraph 3 is closest in meaning to

○ gather. [A]

○ toss. [B]

○ drop. [C]

○ spread. [D]

中譯

3. 在第三段裡，「slather」的意思最接近於

○ gather（聚集）。[A]

○ toss（拋、扔）。[B]

○ drop（丟下）。[C]

✓ spread（塗抹）。[D]

▶ 題型：詞彙題

_____ ○ 雖然 slather 和 gather 看起來相似，但它們並不具有相同的意思。

_____ ○ toss 的意思是將物品扔到空中，文章中沒有暗示這是作者所指的動作。

_____ ○ slather 的意思是在某物上塗抹一層厚厚的物質，這是正確的選項。

_____ ○ 這個選項不合邏輯，因為動物不太可能把殘餘物丟在自己身上。

4. Based on the information in paragraph 4, what can be inferred about toxins?

○ Most toxins that are sequestered by animals are produced by plants. [A]

○ Toxins used by snakes are typically sequestered from frogs. [B]

○ Predators that do not eat plants may sequester toxins originally made by plants. [C]

○ Toxins produced by insects are the main source of poisons used by plants. [D]

4. 根據第四段的資訊，關於毒素，可以推論出下列哪一項？

    ○ 大多數被動物截存的毒素是由植物產生的。[A]

    ○ 蛇使用的毒素通常是從青蛙中截存而來的。[B]

    ✅ 不吃植物的掠食者可能會截存最初由植物製造的毒素。[C]

    ○ 昆蟲產生的毒素是植物使用的毒物的主要來源。[D]

答案解析

▶ **題型：推論題**

    _____ ○ 文章沒有提供任何資訊可支持大部分蛇從青蛙那裡截存毒素的觀點。

    _____ ○ 作者提到掠食者通常吃掉已經從植物等來源截存毒素的動物。這表示即使掠食者不吃植物，也可能從植物來源截存毒素。

    _____ ○ 作者沒有提供任何資訊來支持這個推論。

    _____ ○ 作者說許多昆蟲的毒素來自於植物，而不是植物從昆蟲那裡獲得毒素。

Read the passage about a topic in astronomy.

TOEFL Reading
Question

Origins of the Moon

1   Throughout the nineteenth and twentieth centuries, several astronomers advanced competing theories about how the moon formed. For example, in 1878, astronomer George Howard Darwin proposed the fission theory, which claimed that early in Earth's formation, the planet began spinning extremely fast. Darwin believed that the rapid spinning motion caused a large chunk of Earth to break off and launch into space. This chunk then began orbiting Earth and became the moon. Another explanation, called the condensation theory, stated that while the solar system was still forming, a star exploded and left behind mass amounts of debris. According to the condensation theory, Earth and the moon formed from this debris at roughly the same time and through the same processes.

2   These theories were accepted to various degrees among the scientific community, and there was much debate among scientists about which one provided the most complete account of how the moon formed. Ultimately, the validity of both was **undermined** in the second half of the twentieth century. At this time, newly available data from lunar missions revealed several inconsistencies between the assumptions of the theories and facts about the moon. For one, data collected on the moon showed that, at some point, the moon was subjected to intense heat. However, neither the fission theory nor the condensation theory involved processes that would result in intense heat. Furthermore, there is no evidence that Earth experienced similarly intense heat. Thus, both theories were deemed invalid.

3   Data from lunar explorations also revealed another discrepancy with the condensation theory. According to the theory, the moon and Earth formed through the same process at the same time. Scientists pointed out that if Earth and the moon actually formed this way, they should have the same chemical composition. But when scientists obtained samples from the surface of the moon, they found that the chemical composition of the

moon was different from that of Earth, which severely discredited the condensation theory.

4   Information from lunar explorations played a large role in dispelling previous theories of lunar formation. However, it also helped astronomers formulate a theory that better explains how the moon was formed. Today, the most current and widely accepted explanation is called the giant impact theory. According to this theory, all of the planets in the solar system formed at the same time. In addition to the planets that are currently in our solar system, scientists believe that a planet called Theia also developed at this time. Theia was likely about 4,000 miles in diameter, roughly the size of Mars. During Earth's formation, Theia crashed into Earth and **disintegrated**. Scientists believe that the collision between Earth and Theia caused at least two large chunks of Earth to break off. The larger of these chunks is thought to have become the moon. Meanwhile, scientists believe that the smaller chunk, which was probably about one-third the size of our moon, also orbited Earth for some time. These two pieces orbited Earth together for a period of time that lasted between 10 million and 100 million years. Then, the smaller moon was eventually destroyed when it collided into the larger one.

5   Unlike previous theories, the giant impact theory adequately explains most of the data collected on the moon. For example, the theory accounts for why there is evidence that the moon was subjected to strong heat while there is no such evidence on Earth. Scientists **speculate** that when Theia collided with Earth, intense heat was produced at the point of impact. Moreover, the material that was directly hit by Theia was likely the chunk of Earth that broke off and formed the moon. This also explains why the chemical composition of Earth and the moon is different—the ejected material that formed the moon was primarily from Earth's outer surface. Thus, the chunk that became the moon represents only a portion of the composition of Earth.

字彙 POWERED BY COBUILD

discrepancy 差異：a noticeable difference between two things 兩個事物之間的明顯不同
dispel 消除：to stop someone from having an idea or feeling 停止某人產生某個想法或感覺

1. Based on the information in paragraph 1, what can be inferred about Darwin's theory of moon formation?

   ○ It was the first theory of moon formation to gain wide acceptance.
   ○ It assumed that Earth and the moon were made of the same material.
   ○ It was inspired by other scientists' work on the condensation theory.
   ○ It explained why Earth and the moon developed at different times.

2. The word **undermined** in paragraph 2 is closest in meaning to

   ○ dismissed.
   ○ weakened.
   ○ proven.
   ○ expanded.

3. In paragraph 2, the author implies that

   ○ the majority of scientists favored the condensation theory over the fission theory.
   ○ lunar exploration provided evidence to support the fission theory.
   ○ data from lunar missions was not available to the entire scientific community.
   ○ the chemical composition of the moon was unknown until after the 1950s.

4. The word **disintegrated** in paragraph 4 is closest in meaning to

   ○ became larger.
   ○ softened.
   ○ broke apart.
   ○ disappeared.

5. Based on the information in paragraph 4, what is implied about the giant impact theory?

   ○ Its accuracy is still disputed by many astronomers.
   ○ It cannot explain what became of the planet Theia.
   ○ It describes the creation of multiple moons.
   ○ It is closely based on the condensation theory.

6. The word **speculate** in paragraph 5 is closest in meaning to

   ○ theorize.
   ○ confirm.
   ○ overlook.
   ○ reveal.

097

句子／段落／文章摘要題
Sentence Summary / Simplification Questions and Passage / Prose Summary Questions

Unit 5

5-1 句子摘要／簡化題

句子摘要題要求你選出能為文章中的醒目標示句提供最佳摘要的答案，這類題目也可以稱為句子簡化題。

句子摘要題可能用以下方式表達：

- Which of the following best expresses the essential information in the highlighted sentence? Incorrect answer options change the meaning in important ways or leave out essential information.

  下列哪一項最能表達出醒目標示句中的必要資訊？錯誤的選項會在意思上做了重大改變或遺漏了必要資訊。

句子摘要／簡化題快速指南

內容	句子摘要題要求你選出與文章中的醒目標示句相同意思的答案。醒目標示句通常長達二到四行。
須具備的能力	為了正確回答句子摘要題，你必須能夠： - 理解文章中的主旨（main ideas）和主要支持細節（main supporting details）。 - 確定醒目標示句的論點與其所在段落的其他句子有什麼相關性。 - 判斷並找出正確改述文章資訊的選項。
正確答案	句子摘要題的正確答案會改述和簡化醒目標示句的資訊，它會包含標示句中所有必要或重要的資訊。
錯誤答案	注意包含以下資訊的選項： - 遺漏醒目標示句的重要論點 - 改變了因果關係或錯誤的敘述事件發生頻率，而與文章主旨和事實相互矛盾。 - 包含與標示句一模一樣的措辭和句子結構。正確答案通常會使用同義詞並改變標示句的結構。

5-1-1 句子摘要／簡化題範例

Ⓐ 快速閱讀以下的句子摘要題範例，在題目和選項中，用底線標示出能幫助你確定正確答案的任何關鍵字。

TOEFL Reading

Question

1. Which of the following best expresses the essential information in the highlighted sentence? Incorrect answer options change the meaning in important ways or leave out essential information.

○ Inventors created a new technology that allowed the simultaneous recording of sound and picture in order to resolve problems with sound synchronization.

○ Sound-on-film technology created by filmmakers fixed a problem that they had rarely faced when adding sound to films.

○ To solve the problem of synchronization, filmmakers used technology that allowed them to add sound to pictures separately after filming.

○ The video and audio elements of movies were synchronized using technology that was created by inventors.

Ⓑ 現在閱讀一篇有關電影聲音的文章。在閱讀時，用底線標出包含標示句重要資訊的關鍵概念。當你完成後，在以上選項裡標記出正確答案。

Sound in Early Film

1   In the late nineteenth century, technological innovations led to the birth of a new art form: the motion picture. The first motion pictures could be viewed by only one person at a time. Further innovation made it possible to show films to larger audiences, and the first motion picture appeared before a live audience in Paris in 1895. These early films were silent, although they were sometimes accompanied by live orchestras or narrators in the theater. Silent films were a popular form of entertainment in the United States, Great Britain, Japan, and India in the early twentieth century, but they were soon replaced by "talking pictures," films that incorporated sound as well as images. The rising popularity of talking pictures was made possible by two important advances in technology.

2   One of the most significant barriers to producing films with sound was the synchronization, or simultaneous playing, of sound and pictures. In many early films, the sound was played separately from the film. This system was unreliable, however, as skips or other minor problems with the sound disc could cause the sound recording and the video to play at different times or speeds. **To solve this**

problem, inventors created sound-on-film technology that allowed filmmakers to record the sound and the pictures together, making it impossible for the video and audio elements to become separated.

3   But even when the sound was precisely synchronized with the images on screen, it was often difficult for audiences to hear the recordings. Advancements in amplification technology, or processes for increasing sound volume, were essential to the popularization of films with sound and dialogue. Improvements in microphones made the recording process more effective, and the development of more powerful speakers made it possible to play sound capable of filling larger and larger spaces.

中譯

早期電影的聲音

1   在 19 世紀晚期，技術上的創新促成了一種新藝術形式的誕生：電影。最初的電影一次只能供一個人觀看，而進一步的創新使得電影能展示給更廣大的觀眾群觀賞。第一部電影於 1895 年在巴黎的現場觀眾面前上映。這些早期的電影是無聲的，儘管有時會在戲院裡配上現場管弦樂隊或旁白。在 20 世紀初期，無聲電影在美國、英國、日本和印度是一種很流行的娛樂，但是很快就被「有聲電影」取代，這種電影不僅有影像，還有聲音。有聲電影的普及得力於技術上的兩大重要進步。

2   製作有聲電影最重大的障礙之一是聲音和影像的同步播放。在許多早期電影中，聲音是與影片分開播放的。不過這種系統並不可靠，因為唱盤跳針或其他小問題，都可能導致聲音錄製和影片以不同的時間或速度播放。為了解決這個問題，發明家創造了有聲電影技術，使電影製片人能夠一起錄製聲音和影片，也使影像和聲音元素變得無法分離。

3   但是，即使聲音與螢幕上的影片精確同步，觀眾往往也很難聽到錄下的聲音。擴音技術的進步，或者提高音量的方法，對於有聲音和對話的電影普及至關重要。麥克風的改進使錄製過程更加有效益，而發展更有力的揚聲器也使得播放出來的聲音能夠填滿愈來愈大的空間。

字彙 POWERED BY COBUILD

synchronization 同步化：two activities, processes, or movements happening at the same time 兩個活動、過程或動作在同一時間發生

amplification 放大：ability to increase the strength or intensity or something, usually sound 增加某物（通常是聲音）的力量或強度的能力

5-1-2　掌握要領：句子摘要／簡化題回答技巧

技巧 1

請用你自己的話改述醒目標示句。在看過醒目標示句後，重新敘述一次，並一定要包含原句的所有關鍵概念。看看選項，檢查是否有與你的改述接近的選項。

練習 1　改述 99-100 頁的醒目標示句。在 99 頁的題目中，用底線標出一個與你的改述相似的選項。

技巧 2

刪去那些遺漏了醒目標示句中重要資訊的選項。記住，正確的選項會包含醒目標示句的所有重要資訊。若選項包含文章的事件資訊（factual information），卻遺漏重要資訊，該選項就是錯誤的，應該要刪除。

練習 2　在第 99 頁裡，劃掉一個遺漏了重要資訊的選項。遺漏的資訊是什麼？

技巧 3

留意與文章的事實和主旨相互矛盾的答案。就句子摘要題而言，正確答案必定會支持文章的事實和主旨。錯誤的選項可能調換了事件的因果關係，與文章事實相互矛盾。換句話說，文章中所敘述的原因可能在錯誤選項中被描述為結果。還要注意有頻率副詞的選項，因為這可能會改變句子的意思，使其與文章中的事實相互矛盾。

常見的頻率副詞	
always 總是	occasionally 偶爾
frequently 頻繁	seldom 很少
usually 通常	rarely 很少
often 經常	hardly ever 幾乎從不
sometimes 有時	never 從不

練習 3　畫線刪掉第 99 頁的一個選項，該選項要包含上面表格中的一個頻率副詞。這個頻率副詞如何改變了句子的意思？

技巧 4

檢查一下對於文章的改述。正確選項通常包含原始句的同義詞和改變原始句的結構。如果你看到一個選項與醒目標示句有類似的措辭和／或類似的結構，請務必仔細閱讀後再做出選擇。

練習 4　畫線刪掉第 99 頁裡與原始句措辭相似的一個選項。為什麼這個選項是錯誤的？

在閱讀部分，每篇文章都會有一題摘要題。

段落摘要題會提供一個概述文章主旨的引言句（introductory statement），並提供六個選項，你需要選出其中最能概述文章主旨的三個選項。這類題目也叫做文章摘要題。

段落／文章摘要題快速指南

內容	文章摘要題提供你： ▪ 一個總結文章主旨的引言句 ▪ 六個與文章有關的句子 你必須從這六個句子中選出三個最能概述整篇文章的句子。
須具備的能力	為了正確回答文章摘要題，你必須能夠： ▪ 判斷文章的主旨。 ▪ 了解文章的基本架構。
正確答案	文章摘要題的正確答案會反映文章的主旨。透過閱讀引言句和三個正確答案的句子，一個原本對文章不熟悉的讀者應該就能理解文章的內容是什麼。
錯誤答案	注意包含以下資訊的選項： ▪ 提到文章中的資訊，但並非文章的主旨之一。 ▪ 文章中根本沒提到的論點。 ▪ 與文章中提出的事實相互矛盾的資訊

TEST TIP!

段落／文章摘要題的分數是兩分。如果三個正確答案你都選到了，你會獲得兩分。如果你只選到兩個正確答案，你會獲得一分；如果你只選到一個正確答案或全錯，你會獲得零分。請注意，你的答案不需要按照任何順序。

5-2-1 段落／文章摘要題範例

🅰 快速閱讀以下的文章摘要題範例，在你掃視的時候，用底線標示出能幫助你確定正確選項的任何關鍵字。

TOEFL Reading

Question

1. An introductory sentence for a summary of the passage is provided below. Complete the summary by selecting the THREE answer options that express the most important ideas in the passage. Some sentences do not belong in the summary, because they express ideas that are not presented in the passage or are minor ideas in the passage. This question is worth 2 points.

This passage discusses literature of the American South.

- _____
- _____
- _____

Answer Options

1. Southern writers who worked during the late nineteenth and early twentieth centuries are among the most important literary figures of American literature.
2. The unique aspects of the American South were represented in Southern literature through a number of characteristics.
3. The economy of the American South was largely centered in cities.
4. Family relationships are a central theme found in a lot of Southern writing.
5. Faulkner's stories focused on events that happened to his own family.
6. Southern writers like Eudora Welty often described Southern settings in careful detail.

🅱 現在閱讀一篇有關文學的短文。在閱讀時，用底線標出你認為有助於回答 A 部分題目的資訊。當你完成後，在以上選項裡標記出正確答案。

Literature of the American South

1　The American South has developed a culture that is distinctive in many ways. While the literature of the American South is diverse, Southern writers—especially those who worked in the late nineteenth and early twentieth centuries—often employed similar strategies to explore the distinct character of the region.

2 Family relationships are a central theme found often in Southern writing. Many stories describe the events that affect a family for several generations. For example, William Faulkner, a key writer in the Southern literary tradition, wrote novels that focused on family structure and familial bonds. Perhaps because the economy of the American South is traditionally agricultural, Faulkner's novels are especially concerned with how land ownership is passed from generation to generation.

3 In addition to writing about subjects that reflect the values of Southern culture, Southern writers also created similar settings or locations in their works. Eudora Welty, a Southern novelist and short story writer, describes the Southern landscape in careful detail. The settings of her stories and novels are filled with plants and animals that are specific to the American South, and her writing often makes a place, like a particular river or a certain town, central to the story she tells. While some stories may seem like they could take place anywhere, many of the stories in Southern literature are rooted in a specifically Southern environment.

中譯

美國南方文學

1 美國南部發展出了一種在許多面向上有獨特性的南方文化。美國南方的文學雖然多采多姿，但南方作家——尤其是活躍於十九世紀末至二十世紀初的——常常採用相似的策略來探索該地區的獨特性。

2 家庭關係是南方文學作品中常見的核心主題，許多故事描述的都是影響一個家族好幾代人的事件。舉例來說，威廉・福克納是南方文學傳統中的重要作家之一，他所寫的小說著重於家庭結構和家族關係。也許是因為美國南方的經濟傳統上以農業為主，所以福克納的小說特別與土地的所有權如何代代相傳有關。

3 除了撰寫反映南方文化價值觀的主題之外，南方作家也在他們的作品中創造了相似的背景或地點。南方小說家和短篇小說家尤多拉・韋爾蒂詳細的描述了南方的景觀。她的故事和小說的背景充滿了美國南方特有的動物和植物，而且她的文字經常將一個地方，如一條特定的河流或一個特定的小鎮，放在故事中的核心位置。雖然有些故事似乎可以發生在任何地方，但許多南方文學的故事都根植於確切的南方環境中。

字彙 POWERED BY COBUILD

distinct 有區別的：different or separate from something of the same type 同類型事物中的不同處或有區別的地方

rooted 根植於：strongly influenced by something 受某事物的強烈影響

5-2-2 掌握要領：段落／文章摘要題回答技巧

技巧 1

在文章中尋找每段的主題句（topic sentence）。主題句是介紹該段落主題的句子。文章第一段的主題句可能會出現在該段末尾，而在隨後的段落裡，主題句通常會出現在該段的開頭。找到並重新閱讀文章中的主題句，你就能夠快速選出內容相似的選項。

練習 1　在第 103-104 頁的文章中，用方框圈出每段的主題句。注意這些句子在文章中的位置。

技巧 2

刪除僅包含次要細節的選項。有些選項可能包含了出現在文章中但不重要的資訊。次要細節是指在描述文章主旨時不重要的部分。如果你不確定某個細節是不是次要的，就想像一下，如果你把該細節刪除，一個不熟悉文章的人是否還能理解文章的主旨。

練習 2　在 103 頁用底線標記出一個包含次要細節的選項。

技巧 3

注意選項裡是否包含了文章中未提到的資訊。文章摘要題的正確答案一定會在文章中提到。在某些情況下，選項中的資訊可能看似熟悉或與文章裡的概念有關。但是除非你能在文章中找到直接的參照資訊，否則它不可能是正確答案。

練習 3　在 103 頁用底線標記出一個含有文章中未提到資訊的選項。

技巧 4

留意與文章事實相互矛盾的答案。因為這類題型的正確答案代表文章的主旨，所以它們必須以文章中的事實為根據。為了避免選擇錯誤的選項，一定要回去檢視文章，看看你是否能找到支持每個選項的資訊。如果找不到，你應該刪除該選項。

練習 4　在 103 頁畫線刪掉一個與文章事實相互矛盾的選項。

TEST TIP!

在你完成文章摘要題的答案後，再讀一遍你所選擇的那三個答案。對於不熟悉文章主題的人來說，根據你的選擇，他們能夠理解文章的內容嗎？如果你有疑慮，就重新檢查你的答案，並試著找出更好的選項。

Ⓐ 掃視關於銀匠工藝的短文，用底線標出每個段落的主旨。

Navajo Silversmithing

1   The Navajo are an indigenous group that has lived for centuries in the southwestern part of what is now the United States. The traditional artwork of the Navajo, which includes rugs, baskets, and pottery, is popular around the globe. However, perhaps no Navajo artwork has attracted as much attention as the group's silverwork. In fact, silver jewelry made by Navajo designers is admired among art collectors all over the world. Interestingly, silversmithing is a relatively recent art form in the Navajo culture, but it is one that craftspeople have transformed into a uniquely Navajo creation that is an important part of modern Navajo culture and commerce.

2   The origins of Navajo silversmithing can be traced back to a man named Atsidi Chon, who is widely regarded as the father of Navajo silversmithing. In the late 1860s, Chon learned silversmithing techniques from a Mexican craftsman. He brought his knowledge, as well as tools for working silver, back to his hometown and taught silversmithing to his sons. Within a few decades, many people in the Navajo community had learned the craft, though they faced several obstacles. For example, it was often difficult to obtain the materials required in order to work silver. In the early years of Navajo silverwork, craftspeople frequently melted coins or the silver hardware used in wagons and harnesses in order to obtain the silver for their work. Furthermore, it was equally hard to get the tools for crafting silver, and early silversmiths often resorted to using very basic techniques. Despite these early limitations, craftspeople were able to develop the characteristic style for which Navajo silver items are now known.

3   Today, the work of Navajo silversmiths clearly reflects designs that are culturally important to the group. **Characteristic Navajo silver jewelry often uses the traditional squash blossom bead, a hollow, rounded bead with petal-like carvings that, for some Navajo people, represents strength and** vitality. Navajo silverwork also frequently incorporates turquoise, a semiprecious green or blue stone found in abundance in the American Southwest.

4   Some elements of Navajo silverwork are clearly influenced by other cultures. In the late nineteenth century, the Navajo traded with Mexicans and Spaniards, whose ornate silver belts, spurs, and saddle decorations inspired early Navajo

silversmiths. For instance, early Navajo silver often incorporated designs that resembled pomegranate blossoms, which were very popular among the Spanish who traveled to the American Southwest. The Navajo also traded with other Native American groups. The silverwork they acquired from these groups often referenced British colonial and other styles. Such exchanges of skills and designs from other cultures influenced and inspired their craft, while in turn Navajo silverwork influenced and inspired others.

中譯

納瓦荷銀匠工藝

1 納瓦荷人是一支原住民族，在現今美國西南部地區已經生活了好幾個世紀。納瓦荷的傳統藝術，包括地毯、籃子和陶器，在全世界都很受歡迎。然而，或許沒有任何一種納瓦荷藝術像他們的銀器一樣，引起過這麼多的關注。事實上，由納瓦荷設計師製作的銀飾受到了全球藝術收藏家的讚賞。有趣的是，銀匠工藝在納瓦荷文化中是一種相對較新的藝術形式。工匠們將銀匠工藝轉化為獨特的納瓦荷創作藝術，是現代納瓦荷文化和商業的重要一部分。

2 納瓦荷銀匠工藝的起源可以追溯到一個名叫阿茲迪‧丘恩的人，他被普遍認為是納瓦荷銀匠工藝之父。十九世紀晚期，丘恩從一位墨西哥工匠那裡學習了銀器製作技術。他將自己的知識和用於加工銀器的工具帶回故鄉，並把銀匠技藝教給他的兒子們。幾十年來，納瓦荷社區的許多人學會了這門手藝，儘管他們面臨著幾個障礙。例如，加工銀器所需的材料通常很難取得。在納瓦荷人製作銀飾的早期，工匠們經常利用熔化硬幣或用於馬車和馬具的銀器，來取得他們工作所需的銀材料。此外，取得製作銀飾的工具也同樣困難，早期的銀匠們常常只能使用非常基本的技術。儘管有這些早期的限制，工匠們還是發展出如今納瓦荷銀飾所獨有的特色風格。

3 如今，納瓦荷銀匠的作品清楚反映出對該族群文化來說很重要的設計。獨特的納瓦荷銀首飾常常使用傳統的南瓜花瓣珠，這是一種中空、圓形的珠子，帶有像花瓣一樣的雕刻，對有些納瓦荷人來說，它象徵著力量和活力。納瓦荷銀匠的作品還經常使用綠松石，這是一種綠色或藍色的半寶石，這種石材大量存在於美國西南部。

4 納瓦荷銀飾的一些元素顯然受到其他文化的影響。納瓦荷人在十九世紀晚期與墨西哥人和西班牙人進行貿易，他們華麗的銀製腰帶、馬刺和鞍具裝飾啟發了早期的納瓦荷銀匠。例如，早期的納瓦荷銀飾經常包含類似石榴花的設計，而這種設計在到美國西南部旅行的西班牙人之間非常受歡迎。納瓦荷人也和其他美洲原住民族進行貿易，他們從那些族群裡取得的銀器經常參考了英國殖民地和其他風格。這些來自其他文化的技藝和設計的交流，影響並激勵了他們的工藝，而納瓦荷銀匠的作品又影響和激勵了其他人。

字彙 POWERED BY COBUILD

indigenous 原住民：people who belong to the country in which they are found 屬於其所在國家的人民

vitality 活力：having great energy and liveliness 擁有極大的能量和生命力

仔細閱讀題目。它們屬於哪種題型？在題目和選項中用底線標記你在回顧文章時要尋找的關鍵詞，接著開始作答。留意正確答案，並且閱讀答案解析的原因解釋。

1. Which of the following best expresses the essential information in the highlighted sentence in paragraph 3? Incorrect answer options change the meaning in important ways or leave out essential information.

   ○ Typical Navajo jewelry made out of silver uses a squash blossom bead that looks like a hollow bead with petals.

   ○ Navajo silversmiths use traditional squash blossoms and rounded, hollow beads to represent strength and vitality.

   ○ The characteristic Navajo silver jewelry often employs traditional squash blossom beads, a design that symbolizes strength and energy.

   ○ Hollow, rounded beads called squash blossom beads are often used in traditional Navajo jewelry.

中譯

1. 下列哪一項最能表達出第三段裡醒目標示句中的必要資訊？錯誤的選項大幅改變了意思或遺漏了必要資訊。

   ○ 典型的納瓦荷銀首飾通常使用南瓜花瓣珠，這種珠子看起來像是中空的，帶有花瓣。

   ○ 納瓦荷銀匠使用傳統的南瓜花和圓形的中空珠來象徵力量和活力。

   ✅ 典型的納瓦荷銀首飾往往採用傳統的南瓜花瓣珠設計，這個設計象徵著力量和活力。

   ○ 被稱為南瓜花瓣珠的中空圓珠，常常用於傳統的納瓦荷首飾中。

答案解析

▶ 題型：句子摘要題

   ○ 這個選項遺漏的資訊是：這些珠子對納瓦荷人來說象徵著什麼？

   ○ 這個選項包含了錯誤的資訊。文章中的「Squash blossoms」是銀飾中常用的珠子，而不是一種植物。也沒有在這種珠子之外使用另一種中空珠。

   ✅ 這個選項包含了原始句中有關南瓜花瓣珠的所有必要資訊，以及珠子的意義。

   ○ 這個選項沒有包含珠子對某些納瓦荷人的意義的資訊。

2. An introductory sentence for a brief summary of the passage is provided below. Complete the summary by selecting the THREE answer options that express the most important ideas in the passage. Some sentences do not belong in the summary because they express ideas that are not presented in the passage or are minor ideas in the passage. This question is worth 2 points.

This passage discusses the history of Navajo silversmithing.

- _____

- _____

- _____

Answer Options

1. The Navajo are famous for their rugs, baskets, and silver jewelry.

2. Although it was introduced to the group fairly recently, silversmithing is an important part of Navajo culture.

3. Atsidi Chon is credited as the father of Navajo silversmithing because he created new tools for working silver.

4. Though they often lacked the tools for silversmithing, Navajo artists created a distinctive style soon after the art form was introduced to the community.

5. Navajo silverwork employs designs inspired by other cultures but also features styles that are distinctly Navajo.

6. The design of the squash blossom bead and the use of turquoise are two styles that were borrowed from the Spanish.

中譯

2. 以下是簡短摘要文章的引言句。請完成摘要,選出三個最能表達文章重要概念的選項。有些句子並不屬於該摘要,因為它們表達了文章中未提到的概念,或者是文章中的次要概念。此題總共 2 分。

這篇文章討論了納瓦荷銀匠工藝的歷史。

- _____

- _____

- _____

選項

1. 納瓦荷以他們的地毯、籃子和銀飾而聞名。

2. 雖然銀匠工藝相對近期才被引入該族群,但它是納瓦荷文化重要的一部分。

3. 阿茲迪・丘恩被譽為納瓦荷銀匠工藝之父,因為他創造了加工銀器的新工具。

4. 雖然他們常常缺乏銀匠工藝所需的工具,但納瓦荷藝術家在這項藝術形式被引進族群後不久便創造出了獨特的風格。

5. 納瓦荷的銀器工藝採用了其他文化的設計靈感,但也呈現了獨特的納瓦荷風格。

6. 南瓜花瓣珠的設計和綠松石的使用,是從西班牙人那裡借來的兩種風格。

▶ **題型：文章摘要題**

○ 1. 儘管這個事實在文章中提到過，但它是次要的，並沒有描述文章的主旨。

✅ 2. 在第一段的結尾，作者提到納瓦荷銀匠工藝是最近才被引進社區的，並且是納瓦荷文化和商業的重要一部分。

○ 3. 文章說阿茲迪‧丘恩為納瓦荷社區引進了銀匠工藝，而不是說他創造了用於加工銀器的新工具。

✅ 4. 作者說在阿茲迪‧丘恩首次將這項工藝引進他們的文化後不久，納瓦荷銀匠就創造了他們的獨特風格。

✅ 5. 第四段討論了其他文化的影響，而第三段則討論了納瓦荷銀飾的獨特特徵。

○ 6. 作者說，南瓜花瓣珠和使用綠松石是納瓦荷的創新。

A 掃視關於歷史的短文，並寫下每段的主旨。

1. _____

2. _____

3. _____

4. _____

Ancient Trade Routes

1   In the first millennium, a number of civilizations lived throughout the Eurasian continent. In many cases, there was limited contact between these civilizations, in part because oceans, mountain ranges, and deserts discouraged travel between the east and west. Despite these difficulties, many traders traveled over land and sea in search of new customers and of new items to bring back to their homelands. Historians now refer to these routes, which spanned up to 4,300 miles and connected cultures on the eastern coasts of Asia to North Africa and the Mediterranean, as the Silk Road. Vital to trade from around the first century until about 1400, these routes were important because they allowed the exchange of both goods and ideas.

2   The Silk Road was first developed by Chinese merchants who sought to trade silk and other goods within the Chinese Empire. Soon, the routes expanded as merchants from places like Persia, India, and Egypt sought out rare commodities that they could sell in their home countries. This kind of trade was very profitable because goods that were common in one place were priceless and exotic in another. For example, the Romans were greatly interested in Chinese silk, and the Chinese often bought horses from their western neighbors. Furthermore, traders from the east often carried items like gunpowder, porcelain, and paper, while traders from the west brought ivory, amber, and cosmetics. **People from all over the Eurasian continent exchanged a wide variety of goods, which brought wealth to the merchants who sold the items, to the craftspeople who copied and sold domestic versions of foreign products, and even to people who lived along the trade routes and provided services to travelers.**

3   The trade routes brought many different cultures together, and they often exchanged ideas as well as material goods. Commerce encouraged cultural contact that significantly influenced the development of nations that were very different from one another. For instance, because of trade along the Silk Road, Chinese cities often

housed visitors from many different places. Records show that in 754, one Chinese city was home to at least 5,000 foreigners. These visitors often brought new ideas and ways of thinking with them. Chinese thinkers adopted and adapted some of these new ideas, and they were particularly influenced by Indian philosophies. Many merchants also carried artwork with them on the trade routes. This promoted creative exchanges between cultures, and the similarities between some styles of Greek, Iranian, and Indian sculpture and painting are the result of those exchanges. Additionally, some records suggest that performance art forms, such as music, dance, and storytelling, were transformed by the connections the Silk Road permitted between civilizations.

中譯

古代貿易路線

1　在第一個千年期間，歐亞大陸上存在著許多文明。在許多情況下，這些文明之間的接觸有限，部分原因是因為海洋、山脈和沙漠阻礙了東西方之間的交通。儘管存在這些困難，許多商人仍然跨越陸地和海洋去尋找新客戶，以及能帶回家鄉的新商品。歷史學家現在稱這些路線為絲綢之路，這些路線長達 4300 英里，連接了亞洲東海岸與北非和地中海地區的文化。從公元 1 世紀到 1400 年左右，這些路線對貿易至為重要，因為它們促進了商品和思想的交流。

2　絲綢之路最初是由中國商人開發，他們希望在中國境內進行絲綢和其他商品的貿易。隨著來自波斯、印度和埃及等地的商人尋找可以在自己國家出售的稀有商品，很快的，這些路線擴展開來。因為在一個地方常見的商品，在另一個地方反而是無價之寶且具異國情調，所以這種貿易非常有利可圖。舉例來說，羅馬人對中國絲綢非常感興趣，而中國人經常向他們西邊的鄰人買馬。此外，來自東方的商人通常攜帶火藥、瓷器和紙張等物品，而來自西方的商人則帶來象牙、琥珀和化妝品。來自歐亞大陸各地的人們交換了各式各樣的商品，這為以下這些人帶來了財富，像是出售商品的商人、複製和銷售國內版本的外國商品的工匠，甚至是居住在貿易路線上並為旅行者提供服務的人。

3　貿易路線將許多不同的文化匯集在一起，它們經常交換的不僅是物質商品，還有思想。商業促進了文化接觸，大幅影響了彼此間差異甚大的國家的發展。舉例來說，由於絲綢之路上的貿易，中國的城市經常容納來自許多不同地方的訪客。記錄顯示，在公元 754 年，一座中國城市至少住著 5000 名外國人。這些訪客經常帶來新的思想和思維方式，中國的思想家吸收並採納了其中一些新思想，特別是印度哲學的影響。許多商人也在貿易路線上攜帶藝術品，這促進了文化之間的創意交流。像希臘、伊朗和印度在雕塑及繪畫上某些風格的相似之處，就是這些交流的結果。此外一些記錄指出，像是音樂、舞蹈和說故事的表演藝術形式，也因絲綢之路所促成的文明之間的聯繫而發生了變化。

字彙 POWERED BY COBUILD

commodity 商品：something that is sold for money 以金錢交易的物品
priceless 無價的：worth a very large amount of money 值很多錢的

B 仔細閱讀題目，注意它們是句子摘要題或文章摘要題並作答。於各個解析旁邊填入分別對應的題目選項。請注意，答案解析順序不依照題目選項順序排列！讀者需要判斷各選項為何正確或錯誤，並且找出該選項所對應的正確解析為何，再於解析旁邊填入編號。

1. Which of the following best expresses the essential information in the highlighted sentence in paragraph 2? Incorrect answer options change the meaning in important ways or leave out essential information.

○ People throughout Eurasia traded goods, bringing wealth to merchants and craftspeople and to people who provided services for the residents who lived along the trade routes. [A]

○ Merchants and craftspeople provided services, as did people who lived along the trade routes, and all three groups grew wealthy as a result. [B]

○ Merchants became rich largely because of the trading activities of craftspeople and people who lived along the trade routes in Eurasia. [C]

○ The trading activities throughout Eurasia led to the rise of wealth for merchants, craftspeople, and people who provided services to travelers along the routes. [D]

中譯

1. 下列哪一項最能表達出第二段裡醒目標示句中的必要資訊？錯誤的選項大幅改變了意思或遺漏了必要資訊。

○ 人們在整個歐亞大陸進行商品貿易，使商人、工匠，以及為居住在貿易路線上的居民提供服務的人都變得富有。[A]

○ 商人和工匠提供服務，貿易路線沿線的居民也提供服務，這三個族群因此變得富有。[B]

○ 商人致富的主要原因是和工匠，以及居住在歐亞貿易路線上的人的貿易活動。[C]

✔ 整個歐亞大陸的貿易活動促進了商人、工匠和為沿路旅行者提供服務的人的財富增長。[D]

答案解析

▶ 題型：句子摘要題

_____ ○ 工匠從出售外國產品的複製品中致富，貿易路線上的居民透過為旅行者提供服務來賺錢。文章沒有說明這些族群參與了商人的貿易。

_____ ○ 在文章中，作者說服務是由沿著貿易路線居住的人提供的，而不是由商人和工匠提供的。

_____ ○ 醒目標示句說歐亞大陸上的貿易為商人、工匠和沿途居民帶來了財富。

_____ ○ 文章中沒有提到，為居住在貿易路線上的居民提供服務的人是誰。

2. An introductory sentence for a brief summary of the passage is provided below. Complete the summary by selecting the THREE answer options that express the most important ideas in the passage. Some sentences do not belong in the summary because they express ideas that are not presented in the passage or are minor ideas in the passage. This question is worth 2 points.

This passage discusses the history of trade on the Silk Road.

- _____
- _____
- _____

Answer Options

1. The trade routes known as the Silk Road connected cultures, allowing the exchange of merchandise and ideas. [A]
2. The cultures that lived throughout Eurasia during the first millennium didn't have much contact due to obstacles like oceans, mountains, and deserts. [B]
3. The Silk Road developed when Chinese merchants expanded their trade routes in order to obtain precious goods from Persia, India, and Egypt. [C]
4. While silk originally drove trade along the Silk Road, merchants from a number of cultures eventually began exchanging a variety of goods. [D]
5. In addition to promoting the exchange of goods, the Silk Road also helped people learn about the philosophies and art forms of different cultures. [E]
6. The Silk Road helped people from different cultures exchange ideas and philosophies, which is evident in the art forms produced along the Silk Road. [F]

中譯

2. 以下是簡短摘要文章的引言句。請完成摘要,選出三個最能表達文章重要概念的選項。有些句子並不屬於該摘要,因為它們表達了文章中未提到的概念,或者是文章中的次要概念。此題總共 2 分。

這篇文章討論了絲綢之路上的貿易史。

- _____
- _____
- _____

選項

1. 以絲綢之路聞名的貿易路線連接了不同文化，促進了商品和思想的交流。[A]

2. 在第一個千年期間，歐亞大陸各地的文化之間很少有接觸，這是由於海洋、山脈和沙漠等障礙。[B]

3. 絲綢之路得以發展，是由於中國商人擴展他們的貿易路線，以獲得來自波斯、印度和埃及的珍貴商品。[C]

4. 雖然最初是絲綢推動了絲綢之路上的貿易，但到了後來，來自不同文化的商人開始交換各種商品。[D]

5. 除了促進商品交流外，絲綢之路還幫助人們了解不同文化的哲學和藝術形式。[E]

6. 絲綢之路幫助不同文化的人們進行思想和哲學交流，這在絲綢之路上所產生的藝術形式中顯而易見。[F]

答案解析

▶ 題型：文章摘要題

_____ ○ 在第一段裡，作者說儘管存在障礙，但歐亞大陸的文化之間會彼此接觸。

_____ ○ 作者沒有描述絲綢之路上所產生的藝術形式。

_____ ○ 這一句概述了整篇文章的主旨，寫在文章的第一段。

_____ ○ 在第三段裡，作者描述了透過絲綢之路所做的思想和藝術形式的交流。

_____ ○ 在第二段裡，作者說絲綢之路的擴展是由於來自波斯、印度和埃及等地的商人尋求中國的商品，而不是反過來。

_____ ○ 作者說這條路起初是中國商人為了銷售絲綢而開發的，但後來也有來自不同地方的商人交易其他物品，故而隨之擴展。

Read the passage about a topic in music.

TOEFL Reading

Question

Stradivarius Violins

1 Antonio Stradivari was a famous luthier, or maker of stringed instruments, who lived in Italy during the mid-seventeenth century. Stradivari began his career at the young age of 12, when he began working under another famous luthier named Nicolò Amati. Stradivari learned the basic skills of violin making from Amati, but he eventually developed his own style, for which he is still known today. During his lifetime, Stradivari created an estimated 1,000 violins, 450 of which still survive. The violins of Antonio Stradivari are commonly regarded as the finest stringed instruments in the world, surpassing nearly all others in terms of sound quality as well as in visual appeal. Yet, despite the universal recognition of their exceptional quality, there is much debate over what makes Stradivarius violins so extraordinary.

2 Some experts contend that the violins' superior quality derives from their structure. Though his early violins bore a strong resemblance to Amati instruments, the brilliant luthier eventually altered the standard violin structure by experimenting with the shape of the sound hole. Additionally, he varied the width of the purfling, which is the inlaid border located on the violin's back and front end. **These structural alterations resulted in violins that produced louder sounds, which, in turn, allowed violinists to perform in larger concert halls because the sound could carry to the very back of the venue.**

3 While changes to the violins' structure allowed players to play more loudly, professional violinists argue that these changes do not sufficiently explain the instruments' superiority to other violins. They explain that the excellence of Stradivarius violins is based not only on the volumes that they are able to achieve, but also on their ability to produce loud sound without a loss of quality.

4 One factor that may contribute directly to the superior sound quality is the type of varnish Stradivari used on the instruments. Stradivari stained each of his creations using

the same process. First, he applied a coat of oil similar to that used on canvas paintings. Then, he added a layer of oil resin, a glaze-like substance. Finally, he applied a coat of red dye that gave the instruments the classic color of the Stradivarius violin. Some experts believe that the simple oil varnish preserves the wood's ability to vibrate, a quality that allows the instrument to produce sound. This hypothesis is supported by studies in which researchers tested the effects of different types of varnishes on sound quality. They found that violins that are stained with oil-based varnishes, like the Stradivarius violin, produce the most brilliant sound.

5   It is also possible that the wood used to make Stradivarius violins may explain their unique qualities. Analyses have shown that the violins are made out of dense wood, a characteristic that has important implications for sound quality. This is because the particles in dense wood are closer together, resulting in clear, longer-lasting vibrations. As a result, a violin made with dense wood can carry sound over long distances with no loss in quality.

6   For some time, many people believed that Stradivari acquired this dense wood from ancient cathedrals and castles. However, modern research suggests that, in actuality, it probably originated in the spruce forests that grew near Stradivari's home. Today, the wood from these forests is not very dense, but there are indications that it was denser during a period known as the Maunder Minimum. This period, which lasted from 1645 to 1715, was characterized by unusually cold temperatures in Europe, the coldest that the continent had experienced in 500 years. **The cold temperatures, which probably resulted from a decrease in solar activity, are thought to have slowed tree growth, leading to denser wood than what would have resulted from warmer growing conditions.** One researcher determined not only that the colder temperatures of the period caused the trees in the forests near the home of Stradivari to grow slower, but that the violin maker used the spruce wood from these forests in constructing his instruments.

字彙 POWERED BY COBUILD

universal 普遍的：something that relates to everyone or everything in the world or in a group 與世界上或一個族群的所有人或事相關的事物

venue 發生地：the place where an event occurs 事件發生的地點

1. Which of the following best expresses the essential information in the highlighted sentence in paragraph 2? Incorrect answer options change the meaning in important ways or leave out essential information.

   ○ The changes to the violins' structure increased the instruments' top volume, allowing violinists to perform in larger places because the sound would be heard.

   ○ Violinists could perform in larger performance spaces because the structural alterations to the violins allowed players to perform with greater ease.

   ○ Prior to the structural changes to the basic design of the violins, there were few large performance spaces for violinists.

   ○ Structural changes to the violins resulted in louder sound but a slight decrease in the quality of the sound.

2. Which of the following best expresses the essential information in the highlighted sentence in paragraph 6? Incorrect answer options change the meaning in important ways or leave out essential information.

   ○ Dense wood can grow in warm areas, though it is more common in places that have reduced solar activity and lower- than-usual temperatures.

   ○ Dense wood, which is associated with slow tree growth, resulted from cold temperatures during a period of lowered solar activity.

   ○ A decrease in solar activity led to slower tree growth because growth is affected by cold temperatures and wood density.

   ○ The cold temperatures during the period of decreased solar activity resulted in slow tree growth, which led to less dense wood than what would have grown in warmer temperatures.

3. An introductory sentence for a brief summary of the passage is provided below. Complete the summary by selecting the THREE answer options that express the most important ideas in the passage. Some sentences do not belong in the summary because they express ideas that are not presented in the passage or are minor ideas in the passage. This question is worth 2 points.

This passage discusses the features that contribute to the exceptional sound of Stradivarius violins.

- _____
- _____
- _____

Answer Options

1. With only 450 of these instruments remaining today, Stradivarius violins are among the most valuable musical instruments in the world.
2. Stradivari adjusted the structure of the violins in ways that improved their ability to create loud and clear sounds.
3. Violinists who played Stradivarius violins were able to perform in large venues because the instruments were loud enough to be heard over long distances.
4. Researchers determined that Stradivarius violins had exceptional vibrational quality due to the process in which the varnish was applied.
5. The oil-based finish on all Stradivarius violins likely contributes to their sound quality because it preserves the wood's vibrational ability.
6. The dense wood used to create Stradivarius violins, which likely came from a forest near Stradivari's home, is a factor in the superior sound of the instruments.

Unit 6

文句插入題
Insert A Sentence / Text Questions

6-1 文句插入題

文句插入題要求你判斷題目所給的句子最適合放在文章中的哪個位置。文章中有四個地方可讓你把句子插入,這些位置會用黑色方塊 [■] 標記出來,而你要做出選擇。這類題目通常放在倒數第二道題。

文句插入題可能用以下方式表達:

- Look at the four squares [■] in paragraph 1 that indicate where the following sentence could be added to the passage.

  As a result, scientists disagree about the origins of X.

  Where would the sentence best fit?

  請看第一段標有四個黑色方塊 [■] 的地方,這些方塊指示了下列句子可以插入到文章裡的可能位置。

  因此,科學家對 X 的起源存在著分歧意見。

  這句話最適合放在哪裡?

文句插入題快速指南

內容	文句插入題會給你一個句子,你必須判定這個句子最適合放在文章中的哪裡。句子能夠插入的可能位置會用黑色方塊 [■] 標記。若要放置句子,請點擊文章中適當的黑色方塊,句子便會出現在該位置。黑色方塊通常會出現在同一段裡,但不一定會連續出現在相鄰的句子中。
須具備的能力	為了正確回答文句插入題,你必須能夠: • 理解題目插入句的內容和含義。 • 判斷要放置插入句的段落的主旨。 • 判斷前後文線索,例如文法的一致性(grammatical agreement),這有助於你判定句子最適合的位置。 • 分辨轉折詞(transition word),並知道它們在前後文中的含義。
正確答案	文句插入題的正確答案,在段落的前後文中是合乎邏輯的。
錯誤答案	注意包含以下資訊的選項: • 與插入句的前後句文法形式不一致的選項 • 不依照段落中的邏輯發展的選項

6-1-1 文句插入題範例

Ⓐ 快速閱讀以下的範例題，用底線標示出能幫助你了解題目句子的任何關鍵字。

TOEFL Reading

Question

1. Look at the four squares [▪] in paragraph 2 that indicate where the following sentence could be added to the passage.

   As a result, the agricultural productivity in these areas has declined by 20 percent.

   Where would the sentence best fit?

   ○ a
   ○ b
   ○ c
   ○ d

Ⓑ 現在閱讀一篇有關環境科學的短文。在閱讀時，留意 A 部分題目的句子可以放置的四個地方。當你完成後，在選項裡標記出正確答案。注意：黑色方塊旁邊的小寫字母不會出現在實際測驗中。

Environmental Impacts of Irrigation Systems

1   Over the last 50 years, agricultural production has increased significantly around the world. It's estimated that half of that increase can be attributed to the advancement and spread of irrigation technology. However, recent research shows that the environmental consequences of this technique may be more serious than previously thought.

2   Waterlogging, a state in which the ground becomes oversaturated with water, is a particularly harmful effect of irrigation. When waterlogging occurs, the soil, heavy under the weight of the water, begins to become tightly packed. [a] ■ Thus, it is difficult for oxygen to enter the soil, and without it, plant roots essentially suffocate. [b] ■ According to experts, at least 10 percent of the world's arable land is waterlogged. [c] ■ Additionally, it's difficult to prevent waterlogging from occurring because tests that determine whether a field has a high possibility of becoming waterlogged are very expensive. [d] ■

³ Another consequence of irrigation is salinization, or the accumulation of salt crystals on the surface of a field. Excessive irrigation causes water to collect on the surface of a field. Eventually, this water begins to evaporate, drawing salt and minerals from underground rocks to the surface in the process. Once it reaches the surface of the soil, the salt forms into crystals, which reduce plants' ability to absorb water from the soil. Thus, even if there is plenty of water, salinization makes it difficult for plants to absorb the water they need to survive. When salinization occurs, plants begin to wither and agricultural productivity suffers.

中譯

灌溉系統的環境影響

1　過去 50 年來，全球農業產量大幅增加。據估計，增加的半數要歸因於灌溉技術的進步和普及。然而最近的研究顯示，這種技術所造成的環境後果可能比之前想像的更嚴重。

2　積水，即土壤的含水過度飽和的狀態，這是灌溉上一個特別有害的影響。當積水發生時，土壤在水的重壓下開始被緊密壓實。[a] ■ 因此，氧氣很難進入土壤；沒有氧氣，植物的根部便會窒息。[b] ■ 據專家估計，全球至少有 10% 的可耕地處於積水狀態。[c] ■ 此外，積水的發生很難防止，因為測定一片土地是否存在潛在高積水風險的檢驗非常昂貴。[d] ■

3　灌溉的另一個後果是鹽化，即鹽結晶累積在土地表面。過度灌溉導致水分聚積在土地表面，最後，這些水開始蒸發，並在過程中從地下的岩石中吸收鹽和礦物質。鹽一旦到達土壤表面就形成結晶，這會降低植物從土壤中吸收水分的能力。因此即使有足夠的水，鹽化也使植物難以吸收生存所需的水分。當鹽化發生時，植物開始枯萎，農業生產力便會受損。

字彙 POWERED BY COBUILD

arable 可耕地：land that is used for growing crops, such as wheat and barley 用於栽培諸如小麥和大麥等作物的土地

wither 枯萎：to dry up and die 乾涸並死亡

6-1-2 掌握要領：文句插入題回答技巧

技巧 1

檢視題目所給的句子以及黑色方塊出現的段落。當你閱讀應該插入文章中的句子時，請確定你完全理解它的意思。還有，在閱讀討論中的段落時，請注意該段落的主旨以及作者如何發展論點。同時，一定要考慮題目所給句子要放在該段落的哪裡才適合。

練習： 把 121 頁題目的插入句框起來。接著在第 121 頁的文章第二段，把主旨框起來。

技巧 2

注意任何轉折詞（transition word），並了解它們的含義。轉折詞是作者用來使文章清晰易懂的措辭。學習和認識轉折詞，你便能夠判斷段落的邏輯，從而更容易辨別思路的切換或缺乏邏輯連續性的地方。請參考下表的轉折詞例子。

Indicating Sequence 指示順序	轉折詞	first 首先 second 第二 third 第三 eventually 最後	since 自從 then 然後 until 直到 prior to 在…之前
	舉例	**First**, the volcano erupts, emptying the chamber beneath it. **Eventually**, the land around the empty chamber collapses. **首先**，火山爆發，排空了下方的岩漿庫。**最後**，空的岩漿庫周圍的土地塌陷。	
Continuing in the Same Line of Thinking 在相同的思路中繼續	轉折詞	again 再次 additionally 此外 furthermore 再者	and 然後 equally 同樣 likewise 同樣
	舉例	Fleas have extremely long legs relative to their body size. **Likewise**, grasshoppers also have very long legs. 相對於他們的體型，跳蚤的腿非常長。**同樣**，蚱蜢也有很長的腿。	
Shift in Focus 轉換焦點	轉折詞	although 儘管 despite 雖然 regardless 無論如何	instead 反之 even so 即使如此 however 然而
	舉例	The Atacama Desert is one of the driest places on Earth. **Even so**, it is home to several communities. 阿塔卡馬沙漠是地球上最乾燥的地方之一。**即使如此**，它仍是幾個群落的家園。	

Indicating Cause and Effect 指示因果關係	轉折詞	**Cause** 因 when 當 as long as 只要 in order to 為了 because of 因為 due to 由於	**Effect** 果 for this reason 基於這個理由 as a result 結果 thus 因此 accordingly 於是 consequently 結果
	舉例	**Due to** the speed of the water, the rock becomes eroded quickly. **Consequently**, the channel becomes deep over a short amount of time. **由於**水流速度快，岩石迅速受到侵蝕。因此，渠道在短時間內就變得很深。	

練習 1 在 121 頁的第二段裡，用底線標示出三個轉折詞。

✏️ **技巧 3**

嘗試將句子插入每個位置。記住，你可以不限次數更改答案，因此請試過所有位置。當你這麼做的時候，可以一邊閱讀段落，一邊注意句子位置前後的資訊連貫性，是否符合前後句的邏輯？正確答案會最合乎邏輯。

練習 3 嘗試將句子插入每個位置，並再次閱讀以理解意思。在第 121 頁圈出最適合插入句子的選項。

掃視關於生物學的短文，用底線標出每個段落的主旨。

Control of Malaria

1   Malaria is a disease caused by a parasite in the blood. It has existed since at least 2700 BCE, when its symptoms, including headache, fever, and nausea, were described in Chinese medical writings. However, unlike many other ancient diseases, malaria persists today, with approximately 241 million cases reported in 2020. Advances in medical sciences have made it possible to control the disease, but malaria is difficult to eradicate entirely for several reasons.

2   Though early doctors developed some treatments for malaria using plants and herbs, it was not until the true nature of the disease was discovered that it was possible to formulate a more effective treatment. [a] ■ In 1880, a French surgeon discovered that malaria was not caused by a virus, but by a parasite living in the blood of infected people. [b] ■ The discovery that malaria was not a viral infection led to developments in medicine that focused on destroying the parasite. [c] ■ In 1897, a British doctor stationed in India discovered that malaria parasites were passed from person to person by mosquitoes. [d] ■

3   Today, medical researchers from all over the world have made several developments in controlling the spread of malaria. For one, doctors now have access to a wide array of effective medicines for treating malaria, and many of these can be taken to prevent the disease or even build up a partial immunity to it. Recently there have also been promising advances in the development of antibody drugs and vaccines. Furthermore, scientists have developed pesticides to kill mosquitoes and thus prevent the spread of malaria. Additionally, in some places, controlling malaria is achieved through non-medicinal methods, such as the use of mosquito nets that are constructed from fine mesh cloth. The nets are typically placed over beds in order to protect people from mosquito bites while they sleep.

4   Despite these advancements in treating and preventing malaria, the disease is still a worldwide problem. Because mosquitoes and the malaria parasite are living beings, they can develop resistance to the medicines and pesticides used to kill them. [a] ■ Medical scientists must create new medicines and pesticides to fight these resistant parasites and mosquitoes. [b] ■ Automobiles, airplanes, and other kinds of transportation make it easy for infected people to carry malaria to new

locations. [c] ■ Despite these obstacles, cases of malaria declined between 2000 and 2019. [d] ■

中譯

瘧疾的控制

1　瘧疾是由血液中的寄生蟲引起的疾病，至少自公元前 2700 年就已經存在，它當時的症狀包括頭痛、發燒和噁心，這些都描述在中國的醫學著作中。然而與許多其他古老的疾病不同，瘧疾至今仍然存在，2020 年報告的病例大約有 2.41 億例。醫學科學的進步使得我們可能控制這種疾病，但由於幾個原因，瘧疾很難完全根除。

2　儘管早期的醫生利用植物和草藥，發明了一些對付瘧疾的療法，但直到發現了疾病的根本性質，更有效的治療方法才被制定出來。[a] ■ 1880 年，一位法國外科醫生發現，瘧疾不是由病毒引起的，而是由存在感染者血液中的寄生蟲引起的。[b] ■ 發現瘧疾不是病毒感染導致，促使醫學方面的進展集中在消滅寄生蟲上。[c] ■ 1897 年，一位駐印度的英國醫生發現，瘧疾寄生蟲是經由蚊子傳播再人傳人。[d] ■

3　今天，來自世界各地的醫學研究人員在控制瘧疾傳播方面取得了幾項進展。首先，醫生現在可以使用各種有效的藥物治療瘧疾，其中許多可以用來預防、甚至產生對瘧疾的部分免疫力。近年來，在抗體藥物和疫苗的開發方面也取得了有望的進展。此外，科學家已經開發出殺死蚊子的殺蟲劑，從而防止瘧疾的傳播。另外在一些地方，控制瘧疾的方法並非藥物，而是使用了由細網布製成的蚊帳。這些蚊帳通常被放置在床的上方，用來保護人在睡覺時不被蚊子叮咬。

4　儘管在治療和預防瘧疾方面取得了進展，但這種疾病仍是全球性的問題。因為蚊子和瘧疾寄生蟲是生物，所以會對用於殺死牠們的藥物和殺蟲劑產生抗藥性。[a] ■ 醫學科學家必須創造新的藥物和殺蟲劑來對抗這些具有抗藥性的寄生蟲和蚊子。[b] ■ 汽車、飛機和其他交通工具，使感染者容易將瘧疾帶到新的地點。[c] ■ 儘管存在這些障礙，2000 年至 2019 年間的瘧疾病例有所下降。[d] ■

字彙 POWERED BY COBUILD

nausea 噁心：the condition of feeling sick and that you are going to vomit 感到不適和快要嘔吐的狀態

eradicate 根除：to get rid of something completely 徹底擺脫某件事物

B 仔細閱讀題目。它們屬於哪種題型？在題目和選項中用底線標記你在回顧文章時要尋找的關鍵詞，接著開始作答。留意正確答案，並且閱讀答案解析的原因解釋。

1. Look at the four squares [■] in paragraph 2 that indicate where the following sentence could be added to the passage.

This information led to malaria prevention efforts that involved destroying or avoiding the mosquitoes that carried it.

Where would the sentence best fit?

○ a

○ b

○ c

○ d

1. 請看第二段標有四個黑色方塊 [■] 的地方,這些方塊指示了下列句子可以插入到文章裡的可能位置。

   這項資訊促成了針對瘧疾的預防工作,包含消滅或迴避攜帶瘧疾的蚊子。

   這句話最適合放在哪裡?

   ○ a

   ○ b

   ○ c

   ✓ d

答案解析

▶ 題型:文句插入題

   ○ a:此處之前的句子談到,發現疾病的根本性質才能找到更有效的療法。因此在之後的下一句,應該包含發現該疾病是由寄生蟲引起的資訊。

   ○ b:這句話不能放在這裡,因為作者還沒有提到發現瘧疾是由蚊子傳播。

   ○ c:從文法上來說,這句話不合適放在這裡,因為指示代名詞「this」沒有合理的指示對象。

   ✓ d:這是最合理的位置。句子提到了蚊子,而該段落中只有這裡之前的句子提到蚊子。此外,當插入句放在這裡時,思路最合乎邏輯。

2. Look at the four squares [■] in paragraph 4 that indicate where the following sentence could be added to the passage.

   Another challenge in eradicating malaria is the increased mobility of human beings.

   Where would the sentence best fit?

   ○ a

   ○ b

   ○ c

   ○ d

2. 請看第四段標有四個黑色方塊 [■] 的地方，這些方塊指示了下列句子可以插入到文章裡的可能位置。

根除瘧疾的另一項挑戰，是人類流動性的增加。

這句話最適合放在哪裡？

◯ a

✅ b

◯ c

◯ d

答案解析

▶ 題型：文句插入題

◯ a：在這個位置上，插入句並沒有意義，因為之後的句子繼續討論使用藥物和殺蟲劑來殺死寄生蟲和蚊子的概念。

✅ b：這是最合乎邏輯的位置。插入句提到流動性的增加對於根除瘧疾的努力造成了問題，而之後的句子描述了促進增加流動性的交通工具來支持這個觀點。

◯ c：插入句提出了根除瘧疾的第二個挑戰，把這句話放在這裡會破壞段落中的思路。

◯ d：作者已經討論了流動性在瘧疾傳播中的作用，在描述瘧疾減少的敘述之後加入插入句是沒有意義的。

A 掃視關於地質學的短文，並寫下每段的主旨。

1. _____

2. _____

3. _____

4. _____

History of the Mediterranean Sea

1   The Mediterranean Sea spans 2.5 million square kilometers and is almost entirely surrounded by Europe, Africa, and southwestern Asia. Despite its size, a number of geological discoveries suggest that the Mediterranean may have entirely dried up about 5 million to 12 million years ago. For one, during the 1970s, geologists discovered reflective materials at the bottom of the sea by using a specially designed ship and drilling system to take core samples of the Mediterranean's seabed that were about 30 feet long. [a] ■ These samples revealed that the reflective layer was composed of minerals left behind by evaporated seawater. [b] ■ Geologists also found other materials that were unlikely to exist at the bottom of a sea. [c] ■ For example, they found a layer of anhydrite, a mineral that undergoes a chemical transformation when it comes into contact with water. [d] ■

2   Based on the depth of the layers of non-oceanic materials at the bottom of the sea, many scientists argue that evaporation was caused by the Mediterranean becoming separated from the Atlantic Ocean. Currently, the Mediterranean is connected to the Atlantic at a narrow point, about 8.9 miles wide, called the Strait of Gibraltar. The connection between the two bodies of water is important because the Mediterranean Sea has a negative moisture balance. [a] ■ Because of its negative moisture balance, it's likely that the Mediterranean Sea would dry up in about 1,500 years without extra water from the Atlantic Ocean pouring in through the strait. [b] ■ Researchers speculate that several million years ago, a geological event caused the Strait of Gibraltar to close, cutting off the Mediterranean from its water source. [c] ■ Completely separated from the Atlantic, geologists claim that the Mediterranean dried up in as little as 1,000 years. [d] ■

3   The evaporation of the Mediterranean had significant effects locally and globally. Emptied of water, the region became a vast desert. It's believed that when the Mediterranean Sea dried up, the water level of the oceans around the world increased

by up to 32 feet. Furthermore, a large part of the salt from the world's oceans was stored in the dry seabed. This led not only to decreased salinity in the world's oceans, but also to a hypersaline, or extremely salty, environment in the Mediterranean desert. Because many animals cannot survive in hypersaline conditions, it's likely that many of the species that once lived in the area probably died, resulting in a severe decline in the biodiversity of the area.

4　However, this desert eventually became a sea again. About 5 million years ago, geologists theorize that a major geological event opened the dam between the Atlantic and the Mediterranean, causing an enormous waterfall to flood the Mediterranean basin, refilling it in only 100 years. Such a sudden influx of water would wash away any life growing in the Mediterranean desert and affect the climate of the surrounding regions.

中譯

地中海的歷史

1　地中海面積有 250 萬平方公里，幾乎完全被歐洲、非洲和西南亞所包圍。儘管如此，許多地質發現指出，地中海可能在約 500 萬至 1200 萬年前是完全乾涸的。舉例來說，在 1970 年代，地質學家使用一艘特別設計的船和鑽探系統，在地中海大約 30 英尺長的海床上截取了一些岩芯樣本，發現了海底的反射性物質。[a] ■ 這些樣本顯示，反射層是由海水蒸發後殘留的礦物組成。[b] ■ 地質學家還發現了其他不太可能存在於海底的物質。[c] ■ 例如，他們發現了一層硬石膏，這種礦物在接觸水時會產生化學變化。[d] ■

2　根據海底非海洋性物質層的厚度，許多科學家認為蒸發作用是由於地中海與大西洋分開造成的。目前，地中海與大西洋連接之處是一個很狹窄的點，叫做直布羅陀海峽，約 8.9 英里寬。這兩個水域之間的聯繫很重要，因為地中海有負濕度平衡。[a] ■ 由於其負濕度平衡，要是沒有來自大西洋的額外海水通過海峽，地中海很可能在約 1500 年內乾涸。[b] ■ 研究人員推測，幾百萬年前，一次地質事件導致直布羅陀海峽關閉，切斷了地中海與其水源的聯繫。[c] ■ 地質學家主張，若是地中海完全與大西洋分開，它可能在短短 1000 年之內乾涸。[d] ■

3　地中海的蒸發作用對該區域和全球都有重大影響。失去水分後，該區域變成了一片廣闊的沙漠。一般認為，當地中海乾涸時，世界各地海洋的水位上升了高達 32 英尺。此外，全球海洋中大部分的鹽都儲存在乾涸的海床中。這不僅造成全球海洋的鹽度降低，也造成地中海沙漠的高鹽度環境。由於許多動物無法在高鹽度條件下生存，許多曾經生活在該地區的物種很可能已死亡，導致該地區生物多樣性嚴重下降。

4　然而，這片沙漠最後又變成了一片海洋。地質學家推測，在大約 500 萬年前，一次重大的地質事件開啟了大西洋和地中海之間的堤壩，使一股巨大的瀑布淹沒了地中海盆地，僅用了 100 年就重新填滿了它。如此突然的水流湧入，會沖走生長在地中海沙漠中的所有生命，並且影響周圍地區的氣候。

字彙 POWERED BY COBUILD

evaporate 蒸發：to change from a liquid state to a gas 從液態轉變為氣態

salinity 鹽度：the amount of salt in something 某種東西中鹽的含量

B 仔細閱讀題目並作答。於各個解析旁邊填入分別對應的題目選項。請注意，答案解析順序不依照題目選項順序排列！讀者需要判斷各選項為何正確或錯誤，並且找出該選項所對應的正確解析為何，再於解析旁邊填入編號。

1. Look at the four squares [■] in paragraph 1 that indicate where the following sentence could be added to the passage.

The presence of anhydrite, then, suggests that at some point in the past, there was an absence of water in the region that is now the Mediterranean Sea.

Where would the sentence best fit?

○ a
○ b
○ c
○ d

中譯

1. 請看第一段標有四個黑色方塊 [■] 的地方，這些方塊指示了下列句子可以插入到文章裡的可能位置。

因此硬石膏的存在指出，在過去的某個時間點，現在的地中海區域曾經缺水。

這句話最適合放在哪裡？

○ a
○ b
○ c
✅ d

答案解析

▶ 題型：文句插入題

_____ ○ 此處之後的句子提到了不太可能在海底發現的其他物質，如硬石膏。將插入句放在這裡會破壞段落的思路。

_____ ○ 此處之後的句子繼續討論海底的反射性物質，因此將插入句放在這裡是不合邏輯的。

_____ ○ 此處之前的句子第一次提到硬石膏。這是插入句最合乎邏輯的位置，因為它提供了有關發現硬石膏的更多細節，並支持了地中海曾經乾涸的理論。

_____ ○ 此處之後的句子第一次提到硬石膏，因此插入句不太可能放在這裡。

2. Look at the four squares [■] in paragraph 2 that indicate where the following sentence could be added to the passage.

This means that every year, more water evaporates from the sea than is added to it by rivers and rainfall.

Where would the sentence best fit?

○ a

○ b

○ c

○ d

中譯

2. 請看第二段標有四個黑色方塊 [■] 的地方，這些方塊指示了下列句子可以插入到文章裡的可能位置。

這表示海洋每年蒸發的水量，比河流和降雨所增加的水量還要多。

這句話最適合放在哪裡？

✅ a

○ b

○ c

○ d

答案解析

▶ 題型：文句插入題

_____ ○ 此處之前的句子描述的是，科學家相信大西洋被隔絕後海洋花了多久時間乾涸，這裡並不適合插入負濕度平衡的定義。

_____ ○ 插入句提供了負濕度平衡的定義，因此，它最有可能放在第一次提到負濕度平衡的句子之後。

_____ ○ 此處之前的句子討論了造成地中海與大西洋隔絕的可能事件，在此放置插入句會破壞段落的流暢性。

_____ ○ 此處之前的句子提到了負濕度平衡可能對地中海產生的影響，在此引入定義的可能性不大。

Read the passage about a topic in astronomy.

TOEFL Reading

Question

Detection of Extrasolar Planets

1　An extrasolar planet is a planet that is located outside of Earth's solar system. [a] ■ Like the planets in our solar system, which orbit around the sun, extrasolar planets follow the path around stars in the galaxy. [b] ■ In addition, these planets may be able to provide information about astronomical processes like star formation, which could help scientists understand the beginnings of our own solar system. [c] ■ However, because they are located outside of the solar system, extrasolar planets are very difficult to detect. The task of discovering extrasolar planets is further complicated by the fact that, as mature planets, they do not have their own light source, and the intense light from the stars that they orbit usually obscures them. [d] ■ Despite these difficulties, scientists have devised several methods for detecting extrasolar planets.

2　The primary methods for locating extrasolar planets are indirect, meaning that they involve taking measurements from objects other than extrasolar planets themselves. For example, the radial velocity method involves calculating changes in a star's movement in response to the extrasolar planets orbiting around it. When an extrasolar planet orbits a star, it changes the star's velocity, or the speed at which the star travels. Instruments on Earth that measure the movement of starlight through space can detect changes in a star's velocity from billions of light-years away. [a] ■ By calculating these changes for faraway stars, scientists can determine if there are any extrasolar planets orbiting around them. [b] ■ Furthermore, this method provides researchers with information about the mass of the extrasolar planets that are causing the velocity changes. [c] ■ Typically, extrasolar planets that are discovered using this method are very large. [d] ■ However, researchers are in the process of refining this method in order to be able to detect smaller planets as well.

3　The radial velocity method provides information about the mass of an extrasolar planet, but by using another indirect detection technique called the transit method, scientists can gather other kinds of information about an extrasolar planet's size. [a] ■ Most importantly, the transit method helps observers to determine an extrasolar planet's radius, which is the distance from the center of a planet to its surface. [b] ■ When a planet comes between a star and the instruments used to observe it, the star's light is momentarily dimmed. [c] ■ Thus, by measuring the star's light output, scientists can determine if an extrasolar planet has traveled between that star and their telescopes. [d] ■ Scientists using this method pay attention not only to the intensity of the star's light output, but to the frequency of any changes in output as well. By using this information, along with the size of the shadow that an extrasolar planet casts as it passes in front of a star, scientists are able to figure out a planet's size. Planets with a larger radius cause the light of a star to dim more significantly than it would with smaller planets.

4   In addition to these indirect methods, researchers have been developing new technology intended to make it easier to obtain images of extrasolar planets directly. They are making advancements toward creating instruments that are capable of filtering out the glare of a star's light and producing extremely clear images that allow scientists to distinguish extrasolar planets from the stars they orbit. Some scientists have been researching the possibility of adapting the coronagraph, which is a telescope originally used to block out our sun's light in order to study the fainter light surrounding it. [a] ■ With some modifications, the coronagraph's ability to block out large amounts of light may make it useful for detecting extrasolar planets. [b] ■ Unlike ordinary telescopes, an interferometer uses a system of several mirrors and gathers images from many different angles. [c] ■ By combining the multiple images, the relatively dim light of extrasolar planets is intensified and is therefore more apparent to scientists. [d] ■

字彙 POWERED BY COBUILD
light-year 光年：the distance that light travels in a year 光一年所行進的距離
orbit 繞軌道運行：to move around a sun or moon in a continuous curving path 繞著太陽或月球以連續曲線的路徑運動

1. Look at the four squares [■] in paragraph 1 that indicate where the following sentence could be added to the passage.

   Research on extrasolar planets is driven primarily by the possibility that other solar systems may contain planets similar to Earth in that they are capable of supporting life.

   Where would the sentence best fit?

   ○ a

   ○ b

   ○ c

   ○ d

2. Look at the four squares [■] in paragraph 2 that indicate where the following sentence could be added to the passage.

   This is because planets with a larger mass cause more noticeable changes in the speed of a star's movement.

   Where would the sentence best fit?

   ○ a

   ○ b

   ○ c

   ○ d

3. Look at the four squares [■] in paragraph 3 that indicate where the following sentence could be added to the passage.

   Researchers measure the size of extrasolar planets by observing the light a star produces.

   Where would the sentence best fit?

   ○ a

   ○ b

   ○ c

   ○ d

4. Look at the four squares [■] in paragraph 4 that indicate where the following sentence could be added to the passage.

Other researchers are concentrating on interferometry technology.

Where would the sentence best fit?

○ a

○ b

○ c

○ d

以下將測試你到目前為止所學的技巧。在閱讀模擬試題中,你會閱讀兩篇英文學術文章,並回答二十道問題。文章和題目的難度與托福網路測驗相同。每個問題 1 分,除了每篇文章的最後一道題目,它的分數會高於1分。題目會說明該題的計分方式。

閱讀部分計時說明		
文章	題目數量	答題時間
Passage 1	10 題	35 分鐘
Passage 2	10 題	

開始做模擬試題的時候,請務必按照頁面上的指示進行。在答題時要計時,以免超過規定的時間。完成模擬試題後,請翻至 Answer Key 檢查你的答案是否正確。看看你答錯的題目,並釐清它們是屬於何種題型。你是否對於特定類型的題目感到困難呢?如果有,一定要在參加托福考試之前複習該類型的題目。

Read the passage about a topic in economics.

The Decline of the English Cloth Trade

1   After 45 years of the queen's rule, James I **succeeded** Elizabeth I to the English throne in 1603, at which point the English economy was struggling. The population of England was swelling, food production was insufficient, and prices were high. Despite its instability, a few industries brought reliable income to the English economy. In particular, many merchants relied on the export of cloth to continental Europe. For the first decade of James I's reign, the cloth trade prospered and was an important source of revenue for the English. However, the king was to make a serious mistake that would eventually lead to the fall of the English cloth trade.

2   In 1614, William Cockayne, an English merchant and politician, proposed that James I make a dramatic change to the way the English exported cloth. At the time, the English produced primarily unfinished cloth. This meant that they sold cloth that had not been dyed, bleached, or otherwise processed. Most often, companies in the Netherlands bought the plain cloth from England and finished it themselves. **The Dutch were experts in the complex procedures and technologies required to finish cloth, and these processes added significant value to the unfinished cloth they had purchased from England.** As a result, Dutch cloth companies could sell their goods at much higher prices than the English could. Hoping to transfer these profits to English companies, Cockayne proposed that the English finish the cloth themselves to increase the value of their cloth exports. He also asked James I to establish a company, which was to function under Cockayne's leadership, that would control and monopolize the export of finished cloth to continental Europe. The king was in need of money, and the prospect of increased revenue appealed to him. Thus, he agreed to Cockayne's plan and, per Cockayne's request, founded the King's Merchant Adventurers, a company with a primary purpose of exporting finished cloth.

3   However, Cockayne's plan disrupted the previously steady English cloth trade and was ultimately ineffective for a number of reasons. First, James I's support of Cockayne's company created a rift between the king and many powerful English merchants, particularly the members of the unfinished cloth company called the Merchant Adventurers, which had been cast aside in favor of Cockayne's group. Furthermore, the Dutch, who had previously been Europe's main supplier of finished cloth, responded to English competition by refusing to purchase any English cloth

products, and many other European nations did the same. In addition, merchants in other countries refused to ship English cloth or charged English businesspeople **inflated** fees for shipping. The resistance from abroad was particularly damaging to the King's Merchant Adventurers because it could not afford the ships that were necessary to transport its goods to European markets.

4   In addition to the difficulties caused by its widespread unpopularity, Cockayne's company was unable to produce quality goods. For one, Cockayne did not have the funds to acquire the machines needed to finish cloth. [a] ■ Moreover, English cloth makers were not experts in the finishing process and could not match the high-quality finished cloth produced by their competitors in the Netherlands. [b] ■ By 1617, just three years after the company was established, James I had dissolved the King's Merchant Adventurers. [c] ■

5   The failure of the King's Merchant Adventurers did more than bankrupt those who had supported its efforts. [d] ■ The damage Cockayne's plan inflicted on the cloth trade had disastrous economic effects on other industries as well. Under the King's Merchant Adventurers, more than 500 families had begun producing finished cloth. However, because they could not sell it, their ventures failed. This caused unemployment to rise and even resulted in riots in London and elsewhere. Furthermore, formerly beneficial trade relationships had been destroyed, and sellers of unfinished cloth had to attempt to reestablish contacts with European buyers who were willing to purchase their goods. Though James I had returned power to the members of the Merchant Adventurers, the group resented the damage that had been done to its business. Business relations were strained both internationally and domestically as the English cloth trade made a slow recovery from Cockayne's experiment.

字彙 POWERED BY COBUILD
rift 裂痕、分歧：a quarrel or disagreement 爭吵或爭論

1. The word succeeded in paragraph 1 is closest in meaning to

   ○ did away with.
   ○ came after.
   ○ turned aside.
   ○ kept back.

2. In paragraph 1, the author describes insufficient food production as an indication of the

   ○ need for the expansion of the English cloth trade.
   ○ consequences of heavily emphasizing the cloth trade.
   ○ poor state of the English economy in 1603.
   ○ king's mismanagement of the country.

3. Based on the information in paragraphs 1 and 2, what can be inferred about the English cloth trade prior to the establishment of the King's Merchant Adventurers?

   ○ It was neglected in favor of the shipping and agriculture industries.
   ○ It was the only profitable sector of the English economy.
   ○ It was responsible for driving up prices for necessary items in England.
   ○ It consisted of multiple companies working with international partners.

4. According to paragraph 2, William Cockayne proposed all of the following changes to the English cloth trade EXCEPT:

   ○ The establishment of a company that would exclusively handle the cloth trade
   ○ A focus on increasing the value of cloth created in England
   ○ The interruption of cloth supply to merchants in the Netherlands
   ○ A shift in the primary activities of the English cloth industry

5. Which of the following best expresses the essential information in the highlighted sentence in paragraph 2? Incorrect answer options change the meaning in important ways or leave out essential information.

   ○ The procedures and technologies used to create finished cloth, which were often very complex, were primarily used by Dutch workers.
   ○ Unfinished cloth from England was typically finished by the Dutch, who were experts in the complicated procedures that resulted in more valuable cloth.

○ Finished cloth from England was often more valuable than Dutch cloth due to the complicated processes used to treat the cloth.

○ Unfinished cloth from England lost its value because the Dutch were able to create finished cloth by using expert techniques.

6. Based on the information in paragraph 2, why did the king agree to Cockayne's proposals?

○ He was desperate to improve the English economy quickly.

○ He believed that the changes would allow England to expand the cloth industry.

○ He worried about England's overreliance on trade partnerships with the Netherlands.

○ He wanted to encourage technological advancement in English industries.

7. The word inflated in paragraph 3 is closest in meaning to

○ unfair.

○ special.

○ secret.

○ increased.

8. According to paragraph 4, which of the following was a factor in the King's Merchant Adventurer's inability to create quality goods?

○ It did not have financial support from the king.

○ It couldn't afford to pay cloth-finishing experts.

○ Its employees didn't have the necessary knowledge about finishing cloth.

○ It had an inadequate supply of unfinished cloth.

9.Look at the four squares [■] in paragraphs 4 and 5 that indicate where the following sentence could be added to the passage.

He also reinstated the previous cloth export company, the Merchant Adventurers. Where would the sentence best fit?

○ a

○ b

○ c

○ d

10. Directions: An introductory sentence for a brief summary of the passage is provided below. Complete the summary by selecting the THREE answer options that express the most important ideas in the passage. Some sentences do not belong in the summary because they express ideas that are not presented in the passage or are minor ideas in the passage. This question is worth 2 points.

In spite of economic difficulties in the 1600s, England still had some good sources of income, including cloth production.

- _____
- _____
- _____

Choose 3 answers.

1. William Cockayne was an English politician and business person who knew about the cloth trade.
2. To increase profits, King James established a company to finish the cloth and control the trade.
3. English cloth makers were unable to match the quality of cloth products produced abroad causing the King's company to fail.
4. The merchants in the Netherlands never forgave the King and the cloth trade didn't recover.
5. After the failure of the company about 500 merchants went bankrupt.
6. At that time, the English exported cloth to other countries, where it was finished and sold on at a higher price.

Read the passage about a topic in natural history.

Did Birds Evolve from Dinosaurs?

1   In the mid-1800s, scientists discovered the complete skeleton of a dinosaur called Archaeopteryx lithographica. The creature, which might have grown to a maximum size of about one and a half feet, was thought to have lived approximately 150 million years ago and, curiously, had features that resembled not only dinosaurs, but modern birds as well. For instance, while it had sharp teeth and a bony tail like the dinosaurs of its time, it also had wings and feathers like modern birds. Despite these similarities to birds, the general **consensus** within the scientific community was that the closest living relatives of dinosaurs were reptiles, like lizards and alligators. It wasn't until 1969, when paleontologists discovered the fossils of a dinosaur called Deinonychus antirrhopus, that the debate about whether or not birds evolved from dinosaurs was reopened.

2   **The main problem with the theory linking dinosaurs to modern birds—which was also the main support for arguments that reptiles were, in fact, the closest living ancestors of dinosaurs—was the belief that dinosaurs did not have furculae, or wishbones.** The main function of this fork-shaped bone, which is located at the base of the neck on birds, is to reinforce the skeleton against the many stresses of flight. However, fossil evidence found in recent years has revealed that many dinosaurs did indeed have furculae. For example, the dinosaurs in the Dromaeosauridae family, a group of bird-like dinosaurs, are all believed to have had furculae. This discovery contradicts the theory that the bones are unique to birds.

3   [a] ■ In addition to the observation of furculae in dinosaur fossils, paleontologists have identified a number of other structural similarities between birds and dinosaurs. [b] ■ For example, comparisons between the skeletons of birds and those of dinosaurs like *Velociraptor mongoliensis* and *Deinonychus* reveal that birds and dinosaurs share many unique skeletal features. [c] ■ For instance, *Velociraptor* fossils show that the creature's front limbs, the construction of which would have presumably allowed for great flexibility, are similar to **those** of modern birds. [d] ■ On the other hand, no such likenesses exist between dinosaurs and early reptiles.

4   Such evidence of structural similarities is only one of many reasons that paleontologists now generally agree that birds evolved from dinosaurs. Another **compelling** piece of evidence is the presence of feathers in both organisms. Fossils of

143

Archaeopteryx, which many experts now consider to be both a dinosaur and a bird, feature imprints of feathers that closely resemble those found on modern birds. Since the discovery of *Archaeopteryx*, paleontologists have discovered fossils demonstrating that a number of other dinosaurs that were likely related to *Archaeopteryx* also had feathers. Furthermore, even the fossils of dinosaurs that were not related to Archaeopteryx, such as *Tyrannosaurus rex*, have been found to have long, feather-like structures that are commonly referred to as protofeathers. According to many paleontologists, the main function of protofeathers was to insulate dinosaurs from cold temperatures, not to assist with flight, which accounts for why many flightless dinosaurs may have had them. Because no other animals besides dinosaurs and birds have been found to have feathers, scientists believe that the existence of feathers is a strong indication that the two animals are directly related.

5　Paleontologists have also found evidence that the lungs of dinosaurs were shaped similarly to birds' lungs. Most animals, including primates, lizards, and frogs, have lungs with two compartments. However, birds have extra air sacs in front of and behind their lungs that allow them to keep their lungs inflated constantly. Studies of dinosaur skeletons indicate that some dinosaurs also had lungs with extra chambers. Like the similarities in skeletal structures and the existence of feathers in both groups, the fact that only birds and dinosaurs have these extra lung chambers reveals that birds probably evolved from dinosaurs and are thus their closest living relatives.

字彙 POWERED BY COBUILD
stresses 壓力：strong physical pressures 強烈的物理壓力
compartment 隔間：a separate part or space 一個獨立的部分或空間

11. In paragraph 1, the author mentions wings and feathers in order to

○ point out features shared by Archaeopteryx and modern birds.

○ explain the small size of Archaeopteryx fossils.

○ argue that Archaeopteryx was most likely a bird and not a dinosaur.

○ describe what Archaeopteryx probably looked like.

12. The word consensus in paragraph 1 is closest in meaning to

○ question.

○ debate.

○ evidence.

○ agreement.

13. Which of the following best expresses the essential information in the highlighted sentence in paragraph 2? Incorrect answer options change the meaning in important ways or leave out essential information.

○ The idea that dinosaurs did not have wishbones was the chief difficulty in proving that modern birds were related to dinosaurs.

○ Many people believed that reptiles were the closest living ancestors of dinosaurs because, like dinosaurs, they do not have furculae.

○ The main reason that scientists couldn't link modern birds and dinosaurs was because they could not find furculae in most modern bird species.

○ Dinosaurs' presumed lack of wishbones made people think that birds, not reptiles, were their closest living ancestors.

14. The discovery of dinosaur fossils with furculae was important because it

○ indicated that several bird species had already evolved during the time of dinosaurs.

○ proved that many reptilian animals, including dinosaurs, had furculae.

○ cast doubt on the theory that reptiles were the closest living relatives of dinosaurs.

○ helped scientists determine the purpose of furculae in non-bird species.

15. What can be inferred about dinosaurs in the Dromaeosauridae family?

○ They were closely related to Archaeopteryx.

○ They were able to fly.

○ They were the only dinosaurs that had furculae.

○ They were small compared to other dinosaurs.

16. The word those in paragraph 3 refers to

○ *Velociraptor* fossils.
○ front limbs.
○ likenesses.
○ early reptiles.

17. The word compelling in paragraph 4 is closest in meaning to

○ persuasive.
○ conflicting.
○ recent.
○ sufficient.

18. According to paragraph 5, what do primates and lizards have in common?

○ They have a more elaborate lung structure than dinosaurs did.
○ They are able to keep their lungs full of air constantly.
○ Their lungs have a similar structure.
○ They have other organs in addition to lungs to help them breathe.

19. Look at the four squares [■] in paragraph 3 that indicate where the following sentence could be added to the passage.

Scientists have also observed structural similarities in the skulls and necks of some dinosaurs and birds.

Where would the sentence best fit?

○ a
○ b
○ c
○ d

20. Directions: An introductory sentence for a brief summary of the passage is provided below. Complete the summary by selecting the THREE answer options that express the most important ideas in the passage. Some sentences do not belong in the summary because they express ideas that are not presented in the passage or are minor ideas in the passage. This question is worth 2 points.

Today, there is evidence showing that modern birds, not reptiles, are probably the closest living relatives of dinosaurs.

Today, there is evidence showing that modern birds, not reptiles, are probably the closest living relatives of dinosaurs.

- _____
- _____
- _____

Choose 3 answers.

1. The shape of the forelimb in many dinosaurs would have allowed for great flexibility and movement.
2. Many dinosaurs had feathers or protofeathers, making them the only other creatures besides birds known to have any type of feather.
3. Dinosaur skeletons have revealed that dinosaurs probably had multiple-chambered lungs, as do birds.
4. Dinosaurs and birds have several structural similarities, including the presence of furculae.
5. Like modern birds, not all feathered dinosaurs could fly.
6. Scientists have believed that modern reptiles evolved from dinosaurs since the discovery of Archaeopteryx lithographica fossils in the mid-1800s.

Read the passage about a topic in marketing.

Pricing Approaches in Marketing

1 An important part of marketing is determining what price to charge consumers for goods and services. Companies **aspire** to set prices that are high enough to allow them to make a profit but low enough to encourage people to purchase their products. To determine these prices, marketing specialists must consider a variety of factors and use a number of different pricing approaches.

2 Cost-based approaches determine the price of a product based on how much it costs to make. This is the simplest method because manufacturers can easily determine how much it will cost them to produce their goods. After they calculate the price of materials and labor, they add a set percentage to that cost, called a standard markup, which covers advertising, marketing, and other administrative costs, as well as profit. For instance, rather than determining the exact price of a new building before they start to build it, construction companies will often give estimates about prices based on the cost of materials, equipment, and labor, plus a markup of 20 percent. The final price is not calculated until after the building is completed, when the company adds the markup amount to its total building costs.

3 The main advantage to the cost-based approach to pricing is its simplicity. By using this method, businesses do not need to adjust their prices constantly based on changes in the market for their goods. However, the inability to account for important factors relating to the market is also the weakness of the cost-based approach. This is why many businesses also use more complex approaches to determine their prices.

4 In many industries, producers often pay less attention to their own costs and set prices based on those of their leading competitors instead. This is called competition-based pricing. Competition-based pricing often relies on the going rate, or the average price that consumers expect to pay for a good or service. If five companies are selling plastic tubing for two dollars per foot, a sixth company is unlikely to be successful selling that same kind of tubing for three dollars per foot. Thus, even if the sixth company's production costs are higher, they cannot afford to set their prices higher than their competitors' prices.

5 Competition-based pricing sometimes puts small businesses at a disadvantage. Because they can buy their materials or production machinery in bulk, very large

companies often have lower production costs than smaller companies do. In order to compete, smaller companies cannot depend on cost-based pricing. They often set their prices lower than those of their larger competitors, even though their production costs may be higher, in order to make their products attractive to consumers and build or maintain their customer base. These sellers will also combine cost-based and competition-based pricing in order to find the most competitive price that will yield the highest profit after costs are subtracted.

6   While cost-based and competition-based pricing are largely based on **objective** mathematical factors, like production costs and average prices, buyer-based approaches are based on individual perspective. [a] ■ Perceived value is how much consumers feel an item is worth, as opposed to its actual monetary value. [b] ■ For example, a product like a pet rock, which is simply an ordinary rock marketed as a pet, has very little actual monetary value. [c] ■ Marketers will not use production costs to set their price, because this would make the price too low. [d] ■ Instead, they must determine how much consumers feel their product is worth.

7   Because perceived value is subjective, it is difficult to calculate. **One common strategy for determining the perceived value of a product is to interview people in focus groups, small groups of people who share their feelings about a product with market experts.** The responses of focus groups often change according to the group being interviewed, so experts try to interview a large enough sample to get useful information. Along with focus groups and market experts, some businesses may even employ psychologists to help them understand the minds and emotions of consumers so that they can create products that people will see as valuable. The more perceived value an item has, the more a company can charge for that item, regardless of its production costs or the prices set by competitors.

字彙 POWERED BY COBUILD

in bulk 大量的：in large quantities 大量的
monetary 貨幣的、金錢的：relating to money 與金錢有關的

1. The word aspire in paragraph 1 is closest in meaning to

   ○ decide.
   ○ hurry.
   ○ aim.
   ○ attempt.

2. In paragraph 4, the author implies that a company with higher production costs couldn't afford to charge more than its competitors because the company would

   ○ lose money because customers would choose its competitors' products.
   ○ be expected to lower its production costs to match its competitors' costs.
   ○ have to buy equipment that would lower its production costs.
   ○ be forced to use the same pricing strategies as its top competitors.

3. According to paragraph 5, all of the following are ways that small businesses are disadvantaged by competition-based pricing approaches EXCEPT:

   ○ It provides benefits for companies that buy materials in bulk.
   ○ It favors companies with low production costs.
   ○ It promotes the use of a single pricing strategy.
   ○ It encourages sellers to set prices lower than their costs will allow.

4. According to paragraph 5, what can be inferred about large businesses?

   ○ They are more likely to use only one pricing approach.
   ○ Their prices are influenced by the pricing strategies of small businesses.
   ○ They spend less money on marketing than small businesses do.
   ○ They tend to have higher production costs when using competition-based pricing.

5. The word objective in paragraph 6 is closest in meaning to

   ○ accessible.
   ○ improper.
   ○ impartial.
   ○ precise.

6. According to paragraph 6, what do cost-based and competition-based approaches have in common?

○ They are based on the value of a product or service.

○ They depend on measurable information.

○ They rely equally on personalized information and averages.

○ They focus on the costs to the customer.

7. Why does the author mention a pet rock in paragraph 6?

○ To give an example of a product with a low perceived value

○ To illustrate why using perceived value is appropriate for certain products

○ To contrast the actual and perceived value of a specific item

○ To explain how buyer-based and competition-based pricing can be used together

8. Which of the following best expresses the essential information in the highlighted sentence in paragraph 7? Incorrect answer options change the meaning in important ways or leave out essential information.

○ In order to determine the perceived value of a product, some focus groups interview experts about their feelings on a product.

○ Interviewing people in focus groups is one way that market experts determine the perceived value of a product.

○ Focus groups allow market experts to interview people about how they form their ideas about the value of an item.

○ One strategy for interviewing small groups of people about perceived value involves asking them how they feel about a product.

9. Look at the four squares [■] in paragraph 6 that indicate where the following sentence could be added to the passage.

In buyer-based pricing, companies set prices based on the perceived value of a commodity.

Where would the sentence best fit?

○ a

○ b

○ c

○ d

10. Directions: An introductory sentence for a brief summary of the passage is provided below. Complete the summary by selecting the THREE answer options that express the most important ideas in the passage. Some sentences do not belong in the summary because they express ideas that are not presented in the passage or are minor ideas in the passage. This question is worth 2 points.

Companies need a way to price their products and use at least three methods to do this.

- _____
- _____
- _____

Choose 3 answers.

1. A mark up of 20% is usually applied in the building trade.
2. Cost-based pricing is a method in which a simple percentage is added to the overall cost.
3. Pricing based on a comparison of competitor's charges is often used, although it favors larger companies who have lower production costs.
4. Going-rate pricing is when prices are fixed according to the going-rate of material costs.
5. Psychologists are extremely good at understanding what customer's value.
6. A approach based on buyers' feelings is more subjective and relies on feedback from consumers to set the price.

Writing

Part 2 寫作

Unit 7　寫作測驗指南
Guide to Writing

7-1　寫作測驗概述

寫作部分測試你根據兩種不同類型的題型以書面英文回應的能力。第一個題型，你要閱讀一篇短文，並聽一篇同一個主題的課堂講座，接著寫一篇文章。回答必須整合兩個來源的資訊。第二個題型，會要求你針對課堂討論來敘述和支持某個觀點。

托福寫作測驗

內容	寫作測驗測試你理解書面英文和口說英文的能力，並且以書面英文作答。對於每道題目，你需要了解題目說明，並知道如何撰寫結構良好的回答，以及在回答中融入主旨和細節。
須具備的能力	為了在寫作測驗拿下高分，你必須能夠： • 了解題目說明。 • 在聆聽或閱讀題目時做筆記，整合這些資訊之後撰寫一個結構良好的回答。 • 概述及改述你聆聽和／或閱讀到的文章觀點。 • 表達你對某個主題的想法或他人的想法。 • 在時間內撰寫一個結構良好的回答。
寫作題目	寫作測驗包含兩大題，第一題是整合寫作題，第二題是學術討論寫作題。
計時	準備和回答每一道題的時間，根據題型而有所不同。

Integrated Task 整合題		Academic Discussion Task 學術討論題	
閱讀*	3 分鐘	閱讀	n/a
聆聽	3–5 分鐘	聆聽	n/a
寫作時間	20 分鐘	寫作時間	10 分鐘

你大約有 29 分鐘的時間來完成測驗。

*在整合題部分，你在寫作時能夠從螢幕上看到文章，但無法重新播放聽力部分。文章會在你聽完聽力後消失，但是當你開始寫作時它會再次出現，供你作答時參考。

寫作測驗有兩種類型的題目：整合題和學術討論題。這兩種題型的主要區別在於回答時所需的技巧。

Question 1: Integrated Task 整合題	Question 2: Academic Discussion Task 學術討論題
要求你結合閱讀、聽力和寫作技巧。	要求你針對課堂討論來敘述和支持某個論點。

你在寫作測驗的作答會被發送到 ETS 線上評分網路。托福網路測驗使用 AI 評分來輔助人工評分。你的回答會得到 1-5 的分數，將這些分數相加並轉換為 0-30 分的分數範圍。

在評分你的答案時，評分者要閱讀整個答案並根據你的整體技巧來為你評分。這表示只要你的整體回答滿足了下列所描述的一般評分標準，即使你犯了一些錯誤，仍然有可能獲得最高分。

評分類別	評分者在第 1 題答案中注意的 寫作要素	評分者在第 2 題的答案中注意的 寫作要素
主題發展	• 你整合文章和聽力中的資訊。 • 你藉著提供聽力中的具體細節來解釋教授的立場。 • 你寫了 125 到 225 個字。	• 清晰表達的論點，無論你同意或不同意題目，或者你同意到何種程度。 • 你補充了其他人的想法，而不只是重複他們的論點。要確定你的論述是有相關性的，並且包含足夠的細節。 • 你利用舉例和細節來支持你提出的論點。 • 你至少寫了 100 個字。
結構和 清晰度	• 你寫的是一篇五段式文章，包括引言、三個主體段落和結論。 • 每個主體段落都討論了文章中的重點和教授對該重點的立場。 • 你在文章中使用了轉折詞。	• 你了解題目的背景：如果是針對討論群組的發文，那麼它不用像學術文章那樣正式，但也不能像簡訊那麼不正式。 • 你使用轉折詞來提升答案的流暢性。
措辭運用	• 你使用正確的文法和標點符號。 • 你幾乎沒有拼字上的錯誤。 • 你使用各種句型並展現了豐富的字彙。	

🔧 挑戰 1

我沒有時間寫完一篇完整的文章。

解決方法 1　熟悉能完整回答問題的寫作模板，這樣你就知道你的文章必須包含哪些資訊才能獲得高分。你可以把大部分時間花在組織文章上，並思考適合的支持性細節。

第 1 題的模板	第 2 題的模板
第一段： 包含文章的主題、聽力部分的主題	第一句： 扼要的重述主題，並且敘述和支持你的論點。
第二段： 文章的重點 1； 聽力部分的重點 1； 來自聽力的支持細節	下一句： 在提出你的理由之前，先為議題提供一些背景。
第三段： 文章的重點 2； 聽力部分的重點 2； 來自聽力的支持細節	下一句： 提供你自己對討論的看法。不要重複文章的想法，並確定你的論點有助於討論。 你可以在文章中提出額外的論點，或對文章的論點進行補充，或提出相反的論點，或部分贊成或反對並說明原因。
第四段： 文章的重點 3； 聽力部分的重點 3； 來自聽力的支持細節	下一句： 包含適當的舉例、原因和細節，明確的支持你自己的論點。
第五段： 結論	最後一句： 總結你的立場

解決方法 2　注意你還剩多少時間。在考試當天，你會看到螢幕右上角有一個計時器顯示剩餘的時間。在寫作時，一定要注意計時器。可參考以下的時間運用指南：

第 1 題計時 總計：20 分鐘		第 2 題計時 總計：10 分鐘	
時間	你應該做什麼	時間	你應該做什麼
20:00- 18:00	檢視筆記並迅速寫下大綱。只要寫幾個單字來幫你回想你之後要寫的內容。	10:00- 9:00	仔細閱讀題目說明並對主題做腦力激盪，試著盡可能想出許多論點。根據你的論點決定如何作答。

18:00-4:00	寫作。確定你的作文有五段,而且內容要包含教授所講述的具體細節。	9:00-1:00	寫下答案。確定答案中含有與題目中的論點相關的舉例和說明。
4:00-0:00	檢查並編輯你的作文。一定要檢查有沒有拼錯的單字和不合文法的句子。	1:00-0:00	檢查並編輯你的答案。一定要檢查有沒有拼錯的單字和不合文法的句子。

解決方法③　在考試之前盡可能多練習打字。在考試當天,你必須在電腦上打字。如果你打字速度不夠快,便無法在規定的時間內完成作文。因此你應該在考試之前多練習打字,以提升你的打字速度。

挑戰 2

我擔心評分者不了解我作文裡的論點。

解決方法①　使用轉折詞(Transition Language)。轉折詞是連接兩個句子的表達方式,其作用在於表示焦點的轉移、保持相同的思維路線、導出結論、闡明論點、表示順序等等。如果你的整篇作文都有用到轉折詞,便能夠增加回答的流暢性,讓評分者更容易理解你的觀點。請參考下表的轉折詞及其用法:

功能	轉折詞	
Shift in focus 轉移焦點	but 但是 conversely 相反的 despite 儘管 however 然而 in contrast 與…對照 nevertheless 然而	nonetheless 雖然如此 on the contrary 相反的 on the other hand 另一方面 still 但是;仍然 though 雖然 yet 可是
Continuing in the same line of thinking 保持相同的思維路線	additionally 此外 also 也、還 and 和、而且 beside that 除了那個	furthermore 再者 in addition 此外 likewise 同樣的 moreover 此外
Drawing a conclusion 導出結論	accordingly 相應的、於是 as a result 結果 consequently 結果 for that reason 基於那個原因	hence 因此、由此 indeed 的確 therefore 因此 thus 於是

Clarifying a point 闡明論點	in other words 換句話說 specifically 特別的	that is to say 也就是說 namely 即、也就是說
Indicating Sequence 表示順序	after 在…之後 as soon as 一…就 before 在…之前 finally 最後 in the first place 首先	later 後來 meanwhile 與此同時 next 接著 soon 不久 then 然後
Giving Examples 舉例	For example… 舉例來說… Take X, for instance. 舉 X 為例 One example of X is … X 的一個例子是…	

解決方法② 加強你的拼字。在考試中，你無法依賴自動拼字檢查工具。雖然幾個拼錯的單字不會影響你的分數，但如果你拼錯了很多單字，或許會讓評分員無法理解你的意思。提高拼字能力的一種方法是多閱讀，因為你看過的單字愈多，你就愈明白常用單字的拼法。另一種方法是練習寫作。當你檢查你的作文時，圈出所有拼錯的單字，並學會正確的拼法。

解決方法③ 除非你確定知道那個片語的意思，否則不要使用它。當評分員評你的作文時，他們會看你如何運用片語。但是如果你使用了錯誤的片語，做了不正確的表達，那只會拉低你的分數。

⚒ 挑戰 3
我不知道該怎麼表達我的論點。

解決方法① 了解何時需要表達論點。寫作第 1 題要求你描述教授的觀點，而第 2 題要求你表達自己的主張。下表幫助你知道何時以及如何使用表達論點的措辭。

Question 1：Academic Reading / Listening Synthesis Task 學術閱讀／聽力整合題	敘述教授的觀點 教授會清楚表達對主題的贊成或反對，並提供三個理由來支持他的立場。 ▪ The professor feels that... 教授覺得…… ▪ In the lecture, the professor says that X is a good / bad idea. 在課堂中，教授說 X 是一個好／壞主意。 ▪ The professor says she supports / opposes... 教授說她支持／反對…

	• In the professor's opinion, X is good / bad... 在教授的觀點中，X 是好／壞的… • The professor's view is that X is positive / negative... 教授的觀點是，X 是正面的／負面的… • The professor agrees / disagrees with the claim that... 教授贊成／反對…的主張
Question 2： Academic Discussion Task 學術討論題	表達你自己對某立場的觀點，是贊成或反對。 • While some people think that X, I personally believe that... 雖然一些人認為 X，但我個人相信… • I know that some people feel differently, but it's my opinion that... 我知道有些人有不同的看法，但我的觀點是… • It's my opinion that... 我的見解是… • I agree / disagree with the idea that... 我贊成／反對…的想法 • Other people might disagree, but my view is that... 其他人可能不同意，但我的看法是…

解決方法 2　學習基本的引述技巧。在整合題中，你需要談論文章或聽力段落裡的態度。使用以下措辭來指出所引用的資訊是來自文章還是聽力段落。

指出引文來源的表達方式
The author / professor thinks / feels that... 作者／教授認為／覺得… The author / professor agrees / disagrees / opposes / supports... 作者／教授同意／不同意／反對／支持… According to the passage / professor,... 根據文章／教授的說法，… In the conversation, the professor says / argues / points out / makes the point that... 在對話中，教授說／主張／指出／強調… In the reading / lecture, the author / professor says... 在文章／課堂講座中，作者／教授說… The author / professor supports X by saying / pointing out / arguing / giving an example of... 作者／教授說／指出／主張／舉例…來支持 X

在整合題上，我應該重新表述來自文章和聽力的資訊，但這對我來說很困難。

解決方法 1　確定你完全了解要改寫的段落內容的意思。當你改寫時，你要用自己的話重新表述原本的資訊。如果你沒有完全了解它的意思，改寫的效果就不好。閱讀內容會出現在螢幕上，所以你可以參考文章並回頭檢視你想改寫的部分來確定你理解文章的意思。至於聽力，你應該回頭檢視你的筆記，確定你完全了解教授所提出的主要論點。

解決方法 2　學習托福測驗中常用詞的同義詞（synonyms）。請閱讀本書中整合寫作題的一篇文章來練習。選擇 10-15 個出現在文章中的關鍵詞，並在詞典中查詢這些詞的同義詞，並做成一份單字表。關於如何在改寫中使用同義詞，請參考以下範例。

原文	使用同義詞的改寫版本
A Lazarus taxon is a species that was once believed to have been extinct, but is later found to be alive. 拉撒路物種指的是據信已經滅絕，但後來發現仍然存活的物種。	Types of organisms that were thought to be extinct and are later found to still exist are called a Lazarus taxon. 被認為已經滅絕但後來發現仍然存在的生物類型，被稱為拉撒路物種。
One advantage of using surveys for data collection is that it allows researchers to ask consumers questions about their attitudes and shopping behavior. 使用調查來做資料收集的一個優勢是，它允許研究人員詢問消費者與他們的購物態度和行為有關的問題。	Conducting surveys in order to collect data is advantageous because it gives scientists the opportunity to question customers about their attitudes and shopping behavior. 進行調查以收集資料是具優勢的，因為它給予科學家詢問顧客關於他們的購物態度和行為的機會。

解決方法 3　不要把題目的文字和想法一模一樣的照抄。改寫是把題目中的想法用你自己的話重新表達。如果你只是從文章中複製文字和句子，你的作文會被打零分。為了避免照抄，請在改寫後檢查你的句子結構和詞彙是否不一樣？另外，如果你在筆記裡把教授的話原原本本寫下來，一定要使用引號，這樣你才會記得在你的答案中改寫句子，而不是把這些話當作是自己的。

提高改寫技巧的最佳方法是練習。從本書的閱讀部分找一篇文章，並選擇一段來改寫。完成後，將你改寫的內容與原文做比較。你是否用同義詞置換了關鍵詞？你是否改變了句子結構？每天練習改寫一段，直到你對自己的改寫技巧感到自信為止。

✎ 挑戰 5

在整合題中有太多的資訊需要記住。

在整合題中，你會閱讀一篇文章，並聽同一個主題的課堂講座。你不需要擔心沒有寫下文章的筆記，因為在寫作時，你會從螢幕上看到文章。不過，你需要在聽聽力時做筆記。請使用以下筆記技巧來幫助你記錄最重要的資訊：

I. 使用縮寫。你沒有足夠的時間把一切都寫出來，所以要在可能的情況下使用更簡短的形式。此外，使用對你有意義的縮寫，如果你寫下了東西但不記得意思是沒有幫助的。參考下表以了解縮寫的提示，練習用縮寫寫下你聽到的內容。

縮寫技巧	範例
用阿拉伯數字取代大寫數字	one、two、three… → 1, 2, 3, …
省略單字中的母音	conversation, forest, novel → cnverstn, frst, nvl
用符號取代單字	Jane and Jack → Jane + Jack Jane or Jack → Jane / Jack Everyone except Jack → everyone – Jack The numbers increased → the #s ↑ Eight hundred dollars → $800 Fifty percent → 50% at → @
使用常見的縮寫	without → w/o within → w/in approximately → approx. et cetera → etc. because → b/c before → b4 example → ex. regarding → re.

II. 了解你應該在課堂講座中記下的基本資訊：

你應該寫下的資訊
▪ Whether the professor agrees or disagrees with the main topic from the reading 教授贊成或反對文章的主題
▪ Three reasons that the professor gives for either agreeing or disagreeing 教授贊成或反對的三個理由
▪ Details such as studies or discoveries that support each of the professor's key points 教授每個重要論點都有相應的研究或發現來支持

III. 在寫筆記時要有組織，把你需要記下來的所有資訊寫上標題（Main Idea, Key Point 1, Support...）。

挑戰 6

我在整合題（Question 1：Academic Reading / Listening Synthesis Task）或學術討論題（Question 2：Academic Discussion Task）中選擇要寫什麼的時候猶豫不決。

解決方法 1　練習腦力激盪。腦力激盪時思考一下主題，和迅速提出主要的支持性細節。你也許會發現，花一兩分鐘寫下你能想到的所有正反兩方的論點，是一個很有用的技巧。不用擔心你寫下的論點好或不好──有時候，寫下一個較薄弱的論點會幫助你想到一個更好的論點。

解決方法 2　不要浪費時間考慮支持哪一個觀點。在寫答案時，你應該選擇最容易支持的立場。你可以看一下腦力激盪時所做的筆記來確定立場。哪一方有更多的論述？請記得，在托福測驗中，觀點沒有對錯之分。換句話說，不是根據你的意見本身來評分，真正重要的是你在答案中如何支持你的觀點。

解決方法 3　不要害怕在你的答案中編造個人例子。在學術討論題中，你需要用相關的個人例子來支持論點。然而，沒有人會檢查你的例子是否真實。如果你必須改變一個例子的細節，使它更能支持你的論點，那就做吧！這會使你的文章更強而有力。

解決方法 4　列出熟悉的主題，並練習對這些主題提出論述。給自己大約兩到三分鐘的時間來思考每個主題的看法。這樣，你就會習慣在考試的有限時間內想出支持性的論點。你可以使用下表的主題，或嘗試想出自己的主題：

- Some people think it is important to get a degree from a top school in order to get a good job. Others feel that real-world experience is more helpful for getting a good job. Which do you think is more important and why?

  有些人認為從一所頂尖學校取得學位對於獲得好工作很重要，也有人認為實際工作經驗對於獲得好工作更有幫助。你認為哪個比較重要，為什麼？

- Do you agree or disagree with the following statement?

  你是否同意以下說法？

  Teachers are the most influential people in a child's life.

  老師是孩子生活中最有影響力的人。

- Some people think that having a good diet is the most important factor for physical health. Others think that exercise plays a larger role in health. Which do you think is true and why?

  有些人認為保持良好的飲食習慣是身體健康最重要的因素，也有人認為運動在健康方面起了更大的作用。你認為哪個是對的，為什麼？

- Do you agree or disagree with the following statement?

  你是否同意以下說法？

  It is best to travel before starting a career.

  最好在職業生涯開始之前旅行。

7-4　寫作測驗題型概述

題型	技巧	內容
1. Integrated Task: Academic Reading / Lecture Synthesis Essay 整合題： 學術閱讀／講座整合寫作	閱讀 聽力 寫作	▪ 首先閱讀一篇學術主題的文章。 ▪ 接著聽一位教授對於同一個主題的講述。 ▪ 題目會要求你整合文章和講述中的資訊。 答題時間：20 分鐘
2. Academic Discussion Task 學術討論題	寫作	▪ 托福網路測驗的第 2 道題，會要求你針對課堂討論來敘述和支持某個觀點 答題時間：10 分鐘

整合題
Academic Reading / Lecture Synthesis Essay

在寫作第 1 題中，你會先閱讀一篇學術主題的文章，並聆聽關於同一個主題的聽力段落。接下來你會看到一則題目提示，要求你整合文章和聽力段落中的資訊。

整合題的題目提示，可能用以下方式表達：

- Summarize the points made in the lecture you just heard, explaining how they challenge the points made in the reading.
  概述你剛剛聽到的重點，說明它們如何質疑文章中提出的觀點。

- Summarize the points made in the lecture, being sure to explain how they support the points made in the reading.
  概述課堂中提出的重點，務必說明它們如何支持文章中提出的觀點。

- Summarize the points made in the lecture you just heard, explaining how they cast doubt on the points made in the reading passage.
  概述你剛剛所聽到的課堂中的重點，說明它們如何對文章中的觀點提出質疑。

首先，你的電腦螢幕上會出現一篇簡短的學術文章，字數通常在 250 到 300 之間，會在螢幕上顯示 3 分鐘左右。文章在 3 分鐘之後消失，但在聽力段落結束後會重新出現，你可以在作答時看到它。寫作第 1 題的文章可能與下列其中一項學術主題有關：

- anthropology 人類學
- art history 藝術史
- astronomy 天文學
- biology 生物學
- botany 植物學
- environmental science 環境科學
- literature 文學
- psychology 心理學
- sociology 社會學

文章通常的組織方式如下：
- Introduction of the topic 主題介紹
- Point 1 論點 1
- Supporting details 支持性細節
- Point 2 論點 2
- Supporting details 支持性細節
- Point 3 論點 3
- Supporting details 支持性細節

聽力內容是一位大學教授的課堂講座。你會在作答前聽到這段聽力內容，你只會聽一次，所以要做好筆記！在課堂中，教授會對文章中的觀點提出質疑或支持。「提出質疑」表示教授不贊成文章的主要論點，而且會提供三個理由來說明該論點為何錯誤。在大多數情況下，教授會對文章中的觀點提出質疑，而非支持。聽力內容通常的組織方式如下：

- Statement of agreement or disagreement 說明贊成或反對
- Point 1 重點 1
- Supporting details 支持性細節
- Point 2 重點 2
- Supporting details 支持性細節
- Point 3 重點 3
- Supporting details 支持性細節

接著，題目會要求你概述並整合文章和聽力中的資訊。在作答時，只需要使用文章和聽力所提供的資訊。你不需要具備任何學術科目的專門知識才能作答。

整合題快速指南

內容	學術閱讀／講座整合題需要你用打字作答，描述課堂講座如何支持或質疑呈現在文章中的資訊。
題目	- 在讀完文章並聽完聽力之後，你會聽到旁白提問。 - 題目會問你，課堂中的觀點如何支持或質疑文章中提出的觀點。 - 題目和文章會一直顯示在螢幕上，直到你完成作答為止。聽力只會播放一遍。 - 你有 20 分鐘的時間來規劃和打字作答。螢幕上的計時器會顯示你還剩多少時間。 - 寫作沒有最低字數要求。但是為了獲得高分，你應該在此道題中寫 150 至 225 個字。
須具備的能力	為了在整合題獲得高分，你必須能夠： - 判斷文章和聽力中的主要觀點。 - 判斷教授是支持還是質疑文章中提出的觀點。 - 分析寫作題目提示，並弄清楚你的答案需要包含哪些資訊。 - 為你的答案擬一份大綱。 - 結合兩個來源的資訊，並且正確的引用資訊來源。 - 把你的答案組織好，讓它清晰易懂。

高分作答	一份高分作答的字數應在 150 至 225 字之間。答案應明確指出聽力中的重要觀點或想法，並準確描述聽力如何質疑或支持文章中的資訊。答案應組織良好、使用主題句（topic sentence）、提供具體細節、敘明資訊來源，並且易於理解。
注意事項	1. 做好筆記，確定你明白教授的意思。組織你的筆記，使你能清楚看到文章中的每個重點以及和聽力相應的觀點。 2. 在以打字作答時，先簡明扼要的概述文章和聽力的主旨。一定要描述教授是否支持或質疑文章中的觀點。 3. 你的作文應該有三個主體段落。每個主體段落應該分別討論文章中的一個重點，以及教授在課堂中支持或反對的觀點。別忘了在描述每個重點時，都要提到來自課堂的支持性細節！ 4. 寫一個結論句，重新敘述文章的主要觀點和講述的主要觀點。總計來說，你應該有五個段落：一個引言，三個主體段落和一個結論。 5. 利用既定的時間規劃、寫作和校對你的作文。

TEST TIP!

在寫作部分，你需要以打字作答。請務必在考試前盡可能多練習打字，以提高你的打字速度和準確性。

以下是整合題的範例。閱讀文章，並聽課堂講座內容。在你讀和聽的過程中，在文章和聽力講稿中用底線標出你認為可以用於作答的重要資訊。

TOEFL Writing

Question

Reading

Television has influenced society in many ways since its invention in the early 1900s. However nowadays, with the explosion of streaming services and with on-demand video content available on a range of devices, there are concerns about the effects of children watching so much on-screen content and the impact it may have on their development.

Past studies have shown that educational programs have a positive effect on children's development. There are several arguments to support this view. First, watching a few hours of educational content a week has been proven to boost children's test scores. Researchers found that in a group of 200 preschool- age children, those who watched educational videos had higher reading, vocabulary, and math scores than those who did not. Another study showed that educational videos assist in language acquisition by helping infants and toddlers develop speech more quickly.

Furthermore, watching educational shows together can be an important bonding activity for families. Studies have demonstrated the importance of family bonding time in creating emotionally healthy and well-adjusted children. Family bonding is linked to higher rates of academic success. In addition, research shows that it also promotes increased physical health, as well as a healthy ability to relate to others.

Finally, there is a wide variety of excellent educational television programs and on-demand videos available and the quality of these is closely regulated. Governments in several countries have guidelines and regulations to ensure that children's programs meet certain standards and set standards for video producers to adhere to. This guarantees that children are exposed to only the highest quality of educational content.

中譯

自 20 世紀初發明電視以來，社會在許多方面都受到了影響。然而，今日隨著串流媒體服務的劇增以及各種設備上提供的隨選影片內容，人們對兒童觀看過多的螢幕節目內容，及其對兒童發展的影響感到擔憂。

過去的研究指出，教育節目對兒童的發展有正面影響。有幾個論點支持這一看法。首先，每週觀看幾個小時的教育節目已被證明能提高兒童的考試成績。研究人員發現，在一組 200 人的學齡前兒童中，觀看教育影片的孩子的閱讀、字彙和數學成績，比那些沒有觀看的孩子更高。另一項研究顯示，教育影片有助於語言習得，幫助嬰、幼兒更快的發展語言。

此外，一起觀看教育節目可以是家庭的重要聯繫活動。研究已經證明，家庭聯繫時間對於培養健全情緒和良好適應力的兒童非常重要。家庭凝聚力與較高的學業成就率有關。此外，研究指出它還能促進身體健康，以及與他人建立健康關係的能力。

最後，有各種優質的教育電視節目和隨選影片可供選擇，而且這些節目的品質受到嚴密的監督。許多國家的政府都定立了指導方針和法規，以確保兒童節目符合一定的規範，也定立了製片者必須遵循的規範。這樣才能確保兒童只接觸到最高品質的教育內容。

字彙 POWERED BY COBUILD

boost 增強：to cause something to increase, improve, or be more successful 使某事增加、改善或更成功
adhere to 遵循：to follow or observe regulations 遵守或遵循規定

Lecture

🎧 002

（講稿範例，僅供參考。）

Professor: It seems that video content is everywhere these days: we can access it 24 hours a day, seven days a week on our TVs, laptops, smart phones and other devices. But although streaming and video on demand (or VOD) are part of our daily lives, there are a lot of contradicting views about the impact on families and especially on young children. Overall, though, evidence indicates that watching educational programs is not particularly beneficial for young toddlers and preschoolers.

Although some studies do indicate that watching educational content boosts test scores, there are plenty of studies that directly contradict this notion. In fact, one research team found that watching video of any kind was harmful to brain development in young children. Specifically, children under three years old who were exposed to a well-known educational program showed delayed speech development in comparison to those who watched no video at all.

Second, it's true that family bonding time is an important part of emotional development for children. Unfortunately though, with the number of different ways to access video content and the different devices that may be used, it is often not possible for parents to be with their children when they are watching something on a screen. In addition, watching video together is simply not an effective form of bonding. Even if family members might be physically present while their children are watching something, there is no direct interaction between the individuals. Research shows that for bonding to take place, more contact and communication needs to occur between parents and children. Some good examples of this type of bonding are playing a game or eating a meal together.

Finally, although government regulations aim for good standards of video content and age appropriateness, they often fail to do so. First of all, the regulations only apply to companies that produce professional video content, not to people who make their own content and post it on video-sharing platforms. Although sharing platforms are regulated on what they host, in reality not every video is fact-checked or checked for age appropriateness. This means that a lot of what kids are watching is not very helpful in an educational sense and in some cases can be actually harmful. Although the regulations are in place, they just don't work very well.

中譯

教授：今天，影片似乎無處不在：我們每天二十四小時、每週七天，都可以在電視、筆電、智慧型手機和其他裝置上觀看。儘管串流媒體和隨選影片已經成為我們日常生活的一部分，但是關於對家庭，尤其是對幼兒的影響，有很多相互衝突的觀點。整體而言，證據指出觀看教育節目對於幼兒和學齡前兒童並不特別有益處。

儘管有些研究確實指出，觀看教育節目可以提高考試成績，但也有許多研究直接否定了這個觀點。事實上，有一個研究團隊發現對於幼兒的大腦發育來說，觀看任何類型的影片都是有害的。具體的案例是，接觸一個知名教育節目的三歲以下小孩，其言語發展比那些根本不看影片的兒童要遲緩。

其次，家庭聯繫時間對於兒童的情緒發展是很重要的一部分。遺憾的是，隨著觀看影片的方式和使用的設備種類的增加，父母通常無法在孩子觀看節目時陪在身旁。此外，一起收看節目並不是一種有效的聯繫方式。即使在孩子收看節目時家庭成員可能處在同一個空間，但彼此之間沒有直接的互動。研究指出，父母和孩子之間需要更多的接觸和溝通才能產生聯繫。這種聯繫的一些好的例子包括一起玩遊戲或共進晚餐。

最後，儘管政府的法規是為了讓節目內容有良好的規範和適齡性，但往往未能達到目的。首先，這些法規僅適用於生產專業影片的公司，而不適用於自製內容並將其發佈在影片分享平台上的人。儘管分享平台上的影片受到監督，但實際上並非每個影片都經過事實查核或適齡性檢查。這表示許多孩子觀看的內容在教育意義上並不是很有幫助，有些情況下甚至可能有害。儘管有法規的存在，但它們並不是非常有效。

現在請檢視考生寫下的筆記。注意考生如何將筆記分成兩欄，讓他可以容易看出聽力中的觀點如何質疑文章中的觀點。再次閱讀文章和聽力內容，圈出考生列在大綱裡的資訊。比較你畫底線的部分和你圈出的資訊。你是否注意到所有的重點？

Reading: Edu programs are good for kids	Lecture: streaming and VOD isn't good for kids
1. Boost test scores 　- Study w/200 preschoolers: watching edu videos = better reading, vocab, math scores 　- helps kids learn language faster	1. video content may NOT help test scores 　- Studies show not good for brain dev 　- slower speech dev
2. Bonding for families 　- important for emotional health 　- Fam time = academic success, phys health	2. doesn't help families bond 　- parents can't always watch with children 　- no interaction; need contact and communication
3. Govt regulations and standards = quality	3. Regs only apply to companies, not individuals 　- sites don't always check facts 　- regs aren't working well

中譯

閱讀：教育節目對兒童有益
1. 提升考試成績
　—200 名學齡前兒童的研究：觀看教育影片＝讀、字彙、數學成績更好
　—幫助兒童更快學習語言
2. 家庭聯繫
　—對情緒健全很重要
　—家庭時間＝學業成功、身體健康
3. 政府法規和規範＝品質

課堂：串流媒體和隨選影片對兒童不利
1. 節目對考試成績可能沒幫助
　—研究指出對大腦發育不好
　—語言發展較慢
2. 對家庭聯繫沒幫助
　—父母無法一直陪孩子觀看
　—無互動；需要接觸和溝通
3. 法規僅適用於公司，不適用於個人
　—網站不一定做事實查核
　—法規執行效果不佳

以下是一個整合題的範例題目指令和作答。閱讀時，請注意考生如何利用他在 B 部分的筆記來寫作文。

TOEFL Writing
Question

Directions: You have 20 minutes to prepare, write, and revise your response. Your essay will be graded based on your ability to communicate clearly through writing and on how well your essay demonstrates the relationship between the points in the lecture and those in the reading. An effective response usually contains 150–225 words.

Question: Summarize the points made in the lecture, being sure to explain how they cast doubt on the points made in the reading passage.

中譯

說明：你有 20 分鐘的時間來準備、寫作和修正答案。作文的評分依據的是你寫作清晰表達的能力，以及你的作文如何呈現課堂講座與文章中的觀點之間的關係。優良的作答通常包含 150 至 225 個字。

題目：概述課堂講座中提到的重點，務必說明它們如何質疑文章中所提出的觀點。

SAMPLE ESSAY

The reading passage argues that educational programs have a positive effect on young children. However, the professor disagrees and gives evidence that educational programs are not good for preschool-age children to watch.

The reading passage states that watching educational programs encourages academic success. It refers to studies and statistics showing that watching educational videos can boost test scores and increase language skills. However, the professor points out that there are also a lot of studies that show the opposite result. The professor gives an example of one study where watching a popular educational program was actually harmful to speech development in young children.

Second, the passage says that the quality of educational video content is closely regulated by the government. This means that the educational programs that children watch are guaranteed to be excellent. However, the professor argues that most video content falls below the government standards because they are not produced professionally and the host websites often do not check video content for facts or appropriateness. This means that most videos children watch do not meet the regulations.

Finally, the passage states that watching together can be a good opportunity for bonding between family members. It allows parents and children to spend quality time together. On the other hand, the professor states that there is often no chance for family members to bond while watching because the devices used may make it hard to watch on the same screen, and that there can be little interaction between the people involved. The professor adds that playing a game and eating a meal together are much better ways to achieve family bonding.

To summarize, in the reading the author argues that educational videos are good for young children. However, the professor disagrees with this idea and gives three pieces of evidence to show that watching video content is actually bad for children.

寫作範本

該文章主張教育節目對幼兒有正面影響。然而教授不同意這個觀點,並提出證據,指出教育節目並不適合給學齡前兒童觀看。

該文章表示,觀看教育節目有助於學業成就。它引用了研究和統計數據,證明觀看教育影片可以提高考試成績和增強語言能力。不過教授指出,也有許多研究顯示相反的結果。教授舉了一項研究為例,指出觀看某一個受歡迎的教育節目對幼兒的語言發展實際上是有害的。

其次,文章提到教育影片的品質受到政府的嚴格監督,這表示孩子觀看的教育節目保證是優良的。然而教授認為,由於大多數影片不是由專業人員製作,而且網站平台通常不檢查影片內容是否為事實或是其適當性,因此大多數孩子觀看的影片都不符合法規標準。

最後,文章指出,一起觀看影片是家庭成員之間聯繫情感的好機會,讓父母和孩子共度美好時光。不過教授表示,家庭成員在觀看時通常沒有聯繫情感的機會,因為設備的關係,要在同一個螢幕上觀看可能有困難,而且在場的人和人之間的互動很少。教授補充說,一起玩遊戲和共進晚餐是達到家庭維繫更好的方式。

總而言之,在文章中作者主張教育影片對幼兒有益。但是教授不同意這個觀點,並且提供了三項證據,證明觀看影片實際上對兒童是不好的。

8-1-1 掌握要領：整合題回答技巧

技巧 1

掃視文章以找出最重要的觀點。在第一次閱讀文章時，立即尋找並記下作者的主張以及用來支持這項主張的三個重點。記住，當你寫作的時候，你可以看到文章，所以不必擔心沒有記下每一個細節。不過理解文章中的主要觀點（major point），能幫助你預測聽力中會包含哪些資訊。

練習1　在第 169 頁的文章裡，用方框標記出作者的主張和三個重點。

技巧 2

在聽聽力時做筆記！你只能聽一遍聽力，如果事先知道要記下什麼資訊，你的筆記就會包含所有能幫助你寫出好作文的重要資訊。在聽聽力的時候，寫下教授對文章的主張的立場。教授支持還是質疑這個主張？你也應該記下教授用來支持他的立場的三個重點。

練習2　在第 170-171 頁的課堂講座中，用方框標記出教授的立場和三個重點。

技巧 3

仔細閱讀題目提示。在大多數情況下，提示會問你教授是如何支持或質疑文章中提出的觀點。

練習3　在第 173 頁的題目提示中，用底線標記一個詞組，該詞組告訴你教授是支持還是質疑文章提出的主張。

技巧 4

寫一段清晰的引言和結論。作文的引言應該描述文章中的主張以及教授是支持還是質疑該主張。你可以改寫自己的引言，把它變成作文結尾的結論句。利用下面的詞組來描述文章和聽力的關係。

聽力支持文章	聽力質疑文章
The reading passage says that [main topic from reading]. The professor supports this by providing examples of... 文章指出［閱讀主題］。教授提供…的例子來支持這個觀點。	The reading passage argues that [main topic from reading]. However, the professor disagrees and gives evidence that [main topic from lecture]. 文章主張［閱讀主題］。然而教授並不贊成，並且提供證據指出［課堂主題］。

In the reading passage, the author claims that [main topic from reading]. In the lecture, the professor discusses several studies that show that [main topic from reading] is true.

在文章中，作者聲稱［閱讀主題］。在課堂中，教授討論了幾項研究，都顯示［閱讀主題］是正確的。

The reading states that [main topic from reading]. In the lecture, the professor argues the opposite. He gives evidence to support [main topic from lecture].

文章指出［閱讀主題］。在課堂中，教授提出相反的觀點。他提出證據支持［課堂主題］。

The author of the passage says that [main topic from reading]. The professor agrees with [main topic from reading] and supports it by mentioning a number of specific studies.

文章作者表示［閱讀主題］。教授同意［閱讀主題］，並提到一些具體研究來支持它。

The reading claims that [main topic from reading]. The professor disagrees and says that [main topic from lecture].

文章聲稱［閱讀主題］。教授並不贊成，他說［課堂主題］。

練習④　在第 173-174 頁的寫作範本中，用底線標記出四個描述文章和聽力之間關係的句子。找出上表中提到的句子。

✏ 技巧 5

提及文章中的三個重點。文章一定會包含三個重點。寫作文的組織方式是先寫一段引言再加三個段落，每個段落都分別討論一個重點。除了描述文章中的重點以外，你還必須寫下教授如何支持還是質疑每一點。

練習⑤　在第 173-174 頁的寫作範本中，用雙底線標記出文章中的三個重點。注意答題者用來敘述文章和聽力中的重點的措辭。

🅰 閱讀文章，並且用底線標示出你認為可以用於作答的重點。聆聽同一個主題的音檔，並做筆記寫下重點。🎧 003

Scientists have been testing vegetable oil as a source of fuel for cars since the early 1900s. However, some key factors indicate that vegetable oil is not an ideal source of fuel.

First, using vegetable oil as fuel requires the installation of special equipment in a vehicle, which can be quite costly. Estimates of the total cost vary but could be around $2000 for basic equipment, including a fuel tank, filters, fuel lines, and sensors. Also, when vegetable oil is used as fuel, impurities within the oil can cause the equipment to become clogged over time. These pieces of equipment must be fixed or replaced, which makes regular maintenance more expensive.

Next, using vegetable oil as fuel for cars can be a complicated process. In order for the vehicle to function properly, the special equipment must be turned on when first starting the vehicle and turned off several minutes before stopping. The amount of detail required to use the equipment requires a high level of attention.

Another issue is that using vegetable oil as fuel has the potential to reduce the availability of food crops. Most vegetable oil used for fuel comes from crops that are also used for food, such as corn and sunflowers. In regular production, it takes more than 400 sunflower plants to make just one gallon of sunflower oil. If this vegetable oil were to be used primarily for fuel, then the price of some foods that use the oil, such as French fries or salad dressings, could increase dramatically.

科學家自 20 世紀初以來，就一直在試驗將植物油作為汽車燃料的來源。然而有些關鍵因素指出，植物油並不是理想的燃料來源。

首先，以植物油作為燃料需要在車輛中安裝特殊設備，這可能相當昂貴。對總成本的估計各不相同，但基本設備可能需要 2000 美元左右，包括油箱、過濾器、燃料油管和感應器。此外，以植物油作為燃料時，油中的雜質會隨著時間累積而堵塞設備。這些設備必須修理或更換，使得定期維修變得更昂貴。

其次，以植物油作為汽車燃料可能是一個複雜的過程。為了使車輛正常運作，必須在啟動車輛時也啟動特殊設備，並在停車前幾分鐘將其關閉。在使用設備上所需在意的細節，需要高度的注意力。

另一個問題是，以植物油作為燃料有可能會減少糧食作物的供應。大多數用於燃料的植物油，其來源作物同時也用於食品，例如玉米和向日葵。在常規製造上，需要 400 株以上的向日葵植株才能產出一加侖的向日葵油。如果這種植物油主要用於燃料，那麼有些使用該油的食品，像是薯條或沙拉醬，它們的價格可能會大幅上升。

B 考生為什麼寫下以的資訊？回答有關這個筆記的問題。比較筆記與你在文章中畫底線和聽力筆記的內容。你有注意到相同的重要資訊嗎？

Reading: Veg oil not good source of fuel (A)	Lecture: Veg oil is good (C)
1. Expensive - Need to install special equip; costs approx $2000 - Veg oil clogs; more $ to fix / replace equip	1. Equip pays for itself - Avg miles / tank is 800–1,000 using veg fuel (500 mi for 1 tank of gas) - Price of equip will as tech becomes more common
2. Complicated (B) - Driver needs to turn on / off equipment at certain times; needs lots of attn	2. Not hard to use - Becomes automatic - Automatic converters in dev
3. Reduce avail of food crops - Veg oil comes from corn, sunflowers (food) - 400 sf plants for 1 gallon of oil - Food prices (ex. French fries, salad dressing)	3. Veg fuel is waste product (D) - From factories and rests: used, no intrrptn to food supply

中譯

閱讀：植物油不是優質的燃料來源 (A)

1. 昂貴
—需要安裝特殊設備；成本約 2000 美元
—植物油會堵塞；要花更多錢修復／更換設備

2. 複雜 (B)
—駕駛需要在特定時間打開／關閉設備；需要高度注意

3. 減少糧食作物供應
—植物油來自玉米、向日葵（糧食）
—400 株向日葵才能產出 1 加侖的油
—食品價格上升（例如薯條、沙拉醬）

課堂：植物油是優質的 (C)

1. 很快回本
—植物油平均每箱行駛 800-1,000 英里（汽油一箱行駛 500 英里）
—隨著技術普及，價格降低

2. 使用上不困難
—變得自動化
—自動轉換器開發中

3. 植物油是廢棄物產品 (D)
—來自工廠和餐廳：不會造成食物供應中斷

1. What does item A in the notes tell us?

○ The main topic presented in the reading
○ The first point in the reading

中譯

1. 筆記中的 (A) 告訴我們什麼？

✅ 文章的主題
○ 文章的第一點

2. What is item B?

○ The first point from the lecture
○ The second point from the reading

中譯

2. (B) 是什麼？

○ 課堂的第一點
✅ 文章的第二點

3. What does item C in the notes tell us?

○ The professor's main topic
○ The professor's first point

3. 筆記中的 (C) 告訴我們什麼？

✅ 教授的主題

○ 教授的第一點

4. What is item D?

○ The third point from the lecture

○ The third point from the reading

4. (D) 是什麼？

✅ 課堂的第三點

○ 文章的第三點

閱讀題目指令。它問的是教授是否支持或質疑文章中提出的觀點嗎？閱讀一篇寫作範本，注意答題者用來引入文章和聽力主題、討論重點，以及討論支持性細節的單字和措辭。判斷寫作範本中每句的目的，將以下方框中的編號填在正確的句子前面。

TOEFL Writing
Question

Directions: You have 20 minutes to prepare, write, and revise your response. Your essay will be graded based on your ability to communicate clearly through writing and on how well your essay demonstrates the relationship between the points in the lecture and those in the reading. An effective response usually contains 150–225 words.

Question: Summarize the points made in the lecture, being sure to explain how they cast doubt on the points made in the reading passage.

段落目的

1. Main Topic from Reading
2. Key Point from Lecture
3. Key Point from Reading
4. Professor's Main Topic
5. Support from Lecture
6. Conclusion

寫作範本

[1]　The reading states that vegetable oil is not a good source of fuel for cars. It gives several reasons for this argument.

[　]　However, in the lecture, the professor argues the opposite. She gives evidence to support the idea that vegetable oil is an excellent source of fuel for vehicles.

[　]　The passage points out that it's expensive to install conversion equipment. There are many different pieces that cost money. Maintenance is also expensive.

[　]　However, the professor argues that while it is expensive, the equipment pays for itself quickly by saving money.

[　]　Using vegetable oil as fuel is a lot cheaper than gas. This way, drivers save money in the long term.

[　]　Second, the passage suggests that using the special equipment needed for vegetable oil fuel could be very complicated. It requires a lot of attention.

[　]　The professor disagrees.

[　]　She points out that it's not very hard and that people get used to these motions. Also, she explains that there are new systems that are automatic and don't need a person to turn them on or off.

[　]　Finally, the passage argues that using vegetable oil could affect crops normally used for food, like sunflowers. This could cause the price of certain foods to go up.

[   ]   In contrast, the professor says that the oil used for fuel is a waste product from places like food factories.

[   ]   It's already been used once, so using it for fuel does not affect food production.

[   ]   In conclusion, both the reading and the lecture discuss using vegetable oil as a source of fuel for cars. While the author claims that vegetable oil is not a good source of fuel, the professor disagrees and offers several pieces of evidence to show that vegetable oil is, in fact, a good source of fuel for vehicles.

D 現在，用你自己的詞語填寫以下模版，創作一篇作文。

你的回答

[**Introduction**: Main Topic from Reading, Main Topic from Lecture]
In the reading, the author says that _____.
The professor disagrees and shows that vegetable oil is a good source of fuel by _____
_____.

[**Paragraph 2**: Key Point 1 from Reading, Key Point 1 from Lecture, Support from Lecture]
First, the reading says that using vegetable oil as fuel is _____
_____.

The professor rejects this point and says that _____
_____
_____.

[**Paragraph 3**: Key Point 2 from Reading, Key Point 2 from Lecture, Support from Lecture]
Next, the reading claims that _____
_____.

Again, the professor disagrees. According to the professor, _____
_____
_____.

[Paragraph 4: Key Point 3 from Reading, Key Point 3 from Lecture, Support from Lecture]
The final point in the reading is that _____
_____.

The professor disproves this point as well. She argues that _____

_____

_____ .

[**Conclusion**: Restatement of Introduction]

To summarize, _____

_____

_____ .

現在檢視你剛完成的作文，並閱讀以下敘述。你的回答是否符合整合題的評分要求？繼續練習，直到你能夠完成所有要求。

Checklist		
1. 我的作文準確連結了文章和聽力的資訊。	Yes	No
2. 我的作文有五個段落，包括引言、討論三個重點的三個主體段落，以及結論。		
3. 我提到了文章的三個重點，並描述了教授對每個重點的看法。		
4. 我使用了來自聽力和文章中的具體細節和例子。		
5. 我使用了正確的文法、字彙和標點符號，並且沒有拼錯單字。		
6. 我用標示語和轉折詞指出我的觀點之間的關係。		

Ⓐ 閱讀文章，並且聆聽同一個主題的聽力。 🎧 004

The runic alphabet is a set of letters made up of forms called runes. This writing system was used by various Germanic groups in central and northern Europe as early as AD 150 until about AD 1100. The origins of this alphabet have remained unclear, but archaeological evidence shows that runes most likely developed independently of any other alphabet.

First, Germanic groups had little interaction with people from other parts of Europe until around AD 700, when the Romans conquered many parts of central Europe. Because people in central and northern Europe were culturally isolated from other groups, it is unlikely that the runic alphabet was based on a previous writing system.

Furthermore, runes are thought to have been used by an elite group of high-ranking people for purposes such as burials or for commemoration. We know that runes are most often found at burial sites on grave markers in memory of a wealthy person, great leader, or aristocrat. They are usually carved in stone or wood or bone or on runestones – big rocks covered with runic writing. This indicates that very few people knew how to read or write in runes and that runes could have developed within this very small group for very specific reasons.

Finally, many archaeologists note that the runic alphabet lacks similarities to any other alphabet that existed before or at the same time as the runic system. Any similarities between the runic alphabet and other alphabets are most likely random or coincidental. This makes it difficult to verify that the runic alphabet is a variant of an earlier alphabet.

盧恩字母是由一組被稱為盧恩的符號所組成的字母系統。這個書寫系統早在公元 150 年左右就被中北歐的各個日耳曼族群使用，直到大約公元 1100 年為止。這個字母系統的起源尚不清楚，但考古證據指出，盧恩字母很可能是獨立於任何其他字母系統而發展出來的。

首先，日耳曼族群在大約公元 700 年之前很少與歐洲其他地區的人民互動，當時羅馬人征服了中歐許多地區。由於中北歐人民在文化上孤立於其他族群之外，因此盧恩字母不太可能是根據先前的書寫系統發展出來的。

再者，一般認為盧恩字母由高階的菁英人士用於葬禮或紀念等目的。我們知道，盧恩字母最常見於墓地的墓碑上，用來紀念富人、偉大的領袖或貴族。它們通常刻在石頭、木頭、骨頭或盧恩石刻（刻有盧恩文的大石塊）上。這表示，很少有人知道如何讀寫盧恩字母，盧恩字母可能是在這種很小的族群中、基於很特定的原因而發展出來的。

最後，許多考古學家指出，在盧恩字母之前或與之同時的字母系統，與盧恩字母之間都缺乏相似性。盧恩字母與其他字母系統之間的任何相似之處很可能是偶然的或巧合的，因此很難證實盧恩字母是早期字母系統的變體。

B 閱讀文章，並再聽一遍聽力內容。利用這兩個來源的資訊完成下面筆記。

Reading: Runic alphabet developed independently of other alphabets

1. Cultural isolation of Germanic ppl
   - No contact w/other ❶_____ until 700 (Roman conquest)

2. Runes used by very small number of ppl for specific purposes
   - carved into stone, ❷_____ or wood
   - burial sites, ❸_____

3. No ❹_____ to other alphabets
   - Any sim are coincidental

Lecture: Runes came from ❺_____ (script common throughout Europe)

1. Influenced by groups that used O.I., like ❻_____ and Romans
   - Germanic ppl traded with Greeks and Italians

2. Evidence from Bergen shows runes were used for many things inc
   - business
   - jokes

Because used for memorials, means most people could read them.

3. Similarities between O.I. and runes
   - Use same ❼_____ letters

閱讀：盧恩字母獨立發展，不受其他字母系統影響

1. 日耳曼人文化隔絕
   — 沒有❶_____接觸，直到公元 700 年（羅馬征服）

2. 盧恩字母僅被極少數人用於特定目的
   — 刻在石頭、❷_____或木頭上
   — 墓地、❸_____

3. 與其他字母系統沒有❹_____
   — 任何相似處都是巧合

課堂：盧恩字母來自❺_____（歐洲通用的某種書寫系統）

1. 受到使用古代義大利文的族群的影響，像是❻_____和羅馬人
   — 日耳曼人與希臘人和義大利人進行貿易

2. 來自卑爾根市的證據指出，盧恩字母用於多種用途，包括
   — 商業
   — 笑話
   因為用在紀念物上，表示大多數人都能看得懂

3. 古代義大利文和盧恩字母之間的相似之處
   — 使用相同的❼_____字母

C 請閱讀題目提示，判斷它是否要求你支持或質疑文章所提出的觀點。使用以上筆記完成寫作範本。記得使用引述表達法和轉折詞（如以下所示）來介紹你的主題。

Citing Expressions 引述表達法	Transition Words 轉折詞
The [source] claims / says / argues that... [來源]宣稱／說／主張…	First / Second / Third... 第一／第二／第三…
The [source] agrees / disagrees... [來源]同意／反對…	Next... 其次…
The [source] points out / describes / illustrates... [來源]指出／描述／說明…	Then... 然後…
According to the [source]... 根據[來源]…	Finally... 最後…
The [source] notices / observes... [來源]注意到／觀察到…	In conclusion / To sum up / In summary... 結論是／總而言之／簡言之…
In the reading / lecture... 在文章／課堂中…	On the other hand... 另一方面…

Question

Directions: You have 20 minutes to prepare, write, and revise your response. Your essay will be graded based on your ability to communicate clearly through writing and on how well your essay demonstrates the relationship between the points in the lecture and those in the reading. An effective response usually contains 150–225 words.

Question: Summarize the points made in the lecture, being sure to explain how they cast doubt on the points made in the reading passage.

你的回答

Main Topic from Reading: _____

_____

Main Topic from Lecture: _____

_____

Key Point 1 from Reading: _____

_____

Key Point 1 from Lecture: _____

_____

Support from Lecture: _____

_____

Key Point 2 from Reading: _____

_____

Key Point 2 from Lecture: _____

_____

Support from Lecture: _____

_____

Key Point 3 from Reading: _____

_____

Key Point 3 from Lecture: _____

_____

Support from Lecture: _____

Conclusion: _____

D 現在檢視你剛完成的作文，並閱讀以下敘述。你的回答是否符合整合題的評分要求？繼續練習，直到你能夠完成所有要求。

Checklist		
1. 我的作文準確連結了文章和聽力的資訊。	Yes	No
2. 我的作文有五個段落，包括引言、討論三個重點的三個主體段落，以及結論。		
3. 我提到了文章的三個重點，並描述了教授對每個重點的看法。		
4. 我使用了來自聽力和文章中的具體細節和例子。		
5. 我使用了正確的文法、字彙和標點符號，並且沒有拼錯單字。		
6. 我用標示語和轉折詞指出我的觀點之間的關係。		

Read the passage in three minutes. Begin reading now.

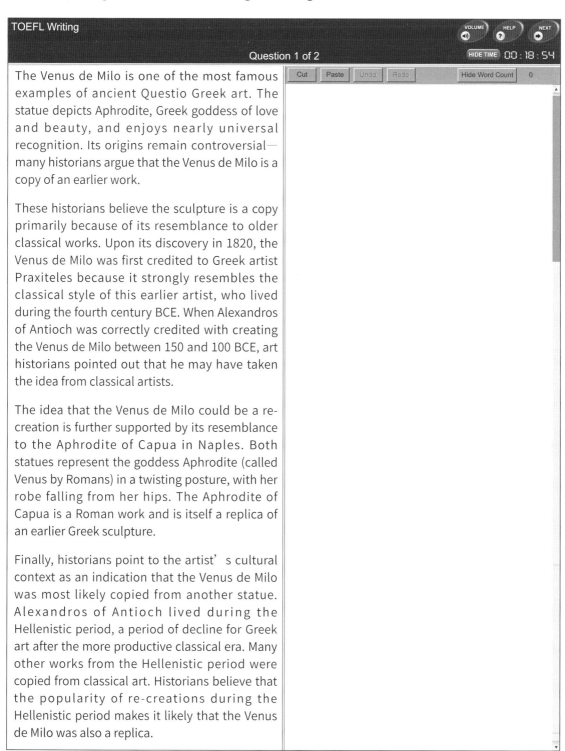

TOEFL Writing

Question 1 of 2

The Venus de Milo is one of the most famous examples of ancient Questio Greek art. The statue depicts Aphrodite, Greek goddess of love and beauty, and enjoys nearly universal recognition. Its origins remain controversial—many historians argue that the Venus de Milo is a copy of an earlier work.

These historians believe the sculpture is a copy primarily because of its resemblance to older classical works. Upon its discovery in 1820, the Venus de Milo was first credited to Greek artist Praxiteles because it strongly resembles the classical style of this earlier artist, who lived during the fourth century BCE. When Alexandros of Antioch was correctly credited with creating the Venus de Milo between 150 and 100 BCE, art historians pointed out that he may have taken the idea from classical artists.

The idea that the Venus de Milo could be a re-creation is further supported by its resemblance to the Aphrodite of Capua in Naples. Both statues represent the goddess Aphrodite (called Venus by Romans) in a twisting posture, with her robe falling from her hips. The Aphrodite of Capua is a Roman work and is itself a replica of an earlier Greek sculpture.

Finally, historians point to the artist's cultural context as an indication that the Venus de Milo was most likely copied from another statue. Alexandros of Antioch lived during the Hellenistic period, a period of decline for Greek art after the more productive classical era. Many other works from the Hellenistic period were copied from classical art. Historians believe that the popularity of re-creations during the Hellenistic period makes it likely that the Venus de Milo was also a replica.

Now listen to part of a lecture in an art history class and take notes. 🎧 005

NOTES:

Read the prompt and write your response.

TOEFL Writing	
Question	
Directions: You have 20 minutes to prepare, write, and revise your response. Your essay will be graded based on your ability to communicate clearly through writing and on how well your essay demonstrates the relationship between the points in the lecture and those in the reading. An effective response usually contains 150–225 words. **Question**: Summarize the points made in the lecture, being sure to explain how they cast doubt on the points made in the reading passage.	

To see sample responses and rater's comments see page 240-242.

寫作範本和評分範例請見240-242頁。

學術討論題
Writing for an Academic Discussion

Unit 9

你要為學術討論撰寫一篇貼文。題目通常會要求你回答教授所提出的問題,並為線上討論做出貢獻。接在教授問題之後是兩位學生的回答,你需要閱讀並做出回應。

學術討論題的題目指令,可能用以下方式表達:

- What is your opinion? Are good public transport systems essential for a town to grow? Why? 你的看法是什麼?良好的公共運輸系統對一個城鎮的進步是必要的嗎?為什麼?
- Some people like to save extra money. Other people prefer to spend it right away. Which of these options do you think is better? Why? 有些人喜歡存錢,有些人則喜歡馬上花掉。你認為這兩者之中哪一個比較好?為什麼?
- What is the best way to understand a person's character before you get to know them and why? 在你認識一個人之前,了解他的個性的最佳方式是什麼,為什麼?

你需要就教授的問題寫出意見。你的意見應該對討論有所貢獻。而且清晰、具連貫性。也應該利用理由和例子來支持和擴展。

你有 10 分鐘的時間來準備和作答,答案沒有字數上限,但一個強而有力的答案通常至少包括 100 個字。在 10 分鐘結束時,你的答案會被自動存檔,並送到 ETS 線上評分網路。

學術討論題快速指南

內容	你要閱讀關於學術討論的三篇貼文。第一篇貼文必定來自於一位教授或學者,他會針對某個話題提供一些背景資料。第二和第三篇貼文來自於學生。
題目	你會在螢幕左側看到說明和教授的貼文,這些資訊會一直保留在螢幕上。題目說明告訴你所討論的一般性的主題,並要求你寫貼文回應。它指示你用自己的措辭表達意見、支持你的觀點,和寫 100 個字。 教授的提示通常包含三個方面: • 關於主題的背景(題目說明已告知一般性主題為何)。 • 該主題比較著重的層面。這可能是選項之間的比較,或者要求最佳選擇,或者要求問題的解決方案。 • 要求把意見發布到討論區。 第二和第三篇貼文來自於學生。每篇貼文都會對教授所提出的主題補充一個贊成或反對的觀點。

須具備的 能力	為了在學術討論題獲得高分，你必須能夠： ▪ 快速分析並理解教授和學生的貼文。 ▪ 明確敘述自己的意見，無論你同意或不同意，或者同意到何種程度。 ▪ 在其他人的想法之外做補充，而不只是重複他們的觀點。 ▪ 確定你的觀點是有相關性的，並包含足夠的細節。 ▪ 利用舉例和細節來支持你的重點。 ▪ 組織你的回答，使內容清晰易懂，利用轉折詞來提升你答案的流暢性。 ▪ 確定你的文法和字彙準確及適當。
高分作答	一個高分作答應該要有 100 個字或更多，但不能少於 100 字。高分作答要能夠清楚回答教授的問題，和提出相關的理由、舉例和說明來支持你的觀點，並且在其他兩位學生提出的觀點之外做擴充。 你必須在討論中補充你自己的想法，而不只是重複已經提過的想法，不過你在提出意見時可以參考其他回應。 貼文的語氣很重要。雖然貼文不像學術論文那麼正式，但仍然是寫給教授看的東西，所以這不是一篇非正式的文章。你的回答應該條理分明，字彙和文法的使用應該正確且多樣，而且貼文通常應該易於理解。如果你不同意其他人的意見，要以尊重的方式表達。
注意事項	1. 閱讀教授的貼文和學生的回應，並且分析和做筆記。 2. 在寫作的一開始先重述主題的重點，並提供問題的背景——在你敘述和支持自己的意見之前先設定情境。 3. 針對討論提出你自己的意見或觀點，要確定你的觀點有助於討論。你可以對貼文中的觀點做補充或提出相反觀點，或者表示部分同意或不同意，並說明原因。 4. 要包含明確支持你個人觀點的適當舉例、理由和細節。 5. 總結你的立場。

TEST TIP!

在考試當天，你需要將答案輸入到一個文字框裡。這個文字框沒有拼字檢查工具，所以要在考試前練習以打字答題，並且不依靠拼字檢查工具。

Ⓐ 以下是學術討論題的範例。注意考生用底線標記重要資訊的方式，這是分析題目、教授貼文和學生回應的一種方法。

Your professor is teaching a class on health sciences. Write a post responding to the professor's question.

In your response you should:

- express and support your opinion
- make a contribution to the discussion

An effective response will contain at least 100 words. You will have 10 minutes to write it.

Dr Singleton

In America today, one of the biggest causes of health issues is poor diet. People eating too many processed foods, such as junk food that is high in fat and salt and drinking sugary drinks, causes thousands of people to have ill health. Some people say that we should have better health care and medical interventions to deal with this problem. Others believe that we should encourage people to have a healthier diet to prevent them becoming ill in the first place. I'd like to know what you think: is it better regulate people's diets or to develop better treatments?

Faik

Eating junk food and drinking sugary drinks can lead to serious illnesses like heart disease and in turn can cost the economy millions of dollars in health care and lost work. In my opinion, the worst thing is that these kinds of food are really cheap, so these health issues are affecting the people who can least afford health care. We need to regulate the sale of these items, so that they can't harm people.

Olga

I acknowledge what Faik says, that we have a problem with our diets. However, my view is that regulation is the wrong way to do this. People will always eat what they like and not everyone suffers from poor health due to poor diet. I think we can provide better health care for people who become ill; after all, the taxes from buying fast foods pay for the health care system.

你的教授正在課堂上教健康科學，寫一篇貼文來回應教授的問題。

你在回應中應該：
- 表達和支持你的意見
- 對討論提出貢獻

合格的回應要包含至少 100 個字，你有 10 分鐘的時間作答。

辛格列登博士
在今日的美國，造成健康問題的最大原因之一是不良的飲食習慣。人們食用太多的加工食品，像是高脂、高鹽的垃圾食物，以及飲用含糖飲料，這導致成千上萬的人健康不佳。有些人說我們應該提供更好的醫療保健和醫療干預來解決這個問題；而有些人則相信，我們應該鼓勵人們養成更健康的飲食習慣，從一開始就預防他們生病。我想知道你們的看法：是更妥善規範人們的飲食，還是開發更好的治療方法？

費克
食用垃圾食品和飲用含糖飲料可能導致像是心臟病等嚴重疾病，進而造成數百萬美元的醫療保健支出和失業。在我看來，最糟糕的是這類食品非常廉價，因此這些健康問題所影響的是最無法負擔醫療保健費用的人們。我們需要規範這些商品的銷售，以免它們對人們造成傷害。

奧嘉
我承認費克所說的，我們的飲食確實存在問題。然而我的見解是，規範並非解決問題的正確方法。人們總是會吃他們喜歡的食物，並不是每個人都因為不良飲食而導致健康不佳。我認為我們可以為生病的人提供更好的醫療保健；畢竟，為了購買速食而繳的稅，是會運用在醫療保健系統上的。

TEST TIP!

我們應給自己足夠的時間閱讀其他同學的貼文和畫出重點。在作答時，我們可以同意、不同意或部分同意其他同學的觀點，但必須提出自己的觀點。自己的觀點應該為討論增添一些新的內容，而不只是重複其他貼文。

B 請檢視考生在分析問題和貼文時所做的筆記範例。雖然你可以在紙條上進行腦力激盪，但在電腦上進行可能會省下一些時間。如此一來，你可以在電腦上將筆記轉為句子，並使用螢幕上的「剪下」和「貼上」功能來改變組織架構。

NOTES

Question: health sciences: Is it better to regulate people's diets or to develop better treatments?

Professor: Biggest cause of health issues is poor diet. Some people say we should have better health care / medical interventions. Others: we should encourage people to have a healthier diet.

Faik: poor diet causes illnesses and costs the economy. Need to regulate. Olga: regulation doesn't work; government should provide better health care.

My opinion: agree with Faik, and add that healthy options and better choices should be encouraged not just regulated.

中譯
問題：健康科學：規範人們的飲食還是發展更好的療法比較好？
教授：健康問題的最大原因是不良飲食習慣。有人說我們應該有更好的醫療干預，也有人認為我們應該鼓勵人們培養更健康的飲食習慣。
費克：不良飲食導致疾病並且造成經濟損失，需要有所規範。
奧嘉：規範不起作用；政府應提供更好的醫療保健。
我的觀點：同意費克的觀點，並補充說應該鼓勵健康的選擇和更好的選擇，而不只是規範。

C 以下是一篇學術討論題的寫作範本。閱讀時，請注意考生如何將 B 部分的筆記轉為一篇完整的作文。

Today you can see the effects of having a diet that contains lots processed foods and drinks with lots of sugar. It is having visible effects on people and the health care system. So, I agree with Faik in many respects, but would like to add my own point. Fast foods are available everywhere, in supermarkets and on the street, and they can even be cheaper than healthier foods. In this situation, there is no surprise that people eat food that is bad for them. However, I don't agree that regulation is the answer. In my opinion, better education and more availability of healthy food is the answer so that people understand the effects of fast food and the benefits of a good diet and make choices based on information. Therefore, I believe that making healthy food as cheap as processed food and teaching people about the consequences of their choices is the best way forward.

9-1-1　掌握要領：學術討論題回答技巧

技巧 1

明智利用時間。利用螢幕上的計時器查看剩餘時間。你應該花大約 1 分鐘分析問題，閱讀貼文和做筆記，並花 8 分鐘寫貼文。最後 1 分鐘應該花在檢查貼文的拼字或文法錯誤上。

練習① 檢視 194 頁範例題中畫底線的文字和筆記範例。你認為你可以在一分鐘左右完成這些嗎？自己計時，並且在限時內完成練習。

技巧 2

確定你了解教授和學生的貼文。畫底線標記主要觀點（main points）和學生是否同意教授提出的問題或主張，或者他們是否反對。

練習② 檢視 194 頁範例題中畫底線的文字。你是否能標記出相同的文字？

技巧 3

趁閱讀貼文時寫下簡要的筆記。

練習③ 檢視 196 頁的筆記範例，注意筆記的精簡性。

技巧 4

在前幾句概述主題，並且敘述和支持你的觀點。

練習④ 檢視 196 頁的寫作範本。在寫作範本中圈出概述主題和敘述考生觀點的引言。

技巧 5

利用一些字詞來連接你的重點，以提高流暢度和清晰度。

練習⑤ 檢視 196 頁的寫作範本。注意考生如何使用連接詞（linking words），例如 so, therefore, however，來連接他們的重點。

在最後一句總結或歸納你的立場。

練習 6　再次檢視 196 頁的寫作範本，用圓圈標記出總結考生立場的句子。

TEST TIP!

在答題時偶爾看一下倒數計時器，確定自己沒有花太多時間閱讀題目，並且留時間寫　100　個字，和檢查你的答案。

Ⓐ 閱讀以下範例題的第一部分，並用底線標記出有助於你答題的兩個關鍵資訊。

Your professor is teaching a class on health sciences. Write a post responding to the professor's question.

In your response you should:
- express and support your opinion
- make a contribution to the discussion

An effective response will contain at least 100 words. You will have 10 minutes to write it.

Professor Braverman

In the middle part of the 20th century, the average human lifespan was 50 years of age. As we saw in the lecture yesterday, this has increased to over 80 years. Of course, there are differences between genders and regions, but overall, the trend for living longer is a fact. As we saw, there are many theories as to why this is happening: better diets, less disease, better living conditions amongst other things. But I'm interested in what you think. What has been the most important development in the last 100 years that has led to increased life expectancy?

Ⓑ 現在閱讀以下完整的範例題。在準備答題時，應該在誰的貼文上做筆記？
- Professor Braverman's 布雷弗曼教授的
- Gezgin's 蓋茲津的
- Sara's 莎拉的
- All three posts 三篇貼文都要

Your professor is teaching a class on health sciences. Write a post responding to the professor's question.

In your response you should:
- express and support your opinion
- make a contribution to the discussion

An effective response will contain at least 100 words. You will have 10 minutes to write it.

Professor Braverman

In the middle part of the 20th century, the average human lifespan was 50 years of age. As we saw in the lecture yesterday, this has increased to over 80 years. Of course, there are differences between genders and regions, but overall, the trend for living longer is a fact. As we saw, there are many theories as to why this is happening: better diets, less disease, better living conditions amongst other things. But I'm interested in what you think. What has been the most important development in the last 100 years that has led to increased life expectancy?

Gezgin

Out of all the developments over the time period, in my view, better water quality is the most important thing. We all need water to survive, and previously people died from diseases carried in dirty water, like cholera, or from diseases associated with dirty water, like malaria. Facilities such as water treatment centres and clean tap water have been the best development in helping us live longer.

Sara

I agree with Gezgin that clean water is incredibly important. For me though, better living conditions, specifically housing, has been the major factor. When people were living in overcrowded conditions and slums, disease could spread more easily, and the chances of survival were limited.

中譯

你的教授正在課堂上教健康科學，寫一篇貼文來回應教授的問題。

你在回應中應該：
▪ 表達和支持你的意見
▪ 對討論提出貢獻

優良的回應要包含至少 100 個字，你有 10 分鐘的時間作答。

布雷弗曼教授
在 20 世紀中葉，平均人類壽命是 50 歲。正如我們昨天在講課中所看到的，現在已經增加至 80 多歲。當然，在性別和地區之間存在差異，但整體上，長壽的趨勢是事實。正如我們所見，有許多理論解釋了這個現象：更優質的飲食、較少的疾病、更好的生活條件等。但我對你們的想法很感興趣。在過去的 100 年裡，導致人類壽命增加的最重要發展是什麼？

蓋茲津
我的看法是，在這段時間內儘管產生了許多發展，但更優良的水質才是最重要的。我們都需要水才能生存，以前人們因為汙水而傳播的疾病（例如霍亂）或與汙水有關的疾病（例如瘧疾）而死亡。像水處理中心和乾淨自來水這類設施，是幫助我們延長壽命的最佳發展。

莎拉

我同意蓋茲津認為乾淨的水相當重要的觀點。不過對我來說，更優質的生活條件是主要因素，尤其是住所。當人們居住在擁擠的環境和貧民窟時，疾病更容易傳播，生存機會也受到限制。

 閱讀筆記範例，用來做筆記的四個標題是什麼？

NOTES

Question: health sciences: What was the most important development in the last 100 years?

Professor: the average human lifespan has increased – better diets, less disease, better living conditions

Gezgin: Poor water quality caused disease. Better water quality (water treatment centres / clean tap water) is the best thing.

Sara: Overcrowding and slum housing caused diseases to spread. Better housing is the main factor in increasing life expectancy.

My opinion: development of antibiotics in the early twentieth century – helped with bacterial infections, e.g. common cold, tuberculosis. These were highly infectious but antibiotic drugs saved many lives.

中譯

問題：健康科學：過去 100 年裡最重要的發展是什麼？

教授：平均人類壽命增加—飲食更好、疾病減少、生活條件更好。

蓋茲津：惡劣的水質導致疾病。更好的水質（水處理中心／潔淨的自來水）是最重要的事情。

莎拉：擁擠和貧民窟居住環境導致疾病傳播，更優質的住所是增加壽命的主要因素。

我的觀點：20 世紀初抗生素的發展——有助於治療細菌感染，例如一般感冒、結核病。這些疾病傳染性高，但抗生素拯救了許多生命。

D 看看下方的筆記格示範本。你認為這對你準備作答會有幫助嗎？

NOTES
Question: _____

Professor: _____
_____

Gezgin: _____
_____

Sara: _____
_____

My opinion: _____
_____

再看一遍前面的範例題，並用下列方框中的詞語來完成寫作範本。

> Therefore, this is the most important factor
> For example,
> Overall, I completely agree
> However, I am of the opinion that

寫作範本

1 _____ with the ideas presented by Gezgin and Sara. There are other things that I could mention too, such as better nutrition, better working conditions and better health care. 2 _____ the most important development has been antibiotics and antiviral drugs. These drugs are used to treat infections that used to kill lots of people. 3 _____ in the 1900s Spanish flu swept the world, but existing medical treatments were ineffective and millions of people died. Since then, a lot of research has been done on developing antibiotics and antiviral drugs, and they have been very effective in preventing illnesses. Furthermore, we are able to produce these drugs more and more cheaply. 4 _____ in helping us live longer.

練習 A 中的詞語有什麼作用？請將功能與詞語配對。

1. Therefore, this is the most important factor

2. For example,

3. Overall, I completely agree

4. However, I am of the opinion that

a. states their position with regards to the thoughts so far

b. sums up and gives a conclusion

c. provides a contradictory view

d. offers an example

用下列模版來回答199-200頁的範例題。

你的回答

Overall, I _____ with the ideas presented by _____

_____

_____

However, I am of the opinion that _____

_____

For example, _____

_____

Furthermore, _____

_____

Therefore, _____

_____

D 現在檢視你剛完成的作文，並閱讀以下敘述。你的回答是否符合學術討論題的評分要求？繼續練習，直到你能夠完成所有要求。

Checklist		
1. 我的貼文仔細回應了教授的問題。	Yes	No
2. 我明確主張我的意見，無論我同不同意問題的主張，或同意到何種程度。		
3. 我在其他人的想法之外做補充，而不只是重複他們的觀點。		
4. 我的每一個重點都有用舉例和細節來支持。		
5. 我使用了正確的文法、字彙和標點符號，而且沒有拼錯單字。		
6. 我用轉折詞來提升貼文的流暢性。		
7. 我了解題目的背景。我的貼文不像學術論文那麼正式，但也不像簡訊那麼隨意。		
8. 我寫了至少 100 個字。		

Read the question and write your response.

Your professor is teaching a class on psychology. Write a post responding to the professor's question.

In your response you should:
- express and support your opinion
- make a contribution to the discussion

An effective response will contain at least 100 words. You will have 10 minutes to write it.

Professor Akdeniz

Stress is a common problem today, especially for students at college. There can be many factors that cause it, including having too much work to do in a short time, no control over your circumstances, or poor relationships with classmates, friends or family. The effects of stress can be harmful both mentally and physically, so it is a problem that must be taken seriously. There are many ways to deal with stress, including participating in physical activity, receiving support from people around you or getting professional help. But what is the best way of dealing with stress? Please post your ideas to this discussion forum before tomorrow's class.

Tracy

I know a lot of people suffering from stress, and it is a serious problem. From my perspective, we don't take mental health seriously enough. The best way of dealing with stress, in my opinion, is to get professional help. There are quite a few psychological therapies for stress, including talk therapy, group therapy and cognitive therapy, and these have good records of success.

Mia

I agree with what Tracy says, but don't think her suggestions work for all kinds of stress. When the issue is really serious, of course you should seek professional help, but before then there are lots of strategies that you can put in place to help reduce stress. One key example is regular physical activity. Doing some kind of exercise helps to reduce stress and boost your overall mood. Just 30 minutes of walking per day will help, and having this as a scheduled thing you do every day really helps.

_____

_____

_____

_____

_____

_____

_____

_____

_____

To see sample responses and rater's comments see page 243-245.

寫作範本和評分範例請見243-245頁。

以下將測試你到目前為止所學的技巧。在寫作模擬試題中,你會碰到與實際托福網路測驗相同的題型。此外,題目的難度與托福網路測驗的題目難度相同。

為了使測驗盡可能貼近實際托福考試,請務必遵循頁面上的指示。當你播放音檔時,你會聽到說明,告訴你什麼時候開始寫作文。以下的計時指南,列出了你在寫作部分每種題型中的作答時間。你需要自己計時。

寫作部分計時說明			
題目	閱讀時間	聽力時間	答題時間
Question 1: Academic Reading / Lecture Synthesis Task 學術閱讀／講座整合寫作題	大約 3 分鐘（顯示於螢幕）	大約 3-5 分鐘	20 分鐘
Question 2: Academic Discussion Task 學術討論題	n/a	n/a	10 分鐘

為了取得高分,你應該在模擬試題中回答針對問題的答案。請記住,在做托福測驗時,你無法使用拼字檢查功能,因此在練習時不要依賴此功能。在書本最後的答案解析中,你會找到每個問題的兩個寫作範本。每個寫作範本都會評分,並附上評分者的分析,說明答案的優缺點。請利用寫作部分的評分分析,來推測你會獲得的分數。

在分析你的作文時,請嘗試找出你的缺點:你是否清楚改述了其他學生的觀點?你是否有支持自己的觀點?透過了解自己的缺點,你才知道需要重點複習哪些部分。

QUESTION 1

Read the passage in three minutes. Begin reading now.

Cut Paste Undo Redo Hide Word Count 0

The Upper Paleolithic Revolution refers to the period during which Homo sapiens, or modern humans, started exhibiting distinctly human behavior for the first time. Among these behaviors was the development of sophisticated stone tools, as well as the creation of language and artwork. According to the available evidence, it is likely that the Upper Paleolithic Revolution occurred in mainland Europe about 40,000 years ago.

First, there are indications that around 40,000 years ago, an earlier type of human, called the European Neanderthal, went extinct. The extinction of the European Neanderthal coincides with the population boom of modern humans in Europe. The population boom is supported by the discovery of large amounts of skeletal remains of modern humans that date to around 40,000 years ago. These discoveries suggest that modern humans took the place of European Neanderthals and were probably able to do so because they had developed superior tools, like stone knives, that helped them catch food and survive.

Next, climate records suggest that Europe provided the conditions necessary for the revolution. According to the records, Europe experienced a period of lower than normal temperatures starting around 70,000 years ago until about 10,000 years ago. Scientists believe that the cold climate prompted modern humans that were living in Europe at the time to create better tools in order to survive. For example, by inventing fishing tools, they were able to catch food despite the abnormally cold weather.

Finally, the first example of modern figurative art appeared in Europe during the Upper Paleolithic Revolution. The Venus of Hohle Fels, a stone statue from Germany, dates to around 35,000–40,000 years ago. This is an early example of sophisticated artwork, and no earlier examples exist elsewhere.

Now listen to part of a lecture in an art history class and take notes. 🎧 006

NOTES:

Read the prompt and write your response.

TOEFL Writing

Question

Directions: You have 20 minutes to prepare, write, and revise your response. Your essay will be graded based on your ability to communicate clearly through writing and on how well your essay demonstrates the relationship between the points in the lecture and those in the reading. An effective response usually contains 150–225 words.

Question: Summarize the points made in the lecture, being sure to explain how they cast doubt on the points made in the reading passage.

To see sample responses and rater's comments see page 245-247.

寫作範本和評分範例請見245-247頁。

Read the question and write your response in your notebook in 10 minutes.

Read the question and write your response.

Your professor is teaching a class on education. Write a post responding to the professor's question.

In your response you should:
- express and support your opinion
- make a contribution to the discussion

An effective response will contain at least 100 words. You will have 10 minutes to write it.

Professor Akdeniz

When students are working together and learning from each other, we call this approach to education peer learning. This way of learning encourages discussion and information exchange between students instead of from the academic to the students. There are many advantages to this approach to learning: it is interactive and stimulating; it includes everyone; and it involves lots of different experience and knowledge. However, there are also disadvantages: students' knowledge tends to be less developed than an academic's; not all students contribute equally; and, finally, there could be a lack of motivation. I'm interested in reading your thoughts on the subject. Let me know if you think peer learning is a good educational approach or whether more formal learning is better.

Laci

Personally, I don't like peer learning. After all, we come to university to learn from experts in our subjects, not from students like ourselves. Other students have limited knowledge or even worse can give you wrong information. Furthermore, we can meet other students after scheduled classes to discuss things, so why spend time in class doing this with them?

Viktoria

I partially disagree with Laci; learning from lecturers and professors is a key part of university education but it's not everything. There can be different perspectives on a question, particularly in subjects like education or sociology or business, and students often have good ideas and opinions – we should listen to everyone and be prepared to learn from them.

To see sample responses and rater's comments see page 247-249.
寫作範本和評分範例請見247-249頁。

2-1-1 細節題範例

A.

1. 根據第二段，關於古印度使用的背誦方式，以下哪一項是正確的？
   ○ 它允許使用者在敘述中添加新細節。
   ○ 它比其他複誦方法更複雜。
   ○ 它需要大家大聲朗讀句子。
   ○ 它要求使用者一次記住整個段落。

2-1-2 掌握要領：細節題回答技巧

練習 1 paragraph 2; true about the repetition strategy used in ancient India

練習 2 some forms of repetition are more complicated; For example, in ancient India, people memorized texts by repeating the words in a different order.

練習 3 It was primarily used to memorize texts.

練習 4 It allowed users to add new details to narratives.; It required users to remember entire paragraphs at a time.

練習 5 One such technique is repetition, which involves saying the words of a story many times.

2-2-1 指涉題範例

A.

1. 第一段中的「it」指的是
   ○ 十五世紀。
   ○ 義大利威尼斯。
   ○ 歐洲。
   ○ 一個頂尖生產者。

2. 第二段中的「they」指的是
   ○ 這座城市留給後世的資產。
   ○ 印刷業者。
   ○ 書籍。
   ○ 歷史學家。

2-2-2 掌握要領：指涉題回答技巧

練習 1 Paragraph 1: the fifteenth century; Venice, Italy; Europe; a top producer
   Paragraph 2: the city's legacy; printers; books; historians

練習 2 Question 1: Europe Question 2: the city's legacy

2-3 題型練習

A.

第一段主旨：England offers a clear example—in the early sixteenth century, a new type of theater, called English Renaissance theater, flourished there. This new theatrical style, sometimes also referred to as Elizabethan theater, developed because of a number of changes in England.

第二段主旨：One major reason for the popularity of English Renaissance Theater was that it reflected the cultural changes that were occurring in England at the time.

第三段主旨：During the same period, English theater companies and performance spaces also underwent a number of changes that helped bolster English Renaissance theater.

2-4 綜合演練

A.

1. Piazzolla's nuevo tango retains elements of traditional tango, but it is also distinct in several ways.

2. Piazzolla began to explore traditional Argentine music by learning how to play the bandoneón, an accordion-like instrument that is often employed in tango music.

3. While there were clear influences of traditional Argentine tango in his work, Piazzolla's nuevo tango also reflected the other types of music he was exposed to as a young man.

4. Another unique element of Piazzolla's nuevo tango music is its experimental tendency.

B.

1.

[D] ✗ 作者指的是新探戈，而不是傳統探戈。

[A] ✗ 如果用「origin」取代代名詞，這個句子沒有意義。

[C] ✓ 這個代名詞指的是探戈。

[B] ✗ 將代名詞替換為「the genre」會改變句子的意思。

2.
[D] ✗ 文章提到了皮亞佐拉的童年，但沒有說這是皮亞佐拉音樂的一部分。

[A] ✓ 作者提到班多鈕琴通常用於探戈音樂中，而且皮亞佐拉使用了這種樂器。

[B] ✗ 作者提到這是阿根廷探戈的一個特點，但沒有說明皮亞佐拉是否在自己的音樂中使用這種歌詞。

[C] ✗ 文章提到皮亞佐拉與阿根廷管弦樂團合作，但沒有說他是否為他們作曲。

3.
[B] ✗ 是皮亞佐拉的作品創造了新探戈流派，所以這個選項不可能正確。

[C] ✓ 該代名詞指的是爵士樂。

[D] ✗ 「classical music」可以取代這個代名詞，但會改變句子的意思。

[A] ✗ 儘管「Argentine tango」可以取代代名詞，但句子的意思會改變。

4.
[C] ✗ 作者說皮亞佐拉與一位作家合作，而不是與其他音樂家合作。

[A] ✗ 作者沒有說詩歌是由皮亞佐拉的實驗音樂所啟發的。

[B] ✓ 最後一句說皮亞佐拉的實驗風格引起了傳統音樂家的抗議，意思就是他們反對。

[D] ✗ 雖然皮亞佐拉在他的祖國很受歡迎，但他音樂的實驗性質卻讓一些人不喜歡。

2-5 實戰演練

TOEFL Reading

Question

戴安‧佛西與大猩猩的研究

大猩猩是世界上最為人所知的動物之一，但在 1980 年代的盧安達，只剩下 250 隻山地大猩猩。靈長類動物學家戴安‧佛西擔心牠們會在世紀末滅絕，因此決心拯救牠們。戴安拯救山地大猩猩的工作是透過揭露牠們與人類的親近和關聯，來阻止這些膽小而善社交動物的滅絕。戴安也改變了保護野生動物的態度，開啟一種新的動物保育法。

戴安前往盧安達的路途並不順遂。她職業生涯的前半段在肯塔基州路易斯維爾做職能治療師，但她自幼對動物十分著迷，並在 1963 年前往肯亞、坦尚尼亞和當時稱為薩伊的地方（現為剛果民主共和國）。她在坦尚尼亞遇見考古學家路易斯‧李奇，他們討論到對大猩猩進行長期研究的重要性，當時她就決定將終身投入大猩猩的研究和保育工作中。在接下來的 20 年裡，戴安與大猩猩在盧安達雨林中生活和工作，她是高山上唯一的人類，因此要獨自應付孤單和對抗獵人偷獵大猩猩的問題。1967 年，她創立了一個叫做「卡里索克研究中心」的研究營地。因她的研究對象天性膽小，且識人類為獵人，所以要靠近研究牠們十分困難，但最後，戴安利用模仿牠們的動作和聲音贏得了牠們的信任，甚至交到了一些朋友。

在戴安的研究中，她觀察到大猩猩是複雜的社會性動物，並說牠們是「有尊嚴、高度社交、溫和的巨人，具有個別性格和牢固的家庭關係」。她發現大猩猩有社會階級制度，並生活在由二到四十個個體所組成的群體中。這些群體被稱為 troops（部隊），由一隻稱為「銀背」的優勢雄性領導，群體中還有其他較年輕的雄性、雌性和幼猩猩。雄性大猩猩帶領牠們的群體到最佳覓食和休息地點，在此期間，大猩猩會玩耍和互動，這讓社交活動變得極為重要。這也代表群體內的溝通非常發達——大猩猩發出聲音來表達痛苦、驚恐，或協調群體。

當牠們發現食物時，可能會唱歌或哼唱，通常幾隻會加入一起唱。當一隻大猩猩想要玩耍時，牠會做出「玩耍的表情」，並表現出類似微笑或打哈欠的樣子——第一種是打鬥後表現出安撫的樣子，第二種顯示焦慮或痛苦。

在戴安剛抵達盧安達時，山地大猩猩的數量只有 450 隻，她確認人類是導致數量下降的直接原因。大猩猩被獵人殺害，除了直接獵捕幼猩猩，也有因為設置陷阱獵捕其他動物而間接捕獲大猩猩。此外，當地人口破壞了大猩猩的天然棲息地，人類將該地清理成農田以提供食物。這為他們和大猩猩帶來了衝突，因他們進入了大猩猩的領域。最後，大猩猩還因為接觸了帶有傳播疾病（例如流感）的遊客而死亡。戴安也反對遊客與大猩猩接觸，因為會改變牠們的自然行為。

戴安的工作產生許多深遠的長期影響，如今山地大猩猩的數量估計超過 1,000 隻。她的書《迷霧中的大猩猩》（後來拍成電影《迷霧森林十八年》）宣傳了山地大猩猩的困境。她成立卡里索克研究中心來保護大猩猩及其環境，現在吸引了來自世界各地的研究人員和學生。最重要的是，戴安開創了一種叫「積極保育主義」的新方法，包括尋找並摧毀獵人陷阱，並讓當地社區參與保護大猩猩族群。現今，卡里索克研究中心為當地居民提供教育和經濟發展計畫，例如重建當地學校和提供健康診所，來改善該地區人民的生活品質。戴安的生活和工作呈現出我們與自然界間的重要聯繫，並指出了與自然共存的新方式。

1. 根據第一段，佛西的工作達成了什麼成就？
   ○ 山地大猩猩的滅絕
   ○ 改變人們對保護動物的態度
   ○ 使大猩猩變得害羞和善於社交
   ○ 人類與大猩猩之間的關係更密切

2. 根據第二段，為什麼佛西決定研究山地大猩猩？
   ○ 因為她對考古學感興趣
   ○ 因為她對動物感興趣
   ○ 因為她喜歡非洲
   ○ 因為她經歷了一場關於研究大猩猩重要性，改變了她的人生的對談。

3. 第二段中的「them」指的是？
   ○ 獵人
   ○ 高山
   ○ 山地大猩猩
   ○ 疾病

4. 根據第三段，為什麼佛西說大猩猩是複雜的社會性動物？
   ○ 因為牠們生活在有組織的家庭群體中
   ○ 因為該群體的領導者是一隻優勢雄性
   ○ 因為牠們會做出不同表情
   ○ 因為牠們具有強烈性格

5. 第四段中的「it」指的是什麼？
   ○ 當地人口
   ○ 食物
   ○ 陷阱
   ○ 自然棲息地

6. 根據第五段，積極保育主義包含什麼特點？
   ○ 吸引研究人員來研究大猩猩
   ○ 使當地居民對幫助大猩猩感興趣
   ○ 宣傳對大猩猩危險的事物
   ○ 為當地社區建立學校

3-1-1 挑錯題範例
A.
1. 根據第一段，下列選項都準確描述了動態定價，除了：
   ○ 它的普及性在二十世紀末開始下降。
   ○ 它賦予買家對一些物品價格的控制。
   ○ 它被賣家使用於網路拍賣。
   ○ 它表示賣家根據情況收取不同價格。

3-1-2 掌握要領：挑錯題回答技巧
練習 1 popularity; buyer's; online auctions; price
練習 2 It gives the buyer some control over the price of an item.; It means that sellers charge different prices according to the situation.
練習 3 It is used by sellers in online auctions.

A.

1. 在第三段中，作者為什麼要討論在特奧蒂瓦坎金字塔上的羽蛇神？
   ○ 為主張馬雅人啟發特奧蒂瓦坎使用羽蛇神
   ○ 為對比特奧蒂瓦坎人和馬雅人所使用的象徵圖像
   ○ 為舉例說明特奧蒂瓦坎人使用的考古技術
   ○ 為指出在馬雅人使用之前，此符就在特奧蒂瓦坎已經很普遍

2. 第一段與第二段有什麼關係？
   ○ 第一段舉例說明一個觀點，該觀點在第二段會進一步詳細解釋。
   ○ 第二段描述了第一段所提及的一個文化背景。
   ○ 第一段定義了一個關鍵術語，該術語對第二段被推翻的理論來說很重要。
   ○ 第二段提供的證據可支持第一段所介紹的理論。

3-2-2 掌握要領：功能題回答技巧

練習 1　feathered serpent; symbols; symbol; Teotihuacanos

練習 2　文章：This is particularly apparent in
　　　　選項：To point out that the symbol was popular in Teotihuacan before the Maya used it

練習 3　To give an example of an archaeological technique used by the Teotihuacanos（為舉例說明特奧蒂瓦坎人使用的考古技術）

練習 4　第一段主旨：Evidence suggests that the Maya were greatly influenced by the Teotihuacanos, especially in the areas of architecture and ideology.
　　　　第二段主旨：The Maya used a variety of architectural styles. However, one that was likely inspired by Teotihuacan was a technique called the slope-and-panel style.
　　　　兩段關係：第二段提供的證據可支持第一段所介紹的理論。

3-3 題型練習

A.

第一段主旨：Active design uses a number of techniques to encourage the occupants of a building to be more active.

第二段主旨：One of the most important strategies of active design is inspiring people to make walking part of their routine.

第三段主旨：Active design encourages physical activity using not only the interior features of a building, but the relationship between a building and its surroundings as well.

3-4 綜合演練

A.

1. Advances in technology have provided modern archaeologists with several methods that give them the absolute age of an object.
2. The most common absolute dating technique is radiocarbon dating.
3. For some inorganic remains, like pottery, archaeologists use a technique called thermoluminescence dating.
4. Thermoluminescence dating is particularly useful for dating pottery because of the process by which pottery is made.

B.

1.
[C] ✕ 作者在第一段裡沒有提到用生物來對物品進行年代測定。
[D] ✕ 當作者提到老鼠時，重點在於舉例說明早期的年代測定技術，而非現代的技術。
[A] ✓ 作者說老鼠可能改變文物的位置，如果考古學家將埋藏的深度作為指標，會導致測定的年代不準確。
[B] ✕ 作者主張早期的年代測定技術是不準確的，而非現代的技術。

2.
[A] ✕ 文章沒有提到灰渣與放射性碳定年法的準確性有關。
[C] ✓ 作者在前一句中定義了有機物質，該句以「For example 舉例來說」開頭。

[B] ✗ 作者並未指明放射性碳是否會被破壞，以及如何被破壞。

[D] ✗ 該句僅提到有機物質，沒有提及無機物質。

3.

[D] ✗ 作者說，陶器的年代是根據它在加熱至極高溫度時釋放多少光。

[A] ✓ 作者說放射性碳定年法對於無機物質不起作用，而不是熱釋光測年法會比放射性碳定年法更普及。

[B] ✗ 作者說放射性衰變導致少量能量被儲存起來。

[C] ✗ 作者說熱釋光測年法用於「結構堅硬的物質」，例如一些陶器中的礦物。

4.

[D] ✗ 在第四段裡，作者解釋當陶器第一次被燒製時，它「讓時間重設了」，表示它沒有存儲放射性能量。

[B] ✗ 在第三段裡，作者說熱釋光測年法對於測定一些像是陶器的無機物質來說，是很好的方法。

[A] ✓ 雖然陶器是一種常見的文物，但這與它是否適合進行熱釋光測年法無關。

[C] ✗ 作者說陶器中的礦物在陶器燒製時「繼續進行放射性衰變」。

3-5 實戰演練

TOEFL Reading

Question

非言語溝通

1　透過口說語言分享複雜、詳細資訊的能力，往往被認為是區分人類與動物的主要因素。然而，除了使用高度發展的語言系統外，人們還可以在完全不使用言語的情況下進行非言語溝通。儘管言語通常被認為是人類溝通的主要形式，但人們也在很大程度上，依賴許多種類的非言語溝通。

2　非言語溝通中最常見的形式之一是肢體語言。肢體語言可以包括面部表情、手勢，甚至眼神交流。人體幾乎能產生無限多種賦有意義的表情、姿勢和手勢，且都能使用於溝通目的。面部表情也許是肢體語言中最常被認出的一種。有些研究甚至指出，表達憤怒、恐懼、驚訝、快樂和悲傷等感受的面部表情可能是普世共通的，表示它們被全世界的人所理解。舉例來說，在某些情況下，即使兩個人可能說著完全不同的語言、來自完全不同文化，他們仍可透過面部表情分享基本情感。

3　然而重要的是，我們要認識到，並非所有的肢體語言都是普世共通的，文化的態度和規範在解釋某些類型的肢體語言時起了很大的作用。例如，將手放在口袋裡，對某些文化成員來說可能表示放鬆的感覺，但對其他文化成員而言可能表示不尊重。因此，肢體語言的含義通常取決於文化或個性。儘管解釋特定類型肢體語言含義有一定的困難，但人類行為研究指出，它是構成人類生活重要的一部分。有些研究人員指出，50-70% 的人類溝通是由肢體語言組成。

4　除了透過動作、表情或其他可見的肢體語言進行溝通外，人類還透過觸碰進行非言語溝通，這通常被稱為觸覺。研究指出，觸覺溝通在嬰兒的發展中尤其重要。在兒童發展語言能力前，父母或其他照顧者可用觸覺來傳達一系列的概念，如關注、照顧和安全。觸覺對成年人來說仍是一種重要的溝通方式，它是建立友誼和其他合作關係的核心部分，這是因為觸覺通常表示鼓勵信任。然而，在某些情況下，觸覺也可能傳達較不正面的訊息。舉例來說，肢體暴力是一種觸覺溝通，為一個人透過威脅或傷害他人來表達自己的心理狀態。

5　儘管大多數透過肢體語言和人際關係所傳送和接收的資訊都是潛意識的，但人類也會有意識的使用非言語溝通。人們通常會在外表上的某些方面做非常仔細的選擇，例如衣服、髮型或其他形式的個人裝飾，

而這些選擇也是另一種非言語溝通形式。透過外表所做的非言語溝通，其主要目的之一是顯示財富或地位。舉例來說，一個人可透過穿昂貴衣服來表示財富。同樣的，一個人也可透過穿戴特殊類型的服裝，例如徽章或制服，來展示他或她的地位。外表可傳達關於一個人希望被認為是認真還是愛玩、傳統還是奇特、專業還是隨意的資訊。例如，被視為正式服裝的傳統服飾，會隨著文化不同而有很大的差異，儘管如此，大多數社會都能識別出正式和非正式服裝之間的某些差異。最常見的情況是，正式服裝是對重要場合表示尊重。雖然大多數人對自己的穿著或外表有一定程度的控制，但也有一些類型的非言語溝通是無意識的。研究發現，在某些文化中，個子較高的人被認為較容易讓人留下深刻印象，且通常比個子較矮的同事容易晉升。在此情況下的非言語溝通並不是有意的，甚至可能傳達錯誤的資訊。

1. 根據第二段，關於肢體語言的敘述，下列哪一項是錯誤的？
   ○ 它包括像手勢和面部表情等行為。
   ○ 有些文化比其他文化更常使用肢體語言。
   ○ 它至少佔了人類溝通的一半。
   ○ 有些肢體語言被認為在任何地方都有相同意義。

2. 在第三段裡，作者提到把雙手放在口袋裡是為了
   ○ 解釋使用肢體語言的一種常見方式。
   ○ 說明肢體語言如何影響情緒。
   ○ 舉例說明肢體語言可能有多種解讀。
   ○ 支持「大部分溝通是非言語」的觀點。

3. 第二段和第三段之間的關係是什麼？
   ○ 第二段提出了一種有關一些肢體語言的理論，而第三段則顯示此理論並非總是成立。
   ○ 第三段比較了第二段中所描述的兩種類型的肢體語言。
   ○ 第二段舉例說明肢體語言，而第三段解釋肢體語言是如何被解讀的。

   ○ 第三段為第二段所提出有關肢體語言的理論提供了證據。

4. 在第四段裡，作者提到下列觸覺溝通的所有功能，除了：
   ○ 給予嬰兒關注
   ○ 促進語言發展
   ○ 建立朋友間的信任
   ○ 傷害他人的身體

5. 在第五段裡，作者說明有意識的非言語溝通可用於以下所有目的，除了：
   ○ 用來暗示個人的性格
   ○ 用來顯示自己有多少錢
   ○ 用來辨識同一族群的成員
   ○ 在特定情況下表示尊重

6. 為什麼作者在第五段提到有關工作場所的身高研究？
   ○ 為說明非言語溝通可能產生意想不到的後果。
   ○ 為指出人們的印象會根據身高而有所不同，是全球一致的。
   ○ 為提供證據證明，大多數類型的非言語溝通都是有意識的。
   ○ 為指出使用非言語溝通可能具有許多優點。

4-1-1 推論題範例

A.

1. 根據第二段，關於巴比倫使用的算盤，可以推論出什麼？
   ○ 它們是最早期的計算機。
   ○ 它們沒有任何教育價值。
   ○ 它們不容易移動。
   ○ 它們啟發了線算盤的發明。

4-1-2 掌握要領：推論題回答技巧

練習 1　abacuses used in Babylon; earliest calculators; did not have any educational value; were not easy to move around; inspired the invention of the wire abacus

練習 2　They were the earliest calculators.（它們是最早期的計算機。）

練習 3　They inspired the invention of the wire abacus.（它們啟發了線算盤的發明。）

4-2-1 詞彙題範例

A.

1. 第一段中的單字「gradual」，意思最接近於
   ○ hurried.（匆忙的）
   ○ continuous.（連續的）
   ○ slow.（緩慢的）
   ○ graceful.（優雅的）

2. 第二段中的單字「imperceptible」，意思最接近於
   ○ dangerous.（危險的）
   ○ insignificant.（微不足道的）
   ○ unnoticeable.（難以察覺的）
   ○ impassible.（不可通過的）

4-2-2 掌握要領：詞彙題回答技巧

練習 1　間接定義：on average, glaciers move a mere 30 centimeters a day
　　　　轉折詞：However
練習 2　字首：im- 定義：不
練習 3　第一題：hurried　第二題：dangerous
練習 4　(answers may vary) gradual: proceeding by steps or degrees; imperceptible: extremely slight or subtle

4-3 題型練習

A.

第一段主旨：its location plays a large role in the climate of the region
第二段主旨：The latitude of the Atlantic Archipelago undoubtedly influences its climate.
第三段主旨：The islands enjoy mild temperatures largely because of their proximity to the ocean.

4-4 綜合演練

A.

1. many animals have developed multiple strategies for obtaining poison through poison sequestration

2. One method of poison sequestration involves obtaining toxins from plant sources.
3. Another poison sequestration strategy involves obtaining poison from other animals.
4. It is also common for poison sequestration to progress up the food chain, meaning that many predators sequester poison from prey that have also sequestered poison.

B.

1.
[A] ✗　雖然 suddenly 可以用在這個句子裡，但它不符合文章的整體意思。
[D] ✗　這種毒素會導致一些動物心臟病發作，所以吃下這種毒物並非無害。
[B] ✗　這個選項不合邏輯，因為沒有理由說掠食者只會吃下部分的毒物。
[C] ✓　攻擊冠鼠的動物並不知道牠有毒，因此牠是意外吃下這種毒物的。

2.
[B] ✗　文章中沒有任何暗示說毒物截存在較大型動物中更為常見。
[D] ✗　作者描述了幾種小型動物截存毒物的情況，因為牠們無法自行產生毒物。
[C] ✗　作者僅提到一種動物將毒物儲存在特殊的囊袋中。
[A] ✓　作者提到大型動物較容易透過捕獵其他生物來獲取毒物，因此推測小型動物更有可能從植物中獲得毒物。

3.
[A] ✗　雖然 slather 和 gather 看起來相似，但它們並不具有相同的意思。
[B] ✗　toss 的意思是將物品扔到空中，文章中沒有暗示這是作者所指的動作。
[D] ✓　slather 的意思是在某物上塗抹一層厚厚的物質，這是正確的選項。
[C] ✗　這個選項不合邏輯，因為動物不太可能把殘餘物丟在自己身上。

4.

[B] ✗ 文章沒有提供任何資訊可支持大部分蛇從青蛙那裡截存毒素的觀點。

[C] ✓ 作者提到掠食者通常吃掉已經從植物等來源截存毒素的動物。這表示即使掠食者不吃植物，也可能從植物來源截存毒素。

[A] ✗ 作者沒有提供任何資訊來支持這個推論。

[D] ✗ 作者說許多昆蟲的毒素來自於植物，而不是植物從昆蟲那裡獲得毒素。

4-5 實戰演練

TOEFL Reading

Question

月球的起源

1　十九世紀和二十世紀期間，幾位天文學家提出關於月球形成的競爭性理論。例如在 1878 年，天文學家喬治‧霍華德‧達爾文提出了分裂理論，該理論聲稱在地球形成初期，行星開始極快旋轉。達爾文認為，快速旋轉的運動導致地球裂掉一大塊，並飛入太空中。接著此碎片開始繞著地球運行，成為了月球。另一個解釋叫做共同形成理論，它聲稱在太陽系形成時，一顆恆星爆炸並留下大量碎片。根據共同形成理論，地球和月球是在大致相同的時間和過程中，從這些碎片中形成的。

2　這些理論在科學界得到的接受程度不同，對於哪個理論提供最完整的月球形成過程，科學家之間進行過多次辯論。但最終，這兩個理論在二十世紀下半葉時被顛覆了。在此時，從月球任務獲得的新資料，揭露了這些理論的假設與月球事實間存有幾個不一致之處。首先，收集到的月球資料顯示，月球在某個時間點曾受到強烈高溫的影響。然而，無論是分裂理論還是共同形成理論都沒有提到導致強烈高溫的過程。此外，也沒有證據指出地球經歷了類似的強烈高溫。因此，這兩個理論都被認為是無效的。

3　月球探索資料還揭露了與共同形成理論的另一個差異。根據此理論，地球和月球是經由相同的過程在相同的時間形成的。科學家指出，如果地球和月球實際上是這樣形成的話，它們應具有相同的化學組成構造。但當科學家從月球表面取得樣本時，他們發現月球的化學組成與地球不同，這嚴重損害了共同形成理論的可信度。

4　來自月球探索的資訊在消除先前的月球形成理論上扮演了重大的角色，而它也幫助天文學家制定了一個能更好解釋月球形成的理論。如今，最新和普遍被接受的解釋稱為大碰撞理論。根據這個理論，太陽系中的所有行星是在同一時間形成的。除了目前在我們太陽系中的行星外，科學家相信還有一個名為特亞的行星在此時期發展。特亞的直徑可能有 4000 英里左右，大約是火星的大小。在地球形成期間，特亞撞擊地球並且瓦解。科學家認為，地球和特亞的碰撞導致地球至少破碎出兩塊大塊物質，其中較大的一塊被認為形成了月球。與此同時，科學家認為，較小的碎片，大概是月球大小的三分之一，也曾繞地球運行了一段時間。這兩塊碎片大約在 1000 萬年到 1 億年之間，一起繞著地球運行。接著當較小的月球撞上較大的月球時，最終被摧毀了。

5　與以往的理論不同，大碰撞理論充分解釋了大部分收集到的月球資料。例如，該理論解釋了為什麼有證據指出月球受到強烈高溫的影響，而地球上卻沒有這樣的證據。科學家推測，當特亞撞擊地球時，在碰撞點產生了強烈高溫。此外，直接受到特亞撞擊的大塊物質，很可能是從地球破碎出來並形成月球的物質。這也解釋了地球和月球化學組成不同的原因——形成月球的噴射物質主要來自地球的表面。因此，形成月球的大塊物質僅代表了地球組成的一部分。

1. 根據第一段的資訊，可以推論達爾文的月球形成理論是什麼？
   ○ 它是第一個被廣泛接受的月球形成理論。
   ○ 它假設地球和月球是由相同的物質製成的。
   ○ 它受到其他科學家的共同形成理論研究啟發。
   ○ 它解釋了地球和月球為什麼在不同時間形成。

2. 在第二段裡，「undermined」的意思最接近於：
   ○ dismissed（不考慮、去除）。
   ○ weakened（削弱）。
   ○ proven（證明）。
   ○ expanded（擴大）。

3. 在第二段裡，作者暗示了：
   ○ 比起分裂理論，大多數科學家更支持共同形成理論。
   ○ 月球探索提供了支持分裂理論的證據。
   ○ 來自月球任務的資料，不是科學界所有群體都能獲取的。
   ○ 直到 1950 年代之後，月球的化學組成才被了解。

4. 在第四段裡，「disintegrated」的意思最接近於：
   ○ 變得更大。
   ○ 軟化。
   ○ 分解。
   ○ 消失。

5. 第四段中的資訊對於大碰撞理論暗示了什麼？
   ○ 許多天文學家仍在爭論其準確性。
   ○ 它無法解釋行星提亞後來的情況。
   ○ 它描述了多個月球的形成。
   ○ 它密切建立在共同形成理論上。

6. 在第五段裡，「speculate」的意思最接近於：
   ○ theorize（推測）。
   ○ confirm（確認）。
   ○ overlook（忽略）。
   ○ reveal（揭露）。

5-1-1 句子摘要／簡化題範例

A.

1. 下列哪一項最能表達醒目標示句的必要資訊？錯誤選項會在意思上產生重大改變或遺漏必要資訊。
   ○ 發明家們創造了一項新技術，可同時錄製聲音和影像，以解決聲音同步的問題。
   ○ 電影製片人創造的有聲電影技術，解決了他們在把聲音添加到電影中時很少遇到的問題。
   ○ 為解決同步問題，電影製片人使用了一種技術，允許他們在拍攝後，另外將聲音添加到影像中。
   ○ 利用發明家創造的技術來使電影的影像和聲音元素同步。

5-1-2 掌握要領：句子摘要／簡化題回答技巧

練習1 改述請自行作答，應要與正確答案相似

練習2 The video and audio elements of movies were synchronized using technology that was created by inventors.（利用發明家創造的技術來使電影的影像和聲音元素同步。）
   缺少的資訊：此選項並未描述發明家創造此新技術想解決的問題。

練習3 Sound-on-film technology created by filmmakers fixed a problem that they had rarely faced when adding sound to films.（電影製片人創造的有聲電影技術，解決了他們在把聲音添加到電影中時很少遇到的問題。）
   對語意的改變：該問題是持續存在的，而不是很罕見的。

練習4 To solve the problem of synchronization, filmmakers used technology that allowed them to add sound to pictures separately after filming.（為解決同步的問題，電影製片人使用了一種技術，允許他們在拍攝後另外將聲音添加到影像中。）
   錯誤原因：此選項所包含的資訊與文章中的事實互相矛盾。

5-2-1 段落／文章摘要題範例

A.

1. 以下是簡短摘要文章的引言句。請完成摘要，選出三個最能表達文章重要概念的選項。有些句子並不屬於此摘要，因它們表達了文章中未提及的概念，或是為次要概念。此題總共 2 分。

這篇文章討論了美國南方的文學。

- 2. 美國南方的獨特性，透過南方文學中的多種特徵呈現出來。
- 4. 家庭關係是許多南方作品中的核心主題。
- 6. 像尤多拉‧韋爾蒂這樣的南方作家，經常詳細描述南方的背景環境。

選項

1. 十九世紀末到二十世紀初活躍的南方作家，是美國文學中最重要的文學人物。
2. 美國南方的獨特性，透過南方文學中的多種特徵呈現出來。
3. 美國南方的經濟活動主要集中在城市。
4. 家庭關係是許多南方作品中的核心主題。
5. 福克納的故事聚焦在他自己家族所發生的事件上。
6. 像尤多拉‧韋爾蒂這樣的南方作家，經常詳細描述南方的背景環境。

5-2-2 掌握要領：段落／文章摘要題回答技巧

練習 1　第一段：While the literature of the American South is diverse, Southern writers—especially those who worked in the late nineteenth and early twentieth centuries—often employed similar strategies to explore the distinct character of the region.

第二段：Family relationships are a central theme found often in Southern writing.

第三段：In addition to writing about subjects that reflect the values of Southern culture, Southern writers also created similar settings or locations in their works.

練習 2　Southern writers who worked during the late nineteenth and early twentieth centuries are among the most

important literary figures of American literature.（十九世紀末到二十世紀初活躍的南方作家，是美國文學中最重要的文學人物。）

練習 3　Faulkner's stories focused on events that happened to his own family.（福克納的故事聚焦在他自己家族所發生的事件上。）

練習 4　The economy of the American South was largely centered in cities.（美國南方的經濟主要集中在城市。）

5-3 題型練習

A.

第一段主旨：Interestingly, silversmithing is a relatively recent art form in the Navajo culture, but it is one that craftspeople have transformed into a uniquely Navajo creation that is an important part of modern Navajo culture and commerce.

第二段主旨：The origins of Navajo silversmithing can be traced back to a man named Atsidi Chon, who is widely regarded as the father of Navajo silversmithing.

第三段主旨：Today, the work of Navajo silversmiths clearly reflects designs that are culturally important to the group.

第四段主旨：Some elements of Navajo silverwork are clearly influenced by other cultures.

5-4 綜合演練

A.

1. these routes were important because they allowed the exchange of both goods and ideas
2. This kind of trade was very profitable because goods that were common in one place were priceless and exotic in another.
3. The trade routes brought many different cultures together, and they often exchanged ideas as well as material goods.

B.

1.

[C] ✗ 工匠從出售外國產品的複製品中致富，貿易路線上的居民透過為旅行者提供服務來賺錢。文章沒有說明這些族群參與了商人的貿易。

[B] ✗ 在文章中，作者說服務是由沿著貿易路線居住的人提供的，而不是由商人和工匠提供的。

[D] ✓ 醒目標示句說歐亞大陸上的貿易為商人、工匠和沿途居民帶來了財富。

[A] ✗ 文章中沒有提到，為居住在貿易路線上的居民提供服務的人是誰。

2.

[B] ✗ 在第一段裡，作者說儘管存在障礙，但歐亞大陸的文化之間會彼此接觸。

[F] ✗ 作者沒有描述絲綢之路上所產生的藝術形式。

[A] ✓ 這一句概述了整篇文章的主旨，寫在文章的第一段。

[E] ✓ 在第三段裡，作者描述了透過絲綢之路所做的思想和藝術形式的交流。

[C] ✗ 在第二段裡，作者說絲綢之路的擴展是由於來自波斯、印度和埃及等地的商人尋求中國的商品，而不是反過來。

[D] ✓ 作者說這條路起初是中國商人為了銷售絲綢而開發的，但後來也有來自不同地方的商人交易其他物品，故而隨之擴展。

5-5 實戰演練

TOEFL Reading

Question

斯特拉迪瓦里小提琴

1　安東尼奧・斯特拉迪瓦里是意大利十七世紀中葉著名的製琴師。斯特拉迪瓦里在十二歲時，開始他的職業生涯，當時他在另一位著名的製琴師尼科洛・阿馬蒂的帶領下工作。斯特拉迪瓦里從阿馬蒂那裡學到了製作小提琴的基本技能，但最終他發展出自己的風格，至今仍然享有盛譽。在斯特拉迪瓦里的一生中，他大約製造了1000 把小提琴，現存於世的有 450 把。安東尼奧・斯特拉迪瓦里的小提琴被普遍認為是世界上最精緻的弦樂器，無論在音質

還是視覺上的吸引力，都幾乎超越了所有其他樂器。然而，儘管人們普遍承認其品質卓越，對於斯特拉迪瓦里小提琴之所以如此不同凡響，仍存在很多爭議。

2　一些專家認為，小提琴的優越品質源於它們的結構。雖然他早期的小提琴與阿馬蒂的樂器有很大的相似之處，但這位才華橫溢的製琴師後來經由實驗小提琴聲音孔的形狀而改變了標準的小提琴結構。此外，他還改變了貫穿在小提琴背部和前端的裝飾線寬度。這些結構性的改變使小提琴能產生更大的聲音，進而使小提琴演奏者能在更大的音樂廳演出，因聲音可傳達到場地的最後一排。

3　儘管對小提琴結構的改變使演奏者能演奏得更大聲，但專業小提琴演奏者們主張，這些改變並不能充分說明它們比其他小提琴優越的原因。他們解釋道，斯特拉迪瓦里小提琴的卓越處，不僅在於它們所能達到的音量，還在於它們能以不損失品質的情況下產生較大的聲音。

4　直接影響優越音質的因素之一，也許是斯特拉迪瓦里用於樂器的漆。斯特拉迪瓦里以同樣的過程，為他的每件作品上色。首先，他塗上一層類似於油畫所使用的油。接著他添加一層油性樹脂，一種像釉的物質。最後，他塗上一層紅色染料，讓這些樂器擁有斯特拉迪瓦里小提琴的經典顏色。一些專家認為，簡單的油漆能保護木材的振動能力，這種品質使得樂器能夠發出聲音。這個假設得到了研究支持，研究人員測試了不同類型的漆對聲音品質的影響。他們發現，使用油性漆染色的小提琴（如同斯特拉迪瓦里小提琴），能發出最優美的聲音。

5　斯特拉迪瓦里小提琴所用的木材或許也能解釋它們的獨特品質。分析指出，這些小提琴由密實的木材製成，為對聲音品質有重要影響的特徵。這是因為密實木材中的

顆粒比較緊密，造成了清晰、持久的振動。因此，使用密實木材製成的小提琴可在不損失品質的情況下，將聲音傳到遠處。

6　有一段時間，許多人認為斯特拉迪瓦里是從古老的大教堂和城堡中獲取這些密實木材。然而現代研究指出，它實際上可能起源於斯特拉迪瓦里家附近的雲杉森林。如今，這些森林的木材不是很密實，但有跡象指出，在被稱為「蒙德極小期」的期間，它曾經比較密實。此期間從 1645 年持續到 1715 年，歐洲出現了異常寒冷的現象，是歐洲 500 年來經歷過最寒冷的時期。寒冷的溫度可能由太陽活動減少引起，據說它減緩了樹木生長速度，使木材比在較暖和的生長條件下更加密實。一位研究人員不僅查明了，該時期的寒冷溫度導致斯特拉迪瓦里家附近森林中的樹木生長緩慢，且還指出他使用這些森林的雲杉木來製作他的樂器。

1. 下列哪一項最能表達第二段裡醒目標示句中的必要資訊？錯誤選項會對意思產生重大改變或遺漏必要資訊。

　○ 小提琴結構的變化增加了樂器音量，使小提琴演奏者能在更大的場地演奏，因為聲音能被聽到。

　○ 小提琴演奏者可以在更大的表演場地演出，因為小提琴結構的改變使得小提琴演奏者能輕鬆表演。

　○ 在小提琴基本設計結構改變前，幾乎沒有大型的表演場地供小提琴演奏者演出。

　○ 小提琴的結構改變使其能發出更大的聲音，但聲音品質略有下降。

2. 下列哪一項最能表達第六段裡醒目標示句中的必要資訊？錯誤選項會對意思產生重大改變或遺漏必要資訊。

　○ 密實木材可以生長在溫暖的地區，但在太陽活動降低和氣溫低於正常溫度的地方更常見。

　○ 密實木材與樹木生長緩慢有關，是在太陽活動降低期間的寒冷溫度中產生的。

　○ 太陽活動降低導致樹木生長緩慢，因為生長受到寒冷溫度和木材密度影響。

　○ 太陽活動降低期間的寒冷溫度造成樹木生長緩慢，使得這些原本應生長在較暖和溫度下的樹木變得較不密實。

3. 以下是簡短摘要文章的引言句。請完成摘要，選出三個最能表達文章重要概念的選項。有些句子並不屬於該摘要，因為它們表達了文章中未提到的概念，或是文章中的次要概念。此題總共 2 分。

這篇文章討論了造成斯特拉迪瓦里小提琴優美音質的特點。

　▪ 2. 斯特拉迪瓦里以改變小提琴的結構方式，提高了它們創造響亮和清晰聲音的能力。

　▪ 5. 斯特拉迪瓦里小提琴上的油性塗層處理可能對其音質有幫助，因為它保留了木材的振動能力。

　▪ 6. 用於製作斯特拉迪瓦里小提琴的密實木材，是樂器音質優越的一個因素，它們可能來自斯特拉迪瓦里家附近的一片森林。

選項

1. 今日僅存450把斯特拉迪瓦里小提琴，它是世界上最有價值的樂器之一。

2. 斯特拉迪瓦里以改變小提琴結構的方式，提高了它們創造響亮和清晰聲音的能力。

3. 斯特拉迪瓦里小提琴的演奏者能夠在大型場地演出，因為樂器的聲音足夠響亮，能夠在遠距離內被聽到。

4. 研究人員查明，斯特拉迪瓦里小提琴的卓越振動品質來自於它的上漆過程。

5. 斯特拉迪瓦里小提琴上的油性塗層處理可能對其音質有幫助，因為它保留了木材的振動能力。

6. 用於製作斯特拉迪瓦里小提琴的密實木材，是樂器音質優越的一個因素，它們可能來自斯特拉迪瓦里家附近的一片森林。

6-1 文句插入題

A.

1. 請看第二段標有四個黑色方塊 [■] 的地方，這些方塊指示了下列句子可插入到文章中的位置。

223

因此，這些地區的農業生產力下降了 20%。
此句最適合放在哪裡？

○ a
○ b
○ c
○ d

6-1-1 掌握要領：文句插入題回答技巧

練習 1　插入句：As a result, the agricultural productivity in these areas has declined by 20 percent.

主旨：Waterlogging, a state in which the ground becomes oversaturated with water, is a particularly harmful effect of irrigation.

練習 2　When; Thus; Additionally

練習 3　c

6-2 題型練習

A.

第一段主旨：Advances in medical sciences have made it possible to control the disease, but malaria is difficult to eradicate entirely for several reasons.

第二段主旨：Though early doctors developed some treatments for malaria using plants and herbs, it was not until the true nature of the disease was discovered that it was possible to formulate a more effective treatment.

第三段主旨：Today, medical researchers have made several developments in controlling the spread of malaria.

第四段主旨：Despite these advancements in treating and preventing malaria, the disease is still a worldwide problem.

6-3 綜合演練

A.

1. Despite its size, a number of geological discoveries suggest that the Mediterranean may have entirely dried up about five million to 12 million years ago.

2. Based on the depth of the layers of non-oceanic materials at the bottom of, many scientists argue that evaporation was caused by the Mediterranean becoming separated from the Atlantic Ocean.

3. The evaporation of the Mediterranean had significant effects locally and globally.

4. However, this desert eventually became a sea again.

B.

1.

[B] ✗　此處之後的句子提到不太可能在海底發現的其他物質，如硬石膏。將插入句放在這裡會破壞段落思路。

[A] ✗　此處之後的句子繼續討論海底的反射性物質，因此將插入句放在這裡是不合邏輯的。

[D] ✓　此處之前的句子第一次提到硬石膏。這是插入句最合乎邏輯的位置，因為它提供了有關發現硬石膏的更多細節，並支持了地中海曾經乾涸的理論。

[C] ✗　此處之後的句子第一次提到硬石膏，因此插入句不太可能放在此。

2.

[D] ✗　此處之前的句子描述的是，科學家相信大西洋被隔絕後地中海花了多久時間乾涸。這裡並不適合插入負濕度平衡的定義。

[A] ✓　插入句提供了負濕度平衡的定義，因此，它最有可能放在第一次提到負濕度平衡的句子之後。

[C] ✗　此處之前的句子討論了造成地中海與大西洋隔絕的可能事件，在此放置插入句會破壞段落流暢性。

[B] ✗　此處之前的句子提到了負濕度平衡可能對地中海產生的影響，在此引入定義的可能性不大。

TOEFL Reading

Question

探測太陽系外行星

1　太陽系外行星是指位於地球太陽系之外的行星。[a] ■ 和我們太陽系中繞著太陽公轉的行星一樣，太陽系外行星在銀河系中也繞行恆星公轉。[b] ■ 此外，這些行星或許能提供有關天文過程的資訊，例如恆星的形成，這有助於科學家了解我們太陽系的起源。[c] ■ 然而，由於太陽系外行星位於太陽系之外，因此非常難偵測。令發現這些外行星任務更複雜的是，作為成熟的行星，它們並沒有自己的光源，而且它們所繞行恆星發出的強光，通常會使它們變得模糊不清。[d] ■ 儘管存在這些困難，科學家已想出幾種偵測太陽系外行星的方法。

2　定位太陽系外行星的主要方法是間接性的，也就是說，它們牽涉到從太陽系外行星本身之外的其他物體進行測量。舉例來說，徑向速度測量法涉及計算一顆恆星對繞著它公轉的太陽系外行星運動的變化。當一顆太陽系外行星繞著一顆恆星公轉時，它會改變恆星的速度，或者說是恆星行進的速度。地球上的儀器可以測量星光在空間中的運動，從數十億光年外就能檢測到恆星速度的變化。[a] ■ 透過計算遠處恆星的這些變化，科學家可確定是否有任何太陽系外行星在它們周圍公轉。[b] ■ 此外，此方法還為研究人員提供有關造成速度變化之太陽系外的行星質量資訊。[c] ■ 通常，使用此方法發現的太陽系外行星都非常巨大。[d] ■ 不過，研究人員正在改進此方法，以便也能偵測到較小的行星。

3　徑向速度測量法提供了有關太陽系外行星質量的資訊，但使用另一種叫凌日法的間接偵測技術，科學家可以收集有關太陽系外行星大小的其他資訊。[a] ■ 最重要的是，凌日法有助於觀察者測定太陽系外行星的半徑，即行星中心到行星表面的距離。[b] ■ 當一顆行星介於一顆恆星和用於觀察它的儀器之間時，恆星的光線會暫時變暗。[c] ■ 因此，透過測量恆星的光輸出，科學家可以判定一顆太陽系外行星是否穿越了該恆星和他們的望遠鏡之間。[d] ■ 使用此方法的科學家不僅關注恆星的光輸出強度，還關注任何輸出變化頻率。利用這些資訊，再加上太陽系外行星在通過恆星前所產生的陰影大小，科學家便能推斷出行星大小。半徑較大的行星與較小的行星相比，會讓恆星光線更明顯變暗。

4　除了這些間接方法外，研究人員也一直在開發新技術，希望能更容易直接獲取太陽系外行星的影像。他們正在開發能夠過濾恆星光芒並產生極其清晰影像的儀器，使科學家能將太陽系外行星與其繞行的恆星區分開來。有些科學家一直在研究改良日冕儀器的可能性。日冕儀器最初用於阻擋太陽光，以便研究其周圍較暗的光線。[a] ■ 經過一些修改後，日冕儀器阻擋大量光線的能力或許能用於偵測太陽系外行星。[b] ■ 不同於普通望遠鏡，干涉儀使用由數個鏡子組成的系統，並從許多不同角度收集影像。[c] ■ 將多個影像結合在一起之後，太陽系外行星相對暗淡的光線被增強，讓科學家可觀察到更明顯的影像。[d] ■

---

1. 請看第一段中標示四個黑色方塊 [■] 的地方，這些方塊指示了下列句子可以插入到文章中的可能位置。

   對太陽系外行星的研究主要受到一個可能性驅使，即其他太陽系可能含有類似地球的行星，具備支持生命的能力。

   這句話最適合放在哪裡？

   ○ a
   ○ b
   ○ c
   ○ d

2. 請看第二段中標示四個黑色方塊 [■] 的地方，
   這些方塊指示了下列句子可已以插入到文章中
   的可能位置。
   這是因為質量較大的行星會使恆星運動速度變
   化更明顯。
   這句話最適合放在哪裡？
   ○ a
   ○ b
   ○ c
   ○ d

3. 請看第三段中標示四個黑色方塊 [■] 的地方，
   這些方塊指示了下列句子可以插入到文章中的
   可能位置。
   研究人員利用觀察恆星所發出的光來測量太陽
   系外行星的大小。
   這句話最適合放在哪裡？
   ○ a
   ○ b
   ○ c
   ○ d

4. 請看第四段中標示四個黑色方塊 [■] 的地方，
   這些方塊指示了下列句子可以插入到文章中的
   可能位置。
   其他研究人員正專注研究干涉儀的技術。
   這句話最適合放在哪裡？
   ○ a
   ○ b
   ○ c
   ○ d

PASSAGE 1

英國布料貿易的衰落

1　英國在經歷了 45 年的女王統治時期後，伊
莉莎白一世的繼任者詹姆士一世於 1603 年
成為英國國王，此時正是英國經濟艱難時
期。英國當時人口膨脹、糧食生產不足，
且物價高漲。儘管不穩定，但一些企業為
英國經濟帶來了可靠的收入。其中特別的
是，許多商人依賴將布料出口到歐洲大陸
來維持生計。在詹姆士一世統治的前十年
裡，布料貿易蓬勃發展，成為英國一項重

要的收入來源。然而，國王卻犯下一個嚴
重錯誤，最終導致英國布料貿易的衰落。

2　在 1614 年，英國商人暨政治家威廉·科克
恩提出，詹姆士一世應對英國出口布料的
方式做出劇烈改變。當時英國主要生產未
加工的布料，這表示他們出售的布料未經
過染色、漂白或其他處理。荷蘭的公司通
常從英國購買未加工布料，並自行完成加
工。荷蘭人是精通於完成布料所需之複雜
程序和技術的專家，這些過程為他們從英
國購買的未加工布料增添相當大的價值。
因此，荷蘭布料公司能夠用比英國更高的
價格出售他們的貨物。科克恩希望將這些
利潤轉移到英國公司，因此建議英國自行
完成布料加工，以提高布料出口的價值。
他還要求詹姆士一世成立一家公司，並讓
公司在科克恩的領導下運作，如此便能控
制和壟斷將成品布料出口到歐洲大陸的事
業。國王需要錢，增加收入的可能性吸引
了他，因此他同意科克恩的計劃，並按照
科克恩的要求成立了「國王商人公司」，
主要目的為出口成品布料。

3　然而，科克恩的計畫打亂了之前穩定的英
國布料貿易，最終由於許多原因無疾而
終。首先，詹姆斯一世對科克恩公司的支
持造成國王與許多強大英國商人間產生裂
痕，特別是為了支持科克恩集團而被忽視
的未加工布料公司「商人公司」的成員。
此外，先前一直是歐洲主要成品布料供應
商的荷蘭人，以拒絕購買任何英國布料產
品來反映其競爭，許多其他歐洲國家也做
出了同樣的反應。此外，其他國家的商人
拒絕運送英國布料，或向英國商人收取提
高的運輸費用。海外抵制重創了「國王商
人公司」，因為它無法負擔運輸至歐洲市
場所需的船隻。

4　除了因普遍不受歡迎而引起的種種困難
外，科克恩的公司也無法生產優質的商
品。首先，科克恩沒有資金購買成品布料
所需的機器。[a] ■ 再者，英國布料製造商
不是加工過程的專家，比不上競爭對手荷

蘭所生產的高品質成品布料。[b] ■ 在公司成立僅僅三年後的 1617 年，詹姆斯一世就解散了「國王商人公司」。[c] ■

5 「國王商人公司」的失敗不僅使支持它的人破產，[d] ■ 科克恩的計劃不但對布料貿易造成損害，也對其他產業帶來了災難性的經濟影響。在「國王商人公司」的領導下，超過 500 個家庭開始生產成品布料。然而，由於產品無法出售，他們的生意失敗了。這導致失業率上升，甚至在倫敦和其他地方引發了暴動。此外，先前有利的貿易關係已被摧毀，未加工布料的賣家必須努力與願意購買他們商品的歐洲買家重新建立關係。儘管詹姆斯一世已經將權力還給了「商人公司」的成員，該組織對業務上所遭受的損害仍感到憤慨。由於英國布料貿易從科克恩的實驗中恢復得十分緩慢，因此國際和國內的商業關係都十分緊繃。

1. 第一段裡的「succeeded」意思最接近於：
○ did away with（廢止、消除某人或某事）。
○ came after（跟隨、接著）。
○ turned aside（轉身避開）。
○ kept back（阻止、保留）。

答案解析
▶ 題型：詞彙題
✗ 「do away with sth」表示「消除某事」。沒有任何線索表明詹姆士一世廢止（殺死）了伊莉莎白一世。
✓ 「succeed」表示接替。詹姆士一世在伊莉莎白一世之後登基，所以這是正確答案。
✗ 「turn aside」表示轉身避開。這個定義在此句話中不適用。
✗ 「keep back」表示阻止某人做某事。沒有任何跡象表明詹姆士一世阻止伊莉莎白一世登基。

2. 在第一段裡，作者描述糧食生產不足為下列哪一事件的跡象：
○ 需要擴大英國的布料貿易。
○ 過分強調布料貿易的後果。
○ 1603 年英國糟糕的經濟狀況。
○ 國王對國家的管理不善。

答案解析
▶ 題型：功能題
✗ 作者說布料貿易是英國經濟的可靠收入來源之一。然而，沒有跡象顯示英國的布料貿易需要擴大。
✗ 在第一段中，作者提到布料貿易是英國少數成功的行業之一。沒有跡象顯示因為強調布料貿易而導致食物生產不足。
✓ 作者提到糧食生產不足和另外兩件事情為英國經濟陷入困境的跡象。
✗ 在文章裡沒有提到國王對國家的管理不善。

3. 根據第一段和第二段的資訊，關於成立「國王商人公司」之前的英國布料貿易，可推斷出下列哪一項：
○ 為了支持航運和農業行業而忽略它。
○ 它是英國經濟上唯一有利可圖的產業。
○ 它導致英國必需品價格上漲。
○ 它由好幾家公司與國際夥伴合作。

答案解析
▶ 題型：推論題
✗ 在第一段裡，作者說布料貿易是英國少數成功的行業之一。因此它不太可能因為政府著重其他行業而被忽略。
✗ 作者說布料貿易是英國少數成功的產業之一，但我們不能假設它是唯一成功的產業。
✗ 作者提到英國的物價很高，但根據文章內容，我們無法得知是不是由布料貿易所造成的。
✓ 作者說「國王商人公司」被賦予出口的壟斷權，表示在這家公司成立前，有許多其他公司從事英國布料的出口。作者還提到，英國未加工的布料被送往荷蘭公司，這些公司被認為是國際合作夥伴。

4. 根據第二段的資訊，威廉・科克恩提出了下列所有對英國布料貿易的變革，除了：
○ 建立一家專門處理布料貿易的公司。
○ 專注於增加英國生產的布料的價值。
○ 中止向荷蘭商人供應布料。
○ 轉變英國布料工業的主要活動。

答案解析

▶ 題型：挑錯題

ㄨ 在第二段裡，作者說科克恩要求詹姆士一世創立一家公司，負責處理所有英國布料的出口。

ㄨ 在第二段裡，作者解釋說科克恩建議英國布料製造商自行加工布料，他們便能以更高的價格出售。

✓ 雖然科克恩希望英國布料製造商自行加工布料，從而與荷蘭人競爭，但他並沒有計劃讓英國停止向荷蘭商人出售布料。

ㄨ 科克恩希望英國人自行加工布料，而不只是將未加工的布料送到其他國家。這代表了英國布料產業主要活動的轉變。

5. 下列哪一項最能表達第二段裡醒目標示句中的必要資訊？錯誤選項會對意思產生重大改變或遺漏必要資訊。

　　○ 成品布料的程序和技術通常十分複雜，主要由荷蘭工人操作。

　　○ 來自英國的未加工布料通常由荷蘭人加工製成，他們利用複雜的程序製造出更有價值的布料，是這方面的專家。

　　○ 由於處理布料的過程複雜，因此來自英國的成品布料通常比荷蘭布料更有價值。

　　○ 來自英國的未加工布料失去了價值，因荷蘭人能利用專業技術製造成品布料。

答案解析

▶ 題型：句子摘要題

ㄨ 這個選項遺漏了已加工布料比未加工布料更有價值的重要資訊。

✓ 這句話包含了醒目標示句中的兩個關鍵重點：荷蘭人通常加工布料，而加工布料讓荷蘭商人能以更高的價格出售。

ㄨ 這個選項包含不實訊息。醒目標示句沒有談論來自英國的加工布料，而是談論了為什麼荷蘭人能以更高價出售他們最初從英國買來的布料。

ㄨ 這個選項包含不實訊息。來自英國的布料並沒有失去其價值，而是來自荷蘭的布料更有價值，因為它經過加工。

6. 根據第二段的資訊，國王為什麼同意科克恩的提議？

　　○ 他急於迅速改善英國經濟。

　　○ 他相信這些改變能使英國擴大紡織工業。

　　○ 他擔心英國過度依賴與荷蘭的貿易夥伴關係。

　　○ 他想促進英國工業的技術進步。

答案解析

▶ 題型：細節題

✓ 在文章中，作者提到英國經濟困難，國王需要錢。這些事實顯示國王渴望改善經濟。

ㄨ 沒有跡象顯示國王有興趣擴大布料貿易。

ㄨ 作者沒有提到英國依賴與荷蘭的貿易夥伴關係。

ㄨ 作者提到荷蘭有加工布料的技術，但並未說國王批准科克恩計畫的動機是鼓勵英國的技術進步。

7. 第三段裡的「inflated」意思最接近於：

　　○ unfair（不公平的）。

　　○ special（特別的）。

　　○ secret（祕密的）。

　　○ increased（增加的）。

答案解析

▶ 題型：詞彙題

ㄨ 雖然「unfair」在句子中是合適的，但無法從上下文中看出這是正確答案。

ㄨ 「special」在句子中是合適的，但它並不是「inflated」的正確意思。

ㄨ 沒有線索指出費用是祕密的（secret）。

✓ 「inflated」表示 increased（增加的），貨運公司提高了對英國商人的運輸費用。

8. 根據第四段，下列哪一項因素導致「國王商人公司」無法生產優質商品？

　　○ 它沒有從國王那裡獲得財務支持。

　　○ 它無法負擔支付布料加工專家的費用。

　　○ 它的員工缺乏有關布料加工的必要知識。

　　○ 它的未加工布料供應不足。

答案解析

▶ 題型：細節題

ㄨ 沒有提到國王是否向該公司提供了財務支持。

ㄨ 作者沒有提及支付布料加工專家的成本，或者

公司是否負擔得起聘起他們的費用。

✓ 作者說英國布料製造商缺乏荷蘭同行的專業知識。因此，他們的成品布料在品質上無法與荷蘭相比。

✗ 作者說在科克恩計劃之前，英國向其他國家提供未加工的布料，因此他們不太可能沒有足夠的布料來加工。

9. 請看第四和第五段中標示四個黑色方塊 [■] 的地方，這些方塊指示了下列句子可以插入到文章中的可能位置。

他也恢復了之前的布料出口公司「商人公司」的營運。

這句話最適合放在哪裡？

○ a
○ b
○ c
○ d

答案解析
▶ **題型：文句插入題**

✗ 前面講述了為什麼「國王商人公司」無法生產質量優良的成品布料。因此，如果將插入句放在這裡，會破壞文意的連貫性。

✗ 後面才討論了「國王商人公司」的失敗，如果把插入句放在這裡並不合理。

✓ 前面討論了「國王商人公司」的失敗，插入句的「also」表示了思路的延續，所以這是最合適的位置。

✗ 前面提到了科克恩計劃失敗的後果，因此，與國王行動有關的句子並不適合放在這裡。

10. 以下是簡短摘要文章的引言句。請完成摘要，選出三個最能表達文章重要概念的選項。有些句子並不屬於該摘要，因為它們表達了文章中未提到的概念，或是文章中的次要概念。此題總共 2 分。

儘管 17 世紀的經濟困難重重，英國仍有一些可觀的收入來源，包括布料生產。

▪ 2. 為了增加利潤，詹姆斯國王建立了一家公司來加工布料並控制貿易。

▪ 3. 英國布料製造商的產品品質，無法與國外生產的布料相比，導致國王的公司失敗。

▪ 6. 當時，英國將未加工布料出口到其他國

家，其他國家加工後再以更高的價格轉售。

選項

1. 威廉·科克恩是一位英國政治家和商人，了解布料貿易。
2. 為了增加利潤，詹姆斯國王建立了一家公司來加工布料並控制貿易。
3. 英國布料製造商的產品品質，無法與國外生產的布料相比，導致國王的公司失敗。
4. 荷蘭商人從沒原諒國王，布料貿易也沒有恢復。
5. 在國王商人公司失敗後，大約有 500 名商人破產。
6. 當時，英國將未加工布料出口到其他國家，其他國家加工後再以更高的價格轉售。

答案解析
▶ **題型：段落／文章摘要題**

✗ 1. 威廉·科克恩是一位英國政治家和商人，了解布料貿易。此敘述不應是文章摘要的一部分。這句話是文章中的一個次要觀點，且含有未提供的資訊——威廉·科克恩了解布料貿易之事。

✓ 2. 為增加利潤，詹姆斯國王建立了一家公司來加工布料並控制貿易。

✓ 3. 英國布料製造商的產品品質，無法與國外生產的布料相比，導致國王的公司失敗。

✗ 4. 荷蘭商人從沒原諒國王，布料貿易也沒有恢復。此敘述不應是文章摘要的一部分。這句話是文章中的一個次要觀點，且含有錯誤的資訊——我們從文章中得知英國布料貿易恢復得很慢。

✗ 5. 公司失敗後，大約有 500 名商人破產。此敘述不應是文章摘要的一部分。這句話是文章中的一個次要觀點。

✓ 6. 當時，英國將未加工布料出口到其他國家，其他國家加工後再以更高的價格轉售。

鳥類是否從恐龍演化而來？

1　在 19 世紀中葉，科學家們發現一種叫做「始祖鳥」的完整恐龍骨骼，該生物的體型最大或許有生長到一呎半左右，據推測生存於約 1.5 億年前。奇特的是，它不僅具有像恐龍一樣的特徵，還有現代鳥類的特徵。舉例來說，它像當時的恐龍一樣擁有鋒利的牙齒和骨尾，但也具有像現代鳥類一樣的翅膀和羽毛。儘管與鳥類有這些相似之處，當時科學界的普遍共識為，關係與恐龍最密切的生物是爬蟲類，像是蜥蜴和鱷魚。直到1969年古生物學家發現了一種叫恐爪龍的恐龍化石，才又重新開啟了關於鳥類是否從恐龍演化而來的辯論。

2　認為恐龍與現代鳥類有關理論（同時也是支持最接近恐龍的現存原型實際上是爬蟲類的主要論據）的主要問題是，人們相信恐龍沒有叉骨（又名如願骨）。這種叉狀骨骼位於鳥類的頸部基部，主要功能是增強骨骼以抵禦飛行中的許多壓力。然而，近年來的化石證據顯示，許多恐龍確實具有叉骨。例如，馳龍科的恐龍（一種像鳥類的恐龍），被認為都有叉骨。這項發現與該骨骼僅存在於鳥類身上的理論相矛盾。

3　[a] ■ 除了在恐龍化石中觀察到叉骨之外，古生物學家還確定了鳥類和恐龍之間的許多其他結構相似之處。[b] ■ 舉例來說，比較鳥類和蒙古伶盜龍、恐爪龍等恐龍的骨骼，顯示鳥類和恐龍共同擁有許多獨特的骨骼特徵。[c] ■ 例如，蒙古伶盜龍的化石顯示，這種生物的前肢構造可能允許極大的靈活性，與現代鳥類類似。[d] ■ 另一方面，恐龍與早期爬蟲類間沒有這樣的相似之處。

4　這種結構相似的證據，只是許多古生物學家現在普遍認同鳥類是從恐龍演化而來的原因之一。另一個令人信服的證據是兩者都有羽毛。許多專家現在認為既是恐龍又是鳥類的始祖鳥化石，其特徵上有與現代

鳥類相似的羽毛痕跡。自始祖鳥的發現以來，古生物學家發現了許多其他可能與始祖鳥有關的恐龍化石，也具有羽毛。此外，即使與始祖鳥無關的恐龍化石，例如暴龍，也被發現具有長而類似羽毛的結構，通常被稱為原羽。根據許多古生物學家的說法，原羽的主要功能是保溫，而不是輔助飛行，這也解釋了為什麼許多不能飛行的恐龍可能有羽毛。由於除了恐龍和鳥類外，並未發現其他動物有羽毛，因此科學家認為羽毛的存在是兩種動物有直接關係的有力指標。

5　古生物學家還發現恐龍的肺與鳥類的肺形狀相似。大多數動物，包括靈長類動物、蜥蜴和青蛙的肺都有兩個腔室。然而，鳥類的肺部前後都有額外的氣囊，可使牠們的肺一直保持膨脹。關於恐龍骨骼的研究指出，有些恐龍的肺也具有額外腔室。與骨骼結構相似性和兩者都有羽毛的事實一樣，只有鳥類和恐龍擁有這種額外肺腔的事實也顯示，鳥類可能演化自恐龍，因此是最接近恐龍的現存生物。

11. 在第一段裡，作者提到翅膀和羽毛是為了

〇 指出始祖鳥和現代鳥類的共同特徵

◯ 解釋始祖鳥化石的尺寸較小

◯ 主張始祖鳥很可能是一種鳥類，而不是恐龍

◯ 描述始祖鳥可能的外貌。

答案解析

▶ 題型：功能題

✓ 作者說始祖鳥具有與恐龍和鳥類相似的特徵。為了指出這種動物與鳥類的相似之處，作者提到了翅膀和羽毛。

✗ 雖然作者描述了始祖鳥的大小，但提到翅膀和羽毛並不能解釋牠的大小。

✗ 作者後來將始祖鳥描述成一種像鳥類的恐龍。然而，作者僅描述了翅膀和羽毛，並沒有說牠是一隻鳥。

✗ 雖然這些特徵的描述有助於讀者想像始祖鳥的外觀，但作者並未特別以翅膀和羽毛來描述動

物的外觀。

12. 第一段中的「consensus」意思最接近於
   ○ question（質疑）。
   ○ debate（辯論）。
   ○ evidence（證據）。
   ○ agreement（同意）。

答案解析
▶ **題型：詞彙題**

✗ 在醒目標示詞出現的句子中，似乎整個學界都同意這個理論，所以 question（質疑）不適用。

✗ 如果 debate（辯論）是正確答案，句子應該會提到正反兩方的辯論。此外，你可以排除這個選項，因為它是正確答案的反義詞。

✗ evidence（證據）在句子中不適用。如果這是正確答案，那麼文章可能會包括這種證據的例子。

✓ 在這個句子中，agreement 的意思是意見一致。根據句子的背景，此字最能取代原字。

13. 下列哪一項最能表達第二段裡醒目標示句中的必要資訊？錯誤選項會對意思產生重大改變或遺漏必要資訊。
   ○ 相信恐龍沒有如願骨，是證明現代鳥類與恐龍有關的主要困難處。
   ○ 許多人認為爬蟲類是最接近恐龍的現存原型，因為牠們和恐龍一樣沒有叉骨。
   ○ 科學家無法將現代鳥類和恐龍聯繫起來的主要原因為，他們在大多數現代鳥類中找不到叉骨。
   ○ 恐龍被認為沒有如願骨，使人們認為鳥類，而非爬蟲類，是最接近牠們的現存原型。

答案解析
▶ **題型：句子摘要題**

✓ 這個選項是醒目標示句的最佳概述，因它包含了原始句子中的所有關鍵概念。

✗ 這句話提到人們認為爬蟲類是最接近恐龍的現存原型，是因為鳥類和恐龍之間的不相似，而不是爬蟲類和恐龍之間的相似性。

✗ 這句話提到鳥類沒有叉骨，這是不實訊息。

✗ 這句話包含有不實訊息，因它說恐龍缺乏許願骨使人們認為恐龍與鳥類有關。

14. 發現具有叉骨的恐龍化石很重要，因為它
   ○ 指出在恐龍時代已經進化出多種鳥類。
   ○ 證明許多爬行動物，包括恐龍，都有叉骨。
   ○ 對爬蟲類是最接近恐龍的現存親戚理論提出了疑問。
   ○ 幫助科學家判定非鳥類物種的叉骨的作用。

答案解析
▶ **題型：句子摘要題**

✗ 作者沒有提到恐龍時代存在任何鳥類物種。

✗ 作者說只有恐龍和鳥類有叉骨。

✓ 作者說，恐龍和爬蟲類是親戚的觀念，是基於人們相信恐龍不像鳥類一樣擁有叉骨。因此，發現擁有叉骨的恐龍，表示牠們最接近的現存原型是鳥類，而不是爬蟲類。

✗ 作者沒有描述恐龍叉骨的作用，只說恐龍是除了鳥類外，唯一擁有這些骨骼的動物。

15. 關於馳龍科的恐龍，可以推斷出什麼？
   ○ 牠們與始祖鳥有密切關係。
   ○ 牠們能夠飛行。
   ○ 牠們是唯一擁有叉骨的恐龍。
   ○ 相較於其他恐龍，牠們體型較小。

答案解析
▶ **題型：推論題**

✗ 作者沒有提供任何線索指出馳龍科的恐龍與始祖鳥有關。

✓ 作者說叉骨的功能是增強骨骼以抵禦飛行中的許多壓力。因此，如果馳龍科的恐龍有叉骨，牠們很可能具有飛行能力。

✗ 作者舉馳龍科作為擁有叉骨之恐龍的例子；作者說許多恐龍都有叉骨。

✗ 作者沒有提及馳龍科恐龍的體型大小。

16. 第三段中的「those」指的是
   ○ 伶盜龍化石。
   ○ 前肢。
   ○ 相似之處。
   ○ 早期爬蟲類。

答案解析

▶ 題型：指涉題

ㄨ「伶盜龍化石」不能取代醒目標示詞。

✓ 作者指的是恐龍的前肢。

ㄨ 作者沒有提及現代鳥類的相似之處。

ㄨ「早期爬蟲類」放在句中不合理。

17. 與第四段中「compelling」意思最接近的是

　　○ persuasive（有說服力的）。

　　○ conflicting（衝突的）。

　　○ recent（最近的）。

　　○ sufficient（充足的）。

答案解析

▶ 題型：詞彙題

✓ 在這句話中，persuasive 表示有說服力的。這些證據是有說服力的，因為它進一步支持鳥類是最接近恐龍的現存親屬之理論。

ㄨ conflicting（衝突的）表示證據不支持這個理論，所以這個選項錯誤。

ㄨ 沒有跡象顯示 compelling 可以用 recent（最近的）替換。如果 recent 是正確答案，作者可能會提及日期或其他時間標記。

ㄨ 如果某物 sufficient（充足的），那表示有足夠的量。這個定義不適用於醒目標示詞。

18. 根據第五段，靈長類動物和蜥蜴有什麼共通點？

　　○ 牠們的肺部結構比恐龍更為精密。

　　○ 牠們能讓自己的肺一直充滿空氣。

　　○ 牠們的肺具有類似結構。

　　○ 牠們除了肺之外還有其他器官幫助呼吸。

答案解析

▶ 題型：細節題

ㄨ 作者說恐龍有多個腔肺，而靈長類和蜥蜴有兩個肺腔。這表示恐龍的肺部結構更為複雜。

ㄨ 作者說鳥類的肺結構（而非靈長類和蜥蜴）使牠們能讓肺部一直充滿空氣。

✓ 作者說靈長類和蜥蜴有兩個肺腔，這表示牠們具有類似結構。

ㄨ 作者沒有提及靈長類和蜥蜴是否有其他器官幫助牠們呼吸。

19. 請看第三段中標示四個黑色方塊 [■] 的地方，這些方塊指示了下列句子可以插入到文章中的可能位置。

科學家還觀察到一些恐龍和鳥類的頭骨和頸部結構上的相似之處。

這句話最適合放在哪裡？

　　○ a

　　○ b

　　○ c

　　○ d

答案解析

▶ 題型：文句插入題

ㄨ 後面提到了上一段的最後一個觀點，並引入了一個新的主題。因此，這不是插入句的正確位置。

ㄨ 後面列舉了鳥類和恐龍之間的結構相似之處，延續了此段第一句的概念。插入句不適合放在這裡。

ㄨ 前面討論了鳥類和兩種特定類型的恐龍共有的骨骼特徵。接下來的句子提供了更多關於這些相似之處的細節。將句子放在這裡會破壞段落的邏輯連續性。

✓ 後面提到了恐龍和早期爬蟲類之間沒有相似之處。段落前面已經討論過肢骨是恐龍和鳥類的第一個相似之處。插入句提到了第二個相似之處，即頭骨和頸部。

20. 以下是簡短摘要文章的引言句。請完成摘要，選出三個最能表達文章重要概念的選項。有些句子並不屬於該摘要，因它們表達了文章中未提到的概念，或是文章中的次要概念。此題總共 2 分。

現今有證據指出，現代鳥類，而非爬蟲類，很可能是與恐龍關係最密切的生物。

2. 許多恐龍有羽毛或原羽，使牠們成為除了鳥類外，唯一具有任何類型羽毛的生物。

3. 恐龍的骨骼顯示，恐龍的肺可能具有多個腔室，就像鳥類一樣。

4. 恐龍和鳥類具有幾個結構相似之處，包括有叉骨。

選項

1. 許多恐龍的前肢形狀可能具有很大的靈活性和運動能力。

2. 許多恐龍有羽毛或原羽，使牠們成為除了鳥類外，唯一具有任何類型羽毛的生物。
3. 恐龍的骨骼顯示，恐龍的肺可能具有多個腔室，就像鳥類一樣。
4. 恐龍和鳥類具有幾個結構相似之處，包括有叉骨。
5. 就像現代鳥類一樣，並非所有具有羽毛的恐龍都能飛行。
6. 自 19 世紀中葉發現始祖鳥化石以來，科學家一直相信現代爬蟲類是從恐龍進化而來的。

答案解析
▶ 題型：段落／文章摘要題

✗ 1. 雖然根據文章這是事實，但這並不是支持現代鳥類，而非爬蟲類，可能是最接近恐龍的現存親戚之主要觀點。

✓ 2. 恐龍具有羽毛或原羽的事實，是文中提到並用來支持鳥類是最接近恐龍的現存原型理論的重要證據之一。

✓ 3. 作者提到鳥類和恐龍擁有形狀相似的肺，這進一步證明了這兩者可能有關係。

✓ 4. 作者描述鳥類和恐龍都有叉骨，以及兩者之間的其他結構相似性，作為牠們有關係的證據。

✗ 5. 這個細節在文章中有提到，但只是一個次要觀點。

✗ 6. 這個說法是錯誤的。在 19 世紀中葉發現的始祖鳥化石，導致許多科學家相信鳥類是恐龍最接近的現存親戚。

補充試題

行銷中的定價方法

1 在行銷中一個重要部分是，決定向消費者收取商品和服務的價格。公司渴望設定的價格要高到足以讓他們賺取利潤，但又要低到足以鼓勵人們購買他們的產品。為了決定這些價格，行銷專家必須考慮各種因素和使用各種不同的定價方法。

2 成本導向定價法是根據產品的製造成本來決定價格。這是最簡單的方法，因為製造商可以輕易判定製造他們的商品要花多少錢。在計算了材料費和人工費後，他們會

將一個固定百分比添加到成本中，這稱為標準利潤，包含了廣告、行銷和其他行政成本，以及利潤。舉例來說，建築公司在開始建造前，不會先決定新建築物的確切價格，往往是根據材料、設備和人工成本以及標準利潤（通常是 20%）來算出價格的估計值。最終價格在建築完成後計算，公司會將標準利潤加到總建築成本中。

3 成本導向定價法的主要優勢在於其簡單性。使用這種方法的企業，無需根據市場對商品的變化而不斷調整價格。然而，成本導向定價法無法考慮到與市場有關的重要因素，也是它的缺點。這就是許多企業也用更複雜的方法來決價格的原因。

4 在許多行業中，生產者通常不太關注自己的成本，而是根據具領先地位競爭對手的價格來設定自己的價格。這種方法被稱為競爭導向定價法。競爭導向定價法通常仰賴市場上的價格，或是消費者期望支付的商品或服務平均價格。如果有五家公司以每呎兩美元的價格銷售塑膠管，那麼第六家公司以每呎三美元的價格銷售同類型的管子就不太可能成功。因此，即使第六家公司的生產成本更高，他們也無法承擔將價格設定比競爭對手還要高的後果。

5 競爭導向定價法有時會令小企業處於不利。因為大型公司可以大量購買材料或生產機械，所以生產成本通常比小型公司的更低。為了競爭，小公司不能依靠成本導向定價法。他們通常設定低於較大競爭對手的價格，即使他們的生產成本可能更高。這樣才能吸引消費者購買，並建立或維持客戶基礎。這些賣家還把成本導向定價法和競爭導向定價法結合，以找到在減去成本後能產生最高利潤的最有競爭力價格。

6 成本導向定價法和競爭導向定價法，在很大程度上根據的是客觀數學因素，例如生產成本和平均價格，而買家導向定價法所根據的則是個人觀點。 [a] ■ 認知價值是

消費者感覺一件物品價值多少，而不是其實際金錢價值。 [b] ■ 舉例來說，像寵物石這種產品，它只是一塊被宣傳為寵物的普通石頭，其實際金錢價值非常低。 [c] ■ 行銷人員不會使用生產成本來設定價格，因為這會使價格太低。 [d] ■ 取而代之的是，他們必須確認消費者覺得他們的產品值多少錢。

7　由於認知價值是主觀的，所以很難計算。確定產品認知價值的一種常見策略，是對焦點小組進行訪談，焦點小組是與行銷專家分享對產品感受的一小群人。焦點小組的回應往往會根據受訪群體而變化，因此專家會努力訪談足夠大的樣本以獲得有用的資訊。除了焦點小組和行銷專家外，一些企業甚至可能聘請心理學者來幫他們理解消費者的想法和情緒，使他們能創造出人們認為有價值的產品。一件物品的認知價值越高，公司就可從該物品收取越高的價格，且不管其生產成本或競爭對手設定的價格為何。

1. 第一段裡的「aspire」意思最接近於
○ decide（決定）。
○ hurry（匆忙）。
○ aim（意圖）。
○ attempt（嘗試）。

答案解析
▶ **題型：詞彙題**

✗ aspire（渴望）和 decide（決定）的意思並不相同。

✗ 如果 hurry（匆忙）是正確答案，作者很可能會給一些有關公司為何想迅速設定價格的資訊。

✓ aspire（渴望）和 aim（意圖）有相似的定義──這兩個詞都表示想要達成某件事。

✗ attempt（嘗試）某事，表示試著去做。這並不是 aspire（渴望）的正確含義。

2. 在第四段裡，作者暗示一家生產成本較高的公司無法承擔收取比競爭對手更高的價格，因為公司會
○ 由於顧客選擇競爭對手的產品而虧損。
○ 預計降低其生產成本來符合競爭對手的成本。
○ 必須購買能降低其生產成本的設備。
○ 被迫使用與頂尖競爭對手相同的定價策略。

答案解析
▶ **題型：推論題**

✓ 作者解釋，如果第六家公司每呎賣得比其競爭對手貴一美元，不會成功。這表示顧客很可能會購買相同產品中價格較低的。

✗ 作者沒提到一家公司如何降低其生產成本，或者它為了競爭必須這樣做。

✗ 作者沒說買新設備會降低生產成本。

✗ 作者說，生產成本較高的公司必須敵得過其競爭對手設定的價格，並沒有說公司的定價策略一定相同。

3. 根據第五段，以下是競爭導向定價法對小企業的不利影響，除了：
○ 它為大量購買材料的公司提供了優勢。
○ 它有利於生產成本低的公司。
○ 它促進了單一定價策略的使用。
○ 它鼓勵賣家將價格設定到低於成本所允許的價格。

答案解析
▶ **題型：挑錯題**

✗ 作者說因大公司可大量購買材料，它們的生產成本通常較低，而且能以較低的價格出售產品。

✗ 作者解釋說，生產成本低的公司可以負擔得起以較低的價格出售物品。

✓ 在第五段裡作者提到，小公司通常把成本導向定價法和競爭導向定價法結合，以找到最佳價格。

✗ 作者說，小公司的生產成本通常較高，而設定與競爭對手的價格相仿，會使它們處於不利地位。

4. 根據第五段，關於大型企業可以推斷出什麼？
○ 他們較有可能只使用一種定價方法。
○ 他們的價格受到小企業定價策略的影響。
○ 他們在行銷方面的花費比小企業少。

○ 在使用競爭導向定價法時，他們往往具有
更高的生產成本。

答案解析
▶ **題型：推論題**

✓ 作者表示，小企業為了獲利，通常會結合不同
的定價策略。因為大公司不必太擔心生產成本
對利潤的影響，所以它們比較有可能使用單一
的定價策略。

✗ 作者解釋了大公司的定價策略如何影響較小公
司的定價策略，而不是反過來。

✗ 作者沒提到大企業或小企業在行銷方面的支
出。

✗ 作者說明小公司的生產成本為什麼會比大公司
高，但沒有關於使用特定定價方法如何影響生
產成本的資訊。

5. 第六段裡的「objective」意思最接近於
○ accessible（易取得的）。
○ improper（不適當的）。
○ impartial（公正的）。
○ precise（精確的）。

答案解析
▶ **題型：詞彙題**

✗ 「accessible」的意思是容易取得，這個單字
在此句中不適用。

✗ 「improper」的意思是不正確，這個單字在此
句中不適用。

✓ 「impartial」表示不受個人觀點或信念的影
響。如果成本導向和競爭導向定價法被描述為
與買家導向定價法形成對比，而且後者所根據
的是個人觀點，那「impartial」一定和「根據
個人觀點」的意思相反。

✗ 「precise」的意思是極其精準，這個單字在此
句中不適用。

6. 根據第六段，成本導向和競爭導向的定價法有
什麼共同點？
○ 它們根據的是產品或服務價值。
○ 它們仰賴可測量的資訊。
○ 它們同樣仰賴於個人化資訊和平均數。
○ 它們聚焦在顧客所評估的成本。

答案解析
▶ **題型：細節題**

✗ 成本導向定價法根據的是產品或服務價值；競
爭導向定價法根據的則是公司競爭對手的定
價。

✓ 作者解釋，成本導向和競爭導向的定價法，根
據的是諸如生產成本和平均價格之類的因素，
這些都是可測量的。

✗ 作者提到，個人化資訊用於買家導向定價法，
並未用於成本導向和競爭導向的策略。

✗ 作者沒有提到消費者成本導向的定價策略。

7. 作者在第六段提到寵物石的原因是？
○ 為舉例說明認知價值低的產品。
○ 為說明為什麼使用認知價值對某些產品是
適當的。
○ 為對比特定物品的實際價值與認知價值。
○ 為解釋如何把買家導向定價法與競爭導向
定價法結合使用。

答案解析
▶ **題型：功能題**

✗ 作者說寵物石的實際價值很低，但沒有描述它
們的認知價值。

✓ 作者提到寵物石來指出一些產品的實際價值很
低，這表示賣家需使用認知價值來設定價格。

✗ 作者沒有提到寵物石的認知價值。

✗ 作者只描述以確定寵物石的認知價值，作為買
家導向定價法的一種策略。

8. 下列哪一項最能表達第七段裡醒目標示句中的
必要資訊？錯誤選項會對意思產生重大改變或
遺漏必要資訊。
○ 為決定產品的認知價值，一些焦點小組對
專家進行訪談，了解他們對產品的感受。
○ 對焦點小組中的人進行訪談，是行銷專家
確定產品認知價值的一種方式。
○ 焦點小組讓行銷專家能夠訪談並了解他們
如何形成對物品價值的想法。
○ 訪問小組關於認知價值的一種策略，牽涉
到向受訪者詢問他們對產品的感受。

答案解析
▶ **題型：句子摘要題**

ⅹ 這個句子對原始句中的行為表達錯誤。是專家們對焦點小組進行訪談，而不是反過來。

✓ 這個句子正確概述了醒目標示句中的重要資訊，它描述了行銷專家訪談焦點小組的原因。

ⅹ 醒目標示句說焦點小組的目的是讓人們與行銷專家分享對產品的感受，而不是分享他們如何形成對產品價值的想法。

ⅹ 醒目標示句描述了判定產品認知價值的一種方式，而不是對焦點小組中人們訪談的方式。

9. 請看第六段中標示四個黑色方塊 [■] 的地方，這些方塊指示了下列句子可以插入到文章中可能的位置。

   在買家導向定價法中，公司根據商品的認知價值來設定價格。

   這句話最適合放在哪裡？

   ○ a
   ○ b
   ○ c
   ○ d

答案解析

▶ **題型：文句插入題**

✓ 前面描述了成本導向和競爭導向的定價法如何運作。因此，作者接著定義買家導向定價法，來和其他兩種定價策略對照，是合理的。

ⅹ 前面作者定義了認知價值。因此將話題轉移到買家導向定價法並不合理。

ⅹ 在前面提供了一個認知價值較低物品的例子。將插入句放在這裡，會破壞認知價值此概念的連貫性。

ⅹ 前面解釋了為什麼公司不會對某些產品使用成本導向定價法。接下來，用「instead」開頭的句子提供了更好的方法來決定這些產品的價格。把題目所給的句子放在此，會破壞此段概念的流暢性。

10. 以下是簡短摘要文章的引言句。請完成摘要，選出三個最能表達文章重要概念的選項。有些句子並不屬於該摘要，因它們表達了文章中未提到的概念，或是文章中的次要概念。此題總共 2 分。

    公司需要一種為產品定價的方式，而且至少使用三種方法來達到這點。

   ▪ 2. 成本導向定價法，是在總成本上再加一個簡單的百分比。

   ▪ 3. 以競爭對手的價售來做比較的定價法常被使用到，儘管它對生產成本較低的大公司比較有利。

   ▪ 6. 根據買家感受的方法也有被使用，但較主觀，且依賴消費者的反饋來設定價格。

選項

1. 建築業通常會加價 20%。
2. 成本導向定價法，是在總成本上再加一個簡單的百分比。
3. 以競爭對手的價售做為比較的定價法常被使用，儘管它對生產成本較低的大公司比較有利。
4. 現行水準定價法是根據現行物料成本來設定價格的定價法。
5. 心理學者非常擅長理解顧客的價值觀。
6. 根據買家感受的方法也有被使用，但較主觀，且依賴消費者的反饋來設定價格。

答案解析

▶ **題型：段落／文章摘要題**

ⅹ 1. 這個敘述不應是文章摘要的一部分，這句話在文章裡是一個次要想法。

✓ 2. 此敘述無誤。成本導向定價法，是在總成本上再加一個簡單的百分比。

✓ 3. 此敘述無誤。以競爭對手的價售來做比較的定價法常被使用到，儘管它對生產成本較低的大公司比較有利。

ⅹ 4. 這個敘述不應是文章摘要的一部分，因句中包含了文章未提及的資訊──價格是根據物料成本設定的。

ⅹ 5. 這個敘述不應是文章摘要的一部分，因句中的資訊在文章中沒提到。文章只提及心理學者可能被僱用來幫助公司理解顧客的情緒和想法。

✓ 6. 此敘述無誤。根據買家感受的方法也有被使用，但較主觀，且依賴消費者的反饋來設定價格。

8-1-1 掌握要領：整合題回答技巧

練習 1　作者主張：educational programs

have a positive effect on children's development

三個重點：First, watching a few hours of educational content a week has been proven to boost children's test scores.; Furthermore, watching educational shows together can be an important bonding activity for families.; Finally, there are a wide variety of excellent educational television programs and on-demand videos available, and the quality of these programs is closely regulated.

練習 2　教授立場：Overall, though, evidence indicates that watching educational programs is not particularly beneficial for young toddlers and preschoolers.

三個重點：Although some studies do indicate that watching educational content boosts test scores, there are plenty of studies that directly contradict this notion.; In addition, watching video together simply is not an effective form of bonding.; Finally, although government regulations aim for good standards of video content and age appropriateness, they often fail to do so.

練習 3　explain how they cast doubt on

練習 4　The reading passage argues that educational programs have a positive effect on young children.; However, the professor disagrees and gives evidence that educational programs are not good for preschool-age children to watch.; To summarize, in the reading, the author argues that educational video content is good for young children. However, the professor disagrees with this idea and gives three pieces of evidence to show that watching educational programs is actually bad for children.

練習 3　The reading passage states that watching educational programs encourages academic success.; Second, the passage says that the quality of educational video content is closely regulated by the government.; Finally, the passage states that watching educational shows together can be a good opportunity for bonding between family members.

8-2 題型練習

C.

[1] The reading states that vegetable oil is not a good source of fuel for cars. It gives several reasons for this argument.（文章中指出，植物油對汽車來說不是優質的燃料來源。它提出了一些理由來支持這個觀點。）

[4] However, in the lecture, the professor argues the opposite. She gives evidence to support the idea that vegetable oil is an excellent source of fuel for vehicles.（然而在課堂中，教授持相反觀點。她提出證據來支持植物油是車輛優質燃料來源的想法。）

[3] The passage points out that it's expensive to install conversion equipment. There are many different pieces that cost money. Maintenance is also expensive.（文章指出，安裝轉換設備的費用很高，有許多很花錢的零件，維護費用也很高。）

[2] However, the professor argues that while it is expensive, the equipment pays for itself quickly by saving money.（然而教授認為，雖然設備費用很高，但很快就能透過省下油錢來回本。）

[5] Using vegetable oil as fuel is a lot cheaper than gas. This way, drivers save money in the long term.（以植物油當作燃料比汽油便宜得多，長期下來駕駛者能省錢。）

[3] Second, the passage suggests that using the special equipment needed for vegetable oil fuel could be very complicated. It requires a lot of attention.（其次，文章指出，植物油燃料所需的特殊設備可能非常複雜，也需要很多注意力。）

[2] The professor disagrees.

（教授並不贊成。）

[5] She points out that it's not very hard and that people get used to these motions. Also, she explains that there are new systems that are automatic and don't need a person to turn them on or off. （她指出這並不難，人們會習慣這些動作。此外她說明，新系統是自動的，不需要人去手動開啟或關閉。）

[3] Finally, the passage argues that using vegetable oil could affect crops normally used for food, like sunflowers. This could cause the price of certain foods to go up. （最後文章主張，使用植物油燃料可能會影響到通常作為食品用途的作物，例如向日葵。這可能導致某些食品的價格上漲。）

[2] In contrast, the professor says that the oil used for fuel is a waste product from places like food factories. （但教授表示，做為燃料用途的油是來自食品工廠等地的廢棄物。）

[5] It's already been used once, so using it for fuel does not affect food production. （它已被使用過一次，因此把它用在燃料上不會影響食品生產。）

[6] In conclusion, both the reading and the lecture discuss using vegetable oil as a source of fuel for cars. While the author claims that vegetable oil is not a good source of fuel, the professor disagrees and offers several pieces of evidence to show that vegetable oil is, in fact, a good source of fuel for vehicles. （綜上所述，文章和課堂都討論了將植物油用於汽車燃料的可能性。雖然作者聲稱植物油不是優質的燃料來源，但教授並不贊成，還提供了幾項證據來證明植物油實際上是車輛的優質燃料來源。）

D.
In the reading, the author says that vegetable oil isn't a good source of fuel for cars. The professor disagrees and shows that vegetable oil is a good source of fuel by describing some of the advantages of using vegetable oil as fuel in cars.
在文章中作者表示，植物油不是汽車的優質燃料來源。教授並不贊成，並描述了使用植物油作為汽車燃料的一些優點，以證明植物油是一種優質燃料來源。

First, the reading says that using vegetable oil as fuel is too expensive because cars using this type of fuel require special, expensive equipment. The professor rejects this point and says that the equipment pays for itself in the end. That's because cars can travel long distances with vegetable oil.
首先，文章指出以植物油作為燃料成本太高，因為使用這種燃料的汽車需要特殊且昂貴的設備。教授反駁了這一點，並表示該設備最終會回本。這是因為汽車可以使用植物油做長途旅行。

Next, the reading claims that the equipment is too complicated to use. Again, the professor disagrees. According to the professor, using the converter becomes automatic, so drivers don't have to really think about it. In addition, she says that automatic converters are available, so drivers don't have to worry at all about switching the equipment on and off.
接著，文章主張設備使用起來太複雜。教授一樣不贊同這個觀點。根據教授的說法，轉換器的使用會變得自動化，因此駕駛不用真的去考量這一點。此外，她表示有自動轉換器可用，所以駕駛完全不必擔心開啟和關閉設備。

The final point in the reading is that using vegetable oil as fuel will lead to higher food prices. The professor disproves this point as well. She argues that the vegetable oil used as fuel is a waste product that typically comes from restaurants and factories. It's used for cooking before it's used as fuel, so it doesn't affect food prices at all.
文章中提到的最後一點為使用植物油作為燃料，會導致食品價格上漲。教授也反駁了這個觀點。她主張，用於燃料的植物油來自餐廳和工廠的廢棄產品。在被用於燃料之前，它先被用於烹飪，

因此完全不會影響食品價格。

To summarize, the author of the reading argues that vegetable oil is not a good source of fuel for cars. The professor disagrees with this idea and discusses three reasons why vegetable oil is a good source of fuel.

總而言之，文章作者主張植物油不是汽車燃料的優質來源。教授不贊成這個觀點，並討論了植物油是優質燃料來源的三個原因。

8-3 綜合演練

B.
❶ Europeans　❷ bone　❸ grave markers
❹ similarities　❺ Old Italic　❻ Greeks
❼ angular

C.

Main Topic from Reading: The reading claims that runes most likely developed as an independent writing system for specific purposes.

文章的主題：文章主張，盧恩字母很可能是為特定目的而發展出來的獨立書寫系統。

Main Topic from Lecture: The professor disagrees and says that there is strong evidence that runes actually originated in an Old Italic alphabet.

課堂的主題：教授不贊成並指出，有強而有力的證據證明盧恩字母實際上起源於古義大利文字母。

Key Point 1 from Reading: First, the reading describes how Germanic groups who used runes could not have based their alphabet on an earlier system, because they were culturally isolated until AD 700.

文章的重點 1：首先，文章描述了使用盧恩字母的日耳曼民族，他們的字母所根據的不可能是先前的系統，因他們在公元 700 年之前一直處於文化孤立狀態。

Key Point 1 from Lecture: The professor says that this is not completely true.

課堂的重點 1：教授說這不完全是事實。

Support from Lecture: He says that Germanic groups interacted with early Romans and traders who used Old Italic scripts long before this.

課堂的支持句：他表示，日耳曼民族與很早之前就在使用古義大利文的早期羅馬人和商人互動。

Key Point 2 from Reading: Next, the passage says that runes are most often found on memorials to wealthy people, which suggests they developed amongst a small group of people for reasons specific to their society.

文章的重點 2：接著，文章說盧恩字母最常見於富人的墓碑上，這表示它們是在一小部分人中，因社會上特定原因而發展出來的。

Key Point 2 from Lecture: The professor, however, points out that there is evidence of runes which were used for many other purposes other than just burials.

課堂的重點 2：然而教授指出，有證據顯示盧恩字母用於葬禮外的許多其他用途。

Support from Lecture: This suggests that runes were read by a wide cross-section of society so must have developed and spread far beyond a small group of people.

課堂的支持句：這表示盧恩字母被社會上廣泛的人群閱讀，因此發展和傳播的範圍必定遠超過一小部分人。

Key Point 3 from Reading: Finally, the reading claims that runic symbols are not visibly similar to letters used in Old Italic alphabets.

文章的重點 3：最後，文章聲稱盧恩字母符號在外觀上與古義大利文字母並沒有明顯的相似性。

Key Point 3 from Lecture: The professor, on the other hand, notices many similarities between the two alphabets.

課堂的重點 3：然而，教授卻注意到這兩個字母間的許多相似之處。

Support from Lecture: In particular, he says that the similar shapes of their letters indicate a relationship between the runic and the Old Italic alphabets.

課堂的支持句：他說，尤其是它們字母在形狀上的相似性，顯示了盧恩字母和古義大利文字母之間的關係。

Conclusion: In summary, while the reading says that runes developed independently from other writing systems, the professor disagrees and provides evidence to show that runes probably came from Old Italic scripts.

結論：總之，雖然文章說盧恩字母是獨立於其他書寫系統而發展出來的，但教授不贊同，並提供證據指出盧恩字母可能來自古義大利文。

8-4 實戰演練

TOEFL Writing

Question

米洛的維納斯是古希臘藝術中最著名的例子之一，這尊雕像描繪的是代表愛與美的希臘女神，阿芙羅黛蒂，它幾乎享譽全球。它的起源仍存在爭議——許多歷史學家認為米洛的維納斯是一件早期作品的複製品。

這些歷史學家之所以認為這尊雕像是複製品，主要是因為它與更古老的古典作品相似。米洛的維納斯在 1820 年被發現時，首先被認為是出自希臘藝術家普拉克西特勒斯之手，因為它與這位早期藝術家的古典風格十分相似，而普拉克西特勒斯活在公元前 4 世紀。後來安提阿的亞歷山卓斯被正確確認為在公元前 150 至 100 年創作米洛的維納斯時，當時藝術史學家指出，他可能是從古典藝術家那裡獲得靈感。

米洛的維納斯可能是一個複製品的想法，得到了進一步支持，因為它與位在那不勒斯之卡普亞的阿芙羅黛蒂非常相似。兩尊雕像都描繪了女神阿芙羅黛蒂（羅馬人稱為維納斯）扭曲的姿勢，她的長袍從臀部滑落。卡普亞的阿芙羅黛蒂是一個羅馬作品，本身為早期希臘雕塑的複製品。

最後，歷史學家指出，以藝術家的文化背景為線索，米洛的維納斯很可能是從另一尊雕像複製而來。安提阿的亞歷山卓斯活在希臘化時代，是希臘藝術在繁榮的古典時代結束後的衰落時期。許多其他希臘化時期的作品都是從古典藝術複製而來。歷史學家認為，希臘化時期的再創作風氣非常普及，因此米洛的維納斯很可能也是一個複製品。

Sample Essay #1:
The reading argues that the *Venus de Milo* is a copy of an earlier Greek or Roman sculpture. The professor, however, disagrees and explains why she thinks the *Venus de Milo* is an original piece of art and not a replica.

這篇文章主張，米洛的維納斯是早期希臘或羅馬雕塑的複製品。然而，教授不贊同，並解釋她為什麼認為米洛的維納斯是一件原創藝術品而不是複製品。

First, the reading points out that this Hellenistic sculpture strongly resembles older classical sculptures, particularly those of Greek artist Praxiteles. The professor disagrees with this because she feels that the *Venus de Milo* is very Hellenistic in style and that its similarities to classical works have been exaggerated.

首先，文章指出這個希臘化雕塑與更古老的古典雕塑非常相似，尤其是希臘藝術家普拉克西特勒斯的作品。教授並不贊成，因她覺得米洛的維納斯在風格上非常希臘化，而且它與古典作品的相似之處被誇大了。

The reading also suggests that the *Venus de Milo* must be a replica because of its similarities to *Aphrodite of Capua*. The professor says that there were so many Aphrodite and Venus sculptures created between the fourth and first centuries BCE that of course some of them look similar, but she points out that the similarities between these two statues are not substantial enough

to prove that the *Venus de Milo* is a copy.
文章還暗示米洛的維納斯一定是複製品，因為它與卡普亞的阿芙羅黛蒂相似。教授說在公元前四至一世紀間創造了非常多的阿芙羅黛蒂和維納斯雕像，當然有些會看起來相似。但她指出，這兩尊雕像之間的相似之處不足以證明米洛的維納斯是複製品。

Finally, the reading claims that because the statue was created during the Hellenistic period, and because so many Hellenistic pieces were replicas of classical works, the *Venus de Milo* must also be a replica. The professor feels that the Hellenistic period is underrated and that it produced many original works.
最後，文章聲稱由於這尊雕像是在希臘化時代創造的，而且由於許多希臘化作品是古典作品的複製品，所以米洛的維納斯一定也是複製品。教授認為希臘化時代被低估了，它也創造了許多原創性作品。

To summarize, in the reading, the author says that the *Venus de Milo* is a replica of a previous work. The professor disagrees with this.
總而言之，在文章中，作者說米洛的維納斯是以前作品的複製品，而教授不贊成這個觀點。

Sample Score #1:
This essay would likely score very well because the testtaker provides an accurate and complete response to the prompt. The essay is organized in such a manner that the relationship between the reading and the lecture is very clear. For example, in the introduction, the test-taker writes, "The professor, however, disagrees." This sentence shows that the student understands the professor's stance with respect to the claim made in the reading.
Furthermore, the test-taker writes about each of the points in the reading and describes how the professor casts doubt on those points. In order to do this, the writer provides plenty of specific details from the lecture.
Finally, the language in the response is clear and easy to understand. The essay is well organized, and the ideas flow very well. The writer uses a variety of grammatical structures and makes no spelling errors.

評分範例 #1：
這篇作文可能會獲得高分，因為考生為題目提供了準確而完整的回答。寫作的組織使文章和教授課堂之間的關係非常清晰。例如在引言中，考生寫道：「然而，教授並不贊成。」這句話顯示考生理解教授對文章中所提出的主張和立場。此外，考生詳細描述了文章中的每一個觀點，並且說明教授對這些觀點的質疑。為了做到這點，作者提供了大量源自課堂的具體細節。最後，答案的措辭清晰易懂。文章組織良好，思路順暢。作者使用了多種文法結構，而且沒有拼寫錯誤。

Sample Essay #2:
The lecture is about the Venus de Milo and why it's not a copy. The reading is opposite of that. The reading first says that it looks like a sculpture that was first discovered in 1820. That sculpture was by an artist who worked during the classical era. But the professor says it actually looks like something from the Hellenistic period. It took place after the classical period. That's why the Venus de Milo looks like that.

該課堂描述的是米洛的維納斯，和它為什麼不是複製品，而文章則持相反觀點。文章首先提到，它看起來像一尊在 1820 年首次發現的雕塑，那尊雕塑是由一位古典時代藝術家創作的。但教授表示，它實際上比較像希臘化時代的作品，其發生在古典時代之後。這就是為什麼米洛的維納斯看起來和它很相像。

Next, the professor says that the Venus de Milo doesn't look like the Aphrodite of Capua that much. The reading argues that the similarity between these two is proof that the Venus de Milo copied the Aphrodite of Capua. So if the

Venus de Milo doesn't look like the Aphrodite of Capua, the professor says that means it's not a copy.

接下來，教授說米洛的維納斯並不那麼像卡普亞的阿芙羅黛蒂。文章主張，這兩者之間的相似性證明了米洛的維納斯抄襲了卡普亞的阿芙羅黛蒂。所以如果米洛的維納斯看起來不像卡普亞的阿芙羅黛蒂，教授認為這表示它不是一個複製品。

Sample Score #2:
This response would likely score poorly because it is difficult to understand and does not completely answer the prompt. After a short introduction, the test-taker discusses only two of the points in the reading. At 138 words, the essay is too short. The score would have been higher if the writer had addressed the third point and, in doing so, extended the word count of the essay. Next, the language used in the essay severely limits understanding. In several cases, the writer uses pronouns without making the referent clear, as in the following sentence: "But the professor says it actually looks like something from the Hellenistic period." In this sentence, the referent of "it" is not clear. The writer also provides inaccurate information about the discovery of the Venus de Milo (the Venus de Milo was discovered in 1820; it did not, as the essay suggests, resemble a different sculpture that was discovered in 1820).

評分範例 #2：
這個答案的得分可能較低，因為它難以理解，而且沒有完全回答題目。在簡短的引言之後，考生只討論了文章中的兩個觀點。這篇作文只有 138 字，太短了。如果作者能處理第三個觀點，並在過程中增加作文的字數，獲得的分數會更高。接下來，作文中使用的措辭嚴重限制了理解程度。在幾個情況中，作者使用代名詞時沒有明確指出指涉詞，例如以下這句話：「But the professor says it actually looks like something from the Hellenistic period.」 在這句話裡，「it」的指涉

對象不清楚。作者還提供了有關發現米洛的維納斯的錯誤資訊（米洛的維納斯發現於 1820 年；它並沒有像作文所說的那樣，與另一尊發現於 1820 年的雕塑相似）。

9-1-1 掌握要領：學術討論題回答技巧

練習 4　Today you can see the effects of having a diet that contains lots processed foods and drinks with lots of sugar. It is having visible effects on people and the health care system. So, I agree with Faik in many respects, but would like to add my own point.

練習 6　Therefore, I believe that making healthy food as cheap as processed food and teaching people about the consequences of their choices is the best way forward.

9-3 綜合演練

A.

1. Overall, I completely agree with the ideas presented by Gezgin and Sara. There are other things that I could mention too, such as better nutrition, better working conditions and better health care.

2. However, I am of the opinion that the most important development has been antibiotics and antiviral drugs. These drugs are used to treat infections that used to kill lots of people.

3. For example, in the 1900s Spanish flu swept the world, but existing medical treatments were ineffective and millions of people died. Since then, a lot of research has been done on developing antibiotics and antiviral drugs, and they have been very effective in preventing illnesses. Furthermore, we are able to produce these drugs more and more cheaply.

4. Therefore, this is the most important factor in helping us live longer.

中譯

1. 整體來說，我完全同意蓋茲津和莎拉提出的想法。我還可以提到其他事情，像是更好的營養、更好的工作條件和更好的醫療保健。

2. 然而，我的觀點為最重要的發展是抗生素和抗病毒藥物，這些藥物從前曾用於治療導致大量死亡的感染。

3. 舉例來說在 1900 年代，西班牙流感席捲全球，但當時的醫療治療方法並無效用，死亡人數高達數百萬。自那時起，有許多研究投入於開發抗生素和抗病毒藥物，那些藥物在預防疾病方面非常有效。此外，我們能以越來越便宜的成本生產這些藥物。

4. 因此，這是幫助我們活得更長久最重要的因素。

B.　1b　　2d　　3a　　4c

你的教授正在課堂上教心理學，寫一篇貼文來回應教授的問題。

你在回應中應該：

▪ 表達和支持你的意見
▪ 對討論提出貢獻

優良的回應要包含至少 100 字，你有 10 分鐘的時間作答。

阿克德尼茲教授
壓力是今日常見的問題，尤其對大學生而言。造成壓力的原因有很多，包括在短時間內有太多事情要做、無法控制自己的情況，或者與同學、朋友或家人之間的關係不好。壓力的影響對心理和生理都可能有害，因此是一個必須認真看待的問題。處理壓力的方法有很多，包括參加體育活動、得到身邊人的支持或尋求專業協助。但處理壓力的最佳方法是什麼？請在明天上課前在討論區發表你的想法。

崔西
我知道很多人都為壓力所苦，這是一個嚴重的問題。我的見解是，我們不夠重視心理健康。在我看來，處理壓力的最佳方法是尋求專業協助。有許多心理治療可用於處理壓力，包括談話治療、團體治療和認知治療，這些方法都有很好的成功記錄。

米亞
我同意崔西的觀點，但我認為她的建議並不適用於所有類型的壓力。當問題真的很嚴重時，當然應該尋求專業協助，但在那之前，有很多策略可以幫助減輕壓力。一個重要的例子是規律做運動。某些運動有助於減輕壓力，提高整體情緒。每天只需步行 30 分鐘就有用，且把它制定為每天例行之事十分有幫助。

Sample Answer #1:
Overall, I concur with the ideas presented by Mia and Tracy. I totally agree that stress can be very serious and have bad effects such

as mental and physical illness, and I also agree that there are different levels of stress. However, I would like to add that the best way to deal with stress is to deal with the causes of stress. For example, if you are worried about how much work you have to do in your job, you should not let it build up into something that makes you stressed. In this case you should speak to your employer about your work. You also need to make time to schedule your days and include time to plan and think about how to cope with the day ahead. Finally, it is really important to understand your priorities. You should not worry about things you cannot do anything about, and don't feel bad about saying 'no' when things become too demanding.

寫作範本 #1：
整體而言，我同意米亞和崔西提出的觀點。我完全同意壓力可能非常嚴重，而且可能導致精神和生理疾病，我也同意壓力有不同程度。然而，我想補充的是，處理壓力的最佳方式是處理壓力的根源。舉例來說，如果你擔心工作量太大，你不應該讓這種擔憂累積成壓力。在這種情況下，你應該和雇主談談你的工作。你還需要空出時間規劃你的日程，預留時間來規劃和思考如何應付未來的日子。最後，了解自己事情的輕重緩急非常重要。你不應為無能為力的事情感到擔憂，當情況變得太嚴峻時，不要對說「不」感到不好意思。

Sample Score #1:
This essay would probably score very well because the test-taker answers the question in a clear and wellorganized manner. The test-taker writes his position at the very beginning of the post, so it's easy to tell whether he agrees or disagrees with the other posts. He clearly makes a contribution to the discussion and supports his opinion with an example. The test-taker makes good use of signalling language so it's clear to the reader what is coming next. Finally, the sentences in the

answer are well written and contain no grammatical or spelling errors, and the post contains more than 100 words.

評分範例 #1：
這篇文章可能會獲得高分，因為考生以清晰、組織良好的方式回答了問題。考生在文章開頭就表明了自己的立場，因此很容易判斷他是贊成還是反對其他文章。他為討論做出了明確貢獻，並用一個例子支持自己的觀點。考生巧妙使用了標示語，所以讀者清楚知道接下來要講什麼。最後，答案中的句子書寫通順，沒有文法或拼寫錯誤，而且文章內容超過 100 個字。

Sample Answer #2:
While at college, there can be many sources of stress: living away from home for the first time, doing exams, assignment deadlines and so on. Fortunately, colleges are big organizations and have people who can help with stress. For example, college writing centres have advisors who can help students when they are struggling with essays. There are welfare officers who you can talk to and also less formal groups that you can join and talk to. I agree that physical activity is very important too, and there are lots of opportunities to get involved in a college sports team or do another activity like walking with a group. So, in my opinion, the best way to deal with stress is to look for people to help you.

寫作範本 #2：
在大學期間可能會有許多壓力來源：第一次離家生活、應付考試、作業截止日期等等。幸運的是，大學是大型組織，有人可以幫忙應付壓力。舉例來說，在大學寫作中心，有顧問可在學生遇到寫作困難時提供幫助。你可以找輔導組職員談話，也可以加入一些非正式小組並參與他們的談話。我同意運動也非常重要，而且有很多機會可以參加大學體育隊或參加其他活動，像是團體步行。因此在我看來，處理壓力的最佳方式是尋找可以幫助你的人。

Sample Score #2:

This response would likely score in the mid-level range. While the post addresses the main topic, the writer does not contribute to the discussion, but instead repeats the ideas in the other posts. The writer does not refer to the ideas in the other posts and although the subject that the professor asks about is a general topic, the student focusses just on stress in education. Having said this, the writer does develop their points with examples. Finally, in their last sentence they only talk about one way of dealing with stress, but in the rest of their answer they include two things. The post contains more than 100 words.

評分範例 #2：

這個答案的得分可能在中等水準範圍內。儘管文章談到了主題，但作者並未對討論做出貢獻，而是重複了其他文章中的觀點。儘管教授所問的主題是關於壓力的廣義話題，學生只著重於教育壓力。雖然如此，作者還是有舉例闡述自己的觀點。在最後一句裡，他們只談到處理壓力的一種方法，但在回應的其餘部分談論了兩種方法。文章內容超過 100 個字。

QUESTION 1

TOEFL Writing

Question

舊石器時代晚期革命，指的是智人或現代人類首次展現明顯人類行為的時期。這些行為包括發展出精細的石器，以及創造語言和藝術。根據現有證據指出，舊石器時代晚期革命很可能發生在約四萬年前的歐洲大陸。

首先有跡象指出，大約在四萬年前，一種叫歐洲尼安德塔人的早期人類滅絕了。歐洲尼安德塔人的滅絕與現代人類在歐洲人口激增的時間點相吻合。支持這項人口激增的證據為，有大量發現約四萬年前現代人的骨骼遺骸。這些發現顯示現代人類取代了歐洲尼安德塔人，可能是因為他們已經開發出更優越的工具，例如幫助他們獲取食物和生存的石刀。

其次，氣候記錄顯示歐洲提供了革命所需的條件。根據記錄，大約自七萬年前開始，歐洲經歷了一個低於正常溫度的時期，此情況一直持續到約一萬年前。科學家相信，寒冷氣候促使當時生活在歐洲的現代人類創造出更好的求生工具。例如捕魚工具的發明使他們能在異常寒冷的天氣中獲取食物。

最後，在舊石器時代晚期革命期間，歐洲出現了現代具象藝術的第一個例子。霍勒菲爾斯的維納斯是一尊來自德國的石雕，可追溯到大約三萬五千至四萬年前。這是一個早期精緻藝術品的例子，且在其他地方不存在更早期的例子。

Sample Essay #1:

Both the reading and the lecture are about the Upper Paleolithic Revolution, which was a period during which humans started displaying modern behavior, like making tools and creating artwork. According to the reading, the Upper Paleolithic Revolution took place in Europe about 40,000 years ago. However, the professor disagrees with this and claims that it probably took place in Africa much earlier than that.

文章和課堂都談到了舊石器時代晚期革命，是人類開始展現現代行為的時期，像是製作工具和創作藝術品。根據文章，舊石器時代晚期革命發生在約四萬年前的歐洲。然而教授不贊同這個觀點，並聲稱它更早發生於非洲。

The first point in the reading is that a population boom among modern humans in Europe was a sign that modern behavior started there about 40,000 years ago. The author also mentions that European Neanderthals, an earlier type of human, went extinct because of the success of the modern humans. In the lecture, the professor disagrees that modern humans emerged in Europe. He points out that sophisticated tools much older than those found in Europe were found in Africa. According to him, this is an indication that the tools were developed in Africa and brought to Europe when people migrated there.

文章中的第一點為，現代人類在歐洲人口激增，顯示現代行為約從四萬年前開始出現在那裡。作者還提到一種為較早期的人類的歐洲尼安德塔人，因現代人類的成就而滅絕。在課堂中，教授不贊同現代人類是從歐洲出現的。他指出在非洲發現了比歐洲更古老的精密工具。根據他的說法，這表示這些工具是於非洲開發，並在人們遷徙到歐洲時帶到了那裡。

Next, the reading argues that a period of cold weather in Europe prompted humans there to develop better tools so they could survive. Again, the professor disagrees by saying that sophisticated tools, like projectile points and engraving tools, were found in Africa that date to about 50,000 years ago. He says that this is a sign that the tools were actually developed in Africa and not Europe.

接下來，文章中論述了歐洲的寒冷天氣促使當地人開發出更好的求生工具。教授同樣不贊成，他說在非洲發現了諸如尖狀器和雕刻工具等精密工具，其年代可追溯到約五萬年前。他說，這表示這些工具實際上是在非洲而不是歐洲開發出來的。

Last, the author says that the earliest piece of art was found in Germany. The stone statue is called the Venus of Hohle Fels, and it was probably created between 35,000 and 40,000 years ago. The professor challenges the idea that this is the first piece of art. He describes two rock carvings that were found in a cave in South Africa. He says these carvings were created in 70,000 BCE, which makes them much older than the piece found in Germany.

最後，作者說最早的藝術品是在德國發現的。這尊石雕被稱為霍勒菲爾斯的維納斯，它可能是在

三萬五千到四萬年前創造的。教授質疑了這是第一件藝術品的觀點，他提到在南非一個洞穴中發現的兩塊岩石雕刻品。他說這些雕刻品是在公元前七萬年創造的，比在德國發現的雕刻品還古老的多。

In conclusion, the reading says that the Upper Paleolithic Revolution took place in Europe 40,000 years ago. But the professor disagrees and provides evidence that it actually took place in Africa earlier than that.

總而言之，文章指出舊石器時代晚期革命發生在四萬年前的歐洲，但教授不贊同這個觀點，且提供證據指出，它實際上更早發生於非洲。

Sample Score #1:
This essay would probably score very well. The essay has five paragraphs, including an introduction, three body paragraphs, and a conclusion. Furthermore, the writer connects information from both the reading and the lecture by giving the main topic of the reading and accurately describing how the professor challenges each key point from the reading. The writer's language is easy to understand and includes a variety of grammatical structures and vocabulary.

評分範例 #1：
這篇作文可能會獲得高分。該作文有五個段落，包括引言、三個主體段落和結論。此外，作者藉著提供文章要點和準確描述教授如何質疑文章中的每個重點，將文章和課堂中的資訊連結起來。作者的措辭易於理解，使用了多種文法結構和字彙。

Sample Essay #2:
The reading and the lecture talk about the Upper Paleolithic Revolution. The reading says that the Upper Paleolithic Revolution happened 40,000 years ago in Europe.

文章和課堂都談到了舊石器時代晚期革命。文章說舊石器時代晚期革命發生在四萬年前的歐洲。

First of all, the reading says that European humans during the Upper Paleolithic Revolution caused Neanderthals to go extinct. The lecturer agrees that the sophistication of human tools was probably the reason for Neanderthal extinction in Europe.

首先，文章說歐洲人在舊石器時代晚期革命期間導致了尼安德塔人的滅絕。而講課者同意，人類工具的精密性可能是歐洲尼安德塔人滅絕的原因。

Next, there's the idea that humans first developed sophisticated new tools during the Ice Age in Europe because it was too cold. The lecture, though, points out that sophisticated stone and bone tools were actually developed even earlier in Africa.

接下來，有一個觀點表示人類在歐洲冰河時期首次開發了複雜的新工具，是因為當時太冷了。然而課堂指出，精密的石頭和骨頭工具實際上在非洲早已開發出來了。

Finally, the reading discusses a rock sculpture from Germany that is 35,000–40,000 years old. But the professor claims in his lecture that sophisticated art began as early as 70,000 BCE.

最後，文章討論到一個約三萬五千至四萬年前來自德國的石雕。但教授在他的課堂中聲稱，精密藝術早在公元前七萬年就開始了。

Sample Score #2:
This response would likely score poorly. While the essay includes an introduction and three body paragraphs, it does not have a conclusion. In the essay, the writer fails to fully connect information from the reading and the lecture, and in some places he describes only information from the reading. The essay also lacks specific details from the lecture, which would have made the points easier to understand. For example, in the second paragraph, the writer says that the lecturer partially agrees with the reading but does not describe the details that the professor gives to challenge the point from the reading. The writer uses many of the same grammatical structures from the reading itself, suggesting that he lacks a strong knowledge of English sentence constructions.

評分範例 #2：
這個答案的得分可能較低。儘管該作文包含了引言和三個主體段落，但缺乏結論。在作文中，作者未能將文章和課堂的資訊充分連接起來，有些地方只描述了文章中的資訊。作文還缺乏來自課堂的具體細節，這些細節原本可使論點更容易理解。例如在第二段裡，作者說講課者部分同意文章中的觀點，但沒有描述教授所提供、用來質疑文章中觀點的具體細節。作者使用了許多與文章本身相同的文法結構，這表示他缺乏對英文句構的深入了解。

QUESTION 2

你的教授正在課堂上教教育學，寫一篇貼文來回應教授的問題。

你在回應中應該：
- 表達和支持你的意見
- 對討論做出貢獻

合格的回應要包含至少 100 個字，你有 10 分鐘的時間作答。

阿克德尼茲教授
當學生一起合作和相互學習時，我們把這種教育方法稱為同儕學習。這種學習方式鼓勵學生之間的討論和資訊交流，而不是單向的從學者傳遞給學生。這種學習方法有許多優點：它是互動和激勵性的、它納入了每個人、它涉及許多不同的經驗和知識。然而，這也存在一些缺點：學生的知識往往不如老師豐富，並非所有學生都能做同等的貢獻，最後，可能存在缺乏動機的問題。我有興趣知道你們對此問題的想法。請告訴我，你認為同儕學習是一種良好的教育方法，還是比較正規的學習更好。

萊斯
就我而言，我不喜歡同儕學習。畢竟，我們上大學是要向各種學科的專家學習，而不是向和

我們一樣的學生學習。其他學生的知識有限，甚至更糟糕的是，他們可能提供你錯誤資訊。況且我們可在課後與其他學生一起討論事情，那為什麼還要花時間在課堂上這樣做呢？

維多利亞
我對萊斯的意見部分不同意。向講師和教授學習是大學教育中很重要的一部分，但並不是全部。在某些問題上可能存在不同見解，特別是在教育、社會學或商業等學科中，學生往往有好的想法和觀點，所以我們應該聆聽每個人的意見，並準備從他們身上學習。

Sample Answer #1:

There are many ways of learning; peer learning is one of these, formal learning from academics or journals is another. In my opinion, both are needed, but the important point for me is how each approach is used and for what reasons. I agree with Laci that the starting point for our education should be the expert who transmits knowledge to the students. They know the most up-to-date information in the area, what is important to highlight and what to recommend students study after class. However, in my view, it is not enough to simply receive knowledge, what you do with that knowledge is important and this is why peer learning is important. At university, we have the opportunity to discuss with classmates and, in addition, when peer learning discussions are guided by an academic, they can be very productive. Furthermore, discussing what you have learned helps you to remember and apply it. So, I think that both have their place in education.

寫作範本 #1：

學習的方式有很多種；同儕學習是其中之一，從學術或期刊中的正式學習是另一種。在我看來，這兩者都是必需的，但對我來說重要的是如何使用這兩種方法以及基於什麼原因。我同意萊斯的

觀點，我們教育的起點應是把知識傳遞給學生的專家。他們掌握了該領域中的最新資訊，知道要強調什麼以及建議學生在課後去學習什麼。然而在我看來，單純接受知識是不夠的，重要的是你如何運用這些知識，這就是同儕學習的重要性。在大學裡，我們有機會和同學討論，而且當同儕學習討論由學者來引導時，效果會非常好。此外，討論所學有助於記憶和應用。因此，我認為這兩者在教育中都有其存在的價值。

Sample Score #1:

This answer would likely score very well because the writer provides a clear and well-organized response to the question in the prompt. In the first sentences, the writer gives some background and states her position. She acknowledges the contributions of the other students by agreeing with one of them, then summarizes why she has that opinion. She develops her point further and adds another point to the second students' post. The language in the answer is clear and includes different types of sentence construction. The writer uses transition language to improve the flow of the answer, and the response is more than 100 words.

評分範例 #1：

這個答案可能會得到高分，因為作者對提示中的問題提供了一個清晰且組織良好的回答。在開頭幾句中，作者提供了一些背景資訊並描述了她的立場。她藉著贊同其中一個學生的意見來肯定其他學生的貢獻，並概述她持有該觀點的原因。她進一步發展了自己的觀點，並在第二個學生的貼文中補充了另一個觀點。答案中的措辭明確，使用了不同的句型結構。作者使用轉折詞來提升答案流暢性，而且內容超過 100 個字。

Sample Answer #2:

In my opinion, we do not need lecturers any more. Think about what is happening online, where we can see videos and presentations or lectures by lots of different people, not just academics. We can learn from students like us or experts in business or industry, researchers or read books and articles. You can see that students today do not really need to be told about the subject they are studying. With content online, we can form groups from around the world and communicate together about the subject we are studying. Also, academics can also put their lectures on the internet, then the students can watch it and then discuss it together.

寫作範本 #2：
在我看來，我們不再需要講師了。想想在線上發生的事，我們可以觀看許多不同人士的影片、演講或課程，而不只是學術性的東西。我們可以向像我們一樣的學生或業界專家、商界專家、研究人員學習，或閱讀書籍和文章。你可見今天學生所要學習的主題，實際上不需有人親自教導他們。透過線上內容，我們可以由世界各地的人組成小組，就我們正在學習的主題進行交流。此外，學者們也可以將他們的課程放在網路上，讓學生們觀看並一起討論。

Sample Score #2:
This response would probably get a low-level score. The writer gives their opinion to the question in the prompt, but does not really say which is a better educational approach: peer learning or formal learning. Instead of comparing, they discuss one side of the argument. They do not refer to the posts of the other students. Although the writer has included examples and explanations to support their point, they should have included more transition language to indicate the relationship between the ideas in the response. The writer often uses the same words and does not display a broad vocabulary. The response is over 100 words.

評分範例 #2：
這個答案的得分可能較低。作者表達了他對題目問題的意見，但並沒有真正說明哪種教育方法更好：是同儕學習還是正式學習，作者並沒有進行比較，而是討論了爭論的其中一方；作者也沒提到其他學生的貼文。儘管作者使用例子和說明來支持他的觀點，但應該多加使用轉折詞來指出答案裡一些想法之間的關係。作者經常使用相同的措辭，並沒有展現出豐富的詞彙。內容有超過100字。

部分講稿已放在題目或解答，在此不重複。

🎧 003

Narrator: Writing Lesson 1: Get Ready
旁白：寫作第 1 課：準備就緒

Narrator: Now listen to part of a lecture in an environmental science class.
旁白：現在聽一段環境科學課堂上的講述。

Professor: As the world's supply of fossil fuels begins to run low, scientists have been exploring alternative sources of fuel for cars and other vehicles. One of the best alternative fuels is vegetable oil. There are a lot of reasons why using vegetable oil is a great idea.
教授：隨著世界化石燃料的供應逐漸枯竭，科學家一直在探索汽車和其他車輛的替代燃料來源。其中一種最佳的替代燃料是植物油。使用植物油是個絕佳的替代方案，也有很多原因支持這個觀點。

First, it's true that people have to invest a little money at first for conversion equipment. However, if you think about it, the equipment soon pays for itself because the car can be driven many more miles on fuel from vegetable oil. Most cars can drive between 800 and 1,000 miles on just one tank of vegetable oil! Compare this to the average gas engine that gets about 500 miles for one tank of gas. The use of vegetable oil saves a lot of money. In addition, the cost of conversion equipment will come down quickly as more people switch to using vegetable oil.
首先，人們確實需要在一開始時投資一些錢來購買轉換設備。但若你仔細想想，這些設備很快就會回本，因汽車可以使用植物油行駛更長的里程。大多數汽車只需要一箱植物油就可行駛 800 至 1,000 英里！相較之下，一箱汽油平均只能讓汽車行駛約500英里，使用植物油可以節省一大筆錢。此外，隨著越來越多的人改用植物油，轉換設備的成本將迅速下降。

It's also very true that the use of a converter requires the driver to pay attention. However, it really isn't that hard to remember to turn the equipment switch on and off. After a while, people who use the equipment just do it automatically. Also, with rapid improvements in technology, soon even that won't be necessary. Already there are automatic converters that sense when to turn the equipment on or off. The driver doesn't have to do anything at all.
的確，使用轉換器需要駕駛的注意力。然而，記得打開和關閉設備開關並不難。使用此設備一段時間後，人們就能自動做到。此外，隨著技術迅速進步，很快連這個動作都不再需要了。已有自動轉換器可感應何時打開或關閉設備。駕駛根本不需做任何事情。

Finally, it's true that vegetable oil comes from crops that are used for food. However, the vegetable oil that we use for fuel in cars is a waste product. Huge amounts of this waste oil are discarded every day from places like restaurants and potato chip factories. This oil has already been used once for cooking, so using it in a car doesn't interrupt the food supply at all.
最後，植物油確實來自當作食物的作物。然而，我們用於汽車燃料的植物油是一種廢棄產品，每天有大量來自餐廳和洋芋片工廠等地的廢油。這種油已在烹飪上被使用過，所以將它用在汽車上完全不會中斷食物供應。

🎧 004

Narrator: Writing Lesson 1: Get Set
旁白：寫作第 1 課：準備就緒

Narrator: Now listen to part of a lecture in an archaeology class.
旁白：現在聽一段考古學課堂上的講述。

Professor: There's this big debate with historians and archaeologists about the origins of runes. Did they develop independently, or were they based on some older alphabet system? Our reading from last night suggests that runes developed independently. I don't really agree with that. I think there's a lot of evidence that runes could have developed from another script. In particular, I think they came from Old Italic, a family of alphabets that originated on the Italian Peninsula in the eighth century BCE. The Old Italic alphabets spread around Europe and were used to write many different European alphabets.

教授：關於盧恩字母的起源，歷史學家和考古學家之間一直爭論不休。盧恩字母是獨立發展的，還是根據某種更古老的字母系統發展而來的？我們昨晚的文章指出，盧恩字母是獨立發展的，但我並不完全贊同。我認為有很多證據顯示，盧恩字母可能來自於另一種文字系統。特別是，我認為它們源自於古義大利文，那是一種在公元前 8 世紀起源於義大利半島的字母體系。古義大利文字母普及於歐洲各地，被用於書寫各種不同的歐洲字母。

First of all, it's true that Germanic groups were more isolated than other people in Europe. But they weren't immune to influences from powerful groups like the Greeks and the Romans, who used Old Italic alphabets. Early Romans probably did travel to central Europe, especially for trade. Actually, I believe that trade with Greeks and Italians, and then conquest by those groups, could have really influenced Germanic culture. So the different languages definitely came into contact, and it's likely that runes were based on the Old Italic system.

首先，日耳曼人族群的確較歐洲其他地區的人更為孤立，但是他們並未免於受到希臘和羅馬等強大族群使用古義大利文字母的影響。早期羅馬人可能真的有到中歐，尤其是為了貿易。事實上我相信與希臘人和義大利人的貿易往來，以及這些族群的征服統治，可能真的影響了日耳曼文化。

因此，肯定有不同語言的接觸，盧恩字母可能是根據古義大利文系統發展而來的。

Also, let's mention the idea that runes were developed in isolation by a very select group of high- ranking people and only for purposes like burials. This simply isn't true. In Norway in the 1950s, an excavation in the city of Bergen discovered lots of runes that were being used in business and other everyday texts. There were runes for personal messages, love letters and even jokes – people understood and used runes widely. And if you think about it, because runes were written on public memorial stones they were there to be read by everyone. Runes weren't a special script developed by and for a few elite people, they were a widespread part of society.

還有需提到此觀點：盧恩字母是由一群非常精英的高階人士，在與世隔絕的環境中發展出來的，且只用於葬禮等目的；事實根本不是如此。在 1950 年代的挪威，從卑爾根市出土的文物中，發現了許多用於商業和其他日常文本的盧恩字母。有用於個人訊息、情書甚至笑話的盧恩字母——人們普遍理解和使用盧恩字母。而且你仔細想想，因為盧恩字母會寫在公共紀念碑上，所以它們是供所有人閱讀的。盧恩字母不是一種由少數精英人士開發並專供他們使用的特殊文字，它們在社會中很普遍。

I also want to address the claim that there aren't many similarities between runes and other scripts. If you compare runic and Old Italic scripts, it's obvious that these two are related somehow. They all use the same angular letters. And while the reading suggests that anything they have in common is probably random or a coincidence, I think that's pretty unlikely.

我還想談一下，關於盧恩字母與其他文字之間相似性不多的主張。要是你比較盧恩字母和古義大利文，你會發現，這兩者顯然在某種程度上有關。它們都使用相同的角形字母。雖然文章指出，它們之間的任何共同點可能只是偶然或巧

合，但我認為這種可能性相當小。

🎧 005

Narrator: Writing Lesson 1: Go for the TOEFL® test
旁白：寫作第 1 課：上場考試

Narrator: Now listen to part of a lecture in an art history class and take notes.
旁白：現在聽一段藝術史課堂上的講述，並做筆記。

Professor: OK, our reading tries to convince us that the Venus de Milo is probably a re-creation of an earlier piece. Personally, I disagree with this stance. I think that the Venus de Milo is an original work from the Hellenistic period, not a copy of something from the classical period.
教授：好的，文章試圖說服我們米洛的維納斯可能是一個早期作品的複製品。我個人不贊同這個觀點。我認為米洛的維納斯是希臘化時代的原創作品，而不是古典時代的複製品。

Let's start by looking at style. The article says that the Venus de Milo resembles classical works by artists like Praxiteles. Really, though, it depends on how you look at the statue. Yes, some of it looks a lot like classical pieces in certain ways, but that's because the classical period lasted from the fifth century BCE until about 330 BCE, and the Hellenistic period immediately followed. And actually, the Venus de Milo looks very Hellenistic. It's very realistic and detailed, and the body is long and lean. These are features of the Hellenistic era. I don't think the artist was copying classical styles.
讓我們從風格開始看起。文章說米洛的維納斯與普拉克西特勒斯等藝術家的古典作品相似。但實際上，這取決於你如何看待這尊雕像。是的，從某些方面來看，它很像某些古典作品，但那是因為古典時代從公元前 5 世紀持續到公元前 330 年左右，緊接著就是希臘化時代。而且實際上，米洛的維納斯看起來非常具有希臘化時代風格。它

非常細緻逼真，且整體修長。這些都是希臘化時代的特點。我不認為藝術家是在複製古典風格。

Also, there's this claim that the Venus de Milo must be a replica because it looks a lot like the Aphrodite of Capua, which we know is a replica of an older Greek statue. But this doesn't make much sense, either, if you ask me. I mean, there were many different artists depicting Venus and Aphrodite between the fourth and first centuries BCE—so many that of course some of them look similar. So I don't think the similarity between these two works proves anything.
此外，有人聲稱米洛的維納斯一定是複製品，因為它看起來很像卡普亞的阿芙羅黛蒂，後者我們知道是一尊古希臘雕像的複製品。但若你問我，我會說此主張也沒什麼道理。我的意思是從公元前 4 世紀到公元前 1 世紀期間，有許多藝術家描繪了維納斯和阿芙羅黛蒂，數量繁多以至於當然有些看起來相似，所以我不認為這兩件作品間的相似性能證明什麼。

And finally, just because Alexandros of Antioch lived during the Hellenistic period doesn't mean that this image of Aphrodite wasn't his own creation. I think that the Hellenistic period was a little underrated. Plenty of beautiful and unique art came out of that time period. I think, um, we can't assume that the Venus de Milo was a replica just because it came from an unknown person at an unlikely time.
最後，不能只因為安提阿的亞歷山卓斯活在希臘化時代，就認為此阿芙羅黛蒂雕像不是他的創作。我認為希臘化時代有點被低估了，許多美麗且獨特的藝術品就是出自此時期。我認為不能只因米洛的維納斯在一個不太可能創新的時代且出自於一位不知名的人，就假設它是一件複製品。

🎧 006

Narrator: Writing Review Test: Question 1
旁白：寫作複習測驗：第 1 題
Narrator: Now listen to part of a lecture in a

history class and take notes.

旁白：現在聽一段歷史課堂上的講述，並做筆記。

Professor: OK, today let's talk about the Upper Paleolithic Revolution. As you know from the reading, this was a period in which people started exhibiting modern human behavior. By that, I mean that humans started developing tools and culture, which earlier types of humans didn't have. Anyway, some scientists argue that the Upper Paleolithic Revolution took place in Europe about 40,000 years ago. But there's actually a lot of evidence that shows that it took place in Africa a lot earlier than that.

教授：好的，今天我們來談談舊石器時代晚期革命。從文章中得知，這是一個人類開始展現現代行為的時期。我指的是人類開始發展工具和文化，而這是早期人類所沒有的。無論如何，有些科學家認為舊石器時代晚期革命發生在約四萬年前的歐洲。但實際上有很多證據顯示，它早在非洲就發生了。

First of all, there's this idea that modern humans emerged in Europe and that's why the European Neanderthals went extinct. But that's not the whole story. I mean, the modern humans had to have come from somewhere, and with the information we have, I'd say they came from Africa. See, it's true that scientists found tools in Europe that date to around 40,000 years ago. But even older versions of those tools have been found in parts of Africa. What does that mean? Well, it means that modern humans migrated from Africa to Europe, and they took their new technology with them when they did.

首先，有一種觀點是現代人類起源於歐洲，這就是歐洲尼安德塔人滅絕的原因，但那並不是事實的全部。我的意思是現代人類必定是從某地方而來，而根據我們擁有的資訊，我會說他們來自非洲。事實上，科學家在歐洲發現了大約四萬年前的工具。但是，在非洲的有些地方也發現了這些工具更古老的版本。這代表什麼呢？這意味現代人類從非洲遷移到歐洲，並在遷移時帶上了他們的新技術。

OK, let's move on. Another theory is that the cold weather in Europe forced modern humans there to develop new tools. Again, I'm afraid this just isn't true. I mean, many stone and bone artifacts appeared in Africa as early as 50,000 years ago. I'm talking about objects like projectile points and engraving tools. So, again, here we have examples of sophisticated human tools that are older than the tools that were found in Europe. It's true that new tools probably allowed humans to flourish in Europe during the period of cold climate, but I don't think the new tools originated in Europe.

好的，讓我們繼續。另一個理論是，歐洲的寒冷氣候迫使現代人類開發新工具。同樣，這也不是真的。我的意思是許多石器和骨器物品早在五萬年前就出現在非洲。我提到的是像尖狀器和雕刻工具這樣的物品。所以，這裡所講的複雜人類工具的例子比在歐洲發現的工具更古老。新的工具確實可使人類在寒冷氣候時期於歐洲繁衍興旺，但我不認為新工具起源於歐洲。

Finally, some experts say that the first example of art was found in Europe. But we actually have evidence of much older pieces of art. And guess what? These older pieces were found in Africa. For example, the oldest rock carvings in Africa are two decorated stones that were found in Blombos Cave in South Africa. Amazingly, these were created in 70,000 BCE!

最後，有些專家說第一個藝術品的例子發掘於歐洲。但事實上，我們有更古老藝術作品的證據。猜猜如何？這些更古老的藝術品是在非洲找到的。例如，在南非的布隆博斯洞穴發現了最古老的岩石雕刻是兩塊裝飾石。令人驚訝的是，它們是在公元前七萬年創作的！

學術字彙表 Academic Word List

以下 570 個單字是在學術文本中最常見的詞彙。請使用柯林斯高級英語詞典（Collins Cobuild Advanced Dictionary）查詢定義、單字的不同形式，參考實際例句，學習發音！也可上網查詢 https://www.collinsdictionary.com/dictionary/english

Coxhead Academic Word List （請注意，托福測驗的單字與本學術字彙表的單字並無直接關係，本表僅作為學術文本中常見字彙的參考。）

abandon	annual	bond
abstract	anticipate	brief
academy	apparent	bulk
access	append	capable
accommodate	appreciate	capacity
accompany	approach	category
accumulate	appropriate	cease
accurate	approximate	challenge
achieve	arbitrary	channel
acknowledge	area	chapter
acquire	aspect	chart
adapt	assemble	chemical
adequate	assess	circumstance
adjacent	assign	cite
adjust	assist	civil
administrate	assume	clarify
adult	assure	classic
advocate	attach	clause
affect	attain	code
aggregate	attitude	coherent
aid	attribute	coincide
albeit	author	collapse
allocate	authority	colleague
alter	automate	commence
alternative	available	comment
ambiguous	aware	commission
amend	behalf	commit
analogy	benefit	commodity
analyze	bias	communicate

community
compatible
compensate
compile
complement
complex
component
compound
comprehensive
comprise
compute
conceive
concentrate
concept
conclude
concurrent
conduct
confer
confine
confirm
conflict
conform
consent
consequent
considerable
consist
constant
constitute
constrain
construct
consult
consume
contact
contemporary
context
contract

contradict
contrary
contrast
contribute
controversy
convene
converse
convert
convince
cooperate
coordinate
core
corporate
correspond
couple
create
credit
criteria
crucial
culture
currency
cycle
data
debate
decade
decline
deduce
define
definite
demonstrate
denote
deny
depress
derive
design
despite

detect
deviate
device
devote
differentiate
dimension
diminish
discrete
discriminate
displace
display
dispose
distinct
distort
distribute
diverse
document
domain
domestic
dominate
draft
drama
duration
dynamic
economy
edit
element
eliminate
emerge
emphasis
empirical
enable
encounter
energy
enforce
enhance

enormous
ensure
entity
environment
equate
equip
equivalent
erode
error
establish
estate
estimate
ethic
ethnic
evaluate
eventual
evident
evolve
exceed
exclude
exhibit
expand
expert
explicit
exploit
export
expose
external
extract
facilitate
factor
feature
federal
fee
file
final

finance
finite
flexible
fluctuate
focus
format
formula
forthcoming
found
foundation
framework
function
fund
fundamental
furthermore
gender
generate
generation
globe
goal
grade
grant
guarantee
guideline
hence
hierarchy
highlight
hypothesis
identical
identify
ideology
ignorant
illustrate
image
immigrate
impact

implement
implicate
implicit
imply
impose
incentive
incidence
incline
income
incorporate
index
indicate
individual
induce
inevitable
infer
infrastructure
inherent
inhibit
initial
initiate
injure
innovate
input
insert
insight
inspect
instance
institute
instruct
integral
integrate
integrity
intelligent
intense
interact

intermediate

internal

interpret

interval

intervene

intrinsic

invest

investigate

invoke

involve

isolate

issue

item

job

journal

justify

label

labor

layer

lecture

legal

legislate

levy

liberal

license

likewise

link

locate

logic

maintain

major

manipulate

manual

margin

mature

maximize

mechanism

media

mediate

medical

medium

mental

method

migrate

military

minimal

minimize

minimum

ministry

minor

mode

modify

monitor

motive

mutual

negate

network

neutral

nevertheless

nonetheless

norm

normal

notion

notwithstanding

nuclear

objective

obtain

obvious

occupy

occur

odd

offset

ongoing

option

orient

outcome

output

overall

overlap

overseas

panel

paradigm

paragraph

parallel

parameter

participate

partner

passive

perceive

percent

period

persist

perspective

phase

phenomenon

philosophy

physical

plus

policy

portion

pose

positive

potential

practitioner

precede

precise

predict

predominant

preliminary

presume

previous

primary

prime

principal

principle

prior

priority

proceed

process

professional

prohibit

project

promote

proportion

prospect

protocol

psychology

publication

publish

purchase

pursue

qualitative

quote

radical

random

range

ratio

rational

react

recover

refine

regime

region

register

regulate

reinforce

reject

relax

release

relevant

reluctance

rely

remove

require

research

reside

resolve

resource

respond

restore

restrain

restrict

retain

reveal

revenue

reverse

revise

revolution

rigid

role

route

scenario

schedule

scheme

scope

section

sector

secure

seek

select

sequence

series

sex

shift

significant

similar

simulate

site

so-called

sole

somewhat

source

specific

specify

sphere

stable

statistic

status

straightforward

strategy

stress

structure

style

submit

subordinate

subsequent

subsidy

substitute

successor

sufficient

sum

summary

supplement

survey

survive

suspend

sustain
symbol
tape
target
task
team
technical
technique
technology
temporary
tense
terminate
text
theme
theory
thereby
thesis
topic
trace
tradition
transfer
transform
transit
transmit
transport
trend
trigger
ultimate
undergo
underlie
undertake
uniform
unify
unique
utilize
valid

vary
vehicle
version
via
violate
virtual
visible
vision
visual
volume
voluntary
welfare
whereas
whereby
widespread

NOTES

NOTES

NOTES

NOTES

絕對攻略 TOEFL iBT 新托福閱讀＋寫作

作　　　者：Collins
譯　　　者：張家瑞
主　　　編：潘亭軒
責 任 編 輯：鄭雅方
封 面 設 計：兒日設計
版 型 設 計：洪伊珊
內 頁 排 版：洪伊珊
行 銷 企 劃：張爾芸
照 片 出 處：shutterstock.com

發 　行 　人：洪祺祥
副 總 經 理：洪偉傑
副 總 編 輯：曹仲堯
法 律 顧 問：建大法律事務所
財 務 顧 問：高威會計事務所

出　　　版：日月文化出版股份有限公司
製　　　作：EZ 叢書館
地　　　址：臺北市信義路三段 151 號 8 樓
電　　　話：(02) 2708-5509
傳　　　真：(02) 2708-6157
客 服 信 箱：service@heliopolis.com.tw
網　　　址：www.heliopolis.com.tw
郵 撥 帳 號：19716071 日月文化出版股份有限公司

總 　經 　銷：聯合發行股份有限公司
電　　　話：(02) 2917-8022
傳　　　真：(02) 2915-7212
印　　　刷：中原造像股份有限公司
初　　　版：2024 年 7 月
定　　　價：420 元
I S B N：978-626-7405-78-9

絕對攻略TOEFL iBT新托福閱讀+寫作/Collins著；張家瑞譯.
-- 初版. -- 臺北市：日月文化出版股份有限公司, 2024.07
264 面； 19 X 25.7公分. -- (EZ talk)
ISBN 978-626-7405-78-9(平裝)
1.CST: 托福考試 2.CST: 考試指南

805.1894　　　　　　　　　　　　　113006310

© HarperCollins Publishers 2024
Collins® is a registered trademark of HarperCollins Publishers
Limited
Academic Word List © Coxhead, Averil 2000